HER MATCH, HER MATE, HER MASTER

VANESSA BROOKS

Published by Blushing Books
An Imprint of
ABCD Graphics and Design, Inc.
A Virginia Corporation
977 Seminole Trail #233
Charlottesville, VA 22901

Vanessa Brooks
Her Match, Her Mate, Her Master

EBook ISBN: 978-1-61258-746-2
Print ISBN: 978-1-61258-682-3
v1

PROLOGUE

"*C*ome back with a wife, son."

John Foster sighed, exasperated. "We've discussed this, Mother; I have made my feelings clear upon the matter. Kiss me goodbye and wish me a safe voyage." His mother reached up to hug his neck; he leaned down to embrace her. He loved his mother dearly but he found this matchmaking between her and his English business partner profoundly irritating. He knew what he wanted in a wife, and a spoiled, aristocratic English girl was not his expectation.

Since his father's death two years ago, he'd taken over the reins of the business. His aristocratic business partner, Sir Edward Wainwright, had written to John's mother explaining that he was ailing and looking to secure his daughter's future. To this end, he'd begged her help in looking favourably upon a match to be made between his daughter Linnet and John. He'd also strongly intimated there would be financial advantage should such a match be realised. Whilst John was of an age and prosperity to take a wife, he was decidedly against this proposal, whatever the inducement.

His mother, a strong, determined woman, absolutely insisted

that he make the arduous journey to England to meet the young woman.

John had other plans. He favoured a home alliance with a colonial girl, a born and bred American woman. One who understood the rigours of this wild country, someone who loved this huge and beautiful continent as much as he did himself.

So he agreed to undertake the long passage across the sea back to the old world, England, in order to cement the ties with his father's old friend, Sir Edward, to please his mother and honour his father. But he had absolutely no intention of taking the Englishman's spoiled daughter to wife.

Aboard The Tempest, he stood on deck and watched as the ship slipped out from Boston harbour, through Cape Cod Bay, and out into the vast Atlantic Ocean, leaving the land of his birth far behind. On deck, he watched as the distant shoreline diminished until all that remained in sight were a line of clouds that marked the edge of his homeland. John remained at the ship's side until there was nothing left to look at but the sea. "I'll be back, Massachusetts," he avowed silently before turning away at last to seek his cabin and rest.

The arduous voyage took longer than he'd anticipated, mainly due to foul weather but, finally, after nine long weeks at sea, land was sighted, and he'd arrived in Devon, England.

CHAPTER 1

The household held its collective breath, waiting for the enraged young mistress to leave for her daily ride. Until that time came, there would be no peace for anyone—and the cause of her rage? The lady's father had informed her, that morning at breakfast, that the man he had chosen for her future husband was due to arrive on this very day. Since then, any of the household staff who had the misfortune to encounter the young mistress had suffered the outraged lash of her tongue. When she had finally slammed out of the house on her way to the stables, her father, Sir Edward Wainwright, emerged from his study, mopping his brow with his kerchief. He'd hidden himself there after imparting the momentous news that so upset his precious daughter.

The staff relaxed, breathing a communal sigh of relief as the girl was seen to gallop away from the house. Meanwhile, preparations continued for the arrival of the important guest. The finest sheets were placed on the bed, flowers arranged throughout the house, silver polished, and cakes and puddings baked in abundance. Despite all the fuss, the staff privately thought the young man's suit bound to fail. Rumour had it that the young mistress's heart was engaged elsewhere. This gossip had spread from the mouth of one Lottie Brown, the young mistress Linnet's very own personal maid.

When word reached Lavenstock Hall that at long last, Sir Edward's ship, The Tempest, had docked at Plymouth, the coachman Davis, who'd been on standby for the past week, made haste to the port to fetch the honoured guest.

It was noted by the staff that Miss Linnet sought refuge from her irritation by taking a long gallop on her beloved horse, Pango.

JOHN FOSTER DISEMBARKED from his ship. Grateful to be ashore again, he climbed into the large, dark green coach that his English host had so courteously dispatched to fetch him, and promptly fell asleep.

When he awoke, John stretched his long legs until his joints cracked complainingly. He gave an all-encompassing yawn followed by a grateful sigh. It had been a rough voyage, and a long one. Normally, at this time of year, the trip from the American Colonies took about eight weeks, but high seas and bad weather had delayed the return to England by another six days. It was a tremendous relief to be ashore. He was not a man who took kindly to long periods of inactivity; an athletic fellow, he was a man who enjoyed physical hard work.

Half opening his eyes, he gazed sleepily out of the small carriage window. It was May in England, the hedgerows full of hawthorn blossom. The leaves on the trees were gently unfurling into soft greens and pale yellows, other trees were already in bud. The scented promise of a summer not far away hung sweet and heavy in the spring air. As the soft rolling green countryside of Devon rolled by, John relaxed, enjoying the sights and smells that only an English spring could offer. He found himself pondering upon the health of his host, his late father's dear school friend and former business partner.

When John had first inherited his father's half of the business, Sir Edward Wainwright had invited him to visit his country estate, Lavenstock Hall in Devon. John had been far too busy learning the ropes of his father's import business for the past couple of years to make time for the journey to Britain. Sir Edward was adamant that his girl and John would suit; both parents were keen to strengthen business ties with a family knot. John felt himself to be a brow-beaten man forced on an unnecessary and arduous journey simply to meet a chit of a girl he barely remembered. The last time he'd seen Linnet, she'd been a small, extremely spoilt, precocious young miss. John doubted the girl's suitability on the grounds that a gently raised English miss would not endure the rigours of the Colonies, let alone the arduous sea voyage required to reach the shores of the Americas.

The cumbersome carriage lumbered on, the rolling motion lulling him into a much needed nap. Eventually, they passed through the lodge gates at Lavenstock. The coach lurched while making the awkward turn and John's head snapped forward, rudely awakening him. Glancing blearily through the half opened window, he could see atop the brow of the hill a horse and rider who, upon seeing the coach, turned towards it, riding at breakneck speed down the slope of the hillside. He held his breath, admiring the fluid movement of horse and rider as they seemed to merge as one; the horse, a large black beast, raced along with its tail held high, the rider lying forward, almost flat over the horse's neck.

At first, he'd taken the rider as male due to the fact that this person rode astride but the length of russet hair that streamed out behind indicated this was a female. Her hair, glinting like a flame, caught in the sun's rays. John noticed her physical outline as she swung her horse around, and he perceived in profile the soft curves and shapely form of a woman. Could this possibly be the girl he had come to meet? Intrigued, he watched her disappear around the side of the hill and then he sat back in his seat, wide awake at last and feeling a strong sense of anticipation.

As the coach swept between rolling hills, a view of Lavenstock Hall emerged, its ancient, twisted chimneys standing high above the trees. The house was nestled in a small valley surrounded by parkland. The structure was originally built around Saxon times, hence the name 'Hall,' but different generations of Wainwrights' had added to the original building over the centuries. For the most part, the house was Elizabethan in style, the windows mainly diamond-shaped, set in stone mullion. The architectural mix worked well, the house had a mellow and welcoming appearance. At last, they drew up outside Lavenstock Hall, scattering gravel as the coachman bought the vehicle to a flourishing halt. John was met by Sir Edward Wainwright himself, beaming a jovial smile as he descended the Hall's wide shallow steps, arms flung wide in welcome. "John Foster, at long last, wonderful to see you, m'boy! How is your dear mother, keeping well, I trust?"

John stepped forward and held out his hand with a warm smile which lightened the dark severity of his rather harsh features. A tall man, he stood a head taller than his host. He silently assessed his host's health, studying him closely. He knew that his partner had suffered a seizure before Christmas, and although Sir Edward had written assuring them of his recovery, John and his mother were extremely concerned. It was partly this concern that had prompted John's final decision to agree to travel to England. He noted Sir Edward's skin held a yellowish tinge, his lips underneath the large white moustache showed the thinning of age, and his hazel eyes appeared to have a film across the surface. John frowned. It was a good thing he'd decided to visit.

"Something troubling you, m'boy?" Sir Edward asked his guest.

"No, sir, not at all. Mother is well, I thank you. She sends you her regards and trusts that your health has improved."

Sir Edward placed a friendly hand on John's shoulder. "I could be better, lad, but I tell you, leeches are the answer. A good bleed put me to rights. Upset m'daughter, I can tell you, she don't take to me being bled, disagrees with the practice. I think it's just a case of a female's natural squeamishness. My wife was the same, don't you know. Now come along inside, you must be exhausted!"

Gravel crunched as the coach pulled slowly off to the coach yard situated at the back of the house. Two footmen hastened down the steps and gathered John's luggage. Sir Edward led the way into the house and John followed, answering his hosts questions regarding his journey as they went.

Arriving in the inner hall, they met a young woman coming through from the rear of the house. She wore a dark green riding habit, her skirts unusually split down the middle. John guessed that this must be the rider he'd seen from the coach. Sir Edward went to greet her. "Well met, Linnet, m'dear! You remember John Foster, do you not?"

Sir Edward Wainwright beamed cheerfully at his daughter. She drew herself up ramrod straight, her back rigid. The girl's haughty but beautiful face remained expressionless. She waited, one foot poised upon the bottom of the stair, ready to ascend. Casting a brief glance over John, she spoke directly to her father. "I was a child when last we met but I do vaguely recall him, Papa," she replied in a disinterested tone.

John stared, drinking in her good looks. Such an exquisitely lovely young woman, with a mass of titian hair, her build slender but full breasted. It was her eyes, however, that caught his attention; they were certainly her most striking feature, a clear translucent green, almond-shaped and almost uncannily cat-like. John took a step forward, determined the beauty should notice him.

"How do you do, Miss Wainwright?" he enquired politely.

She raked her gaze over him somewhat insolently before turning her back on him rudely. "Papa, I intend to bathe before dinner." She spun away and ran lightly up the stairs, disappearing from view.

John raised an eyebrow. Phew, she may be a rare beauty but no one had taught her manners. Sir Edward Wainwright was florid with embarrassment.

"Sorry about that, John, my fault entirely, I've quite spoiled her, don't you know! I expect you find that understandable now that you've see what a delectable beauty she is. Actually, she doesn't mean to be ill-mannered. Well now, come along, how about a brandy, m'boy? Follow me." He led the way into his comfortable library, where a fire burned cheerily in a large stone hearth, the yellow flames throwing reflections onto the many richly adorned books that lined the walls. The warm flickering light picked out the odd gleam of gold lettering on the books' spines. After pouring out two goblets of brandy, Sir Edward gestured John toward two chairs placed invitingly either side of the welcoming fire. They sat in companionable silence, ruminating for a while, sipping the warming liquid and contemplating the flames.

Eventually, Sir Edward spoke, "So then, down to business. Have you any more information about that pirate rogue, Jacques?"

John shook his head. "Nothing. The man is like an eel—each time, he slips away without a trace. Still, we are lucky, we've not lost as much to him as others. George Hayden has been unlucky, a whole cargo of the finest silks and satins, gold leaf for braid and ribbon. He has lost a small fortune."

Sir Edward reached up and scratched under his wig thoughtfully. "All that finery being worn by poxy French whores by now, I shouldn't wonder. Godsdamn the man to hell and back! Those Frenchies don't even drink tea! Wonder where our cargo ended up, eh?"

John laughed and shook his head. "We shall never know. He'll have got a good price for it, of that you may be sure. Tea is worth almost as much as gold these days! Providing we don't experience any more misfortunes of the kind, we can cope with the loss of one cargo. We were lucky not to lose the ship as well. Our next shipment due out is in three weeks, aboard The Tempest."

Sir Edward rose to fetch the brandy decanter. John nodded his assent to his host's enquiring gaze, holding out his goblet for a refill.

"We have a problem. This tea levy that Lord North has introduced—the colonists are enraged by what they see as an attempt by the English Government to redeem their losses from the war with France by exploiting them. So they are simply not buying our tea," John explained.

Sir Edward looked thoughtful. "Well, there was a great fuss made about the Declaratory Act in '66, after the Stamp Act was repealed in Parliament. That blew over. I tend to think this will lead to a temporary dip in relations with America, only a minor business setback, I am sure."

John shook his head pensively. "I wish I could share your confidence, sir, but the mood in Boston is very anti-English, especially now, with a garrison stationed in the town. Mother, however, continues to hold her lavish tea parties, she has managed so far, at least, to keep up our regular local sales."

Sir Edward chuckled. "Wonderful woman, your mother, has a head for business as sharp as a whip! Still, it wouldn't hurt to look at the possibility of carrying some other cargo, just in case this all gets out of hand. You are still adamant, I suppose, that we shouldn't touch on the slave market?"

John nodded, his face grim. "I will not be involved with trading in human misery, Sir Edward."

"Well, well, I tend to agree, but we might think about cloth, eh? The mills in the North of England are churning out some wonderful material, thanks to new machinery, and at a damned good price, too. We could turn a profit, I'd be bound. Leave that to me, I'll make enquiries. Now my boy, what do you think of my girl Linnet, a little beauty, eh?"

John sipped his brandy, pondering a careful reply. "She is certainly blessed with good looks. I wonder, though... will I have enough time to court her? She seemed a trifle frosty when we were introduced. Three weeks seems a very short time to woo a reluctant bride. Have you told her of your intention to arrange a match for her?"

"Well, yes… I told her what a handsome fellow you were. I explained to her that you were my partner in business now that your father had passed on. I said it would be a splendid thing if the two of you made a match. Linnet's a little highly strung. It came as something of a shock to her that I was contemplating matrimony for her but I want to see her settled and financially secure. Should anything happen to me, she will be without a roof over head. Lavenstock is entailed down the male line, my second cousin inherits the title." Sir Edward refilled John's glass. "Just give her a few days, John. I know my girl, she'll come around. Why, I'd wager this time next week, you will have a ring on her finger."

CHAPTER 2

*D*uring the next few days, John had difficulty spending any time at all in Linnet's company. She was always out of doors, generally riding. Sir Edward's appeal to her to show John over the estate was simply ignored. After spending a day or two trying to track the elusive Miss Wainwright down, John was despairing of ever having the opportunity to acquaint himself with her. He enlisted the help of an under-groom at great cost—a gold sovereign, no less. The groom was to let him know when she next went riding. He was also to have a horse saddled ready for John's use. Word duly came that Linnet had requested her horse Pango to be tacked ready for ten o'clock that morning, the third day since John's arrival at the Hall.

He hurried to his horse only to watch his quarry disappear from the stable yard at a canter. She sped off into the chilly morning lit by bright, pale sunshine. Muttering a curse, he yelled for the boy to bring his horse about, but by the time John had ridden after her, she was out of sight. John rode in the direction he'd first seen her on the day of his arrival. He gave the horse its head and urged him on at speed, enjoying the freedom and exhilaration of the ride.

He slowed his horse to a trot as they approached a thicket of trees. A rider burst forth and galloped off in the opposite direction. It was, without a doubt, Linnet Wainwright. Her hair flew out behind her like a streak of bright lightning. John urged his horse forward, giving chase. Linnet must have realised that he was pursuing her and was determined to lose him. John, however, was an excellent horseman and had no intention of losing sight of his quarry. They raced on until, to her obvious dismay, he drew alongside of her mount, riding at breakneck speed for a mile or so until he drew close enough to lean over and grab her horse's reins. Holding tight to the leather halter, he gradually slowed both horses to a walk, all the while calming her mount with soothing words in his deep American drawl.

Indignantly, she tried to slap his hands away from the reins, but to no avail. She turned on him furiously, her green eyes flashing with rage as she exclaimed, "You utter fool! What do you think you are doing? You might have killed me!"

John studied her flushed face and his eyes strayed to the swell of her rounded bosom, immediately experiencing a tightening in his loins. He shifted uncomfortably in the saddle, trying in vain to ease the uncomfortable increased tightness of his breeches. He was most pleasantly surprised by his body's instant reaction to the girl. A smile twitched at his lips as he attempted to smooth her ruffled feathers. "Oh, come now. I think you exaggerate, Miss Wainwright, a fine horse woman such as yourself? It would take at least a thunderbolt to unseat you." *Or a lusty fellow such as myself!*

"What is it that you want of me, Mr. Foster?" she interrupted impatiently. He raised an eyebrow at her abruptness but made no comment, deciding it was a good thing she was no mind reader, for she would flee if she could discern his lewd thoughts.

She sat awaiting his reply; a glowering, mulish expression marring her pretty features. When he made no attempt to answer, she tossed her head, gazing haughtily in the opposite direction. It was obvious to him she'd decided that, since he'd engineered their encounter, he could carry the conversation—he knew that she preferred to be left alone to her own devices. They sat in an uneasy silence until the horses, growing restless, began to dance around, snorting and stamping their hooves, impatient to be on the move again.

John openly assessed her. He admired her proud profile and straight back, and the soft wisps of her fiery hair that had escaped the chignon in which she'd tried to arrange it and floated around her pretty, if rather sullen, face. He had the sudden urge to reach out and smooth back the silky strands but he resisted, keeping a firm hold on the reins. Shifting his weight in the saddle, he sighed. "I suppose," he drawled, "it was too much to expect courtesy from you, Miss Wainwright, although I thought at the very least you would honour your father's request that you show me over the Lavenstock estate. Perhaps you are unaware that I am a very stubborn man and I shall not leave your house until I have spent time with you, especially since it is your father's wish that we become further acquainted. I would have thought that, to accomplish this, you would see sense in our continuing to ride together to at least fulfil your obligation to your father."

A flush spread across her cheeks. She was obviously feeling uneasy in his presence—for whatever reason, he appeared to make her nervous. He observed her taking a sidelong peek at him from beneath lowered lashes. Taking a deep breath, she spoke coldly, "Very well, Mr. Foster, I will escort you on a tour of our estate because my father has requested it of me. Will you then agree to leave me in peace?"

John frowned thoughtfully. "Do I invade your peace of mind so much, Miss Wainwright?" he asked mildly.

She flushed. Lifting her chin, she glared at him. "You seem to be ignorant of the fact that since my mother is dead, I am not *Miss* Wainwright but *Lady* Wainwright. Please try to remember that fact, Mr. Foster. Come along... if you still wish to see the estate, that is?" Without waiting for a reply, she turned her horse with a flourish and cantered off. John urged his mount forward whilst muttering an acerbic curse, one definitely not for a lady's ears. He galloped after her.

First, they rode the estate boundaries but then she led him to a small row of farm cottages. All appeared to be in reasonably good repair except the first, which had a battered, dilapidated front door. Shutters were missing from most of the windows. Linnet leapt from her horse and was greeted by a pair of yapping mongrels which she stooped to pat before walking to the cottage and rapping at the door with the end of her silver mounted riding crop. John dismounted and followed her, assuming that was what she expected.

The door was opened by an elderly, unkempt man. His hair, what remained of it, hung in thin, greasy strands. His clothing was stained, and he emitted a pungent odour of unwashed body. At the sight of Linnet, however, his face broke into an almost toothless grin. "Ah, 'tis yerself is it? Come to see Esmeralda, have 'ee?" He flung the old wooden door wide for Linnet to enter. John followed behind, listening to Linnet chatting easily with the old man.

"Has she whelped yet, Jacob?"

"Ay, that she has, Miss, yesterday 't was."

"How many?" she asked.

"Would ye believe nine?"

"Nine?" Linnet exclaimed, clapping her hands.

Jacob led them through the untidy, fetid cottage and out to the back, where a large brick pen, smelling strongly of pig, stood. Linnet leaned over the wall, excitedly exclaiming over the nine small piglets that lay nestled close to their large pink mother. "Hello, my darling, what a clever girl you are. Nine little babies just as lovely as their mama! You will let me hold them in a day or two won't you, Esmeralda? Ah, look at the sweet things!" she cooed, turning her shining green eyes to John. He listened in amazement as this aloof and beautiful girl chatted lovingly to a large, rather dirty, not to mention smelly, porcine mother. All her past animosity toward John seemed forgotten as she explained that pigs liked to keep their piglets to themselves for a few days before they allowed others to hold them.

"How did you become so enamoured with hogs, Lady Wainwright?" he asked curiously.

Linnet gave Jacob an impish grin. He winked, breaking into a phlegm riddled cough before saying, "Ah, well 't was like this, I've two dogs, d' you see, always 'ad two, blest if I knows why?" Jacob stopped and scratched his stubbly chin thoughtfully.

Linnet chuckled then continued the tale. "One of Jacob's dogs was known to be fierce; in fact, my father was always saying that he would knock it on the head if it should ever bite anyone. When I was eight or thereabouts, I was down here in the apple orchard, scrumping apples with the village children... well, strictly speaking *they* were scrumping but since we own the orchard, I was not." She waved a hand at the orchard that ran up almost to the back of the cottages.

"I just couldn't manage to climb a tree, constrained as I was by my long skirts, so I stayed on the ground while the boys threw apples down to me and I caught them in my apron. Suddenly one of the boys yelled a warning, 'Run, it be Jacob's dog!' So up I flew and ran as fast as I possibly could while this awful dog streaked after me, barking like mad! It was at my heels already by the time I had reached here. I scrambled up the wall and flung myself over the other side, straight into Esmeralda's grandmother Primrose's stall! I landed covered in pig filth and slid over to the far side of the pen, squashed up against the wall, covered with muck. Goodness, I was terrified! This simply enormous pink pig started to come toward me; I had heard that pigs could give a very nasty bite. Their teeth lock like so." Linnet linked her fingers to demonstrate.

"Then I remembered the apples in my apron pocket. Luckily, I still had three, so I rolled one across to Primrose; she gobbled it up and came a bit closer. So I rolled another, she ate that one, too, and walked right up to me! I dropped the third apple in fright onto my knee. Primrose ate it and then snuffled my apron, looking for more. When she couldn't find any more apples she lay down like a dog and rested her head in my lap!" Linnet laughed.

"Aye," Jacob confirmed with a shake of his head. "When I comes out to see what the racket was about, I looked over the wall to see Milady sat, covered in pig filth, petting old Primrose like she was a little pet dog! She's a' scratching 'er ears and patting old Primrose an' that pig is a lying' there adoring yon lass! Never seen nothing like it in me life before, an' that's a fact."

Linnet giggled with infectious laughter, she flapped her hand at John. "Wait, though," she chirruped, "the b-best part!"

She tried to speak but was doubled up with gales of infectious laughter. John began to chuckle along with her. "The dogs!" she spluttered, "Jacob's dogs, one was fierce, and one that soppy old lump over there!" She pointed at the larger of the two hairy mongrels, who sat with a lolling tongue, basking in a patch of sunlight. "It was that dog, you see, that had chased me, not the fierce dog at all!" Linnet clutched Jacob as they howled with laughter together.

It was at this point John realised with a jolt that he very much wanted to marry this bewitching, mercurial girl.

CHAPTER 3

*T*he rain lashed the windows of Lavenstock and the howling wind rattled the old panes. The trees beyond the driveway bent double with the ferocity of the elements. John turned away from this depressing scene and glanced over at his host. "Filthy weather for spring, even for England," he muttered. Walking from the sight, he moved to stand next to the blazing fire where he rested his booted foot up on the fender, his elbow on the mantle. He released a long, deep sigh. He had been at the hall for a number of days now and Sir Edward was pressing him to propose to Linnet. Since his ride about the estate with her, John found that now he was himself keen to marry the girl, and this surprised him. He'd been so determined to marry a woman from his own country and although Linnet was extraordinarily beautiful, she was the most bad-mannered, discourteous young woman John had ever met. Had he not seen that other surprising side to her character while at Jacob's cottage, he would certainly have given up on the idea of a match. He was surprised by just how much he desired this spoilt, wilful, proud girl, yet she inflamed his blood and possessed his thoughts until he knew he had to have her.

Coming to a decision, John swung away from the fire and

seated himself opposite his friend. Leaning forward, he looked earnestly into the worried face of his host. "Sir, if Linnet will have me, I should like to take her as my wife. Yet so far, most of our encounters have been at best… chilly. It pains me to have to tell you it is not simply that your daughter is spoilt, but she is also contrary, perverse, arrogant and extremely rude. Her only saving grace is her sense of humour."

Sir Edward chuckled and said, "Oh come now, her beauty sweetens the list of her faults, surely?"

John grinned and nodded affirmation; her beauty and shapely form were on his mind rather a lot of late.

Sir Edward sat back, quietly contemplating for a moment or so before straightening up and leaning forward in his chair. "Very well, John, if you should marry my Linnet, you should know that on my death, everything goes to my daughter—and so to you, as her husband. Now, for her wedding portion, I will sign over The Tempest and one quarter of my interest in our company. Well now, what do you say to that?"

John held up his hands. "You misunderstand me, sir. I am much taken with your daughter. Her beauty is unrivalled and her spirit admirable. It is just that I need a wife who needs must leave all that she knows and travel across the sea to a new world. I intend to propose to her, but there is little I can do if she will not have me."

Sir Edward slapped his knee. "Nonsense! A red-blooded young buck such as yourself knows how to tame a horse. Use that knowledge. Skittish things, horses, much like women, I always think! Linnet must be settled with a man, not some milksop boy who won't be able to deal with her hissy fits! I know my gal, John, and she just won't be happy unless she can respect her man."

"That remains to be seen, sir; your daughter is not impressed with my presence so far. As to my wealth, well, our partnership will, I hope, prevail, whatever the outcome." John smiled, and Sir Edward relaxed, nodding.

"Of course, dear boy, of course. However, you are, I am sure, wrong about Linnet's opinion of you. Why, only this morning I overheard her speaking to her maid, Lottie. She said you were a most handsome man and that if she could take a hand in your choice of dress, she would soon have all the ladies swooning at your feet."

Both men laughed.

Sir Edward had not been quite truthful with his account of eavesdropping, for what he failed to add was that the young lady in question had also said, "The ladies would swoon at his feet but no doubt he would simply glare at them for getting in his way. I assure you that would be the only notice he would take of them!"

LINNET WAS the only daughter of Sir Edward and his late beloved wife, Arabella. She was so named for her maternal grandmother and had been extremely over-indulged by her father. Even the servants were inclined to spoil the bewitching little Linnet. Her mother had been the toast of London during her coming-out season. A stunning young woman with classic pale beauty, Linnet had inherited her mother's loveliness, along with her amazing green eyes. Her hair was much darker than her mother's, a deep burnished copper. From her father, she had inherited something of a temper, along with his stubborn determination. She could outride all her friends and many young gentlemen of her acquaintance. She loved her horses.

When she was ten, she and two stable lads had stolen four old nags from the local horse fair. Actually, the stable lads were unwilling accomplices, coerced by an avenging Linnet. The poor animals were in a terrible condition, they would probably be sold to a knackers' yard. Linnet, however, seeing the beasts tethered the day before, determined to liberate them from their plight. In the dead of night, she and her accomplices crept from the estate and rode into the village. There was nobody about. Certainly the owner of the ancient nags did not expect anyone to steal what he had been unable to sell, dragging the sorry creatures from fair to fair, eventually resenting them any kind of care. The 'horse thieves' simply unfettered the ponies and led them home to Lavenstock Hall.

Even after the experienced care of Sir Edward's stable hands and a goodly diet of oats, the poor animals failed to thrive, eventually succumbing to old age. They died one after the other. Linnet consoled herself with the fact that the poor things had known some comfort at the end of their lives. Sir Edward had bawled his daughter out after the escapade, but even she could tell that he was rather proud of her action. Sir Edward had admired her courage; he told everyone of their acquaintance the tale of her rescue and always ended by praising her 'pluck.'

Meanwhile, Linnet was preparing for that night's ball, her maid Lottie was helping her to dress. "Lottie, do you prefer the green silk or the cream?" She held up the cream gown adorned with tiny pearls, gazing at her reflection in the mirror. Her head was tilted to one side, the tip of her pink tongue caught between her front teeth in concentration.

Lottie stood behind her. "I really cannot say, miss, both are lovely. Hold up the green again, only this time I'll hold the cream next to it, that way we can compare them both, maybe that'll help us decide." She lifted the beautiful green satin up against her mistress and they both gazed intently into the mirror.

"I just don't know," Linnet mused. She glanced sideways at her plump little maid. "What do you think?"

"The green do bring out your eyes, miss. I know you always like to wear green because of your eyes and this gown do make them all glittery an' bright. Wear the green, please, miss!"

Linnet was pleased with the compliment. "All right," she agreed as she twirled around with the chosen gown.

"Come, miss, let me help you into your hoop and petticoats."

"Oh, I do hope he is there tonight. I know he received an invitation because Lady Margaret told me so."

"Mr. Foster, miss?" Lottie laid the green silk upon the bed. Moving across the chamber, she opened the jewellery casket on the dressing table and withdrew an emerald and pearl choker.

"No, of course I don't mean Mr. Foster! I was talking about Lord Charles. Oh, where is my fan?"

"Here it is, miss, I have it!"

"Lottie, why did you think I meant Mr. Foster?" Linnet asked.

Lottie giggled. "He's that handsome miss! I naturally thought it was him you meant."

Linnet gazed thoughtfully at the little maid. She mulled over the time they had spent together. She saw John as an arrogant, darkly forbidding man, not at all the type of gentleman she would consider as husband. The stern, hawk-like profile of his hooded pewter gaze unsettled her. She remembered his self-assurance astride his horse, the powerful shoulders, sturdy thighs clad in fawn riding breeches, muscles that bulged as he'd controlled the restless movement of the beast between his thighs. She shivered at the very thought of enduring such a man as her husband. Her taste ran to an altogether different breed of gentleman—one man in particular, a gentleman with merry blue eyes that held humour and sparkle.

"You think him handsome? He is so dark and forbidding, not to my taste at all. Why, when you compare him to Lord Charles, he seems like an old man, always so critical. Have you noticed his frown?" Linnet pulled a horrible grimace as she plumped down onto the bed.

"Mind your dress, miss!" Lottie gave her mistress a hard shove and retrieved the lovely gown Linnet had just crushed.

Maid and mistress had known each other for a very a long time. Their relationship had developed into a friendship that went beyond their societal roles. Lottie, a pretty, but rather plump girl, had grown up on Sir Edward Wainwright's estate; her father was one of Sir Edward's tenant farmers. She was one of six children and, being the eldest; she was sent into service up at the 'Big House' when only twelve years old. She was a bright and capable girl and soon caught Sir Edward's eye. He was very aware of Linnet's wild streak and thought a young, intelligent girl would have more influence over her more extreme behaviour than an older, duller maid. So far, his judgement had been sound and the two girls, similar in age, had quickly become friends.

Lottie shook out the crumpled green silk and, pushing her arms into it, held it up high. "Come on, miss. Let's get you into your gown now."

Linnet stood up and bent her head into the dress opening. "Lottie," she spoke from the depths of green satin, "have you heard any talk of marriage between this John Foster and myself?"

"Talk, miss? Why no, miss." Lottie pulled the ball gown downward, holding out each sleeve in turn for Linnet to push her arms into.

"It's just that Father keeps on and on about him, continually asking me what I think of him. I feel sure he is planning a match for me, despite my refusal to countenance one. Oh, I do wish Charles would hurry up and propose to me. It would take care of this John Foster problem that Father is fixated upon." Linnet sighed heavily but youthful exuberance meant she quickly forgot her woes as she twirled delightedly about the room. "Do you know, Lottie, you are quite right about this gown. I agree it does make my eyes more noticeable, even though I say so myself! I look quite stunning! Surely Lord Charles won't be able to resist me tonight?"

CHAPTER 4

*L*innet descended the wide staircase. Her hair was piled high, arranged in an artful array of loose curls. Her swan-like neck was adorned with the emerald and pearl choker. The green gown swirled and shimmered around her shapely form. John could see Linnet's uncanny cat's-eyes glinting from where he stood in the hall, waiting for her to descend. When she reached the bottom stair, he stepped forward and offered her his arm gallantly. "You look absolutely beautiful, my dear, your gown is exquisite."

She took his proffered arm, glancing up at him coyly through her lashes. "Mr. Foster, you do surprise me. Such pretty words! Who would have thought you actually capable of flirting? Certainly not I... So, are we ready to depart? My cloak, ah, thank you, Lottie. Do not wait up for me, I shall manage on my own tonight."

Lottie slipped a long, fur-lined hooded cape around her mistress, then curtsied to the group before turning away back up the curved staircase. The merry little entourage, consisting of Linnet, John Foster and Sir Edward, made their way outside to the waiting carriage.

On the short journey, the two men attempted conversation that included Linnet but she wished to be left alone with her thoughts and gazed out of the window. John and Sir Edward eventually reverted to discussing business. They continued their exchange until the coach swept up to the entrance of Sir Henry James and Lady Margaret Peabody's imposing residence.

Linnet gazed about in amazement as she entered the ballroom. The magnificent chandeliers twinkled, sparkling in the light of a hundred candles. The large ornate mirrors that hung on all four walls reflected the soft flickering glow as colourful twirling couples danced to the tune of violins and harpsichord. The music was provided by a group of local ladies who had volunteered to play for the ball. The block wooded floor had been highly polished until it gleamed, rich and mellow. The silks and satins of the guests' clothes shimmered and their jewels sparkled, reflecting the light caught from the sputtering candles in sconces that lined the walls. Linnet gazed about her with delight, one foot tapping in tune with the music. "There you are, puss! My dear, may I present you to Captain and Mistress Pettigrew." Sir Edward beamed at Linnet as she dutifully smiled and curtsied to the older couple.

"Captain, Madam," she murmured politely.

"The captain will shortly be leaving to return to the Colonies, Linnet," her father began, but a cough from behind startled her so she spun around rather too quickly and collided with John Foster. She unbalanced, then tripped sideways over his feet. She stumbled but before she could fall further, she found herself caught up in a pair of strong arms and pressed firmly against a broad chest, a pair of amused grey eyes gazing down into her own.

Linnet felt the vibration rumble deep in his chest as he apologised. "My fault entirely, I believe I may have startled you. Please forgive me. Are you quite recovered, Miss Wainwright?"

She glared up at him and stepped back. "You simpleton," she hissed. "What do you think you are doing creeping up behind me in such an ignoble fashion? Now everyone is staring. Leave me at once! Oh, and Mr. Foster, do remember I am *Lady*, not *Miss* Wainwright!"

Shockingly, he held her fast. He even shook her arm. "Stop this quite unnecessary behaviour. I simply wished to reacquaint myself with the good Captain. I travelled over with Pettigrew from my home, which is in Boston, where the Captain often resides. In a crush such as this, people are bound to fall over one another. Becalm yourself and come dance with me."

He smiled roguishly down at her and for a moment, she was tempted. He looked rather dashing when he smiled that way. She realised Lottie had been right, he *was* good-looking and impeccably dressed for the occasion, although he lacked the fashionable touches that Linnet so admired in Lord Charles's choice of attire. John wore plain knee breeches and silk stockings in white, a plain, high-necked white shirt and stock, topped by a deep wine-coloured dress coat edged with black velvet. His highly polished black shoes were unadorned by fashionable buckles or bows. His dark brown hair was un-powdered and simply tied back in a queue with a black velvet ribbon.

Linnet caught sight of Miss Nancy Trubane, her rival for Lord Charles's affections. The pretty brunette was giggling and pointing over in their direction. She realised with horror that the person Nancy was chuckling with was none other than her beloved Charles. He stood watching them with one knee nonchalantly bent, one hand lazily swinging his eye glass. A tall young man with fair good looks, twinkling blue eyes and an affable, if slightly affected, nature, he was dressed in the very height of fashion, sporting a tall powdered wig and a beautiful satin coat of pale blue frocked in gold. A large diamond pin in his white silk stock winked and sparkled, catching the light as he turned, laughing and chatting to the dimpling Miss Trubane.

Linnet looked about for a distraction but her father and his acquaintances had wandered away. She swung her attentions back to John, who seemed to have given up the idea that she might agree to dance with him and was about to walk away.

"Stop, do not leave me standing here alone! Quickly, take me over to the refreshment table!" She grasped his arm.

"I thought you wished me to leave you in peace?" He raised a quizzical brow.

"I've changed my mind—a lady's prerogative, you know! After all, it is the very least you can do after knocking into me." She held onto his sleeve in an attempt to stop him walking away.

"Linnet, for the last time, I did not knock you over, you cannoned into me. Since you have no wish to dance, I shall waste no more of your precious time. I bid you a good evening." He plucked her hand from his sleeve and strode away, quickly disappearing into the press of people.

"Odious, pig-headed man," Linnet gasped. "What an objectionable and vile creature!"

"To whom are you referring… surely you cannot mean, *moi?*" asked an affected, amused voice at her side. Linnet spun around, startled.

"Charles, my dearest, hullo… No, *never* you! I was speaking of that odious man, John Foster of Boston America. He is my father's business partner. Such a rude ignoramus! Did you witness him cannon into me? I cannot believe he nearly knocked me over completely."

"I believe I might have seen something of the kind." After years of living with a difficult mother, Charles found it advisable to wholeheartedly agree with any female whose ire was up.

"An oaf indeed. I declare, what a crush!" he said. "Come, dear girl, let us dance. I have something I *particularly* want to discuss with you tonight."

Charles took Linnet's hand and led her through the crowd onto the dance floor where they danced a reel. Afterwards, breathless and laughing, they made their way over to the refreshments. Linnet took a lemon drink, sipping the cool, deliciously refreshing liquid. She cast her eye over the dancers, spotting John amongst them. He was partnered with a pretty red-headed girl. Linnet was surprised by the twinge of envy she felt as she watched their progress on the dance floor. John, it seemed, was an accomplished dancer. She wondered how an American trader had learned to dance so well. Charles interrupted her musings. "Miss Wainwright—Linnet— would you care to step outside onto the balcony with me? I do rather need to speak with you."

This is it, thought Linnet, shivering with excitement. *At last, he is going to propose!* "Of course, Charles dear, but I rather need to visit the powder room first…"

Charles's mouth turned down. "Linnet, you look absolutely fine, you have no need of powder or whatnot. Come along with me."

She found herself propelled none too gently across the dance floor. "Charles, for heaven's sake, stop!" Lord Charles obviously wasn't listening. He reached the other side of the dance floor and opened the French doors that led out onto a large balcony. The walls surrounding were covered with roses and honeysuckle, forming an arching bower that gave them some privacy from within. The flowers gave off a deliciously heavy perfume. He closed the doors quietly behind them and then walked to the stone balustrade of the balcony that looked out over the gardens.

Linnet took a deep breath of sweet scented air, leaning on the edge of the balustrade before turning to Charles. "What a heavenly place. It reminds me of the balcony scene in Romeo and Juliet, it is so romantic. Don't you think so, Charles? Charles, are you even listening to me?"

He was distractedly plucking the petals from a pink rose and frowning. "I beg your pardon? Oh, yes, it is quite lovely, I do agree. The thing is this, Linnet… we've known each other nearly all our lives and we are good friends, are we not?"

Excitedly, Linnet held her breath, her heart beating a fast tattoo.

Charles finally blurted, "I really value your friendship. I would like to ask your opinion about something, um, well something rather delicate…"

Linnet's eyes shone as she cried, "Oh, Charles, yes! The answer is yes! Oh my darling, darling Charles! Charles, is something wrong? *Charles*!" He had taken a step backwards. There was a look of absolute horror on his face.

He grasped Linnet's wrists, pulling them from about his neck where she had reached up and entwined them. "I say, old girl... No, Linnet! No, no, huge misunderstanding. Sorry... so sorry! Not us, not you, not you at all, but Nancy!"

Linnet felt her face freeze. Suddenly she felt nauseated. Nancy? Oh, dear God.

"Nancy! Charles... Nancy! For goodness' sake, you mean to tell me... you dragged me out here to talk about... Nancy?"

Charles looked wretched.

"Yes. I am so sorry, Linny, I thought you'd guessed! My wretched mother has had us paired off since babyhood."

Linnet knew that Lord Charles was in awe of his forceful mother. She'd even heard that this formidable Lady had decreed her only son should marry her best friend's daughter, Nancy. This was a match that the two mothers had contrived to bring about since their children were in short skirts but Linnet had assumed—wrongly, it appeared— that she would be able to turn his head and heart in her own direction.

"Nancy's mother is my mother's closest friend, don't you see?" Charles ran a hand distractedly through his hair. He was quite unprepared for what happened next.

He was suddenly propelled backwards over the balustrade, his white satin-clad legs disappearing over the ledge, leaving one shiny black buckled shoe behind on the balcony floor. Linnet leaned out over the edge and peered down into the darkness. There had been a loud splash shortly after Lord Charles had fallen, but since then, only silence.

"My word, but we are out of sorts this evening," a deep male voice drawled from behind her. Linnet spun about and her hand flew to her mouth in surprise. "Mercy... Oh. It's you! You scared me half out of my wits!"

John stood leaning against the wall, one eyebrow quirked. "I do hope you haven't killed that poor unfortunate boy." He studied Linnet's flushed face.

"I'm sure I don't know what you mean." She lifted her chin defensively.

John leaned forward and stooped to retrieve the black shoe that Charles had left behind when he fell. Holding it up, he examined it critically. "Oh come now, this is hardly Cinderella's slipper, is it? I watched the whole thing, Linnet. You didn't think I would let my future wife disappear out onto a balcony with another man and not keep a close watch on the pair of you? You pushed him over the side... oh yes, you did!" He wagged his finger at her as she shook her head in denial. "I saw you do it!"

Linnet spun away from him, vexed, giving a snort of derision. Oh, why couldn't the wretched man go away and leave her in peace? Ignoring John, she peered over the balustrade down into the darkness, calling in a loud whisper. "Charlie, Charles, are you all right? CHARLIE CAN YOU HEAR ME? Perhaps, Mr. Foster, you would be good enough to shout? Your voice will carry better than mine."

John stayed where he was. "I have no intention of leaning over that wall and ending up as the erstwhile Lord Charles did."

She instantly whipped about to face him. "What do you know about it? Absolutely nothing, and I don't know where you acquired the idea that I would consent to marry you! Since you are here, let me put you straight once and for all, *Mr. Foster.* I would not marry you if you were the last man on this earth! Is that clear enough for you? You may finish whatever business you have with my father and return to those uncivilised Colonies that spawned you, but until that happy day, *leave me in peace!*"

He stepped close and grasped her by her shoulders, shaking her once for emphasis. His slate-coloured eyes bored into her wide-eyed pools of green and her face turned mulish as she glowered up at him, defiantly. She shoved her hands up between them, attempting to push him off, but he was having none of it.

"Let go of me, you arrogant swine!"

His grip tightened, his fingers digging in to her tender flesh as he yanked her into his arms, crushing her tight against his chest. His mouth came down hard upon hers, he intended kissing her thoroughly.

Her reaction, when he finally released her, appeared sluggish. She was paralysed with shock, frozen, obviously amazed by his audacity. She struggled to be free of him and succeeded in kicking him in the shins, followed by a stamp upon his foot but he didn't flinch. Instead he pulled her back into his firm embrace, arms tight about her. Perhaps because he held her fast and she couldn't pull away, she relaxed into him.

Then, without warning, he released her. She staggered backward, befuddled and unbalanced by his sudden withdrawal. Startled, she stared up into his face, noticing his tightly clenched jaw and disapproving expression. "J-John?" Her faltering voice sounded breathless, he realised she was panting and watched as she placed her hand over her heart to slow her breathing.

"So you like a kiss, my girl?" he drawled with acid sweetness. "Did Charles not come up trumps tonight... hmm? You thought that I might do as the consolation prize perhaps?" He raised a sardonic brow.

She looked bewildered, hurt and confused by his sarcasm. She lashed out with her foot, catching him a painful blow on the shin then, raising her fist, she cracked him hard across his jaw. Spinning, she flew inside through the door, dashing back into the ballroom.

John stood stunned for a moment, then, turning, he rested his forehead on the edge of the cool stonework of the balustrade. Putting his arms up on either side of his head, he closed his eyes. God, he had been so wrong! How could he have mistaken her ardour for that of a wanton? Indeed, her passionate response had been a real surprise to him, and now that he had so wounded her feelings, it would be well-nigh impossible to court the chit! Damn her pride—*damn his*! He grinned ruefully, rubbing the side of his face. He'd got rather more than he'd bargained for, certainly not a maiden's chaste slap. He'd had lesser blows in taverns back home!

Linnet, meanwhile, had made her way down into the garden. She slipped through the warm, moist heat of the conservatory, out into the cool spring air.

"Charles, where are you? Are you all right?" she called softly.

She walked along the gravel pathway that wound between dark hedges and led to the pond beneath the balcony. The pale moon cast eerie shadows in front of her, the gaps in the hedges loomed dark and menacing. She shivered, glancing nervously from side to side. At last she came to the pond, the black waters glinting still and oily in the moonlight, but there was no sign of Charles anywhere. Linnet wondered whether the pond were deep enough for poor Charles to have drowned. Gingerly, she reached down, placing her hand into the cold dark water. Shivering, she leaned further forward on tiptoes, her feet on the very edge of the pond. She was unprepared for the sudden shove in the middle of her back. She fell, landing face first in the shallow water.

Coughing and spluttering, she surfaced, gasping with shock. She half swam and half stumbled to the edge of the pond, her hair falling in a sodden mass over her face so that she could hardly see. A strong arm reached for her and pulled her out onto the path. She grasped hold of what she realised was a body as wet and as cold as her own. "Charles?"

"Yes, you hellion, it's me!" he hissed venomously.

"Oh, Charlie, I'm so very sorry, really I am! I suppose I deserve the fright you gave me but Charlie… really, *look at me!*"

Charles did as she asked, then he began to chuckle. "You look awful, Linny, but you deserve that… and worse. You could have killed me, you little witch!"

Linnet was relieved he was laughing and seemed unhurt. "I did know there was a pond there but not actually how deep it was. I was so afraid you'd drowned! Oh, my blessed temper, I don't wonder you'd rather marry Nancy," she wailed.

Charles slipped his arm about her shoulders and gave a squeeze. "Linny, I am sorry about our misunderstanding. I honestly thought Nancy had spoken to you of our mothers' plans for the match."

Nancy had, but instead Linnet had chosen to think that Nancy was warning her off a gentleman she fancied. Not for a moment had Linnet believed that Nancy was telling her the truth. After all, they'd both known Charles for years; they were all playmates as children. They had met up many times throughout the intervening years, mainly at social occasions. Then Charles had gone on the grand tour and she had not seen him again until he'd been invited to her coming out ball. At their re-acquaintance, she'd been enamoured of him immediately.

He had grown into a very pretty but vain young man, his character weak; he was very much in awe of his domineering mama. Linnet was captivated by his blond, foppish, fashionable good looks. She'd ignored Nancy's proprietary air and set her cap at him, flirting outrageously, claiming dances with him whenever she could. Charles, who remembered Linnet and their escapades as children, took her interest as renewal of a childhood friendship but nothing more. He now felt wretched at the awful mix up and at his own lack of perception. He looked at her standing in the moonlight, her lovely green dress soaked and dripping in a ruin around her. Her usually pale hair looked dark as it hung in rat-tails, covered in green slime that trailed over her shoulders. She looked frozen.

"Come, Linnet, we can use your coach to travel home. We will drop you at Lavenstock Hall, after which I shall go onto my house, change my clothes, and then return to the ball. I will seek out your father to explain that you were feeling unwell and have withdrawn home." Charles, pleased with his plan, walked briskly away down the gravel pathway in the opposite direction to the house. "Come along, the stable yard is this way, there is a gate to where the coaches stand, follow me!"

Linnet was by this time too cold to argue. Besides, the plan seemed to be a good one and she certainly had no intention of returning to the ball in her present condition. They crept across the stable yard. Yellow light shone out from the groom's quarters above the stables but all was quiet and no one saw them. Opening the gate, they edged along in the shadow of the wall, taking care that the coachmen should not see them. Linnet spotted her father's coach. "It's over there, Charlie! The large dark green one, you can see my father's crest on the side."

"Wait here," Charles whispered. "I'll check inside and see if your man is there."

Luckily, Charles found Davis the coachman happily snoozing inside. Not a social sort, he preferred not to join the other coachmen for a chat and a jar of ale. If Davis was surprised to see his mistress dripping wet, accompanied by a young man in the same condition, well, it really was not his place to comment. He pulled himself up onto the driver's seat, grumbling acerbically as he did so. As soon as they were inside the coach, Charles wrapped a plaid rug over Linnet's knees. He bade Davis to drive them back to Lavenstock Hall.

However, just as Charles had settled onto the seat, the door of the coach was flung wide and John Foster leapt inside. He pulled down the window then bellowed up to Davis, "Hold hard there, man, I will tell you when to drive on!"

Davis tutted, he grumbled but obediently held the horses in check.

"Well!" John looked at each of them in turn, "You two look a sorry sight, I must say!" He settled himself comfortably onto the seat next to Linnet, who flounced as far away from him as the plaid blanket would allow.

"You!" she spat furiously. "What on earth are *you* doing here?"

Linnet was extremely agitated by this unexpected turn of

events. Her plan to put Charles into an uncompromising position so that he had no choice but to marry her was going swimmingly up to the point when John had arrived.

"Let's just say I feared for young Charles's safety, my dear. Well now, how cosy we are! Setting off to Gretna Green perhaps? I must say you have chosen a most interesting fashion to wear for your wedding, not so much *Lady Greensleeves* as *Lady of the Lake!*" John grinned. Covering his fury, he leaned back against the seat and made himself comfortable.

"You insufferable prig, answer my question! What in Hades are you doing here, following me again?" Linnet sneered as she pushed her wet hair back from her face. Leaning forward, she glared venomously at John.

Her intensely green eyes flashed dangerously. John recognised the warning signs of a temper tantrum, so he responded mildly. "I thought I had answered your question, Miss, uh, I apologise... *Lady Wainwright*. I followed you from the garden because I was concerned for Lord Charles's safety. After all, you did push him off a balcony!"

Charles hurriedly interjected, "Yes, but as you see, sir, I have had my revenge!" He gestured towards the bedraggled and dripping Linnet. "We are friends again now, are we not, Linny? I am sorry, but who are you again?" Charles was having trouble keeping up with this evening's strange events.

"So, you have had your revenge, but what of mine?" John asked.

"Yours, sir? I'm afraid I don't quite follow." It appeared that events were becoming rather too complicated for Charles.

"Let me enlighten you, Lord Charles. After you plunged from the balcony this evening, I came upon this young lady leaning over the balcony, shouting for a 'Charles.' I assume that you are said Charles, and not some other poor unfortunate my fiancée has plunged into the pool tonight?"

Linnet spluttered with outrage as Charles first shook then nodded his head. It was obvious to John that he was having difficulty following the tale. John continued, "I was not pleased to hear my fiancée calling out after another gentleman. I took the opportunity to remind her of our betrothal which was arranged this very afternoon by her father, Sir Edward Wainwright, whereupon... I kissed her. This young, um, *lady*, brutally attacked me! Allow me to show you the bruising to my face?"

John tilted his head so the light caught the darkening bruise adorning his cheekbone.

"What?" Linnet shrieked, staring at him in disbelief. "This is complete and utter nonsense! I cannot believe I am hearing this- this tissue of lies! How *dare you* distort what happened tonight! Have you forgotten that I rejected you outright, that there is no engagement?" Obviously incensed, she leapt up then, hitting her head on the coach roof, she dropped straight back down into her seat again. Rubbing her head, she glowered at John. His lip twitched.

Meanwhile, Charles was feeling rather tired and incredibly confused. His head hurt and he thought perhaps he may have banged it during his fall from the balcony. He was finding it difficult to follow the present chain of events. In desperation, he clung to what had just been revealed by John.

"Sir, can it be true?" he asked in a bemused tone. "Sir Edward Wainwright approves your suit and supports your match?"

John looked Charles in the eye. "Yes, I assure you that Sir Edward Wainwright himself arranged our match and will soon announce our betrothal. Tell me, young man, do you feel you have prior claim on Miss—*Lady*—Wainwright's affections?"

Charles was horrified. "Good Lord, no, sir, I had no idea that Linnet was about to become betrothed! Please let me assure you that this evening's circumstances are entirely innocent. Linnet's er, *integrity* should not in any way be held in question. Although her *reputation...*"

Here he faltered and mopped his brow with a wet handkerchief pulled from his sodden waistcoat. Gad, what an awkward situation this was, to be sure. If the American was indeed betrothed to Linnet, then at least he would be free to seek the restful charms of Nancy, which was what he had originally planned before this evening's fiasco. The scandal that seemed only a step away in this present compromising situation could possibly be averted if one of them was engaged to Linnet. Charles was under no illusion that found alone and in their present bedraggled state, he would be honour-bound to offer for Linnet should John decide, in view of present circumstances, to break their betrothal. Charles realised after tonight's escapade that life with Linnet as his wife would be little better, if not much worse, than life with his mother. He was a rather weak man who hated confrontation and felt contented in the company of the mild-mannered and frivolous Nancy. Whenever he complained about his Mamma's high-handedness to Nancy, she would soothe and restore his good humour. Life with Linnet as his wife would be as stressful as living with his mother had been.

Here, then, was Mr. Foster, offering him a splendid solution to his problem, and he was going to do his damndest to accept this olive branch and escape the melodrama Linnet Wainwright was enacting.

Lord Charles's musings were interrupted by a howl of incredulous rage from Linnet. "I am *not* betrothed to you, you imbecile! *Charles, you have to believe me—he is lying!*"

Charles and John snapped in unison, "Be quiet, Linnet!"

John suddenly held out his hand to Charles. "I accept your assurances as a gentleman of honour that nothing unseemly has occurred here tonight. I will endeavour to keep this evening's scandalous events between ourselves but that is on the understanding that you undertake not to see my fiancée alone again."

Both men ignored yet another spluttering yelp. Charles shook John's proffered hand and readily agreed. "I suggest that I leave the pair of you alone to make your arrangements while I find an alternative way home. I congratulate you both on your engagement and wish you good night!" So saying, he hastily opened the coach door and leapt out into the darkness. He could hear Linnet pleading with him the whole way through his pretty speech, but he focused solely on John and ignored Linnet completely. As he squelched away, leaving behind the drama, he counted himself lucky to be leaving this mess totally unscathed and unencumbered by an unwanted fiancée!

John was extremely satisfied by the way things had turned out. Linnet's lack of decorum had placed her in a position where she would have no choice but to accept his proposal of marriage, and when she had calmed down sufficiently, she would realise that this was indeed the case.

Linnet was incensed at Charles's sudden departure and pulled down the carriage window, calling after him, "Charlie! Oh, Charles, do come back!"

She tried to stand up and follow him but the plaid rug caught around her legs and she ended up sprawled across the seat of the coach. John reached over and hauled the wet, seething, angry girl upright. He moved to sit beside her and she immediately begun to berate him for ruining her chances with Charles.

John laid his fingers gently against her lips. "Hush now, and just listen to me, young lady. You *are* going to marry me. You really have no choice in the matter, for if you refuse me, your reputation will be ruined. Lord Charles is very much afraid that if I do not marry you, he will have to, and he so obviously does not wish to!" He held up his hand for silence as she vehemently protested. "Yes, I am very much aware that such was your intention, my girl, but as you see, Lord Charles..." John paused and suddenly leant forward, pushing open the door to the coach which, in his hurry to leave, Charles had left slightly ajar.

It swung open, revealing Davis the coachman standing with his ear pressed to the door, eavesdropping. Caught red-handed, he stepped back, his face flushed. "Sir, er, shall you want to leave now?" he stammered.

"Yes," John replied smoothly. "Drive us back then return for Sir Edward. I shall pen a note for you to take to him on your return which will explain the situation." He calmly leaned over and tugged the door fully closed.

He then pulled the curtains across at both windows. "That will prevent draughts and any other eavesdroppers. I am sure that you saw Davis's face, my dear? This juicy titbit of gossip will be talked of in all the best drawing rooms before the week is out. Accept our betrothal, for you really have no other choice."

His grey eyes flicked over her, taking in her bedraggled appearance. "Come, let me see to you. Look at you, completely drenched. Move over here, closer to me."

He watched as her eyes filled with foreboding. She shuffled across the seat away from him. She pulled the rug up under her chin, staring warily over it with narrowed eyes while failing to suppress her shivering.

"Now what is the matter?" he asked. "Look, as much as I would like to put you over my knee and spank you soundly—which, incidentally, you do very much deserve—I think we must concentrate on getting you warm, if not dry, before you catch your death from cold. Just look how wet you are!" He took hold of the blanket and pulled it away from her. "Come now, there's a good girl, let's get you as dry as we can," he coaxed.

He'd intended to rub her briskly with the blanket, but when he stretched out his hand, she whipped forward and sank her teeth deep into his wrist, drawing blood. "Yee-ouch! Why, you spiteful baggage! I have a good mind to— You have been asking for this, you little brat. That's it, I'm going to warm you properly!"

Provoked beyond endurance and recalling her vicious attack upon him earlier in the evening, not to mention her ill-mannered behaviour over the past few days, he hauled Linnet across his knee, determined to teach her a much-needed lesson in manners. Raising his arm, he proceeded to spank her with emphasis. Her head was smothered in the wet wool rug, which hampered her struggles and muffled her cries. She managed to sink her teeth into John's thigh. Although the blanket took the worst of the bite, he jumped and gritted his teeth, compelled to teach the English harridan a lesson she'd not soon forget.

He flung up her wet gown and petticoats, baring her peachy behind. She stilled for a moment, and he surmised that she was in shock. He took his time admiring the pair of alabaster orbs lying face up across his lap and stroked her silken skin before raising his hand. He landed a satisfying slap on her exposed bottom, more than pleased by the pink hand-mark now blooming on her pale skin. She shrieked, no longer still. John continued to spank her, catching her hand as she tried to protect her pink posterior.

"Oh no you don't," he scolded, his voice dark with warning.

He continued slapping her rear end, his arm swinging in a repetitive arc, delivering the chastisement with immense pleasure. "You have been spoiled, a privileged brat all your life. Your father should have taken you in hand years ago but never fear, you are about to take a husband. I shall see to all your needs. After we are wed, I will address the subject of your neglected discipline."

She howled, she kicked, but to no avail. It was obvious to John that no one had ever dared to treat her thus before. "You earned this spanking. Once we are wed you will find I have a low tolerance for sassy, brattish behaviour." Her flesh felt heated under his chastising hand. She began to weep in earnest.

Finally, her writhing behind well and truly punished, he released her.

"Don't you d-dare laugh at me!" she cried. "As soon as my father hears about this, he'll k-kill you, you brute!"

Her mouth wobbled precariously. He grinned, for with her narrowed green eyes, she resembled a spitting kitten.

Once the coach had finally arrived at the house, Davis jumped down and opened the carriage door. He leapt back in surprise as his mistress tumbled down from the coach and streaked headlong across the gravel and into the house. John leaned forward to watch as she disappeared, shaking his head pensively. Slowly he clambered down from the coach himself and followed her path into the entrance.

Once inside, he went straight to the library, where he knew Sir Edward Wainwright kept his brandy. He poured himself a generous tot then wrote a brief note to Sir Edward, handing it to a footman before settling himself into a comfortable fireside chair to await his host's return. He knew that he should be the one to tell Linnet's father what had occurred that night, and wondered how the elderly gentleman would react to John spanking his darling girl.

Linnet, meanwhile, ran straight up to her bedroom. She was sorry now that she had told Lottie not to wait up for her. Trying to remove her soaking wet satin ball gown by herself was no easy task, particularly when her fingers were stiff with cold and she was shivering violently. Eventually, she managed to free herself of the cumbersome gown. Using an old soft blanket, she rubbed her hair and body vigorously dry. After throwing some coal onto the dying fire, she gave it a rattle with the poker that brought it back to life. She hurried to the bed, snuggling into the soft inviting depths.

As she lay waiting restlessly for sleep, she reflected miserably upon her disastrous evening. First, she pondered that extraordinary kiss. She wondered at her reaction to the American. That intoxicating male smell, overlaid by the scent bay rum which so aroused her senses. Her awareness of his body warmth as his heat had seeped through the flimsy material of her gown, warming her flesh, lulling her into a false sense of security. She remembered the steady beat of his heart as he held her close. The slow, sensuous pressure of his lips pressed to hers, which caused such languor as her lips responded to his.

She had been suddenly and acutely aware of her own body, of her breasts and hardening nipples pressed up against the hard planes of his chest. Her heart had pounded, the blood racing through her veins as desire held her enthralled. It was as if time had ceased, and all that remained was his kiss. Her lips had moved involuntarily, responding to the hypnotic, sensuous rhythm he'd set, with the impudent flicking of his tongue. Compliantly, she'd parted her mouth, allowing his tongue entrance. Even now she felt intensely excited by the thought of his unexpected invasion of her virginal ingress, her first ever kiss. Then the hurtful rejection as he'd shoved her away, heaping scorn upon her, confusing her, playing with her fragile emotions.

Tears of self-pity filled her eyes. Oh, how she loathed the odious man! How dare he treat her in such a barbaric way! She'd never been so humiliated in all her life and then to top it all he'd spanked her! She tossed in the bed, trembling with ire and indignation. No one, but no one, had ever subjected her to such treatment before. Oh, how she hated this arrogant fellow, this American interloper, John Foster! She'd never marry him, no, not even if he were the last man on this earth. Her father would be utterly livid with John Foster; he would probably hang him for what he'd done to his precious daughter. She enjoyed a satisfying vision of John Foster hanging from their huge oak tree in the garden. At the very least, Sir Edward would cut business ties with the man.

Her father would see that she had been right all along and stop this foolish plan to marry her off to the colonial lout. She knew Sir Edward would be absolutely horrified by tonight's events, there was no doubt in her mind that when she arose in the morning, John —*bloody, yes that's the word for him, bloody*—John Foster would be exiled from the house for good! She smiled drowsily to herself, content at the thought as she drifted away into a deep sleep.

THE NEXT MORNING dawned chill but bright. Linnet awoke and, refreshed, she lay listening to the bird song outside for a moment then stretched and threw off the covers. Lottie tapped at the door and walked straight in as she was wont to do every morning. She carried a pail of steaming hot water.

"I thought after your escapade last night, you might like to soak in the tub. Hattie and Jane are following me with more hot water. I'll leave this here and fetch the tub. Mr. Foster had a bath this morning, so—"

Linnet interrupted her. "*What?* That man is still here?"

"Why yes, miss, an' there are secrets afoot if you ask me," Lottie said, tapping the side of her nose, nodding sagely.

"Whatever do you mean, Lottie, *secrets*?" But before Lottie had time to answer, the upstairs maid arrived with more hot water. Lottie slipped out of the door to fetch the copper tub used by the family for bathing.

Later that day, Linnet sat alone on the pinnacle of a hill some way from Lavenstock. It was a favourite spot of hers. The fragrant meadow afforded a lovely view that swept as far as the sea. She was reeling from shock at the interview she'd had with her father. Fully expecting outrage on her behalf, after the previous night's spanking incident, she had been unprepared for his hostile reaction toward her.

He'd summoned her to his study after she'd breakfasted, and castigated her. Seating herself confidently in the chair opposite his desk, it had taken her a few moments to understand that it was *she* he was berating and not the odious Foster! Sir Edward had not even let her interrupt him to explain the true version of the previous night's events. She realised that she'd never before seen her father so angry with her. He'd left her no choice but had outlined a course for her, demanding in no uncertain terms that she marry John Foster. Without the marriage, he insisted, she would be ruined by her behaviour the previous evening. He would brook no disobedience from her. He berated himself for sparing the rod and spoiling her.

It was at this point that Linnet had indignantly raised a protest but, holding a hand up to silence her, Sir Edward had bellowed at her, his face purple with rage. Linnet had found herself nervous of her father for the first time in her life, and had subsided quietly into her chair, listening without further interruption until he'd finished.

The essence of the scolding was that she would marry John Foster. Her dowry would ensure that John would become sole heir to the business. As the dry financial details were explained to her, Linnet realised that John Foster would, in effect, own her. She was informed that they were to marry a fortnight hence and leave for Boston America from Plymouth on the following day. They would travel on one of the company's ships, The Tempest, which her father had given to Foster as a wedding gift. It would be carrying a cargo of tea and cloth back to Boston. When Sir Edward finished his litany, Linnet had fled to her room, hastily donned her riding habit, and left the house. She'd galloped away at speed a short while later, riding her beloved horse, Pango.

She now sat upon the ground, wondering what on earth she should do about the whole tangled situation. Desolately, she plucked at the soft spring grass. She'd always assumed that she would be allowed to choose her own husband. Her father had always indulged her; it had not even occurred to her that he might select a husband for her, let alone a man she did not like!

Oh, she knew well enough that it was common practice for parents to make matches for their daughters. But having grown up without a mother, she'd become accustomed to thinking for herself. After all, her father had encouraged her to do just that.

She found her thoughts drifting to this man, Foster. She grudgingly admitted he was handsome, if you liked dark brooding men, which she most certainly did not. There was something dangerous about him—there had to be, for her to feel so unsettled around him—especially after the humiliating way he'd treated her the previous night. The situation was so unfair. She wanted to marry someone easy-going like Charles, someone who would not interfere overmuch with her perfect life, someone who would leave her to plan their social calendar, giving her free rein to do pretty much as she liked. Not some overbearing tyrant like this Foster, a man who resorted to violence when he was disagreed with. She sniffed disdainfully. What was it her father had said? Ah, yes. "John tells me that you are a wilful and heedless young woman who is in need of a strong man for your husband, one who will know how to quell and modify your behaviour." Linnet squirmed, absolutely mortified. She was furious. Imagine the nerve of the man, his insufferable cheek unbelievable!

"Oooh, he is a detestable, bullying oaf!" she squealed aloud, startling Pango, who swung his head up from where he was quietly cropping the lush spring grass. His dark intelligent eyes watched his beloved mistress, apparently waiting to see if she was about to call him to her but since Linnet continued to sit, quietly frowning into the distance, he dropped his head back down to tear at the turf once more.

She decided that if things did not change within two weeks and she did end up married to that insufferable bastard, she'd run him a merry dance. If she could make his life difficult enough, perhaps she'd be able to come to some agreement with him. She'd suggest that he return to Boston alone, leaving her behind with her father. After all, plenty of marriages continued in just such a manner. The more she thought about her plan, the more sensible it appeared to be. Fairly soon, she felt much better about her situation, so much so that she decided that when she saw John next, she'd suggest her proposal immediately. She intended to use her father's age and frailty as a lever to her remaining in England while he returned, with good riddance, to the New World. Having solved things to her own satisfaction, she re-mounted and turned in the direction of home.

On her return to Lavenstock, Linnet was dismayed to find that John had left the house. She was told that he would not be returning until the day of their proposed wedding. The reason given was that he had business to attend to in Plymouth.

In actual fact, although he did have some tasks to attend to, the real reason was that he suspected Linnet would attempt some sort of hare-brained scheme to scupper their wedding. He had no wish to antagonise or irritate her with his constant presence and so he concluded the sensible solution was for him to remove himself as far from her wrath as possible.

Sir Edward Wainwright was adamant that the wedding would take place; he was extremely pleased that his plans had come to fruition. He was most reassuring and jovial whilst seeing John into his coach after luncheon.

Linnet was at first dismayed by John's absence but then relieved to find him gone. Embarrassed by the treatment he'd meted out to her in the coach the previous evening, she was pleased not to have to face him again so soon, reasoning that with him out of the way, she could persuade her father to let her remain behind in England while John returned to the Americas.

Now that she felt calmer, Linnet began to face the fact that in the society in which they lived, where the slightest hint of scandal ruined a young girl's reputation, she really had no other option but to accept John's proposal of marriage. Of the marriage bed, well, whenever her thoughts drifted to that terrifying, rather embarrassing subject, she remembered their kiss upon the balcony at the ball and her confusion grew, so she decided not to dwell any further on the matter.

The days passed quickly in a whirl of activity. Linnet settled down, she began to enjoy the fuss and attention afforded her as a bride. Her mother's wedding gown was brought down from the attic; it had been carefully wrapped and preserved in camphor and linen. The heavy garment had once been pale yellow but was now aged to a deep golden cream. The high, rounded neckline had a border ruff, edged with tiny seed pearls. The sleeves hung below the elbow. The bodice was silk with a layer of lace, sewn with more seed pearls. The front was a stiff panel with an attached skirt of flounced edges, each flounce decorated with a cream embroidered rose which was embellished with seed pearls. A train of the same material hung from the shoulders of the gown. The style was not of today's fashion, but for once, Linnet did not care. This was her beloved mother's wedding gown, and she was thrilled with it. After all, it was still a strikingly beautiful dress of quality and richness, and she loved it.

Linnet had put forward her post-marriage plan to her father, and he had rather surprisingly listened to her. Sir Edward even appeared to agree with her plan. He told her that, contrary to her opinion, John was a very reasonable and kindly young man, one who would no doubt consider what she had suggested most seriously. Since this conversation, Linnet had convinced herself that the problem was as good as solved. Her troublesome husband would soon be gone from whence he came, while she would remain behind at Lavenstock Hall. Free to continue the life that she loved.

CHAPTER 5

*T*he day of Linnet's wedding dawned cloudy and dull. *So much for good omens*, she brooded as she gazed out of her bedroom window at the depressingly dull weather. She'd breakfasted in bed then bathed in the linen-lined copper tub. Lottie put up her hair, parted at the back with a profusion of burnished ringlets and leaving a few wispy tendrils that framed Linnet's face. She planned to wear her mother's pearl drop earrings but no other jewellery.

Linnet turned away from the window and slipped her feet into her soft satin slippers. Standing quietly in her shift, she waited for Lottie to place her wedding dress over her head. Amazingly, she felt calm and rather dreamy. Lottie needed Hattie's help to lift the layers of foamy petticoats over Linnet's head and smooth them down. Then, carefully, gently, they put the precious wedding gown on their mistress while she stood patiently. Lottie fastened the many laces at the back of the gown. "There! All done, miss. Ah, mistress Linnet, you look like a princess from a fairytale, you do," Lottie cooed as she turned Linnet to see herself in the looking glass.

Linnet gazed at her reflection; she did indeed look like a regal princess. She swished to and fro in front of the mirror, the voluminous dress and petticoats rustling pleasingly as she moved.

"My roses please, Lottie."

Handing Linnet her bouquet of the palest pink and cream roses, bound up in a creamy satin ribbon to match her dress, Lottie's eyes misted over. "Miss Linnet, might I wish you every happiness?"

"Why, thank you, Lottie dear."

Linnet kissed her little maid's warm, flushed cheek. The maid took out her handkerchief and blew hard. Linnet patted her shoulder. Taking a deep breath, she turned and walked out of the door, head held high, accepting of her fate.

Sir Edward Wainwright was pacing downstairs. Wandering from his study into the hall then back again, luckily, he happened to be in the hall as Linnet descended the staircase. Hearing a faint rustling of skirts, he glanced up and his breath caught in his throat as he watched his beautiful, beloved daughter slowly make her way down the curved stairway. She looked for a moment just as his dear Arabella had on their wedding day so many, many years ago.

He wiped a tear from his rheumy eye and blew his nose loudly. How could he bear to part with his enchanting, green-eyed puss? The last link, it seemed, with his darling Arabella. He had put forward Linnet's suggestion that she remain here at Lavenstock with him while John returned to the Colonies but John had kindly and firmly refused to consider the idea. Truth be told, Sir Edward would not have respected the man had he agreed to Linnet's plan. A man should have his wife beside him, why else take a wife? He knew he would miss his daughter's presence dreadfully but at least he felt assured that she would be well cared for when his own end came about.

Linnet stepped down from the last stair and stood in front of her father. He placed his hands upon her shoulders, holding held her at arm's length, he studied her. Smiling down at her, he nodded, satisfied. Then he took her into his embrace, gently rocking her.

"Papa?" Linnet queried softly.

"My dearest child, a child no longer, you looked so like your dear mother coming down those stairs. You look beautiful, my green-eyed puss. Make John a good wife, this man is my own choice of husband for you and I am sure he will make you happy, my dearest. Be kind to him, and he will be kind to you. Now, come... t'wouldn't do to be late for your own wedding!" He kissed her forehead then drew her arm through his own as he walked her to the entrance.

Outside, an open-topped carriage awaited, festooned with cream and pale pink ribbons. The air was still damp from the earlier rain, and droplets of water sparkled in the weak sunlight. She climbed into the carriage in a daze. As she gazed about her, she was suddenly acutely aware of every detail, the way the hairs on her father's wrist curled at the cuff of his sleeve as he placed his hand upon the carriage door, the rainbow of colours mirrored within each tiny droplet of moisture standing on the surface of the coach, the hairline criss-cross scratches upon the leather seats inside the carriage.

In next to no time, they'd arrived at the chapel situated within the estate grounds. The little grey stone building seemed to be packed with people whereas, in actual fact, there were only around fifty or so guests gathered inside. The chapel was rarely as full as this; usually only the estate workers and household staff joined the family for services on a Sunday. Today, most of those people were there, plus other local folk such as the doctor, who had seen Linnet through all her childhood ailments, and her old governess, Miss Spires, now retired and living with her sister in Portsmouth. Of course Charles and his mother had come, together with Nancy, accompanied by her parents. A brace of Sir Edward's business friends had also been invited. On John's side, only the captain from one of his ships and his wife were there. John's English lawyer stood as his best man.

Linnet seemed to float down the aisle in her dream-like state.

Dust motes hung suspended in the stream of refracted golden light that spilled inside from the chapel's stained windows. Thick candles sputtered softly, adding an ethereal quality to the occasion. As she glided past the wedding guests, each person turned to watch her pass by and then sighed. It appeared to Linnet as though she walked through a sea of whispering, swaying corn.

At last, she stood before the altar, and she turned to look at the man she was to marry, studying him frankly. He was a tall man with the healthy tanned complexion of one who spends much of his time out of doors. His dark brown hair was tied back with a black velvet ribbon. His lips were well defined, his chin square and firm—in all, his was a rather severe face. Finally, she raised her eyes to meet his compelling gaze, thick dark lashes that surrounded pewter grey eyes unusual in their intensity. She found it hard to maintain eye contact and blushed. John nodded graciously to his bride, a small smile twitched at the corner of his mouth as he witnessed the heat suffusing her face.

She had not seen him since he'd spanked her inside the coach. There was no sign of the hoyden today as she stood demurely by his side. He was entranced by her fey beauty as he watched her study him from under her lashes. His bride looked like an angel; how could this ravishing creature be so stubbornly wilful? The service flowed smoothly, and finally, they emerged from the chapel into a watery sunlight as Mr. and Mistress John Foster.

Suddenly, it seemed to Linnet that everyone around her was shouting. The noise burst in upon her inner world as she emerged from her dream, jolted. Voices seemed extraordinarily loud. Overwhelmed by people's good wishes, Linnet was jostled and kissed, turned this way and that. Finally, she could cope with no more; she was close to tears. She felt her elbow grasped firmly as she was led forward to the waiting coach. John guided his new wife to the carriage step. "Are you unwell?" he inquired quietly.

"Pardon?" Linnet asked faintly then realised what he'd asked. "No. I-I don't know. I-I feel most peculiar."

She swayed as she spoke. John immediately swept his arm under her. Lifting her, he cradled her against his chest and studied her pale, upturned face with a frown of concern. Instinctively, Linnet slipped her arms around his neck. A slight smile softened his mouth as he whispered into her ear, "Mrs Foster, you are an extremely beautiful woman."

Lowering his head, he kissed her gently upon her mouth, moving his lips over hers in a soft caress. Shyly, Linnet yielded to him. John lifted his head and gazed into her intriguing green eyes, wondering if her thoughts were of the marriage bed. He had thought of little else these past few days.

The crowd of guests witnessing this romantic kiss began to clap and cheer. John grinned at them and stepped up into the carriage, where he placed Linnet upon the seat before sitting opposite her.

On their arrival at the Hall, they were met by a footman who handed them up a glass of mead each, an old tradition in this area of Devonshire. Linnet began to feel much better after the mead had warmed her stomach and lightened her spirits. The party feasted well on cold salmon, followed by roast meats of venison, duckling and beef. Followed by Jellies, sweet flummery, fruit pie and thick clotted cream. Linnet and John sat at opposite ends of the long table. They stole sly glances at one another, each when they thought the other wasn't watching. John thought her the most desirable and beautiful bride ever, but as Linnet nervously observed John's brooding dark looks, she feared his masculinity.

After the meal, there was dancing outside in one of the barns, mainly for the servants and farm workers. But a few guests joined in, attracted by the jaunty music; a wedding was always a great leveller of people.

As Linnet stood talking to Jackson, her father's bailiff, Lord Charles and Nancy approached.

"Dearest, you look breathtaking!" Charles exclaimed.

"Why, thank you, Charles. Regretting letting me go now, are you?" Linnet teased as she bent forward, accepting his kiss before turning to Nancy and embracing her. Nancy, upon receiving her kiss, gave Linnet a little hug. "You shall be nearly the first to know, outside of the families, of course, that Charles and I are to be engaged next week!" Nancy beamed.

"Yes, we are to become engaged, Linnet. We shall shortly be joining you and John in wedded bliss!"

Charles sounded exuberant and Linnet could see he was relieved by the way things had resolved themselves.

"I am very pleased for you both. When do you expect your wedding will take place?" she asked politely.

"Not until sometime next summer, I should think." Nancy answered for the both of them. "I have to prepare my trousseau; oh, there is so much to do!"

Sir Edward walked over and stood behind them. Listening quietly, he placed his hands on each of their shoulders. "I couldn't help overhearing; congratulations to you both. About time you two tied the knot, eh?"

He clapped Charles on the shoulder in a congratulatory manner then turned to Linnet. "Can I have a quiet word, my child? Please excuse us."

He bowed graciously to Nancy and Charles and escorted Linnet out into the hall. "Lottie awaits you up in your chamber, my dear. She has had the rose guest room prepared for you both tonight."

Somewhat embarrassed, Sir Edward kissed his daughter's forehead then pushed her gently towards the stairs. "I shall bid you good night, darling girl." He turned, hurrying back to his guests, most of whom would shortly leave now that the bride had retired.

Linnet reluctantly made her way up to the rose bedroom, so named for the rose-patterned wall paper and deep pink bed hangings. Lottie undid all the lacings she had carefully laced together only a few hours previous. A little while later, Linnet found herself lying beneath starched linen sheets, and her stomach lurched while her heart beat a fast tattoo. A fire burned merrily in the hearth, the flickering light sending out a cheery orange glow, banishing the strange shadows into the darkened corners of the room. Linnet, freshly washed and scented by Lottie, had reluctantly climbed into the enormous bed.

She wore a diaphanous nightgown of white silk, which kept sliding from her shoulders. It was newly made by Lottie as a wedding gift for her. The material was of finest silk and, in the candlelight, quite revealingly transparent. Lottie had sewn lace ruffles at the cuffs and added a pull string at the open neck. She was a good needlewoman, and although she had not had very much time to make the nightgown, she had made an excellent job of it.

Linnet lay abed, nervously awaiting the arrival of her new husband. She felt so nervous that she had to grit her teeth together to stop them from chattering. Yet there was an inner excitement, for at last she would share the secrets of the marriage bed. She attempted to relax, only to freeze a moment later at the sound of the door opening. More candlelight spilled into the room as John entered, softly closing the door behind him.

"Linnet," he whispered into the shadowy room.

"Yes?" she queried softly.

"Lordy but it is dark in here! I shall light some additional candles."

She could hear John as he rustled around looking for tapers.

"No! No please don't," she cried, sitting up flustered.

John moved over to the bed and sat beside her. Looking at her wan face, he reached out a finger and stroked her pale cheek before letting his hand drop to her lap, whereupon he took hold of her cold hand. He rubbed the back of her hand with his thumb while he watched her, a thoughtful expression on his face. "You are afraid," he stated. She nodded. He reached out and lifted her chin with his finger.

"No, don't pull away, let me look at you. You have no need to fear me, Linnet. I am your husband. As such, I promise that I shall love, cherish and protect you always, until the day I die." Gently he gathered her against his chest, his arms encircling her.

She started to speak, but he interrupted her. "Hush, hear me out. Your father wrote to me many months ago, asking me to consider taking you to wife. I only remembered you as a young child. I worried about how an English lady, gently bred, would cope living in the Americas. The Colonies are quite unlike England; much of the land is wild, untamed. Oh, it is beautiful, far more so, I think, than England, but it is not a safe and cosy country, no place for a delicate English rose. Eventually, under pressure from my mother and your father, I decided to travel here in order to assess the possibility—not expecting anything to come of my trip. Imagine my surprise when I found that I liked what I saw. You were beautiful, strong, healthy and feisty!"

Linnet went rigid in his arms. She shook with the fury that filled her. "How dare you? Just as if I were some brood mare or… or prize cow!"

She bounced off the bed, yanking out from his embrace. Her eyes blazed furiously at him, especially when he laughed. "Your reaction now is exactly why I *did* marry you! Your courage has the ring of true fighting pioneer spirit!"

Linnet was completely nonplussed. He grinned. "I require that you grow out of your selfish and, if I may say so, somewhat childish behaviour, but you are now mine, my lovely, brave wife. I think you will cope admirably with the rigours of the Colonies." He swiftly reached out and pulled her down upon his lap, keeping her arms pinned. She was annoyed that thus restrained she would be unable to slap him if she felt inclined. He lowered his head and kissed her with searing passion.

Furiously, she struggled. How dare he kiss her after saying those unflattering things about her? She wanted to claw his eyes out! She had things she wished to say to the beast! His lips were distracting, persistent and demanding. She looked into those hooded grey eyes and, seeing his determination, she quickly closed her own. After a while, all she could think about were the delicious feelings he aroused within her treacherous body. She responded to him despite herself.

Her limbs began to feel loose and languid, the pebbled tips of her breasts tingled. She was acutely aware of her thinly clad bosom pressed firm against his open shirt front. His hand roved; cupping her breast, he rolled her pert nipple through the gossamer thin material of her nightgown. "My own darling girl," he murmured.

She shivered, goose bumps lifting across her skin at the erotic sensation of masculine hands touching her flesh intimately for the very first time. He tipped her over onto her back, not once breaking their kiss. When his tongue flicked at the inside of her lips, she sighed. He pulled up her gown, one hand on the firm mound of her breast, rolling and squeezing the aching nub. She arched her back, moaning inarticulately, softly compliant, open and trusting. It was as if all that existed in the world were the wonderful carnal sensations he created deeply within her. She quivered under his questing fingers as his hands slowly explored the soft slopes of her body, stroking and knowing. She writhed beneath him as arousing shivers pulsed through her. Finally, he slid his hand between her thighs, his fingers going to the heart of her newly awoken desires, that slippery cleft betwixt her legs. She called his name aloud as the thrumming pulse ignited at his touch.

She noticed his dark hand lying between her smooth pale thighs and at the copper-haired mons of her sex. He moved away, leaving her feeling strangely bereft as he quickly stripped off his clothing. As he turned toward her she saw his shaft had stiffened, lengthening to its fullest extent.

She did not know that it had been a long time since he had been with a woman, and never one as beautiful as his new bride.

She hoped that he would be able to control the beast she appeared to wake in him and he would take her as gently as she deserved on her wedding night. His fingers caressed her sweet, wet divide, igniting an erotic rhythm within her. She was overwhelmed by her body's powerful response to his caresses as the sensation of fluttering swirled deep in her belly.

Raising himself up until he was poised over her, his hands either side of her face, his thumbs caressed her soft cheeks. "I will attempt to make this easy for you, my love; the first time is always bad for a woman, but next time, I promise that it shall be different."

The soaring sensation ended abruptly, leaving her feeling needy and confused. John's weight pressed down upon her, replacing the sweet spiralling sensation with a forceful and intruding pain. "No!" she cried, attempting to push herself up the bed and out from under him. "Stop, no, please it hurts!" she cried.

John held her shoulders firmly and penetrated her with a powerful thrust. She felt her virgin flesh tear and he pulled back. She breathed a sigh of relief that it was over but as he moved again, she realised that he'd only paused momentarily. At least the small lack of movement had allowed her breathing space to become accustomed to the feel of his shaft deeply embedded in her virgin flesh. He slid in and out again. She gasped, digging her nails deep into his shoulders, not quite sure if she was pushing him away or pulling him to her. Nothing else existed, only the sensation of being joined at the hip with the alien feel of his swollen member centred within her apex.

He lowered his head to kiss her, she nipped his lip. With a quiet ferocity he snapped his hips, pushing deeply within her. He then began pounding into her as he moved toward his obvious need for release.

For her, it was a burning, stinging ordeal which ended suddenly, with John stiffening as he gave a loud bellow. He slumped forward, lying still, the sudden dead weight a shock to her. He appeared relaxed as he lay with his full body weight pressed down heavily upon her. Linnet lay there feeling sore, sticky and slightly nauseous. How did women endure it? This was meant to be love? Those wonderful sensations that she had begun with, they led to this, this *disappointment*? She pushed at John's inert body, wanting him away from her. She wanted to weep and to scold.

He rolled off, murmuring her name sweetly but Linnet moved onto her side, shifting to the far edge of the bed. She pulled the covers high about her ears, curled in a ball.

John sighed heavily. He turned upon his side so that he was spooned around her stiff back. Putting an arm about her, he lifted the cascade of her hair and kissed her shoulder. "I know that I have hurt you, my love. I am sorry but I assure you, it will be different for you next time. It is always difficult for the lady on her first time. Sleep now, my sweet. We have an early start on the morrow. Good night, Mistress Foster." She tolerated his kiss on her unresponsive cheek. He yawned, then, settling himself, he promptly fell asleep.

Linnet lay in her tight knot, wishing her mother were still alive so she might go to her with her many unanswered questions. Silently she wept as she listened to John's deep, even breathing. At last she, too, fell into an exhausted sleep.

When she awoke, she knew instinctively that she was alone. Rolling onto her back, she glanced around the room. Sure enough, there was no one there. It was early; dawn. Perhaps John had already left on his journey to America. She hoped so. At least, unlike many other women, she would not have to endure *that* more than once or twice a year. There was a light tap at her door and Lottie entered bearing a tray full of breakfast things.

"Good morning, miss, I mean ma'am," she sang brightly. "Your husband bade me fetch you a tray. Sir Edward is up and already dressed. He is going to travel to the port as well."

She set the tray down on a small table near the fire. "I'll just give the fire a rattle and get it burning again. You sit here and get warm, it's that chilly this morning!"

Linnet sat up in bed and shivered. So, her father intended to see John off from the port. No doubt he thought that she would go to see her new husband on his way and wanted to keep her company. Well, it was the least she could do—after all, he was her husband.

After Linnet had breakfasted, she made her way to her own chamber in order to dress. She looked around, frowning. Lottie had tided everything away; her room was very bare.

"Lottie," Linnet called. Lottie was in the little dressing room next door, fetching Linnet's warm travel dress. "Yes, miss?" She came into the room carrying the heavy clothes.

"There was no need to clear my room, I won't be staying in the Rose Room," Linnet said, taking the matching cape from the top of the pile of clothes that Lottie held in her arms she laid the garment on the bed.

A deep voice called cheerily from the direction of the doorway, "What, not dressed yet? Your father is already outside in the coach awaiting us. Incidentally, good morning, wife!"

Linnet stood in her corset and shift she glanced sourly at her new husband. He leaned against the doorway with an odious grin on his face, dressed for travelling in high hessian boots of dark brown, and tight fawn britches. A brown greatcoat was slung over his arm. Linnet, with an outwardly cool demeanour, replied, "Good morning to you, husband. If you would be so kind as to leave me in peace, I shall be ready to join my father directly."

John raised an eyebrow at her formality. "Very well, I will await you outside. I shall go and keep your father company."

Hurriedly, Lottie arranged Linnet's hair and dressed her. Linnet thanked her, kissed her briefly and, as she ran out of the room, called over her shoulder, "I shall want to go riding later, Lottie, so leave my blue riding habit out for me, would you?"

Lottie's mouth dropped open. She ran after her mistress, calling, "Miss, miss! What's that, whatever d' you mean, miss? You cannot go riding, miss, *you'll be at sea.*" The last part was whispered. What could her mistress have meant? Surely she couldn't be going out on her horse; she was off to America. After all, Lottie should know, as she had supervised the packing of Linnet's belongings into trunks sent on to the port. No doubt by now they were stowed aboard in their cabin. She tripped over Linnet's discarded nightgown, the one she had spent so many nights sitting up and sewing by candlelight. Lottie picked it up and held it to her face. She wept, holding the soft gown against her cheek.

"Oh my dear, I shall miss you so, and no proper goodbye for Lottie." The poor maid sat down abruptly and sobbed.

CHAPTER 6

*C*limbing the gangway onto The Tempest, Linnet clutched the rope support and looked at the huge drop downward into the harbour while the murky waters churned about between the wall and the ship's side. The ship swayed backwards and forwards, nearing the wall but never quite touching the stonework. It creaked and groaned, as if moaning to itself. Linnet shuddered. It was as if the ship were a live creature.

She had never been to the port before; her father rightly supposed that it was not the place to take a young girl of gentle upbringing. The language and behaviour of the sailors was coarse and rough. Once on board the ship, Linnet looked about her with fascinated interest. There were men everywhere, scurrying around like ants, each seemed to know exactly what he was about. Men shimmied up and down masts, others carried barrels aboard, while others wound thick ropes, the width of a man's wrist. All the while, they called out, swore, and some even sang.

There was a sense of anticipatory excitement all around. Overhead the gulls wheeled, dipping and diving, their screaming calls adding to the noise and confusion. The captain came towards them. He waved jauntily, his progress somewhat hampered by men stopping to speak to him every few feet or so. Eventually, he reached them. He was a short man, with a large girth, and he looked to be in his fortieth year. His face was clean-shaven, although he sported huge side whiskers which looked startling, but not so much for their size as for their colour, a bright gingery red, as was the thick wiry hair on top of his head.

"My dear sirs, miss, *excuse me*, I mean *Mistress* Foster! Captain Pettigrew at your service, ma'am, welcome aboard The Tempest! The weather is favouring us, yes indeed! Now, please, I insist that you join me below. I have some fine brandy and a Madeira ready in anticipation of your arrival. Please, to follow me!"

He waved his arm expansively in the direction of the bridge and walked away from them in that direction, assuming they were obediently behind him. They did their best to keep up but kept having to stop as the seamen ran across their path, hampering their progress. They also had to avoid obstacles such as open hatchways, piles of rope, barrels of tar and supplies not yet stowed away.

The captain, obviously at home on his ship, leapt around these potential death traps with the grace and ease of a nimble but portly cat. Eventually, they arrived safely by his side, and the captain gestured to a small dark stairway leading down. "Ladies first!" he shouted genially.

Linnet took a firm hold of the rail and stepped down. She waited at the bottom of the stairs for the captain, whom she now recalled seeing at her wedding. He led them to a cabin, flinging the door open into a pleasant, if smallish, room. She glanced around curiously. In one corner stood a large table or desk covered with charts, and on the side of this was a box with many rolled up maps, tightly packed together. Various strange brass instruments were dotted about on the table, along with quills and an ink stand. At the other end of the cabin, a table was laid with a white cloth. Set out on this were glasses and bottles, along with plates of small pasties and sweetmeats.

Linnet suddenly felt extremely hungry. The captain poured

them drinks and handed out round pewter plates. Linnet barely listened to the conversation, so intent was she on eating pasties and sipping her Madeira wine. She realised that the men had all turned to look at her and that the captain had spoken to her. "I am so sorry, Captain Pettigrew, could you repeat that please?"

"Of course, my dear, I asked if you had been to sea before now."

"Well, no, actually. Why?" Linnet asked curiously.

"Just wondered how your sea legs would be, that's all, m'dear. We'll soon find out!" He winked and chuckled.

She was surprised, but not concerned. Naturally, he assumed she was returning with John to the Colonies, she supposed. She was about to put him right on the matter when he suggested that he guide them to the owner's cabin. They all followed the captain into the passage as he led them down the steps. The passage was lit by oil lamps that hung from the ceiling, they swung gently to and fro with the ship's gentle movement.

They turned right and came to a door where the captain halted. He withdrew a large key from his coat pocket to unlock it. "Here we are, then. Now, anything you need, just let my first officer know, he'll see to it. I will leave you to settle in. Dinner is early aboard ship; we eat at eight bells."

He turned to Linnet's father. "Sir Edward, your servant, sir! We set sail in an hour, don't get caught on board!" With another of his irrepressible chuckles, the captain bowed to Sir Edward then left the three of them alone. John held open the cabin door and they all entered. Sir Edward coughed. "I think I shall leave you to unpack and get your things stowed away. I'll say my goodbyes now." Alarmed, Linnet spun around to face her father. Had she understood his meaning?

Her father took her in his arms in a great bear hug, holding her tightly against him. "My dear, I wish you all the happiness in the world. God willing, we shall see each other again one day."

Linnet gasped. "B-but I am not going, Papa. I am coming home with you!"

Sir Edward Wainwright gripped her shoulders firmly and looked into her face sternly. "No, child, your place is by your husband's side and that is where you will be. Enough protestation, you are John's wife, Linnet!" he chided. His heart ached for them both as she started to protest but he remained adamant. "You are married. There is no more to be said, so kiss your father and let me remember you with pride. Stand bravely beside your husband and enjoy the adventure of a new life together."

John stepped forward and placed his arm around his wife's waist, giving her a squeeze. "Be brave for your father's sake, dearest. Do as he bids; you wouldn't want his last memory of you to be a sad one."

"My dear, I wish you all the happiness in the world. As I said, God willing, we shall see one another again."

She trembled. "No, Papa! No! I cannot leave you! How can I possibly leave? I may never see you again!" She flung herself into his arms. Tormented, she sobbed with disbelief, her hands clutching his coat front.

Sir Edward lifted a hand to stroke her hair. "My precious child, you know that you could return with me and I might die tomorrow. I am an old man now, puss. If I should die, then what would become of you? John is a good man, he will look after you and, God willing, you will give me many grandchildren, each of whom will come back to England in order to visit their old grandpapa! Life goes on my child, life goes on."

He placed his hands over hers and lifted them from his coat. He turned to John, holding her clasped hands out towards him. "Take my girl, John. Protect her and cherish her."

John took the weeping Linnet by her hands and drew her to him, folding her in his arms, "You know I will, sir, and thank you."

Sir Edward Wainwright reached forward and placed a hand on John's shoulder, giving it a hearty squeeze. "Good man," he said, his voice gruff. With one last lingering look at his weeping daughter, he turned and left the cabin.

Linnet screamed. She tore herself from John's arms to hurl herself after her father but John caught her about the waist, restraining her. He held her tight against him before leading her over to the bed where he sat and cradled his wife on his lap. John clasped her against his shoulder, his arm about her protectively, and so they stayed while Linnet wept. Eventually, when she was a little calmer, John laid her, curled up, on the box bed. He pulled the eiderdown over her and stroked her hair tenderly back from her forehead.

"Sleep now, sweetheart. I'll wake you later for dinner. Just rest; all will be well, you'll see." He left her to sleep and began to sort out the various trunks piled high in the corner of the cabin.

When she awoke some two hours later, she found herself alone. At first, she simply lay upon the bed feeling desperate and very lonely. As she pondered, a white hot blaze of fury shot through her. This was all that man Foster's fault; he had tricked her into marrying him and under false pretences. Linnet sat up and looked around, noticing various details that in her distress earlier she had missed. The bed she was lying upon was a box bed, a square wooden frame, in-filled with a horse-hair filled mattress, topped off with a downy quilt. A rail ran around the bed, secured above to the wooden ceiling. Dark red curtains hung from them on either side of the bed, enabling it to be surrounded, enclosed from the rest of the room. It was secured to the floor in order to stop it moving in high seas. To the right of the bed there was a window, made up of tiny diamond-shaped pieces of glass, and this was framed by some rather ragged dark red curtains. Under the window sat a pair of large ornate oak chests.

Linnet noticed that her set of silver hair brushes and combs had been laid out atop one of them. Sitting up in the bed, she looked over to the other end of the cabin where a round table stood, fixed to the floor by its central pedestal. Set on either side were two brown, leather-covered chairs. In the far corner, beyond the table, was a screen. She assumed that behind this, the pitcher and ewer could be found. Of their larger travelling trunks there was no sign.

Linnet leaned back on the bed. Pulling the counterpane up under her chin, she began to think about her home. Why had Lottie not informed her that she was to travel with John to the Colonies? Linnet recalled her final conversation with her maid as she was leaving that morning. It began to dawn on her that Lottie had assumed that she had known about the travelling arrangements. Linnet closed her eyes in pain. She hadn't even said goodbye to dear Lottie—or any of the other household staff, for that matter. She had known all of them since she was a small child. Huh, and Pango! Who would exercise him now? Oh, this was terrible!

Tears began to slip down her cheeks as she remembered all she had left behind. If only she had been able to marry Charles, she could have remained near her home and her father, maintaining her way of life, one that she loved. Instead, here she was, cast adrift out on the wide Atlantic Ocean, with a man she called husband but whom she barely knew and was certain she disliked. All this trauma and unhappiness was down to him and his interference. He had deliberately scuppered her carefully laid plans. Gradually, the resentment she already felt towards John intensified until it burned hotly within her.

John unwittingly chose that moment to quietly enter the room bearing a tray with a teapot, cups and saucers, alongside a plate of freshly baked scones.

"Oh, good, you are awake," he said cheerily. "The captain has an excellent cook. I've brought you some of his delicious soft biscuits to try. He called them scones; I think that is what he said."

John set the tray down on the table and went over to the bed where he sat upon the edge and took Linnet's hand. He was moved to see the tear stains tracked upon her cheeks. "Poor darling girl, please don't fret. I swear to you that if we can, we will visit your father, possibly even next year—provided you are not in a delicate condition, of course."

John gave a slow smile and pinched Linnet's cheek affectionately.

He couldn't be certain of what happened next. Suddenly he appeared to be covered in bed clothes and lying in a heap upon the floor. As he struggled to sit up, pushing his head free of the constricting covers, he was doused in cold water, the shock of which left him gasping.

"*Delicate condition?*" she screeched from where she stood, clutching the empty water pitcher. "Let me tell you, sir! I have no intention of sharing a bed with you *ever again*, let alone becoming in a 'delicate condition,' as you put it! When we reach the Colonies, I shall arrange my passage straight back home to England, to Lavenstock Hall, which is where I belong, and not with some colonial half-wit who has decided to drag me halfway across the world on a whim!"

Linnet, exceedingly angry as she was, nevertheless took a stumbling step backwards as he presented dark, open fury on his face. His eyes narrowed to steely slits as she ranted. Any sympathy he had felt for her earlier was obviously gone, and it appeared to have been replaced by rage.

Slowly he hauled himself upright and, kicking the bedclothes aside, he shook his head. He looked like a wet wolf shaking himself dry. John passed a hand over his head and slicked his wet hair back. What sort of a harridan had he married? Well, he intended to start as he meant to go on.

He took a deep breath, recalling that she had just left her homeland—possibly forever. Therefore, he would not allow her to goad him into losing his temper. He intended to make things absolutely crystal clear to her. Surely, once she understood, she would settle down and remain calm. He walked over to the table where he picked up a cup and saucer, enquiring in an icily polite tone, "Shall we take tea now, my dear?" When he got no reply, he went on, "Sit down, my dear, for I have a few things that I wish to say to you."

Linnet flounced into a chair, her expression sulky. She was somewhat relieved that John was behaving in so civilised manner after her attack, but she was also somewhat disappointed in his lack of reaction.

She would have quite liked to have had the opportunity to vent more of her anger. She was still simmering, and wanted to throw something hard at his vile head. John, fully aware of her volatile nature, nevertheless felt some sympathy for her state of mind. He decided that he would naturally subdue her, teaching her to respect her husband. He was determined to soothe Linnet and make her understand that their marriage was a fact that she could no longer change.

He poured them both a cup of tea and sat across the table from her. "I trust that you are now feeling calm enough to talk?" When she failed to respond, he continued regardless.

"As you know, Linnet, your father wished for this marriage to take place, but it did so because I wanted you as my wife. I want our union to work for both our sakes. As your husband, these are the things that I expect from you: first and foremost, respect, as I shall respect you. Your loyalty, as you have mine. Your obedience—in fact, I expect you to fulfil your wedding vows to me absolutely. I hope that, in time, you will learn to love me. I am a fair and patient man, but I am fully prepared to teach you to love, respect and honour me. This can be done most pleasantly, or unpleasantly. At the end of the day, the choice is yours. As for the marriage bed, well, you do still have a lot to learn, but it will be my pleasant task to teach you the joys of that too. You are my wife, Linnet, as such, you *will* share my bed and you will respect me as your husband. Otherwise, there shall be consequences. In return, you have my love and protection in all things."

John picked up his teacup and drank from it, watching her reaction to his pretty speech over the rim. Linnet's emotions swung from a resentful anger to incredulous embarrassment. Her face blanched and then flushed.

She took a deep breath then replied in a shaky voice, "Firstly, sir, you have to earn my respect. Secondly, I make my own decisions. Thirdly, I loathe you, Mr. Foster, and I promise you that I will not be falling in love with you now or in the future! As a gentleman, you will be bound to leave me in peace at night and take your base pleasure elsewhere, for I tell you that I will not endure it, sir!" Linnet lifted her chin haughtily, her green eyes flashing.

A muscle twitched once in John's cheek. "I warn you, Linnet: do not push me, for you would not enjoy the outcome."

"Do you *threaten* me, sir?" She stood up and faced him as he watched her performance, for a performance it was. He admired his new wife, he was inwardly proud of her strength of character but she needed to learn quickly that he was her destiny, and it would be dangerous for her in the Colonies to try and go her own way. She must learn to trust his judgement, to do as he instructed her. This voyage would be a good opportunity for him to school her in her wifely duties, and he found himself looking forward to the prospect. He gazed at Linnet's heaving bosom and flushed cheeks. His new wife had no idea of the effect she had on a man, and that was going to be part of the danger that lay ahead for someone as lovely as she, in a country as untamed and wild as The Americas.

John brushed down his knees and rose, choosing to ignore her statement. After all, she'd had a shock, perhaps she simply needed some time to adjust. He considered himself a kindly fellow. He hoped his wife would settle down and accept her fate.

"I shall return the tray to the galley. We dine with the captain at six o'clock, which is eight bells, and your clothing for the voyage is in the trunk on the left. Please be ready at ten minutes to the hour, I shall return for you then."

He collected the tea things then, turning at the doorway, he spoke quietly. "I think it would be wise for you to ponder the outcome of our disagreement before our marriage, young lady, and try to achieve a more biddable nature from now onward,"

He gently pulled the door shut behind him and left the cabin.

Linnet sank back down upon the chair and stuck out her tongue at the closed door. She was livid. How dare he threaten her, the pompous oaf! *He is your husband now*, pointed out a little voice of reason. *Yes, but not by my choice!* she countered. He was so smug! Linnet thought of him earlier, lying on the floor, wet and dishevelled. She giggled. That had dented his damn American pride all right. Then she remembered his instructions to be ready at ten to six. *Very well*, she mused, *I shall be ready, but perhaps Mr. Foster may not be!*

She skipped over to the wooden trunks and lifted the lid of the chest. It was full of his clothing and all made from fine cloth, she noted as she fingered the rich, soft materials. It did seem a pity to mar such beautiful clothes. She for pondered a moment, chewing her bottom lip indecisively, finally concluding that he deserved retribution for the way he'd treated her.

She fetched her small nail scissors. Returning to the trunk, she knelt and lifted out a shirt. Holding the garment by the sleeve, she hesitated but a second before she cut. From every shirt in the trunk, Linnet took off one shirt sleeve. She then stuffed all the loose shirt sleeves down at the bottom of the trunk before folding the other clothing neatly on top in order to hide the destruction she'd wrought. A small shiver of misgiving trickled down her spine as she wondered what John's reaction might be. However, the deed was done, and what could he possibly do about it?

A brief memory of their encounter in the coach came to mind but she hastily dismissed that episode—she'd bitten him on that occasion. John had not reacted over the water incident earlier that day, had he? She was a married woman now; her husband was required to cherish her and show her due respect, he'd even said as much earlier. Anyway, by the time he discovered the deed, she would be safely at dinner sat amongst the captain and his officers. Linnet then opened her own trunk and pulled out a couple of gowns, finally deciding on a pretty blue silk with front lacing and a pale bronze under skirt. This dress had always drawn compliments; the soft golden bronze of the underskirt matched her hair colour perfectly.

When John returned, it was already a quarter before six. He'd spent the afternoon on deck watching the crew as they handled the ship, taking her far out to sea. John had become reacquainted with the first officer, Duncan Snow, a fresh-faced young man with fair hair and freckles. John had liked him immediately on his voyage over from Boston. Duncan had been with Captain Pettigrew since he was a lad, and looked upon the jovial captain as a father figure.

Duncan was not as young as he looked; he was thirty, married with a wife and two young daughters, who resided in Plymouth England. Duncan accompanied John back to the cabin to make Linnet's acquaintance. If she was surprised by his arrival, she did not show it, inclining her head graciously upon John's introduction, holding out her hand to Duncan, who gallantly took it and raised it to his lips. "Your servant, ma'am. If there is anything at all you need, please do not hesitate to ask. Tomorrow, I shall bring the cabin boy, Pat, to meet you. He will be your servant for the voyage and will happily carry out chores for you, run messages and any errands that you care to set him," Duncan assured her.

"I thank you, Mr. Snow, how very thoughtful of you. My husband seemed to forget my need of a maid on this voyage. It is so refreshing to meet a man who thinks of these things."

John cocked his brow, a smile twitching at the corner of his mouth. "Yes, most kind of you, Snow. Perhaps you would like to accompany my wife in to dinner? I need to change but will follow on directly."

Duncan offered his arm to Linnet and they left the cabin. John untied his cravat and began to change.

Linnet made polite conversation with Duncan Snow as they made their way to the captain's quarters, where they discovered two other officers conversing with Captain Pettigrew. The conversation stopped as she and Duncan Snow entered. The captain stepped forward. "My dear, welcome! How lovely you look. Come in and meet my officers, Mr. Dexter and Mr. Edward. Gentlemen, allow me to introduce Mistress John Foster." He gestured to Linnet and the officers gazed at her with open admiration. Both wore the same uniform of dark blue frock coats and white breeches.

They bowed low.

"Ma'am," they chorused.

"Gentlemen," Linnet replied coyly, sketching a curtsy.

The captain looked beyond them towards the open door. "Mr. Foster is not accompanying you into dinner, madam?"

"Why yes, he shall join us shortly, Captain," Linnet reassured him.

She was starting to have doubts about the wisdom of her revenge. What if John should burst into the room in a rage? Surely he wouldn't create a scene in front of the captain and his officers? Linnet had a particularly nasty vision of being turned across John's knee—and in front of all these gentlemen. She blanched. Oh, why had she been so rash? John wouldn't treat his wife thus, surely? Nervously, she waited for John to arrive. She sat, twisting her lace handkerchief whilst trying to make polite conversation with the captain and his men, her thoughts in turmoil elsewhere.

Linnet started when John placed his hands upon his wife's shoulders. "So sorry, captain, gentlemen, to keep you waiting," he apologised.

John bent forward and kissed the nape of her neck. She shivered as his hot breath caressed her skin.

"You look ravishing, darling," he said clearly before lowering his voice so that only she could hear, "I shall need your help sorting through my clothing on the morrow, especially my shirts. You have a better dress sense than I."

She tittered nervously. "Oh, do you really think so?" Linnet could not be sure whether John knew about his damaged shirts and his comment was telling her so. But would he be this calm if that were the case?

Captain Pettigrew picked up a wine glass and tapped it with a spoon, attracting everyone's attention. "Gentlemen, I should like to make a toast to the newly wedded Mr and Mrs John Foster, who are now the proud owners of our lovely ship, The Tempest!"

Dinner was plain but delicious; tender chicken served with herbs and root vegetables, followed by fresh fruit and cheese. Linnet, however, could have been eating sawdust, she was so nervous. She would have perhaps enjoyed her meal more if she had known how the ship's food would decline as the long voyage continued, but all she could think about was the fact that John was wearing the same shirt that he had worn all day. He had simply changed his waistcoat for dinner, and she could see the white stock at his neck was a fresh one. Did this mean he had found the mutilated shirts? She had to know; she had to get back to their cabin to take a peek and check.

John surreptitiously watched his new wife's discomfiture. When he had discovered the vandalised shirts, he had wanted to find the vindictive little witch, turn up her skirts and tan her backside. Instead, he had made himself calm down. He'd poured a whisky and sat a while, sipping thoughtfully while he decided how best to react to this blatant challenge to his authority. John reasoned that since Linnet had still not experienced the full potential of her womanhood, after all, the two of them were still strangers, unbound as yet by the physical act of love. Last night had been pleasurable for him but he'd hurt her and now she was wounded and angry. If he alienated her, he may never gain her trust, particularly in the bedchamber. That would mean the perfect partnership he knew them capable of would possibly never flourish. After all, Linnet was still shocked at leaving her home and her beloved father behind.

He'd come to a decision. He would pretend, at least for the time being, that he had not discovered the results of her malicious deed.

Tonight, he would teach her about the act of love. Afterwards, he hoped that she might confess all to him, in which case he would magnanimously forgive her. If not, well then, he would make sure she received a lesson that would ensure that she would never again repeat her underhanded act of petty vengeance.

Linnet had been placed opposite John at the dinner table. The talk was all of politics, and Captain Pettigrew sought John's views on the reaction of the Colonies to the taxes imposed by Lord North, the prime minister. "My own view," the captain explained, "is that the new cabinet changes will be seen in a positive light."

John shook his head. "I would have to disagree with you sir; Lord North is not known to be sympathetic to the Colonies' plight. Providing he can be persuaded that the taxes should be reduced, I can see mutual co-operation and a return of the free trade, such as we enjoyed before England's war with France. Now that Lord North has introduced the Tea Levy, things could become substantially worse."

The conversation wore on, until Linnet tired of dull discussion and turned to the captain with a bright smile. "Do tell me, Captain, what do you make of these salacious rumours that Lord North is the king's bastard brother? The resemblance between the two is said to be almost uncanny. One wonders which of his parents was guilty of such indiscretion." An uncomfortable silence fell as one by one, the officers seated around the table turned to stare at Linnet. John shook his head, deeply annoyed with her.

"I must apologise for my wife's indelicacy, gentlemen. She has the typical female nose for a scandal!" The captain gave a polite laugh. "Mr Foster, your pretty wife seems quite worn out by the day. Escort her to your cabin, sir, why don't you?"

John looked thoughtfully at Linnet. Did she not realise the offence she had caused these good, loyal English men with her silly, flippant remark? It had been rumoured, certainly, that due to a strong physical likeness, the king and Lord North may be in some way be related. But loyal subjects of King George did not tend to repeat such libellous slander. The captain would hopefully put Linnet's tactless comments down to her youth and the female propensity for gossip. John thought it best to remove his naive wife from an embarrassing situation.

He pushed back his chair and, dipping his head to the captain, he became the picture of a concerned husband. "My dear, you are tired," John told her solicitously. Linnet was eager to get back to the cabin and check upon the status of John's ruined shirts, so she willingly acquiesced.

"Actually, yes, but I should like to retire to my room alone. Please stay here, my dear, and enjoy the gentlemen's company." It was killing her not knowing whether or not he had discovered the shirts. Surely not, he had been so lovingly attentive toward her all evening.

"Cabin, my love," John corrected her. "The rooms on board a ship are called cabins. I insist on accompanying you."

Linnet gritted her teeth but said with a saccharine smile, "I quite forgot they were called cabins, how kind of you to remind me, my dear!"

John pulled out her chair and helped her to her feet but Linnet shook his hand away and flounced to the door, furious that he had not only shown her up by correcting her in public, but that he intended to escort her. Amidst an amused chorus of good wishes, they took their leave.

On the way to their cabin, John pointed out to his sulky wife the inadvisability of spreading drawing-room gossip while aboard the ship. Linnet simply shrugged disinterestedly; she had only been trying to liven up what, to her, had been an otherwise tedious evening.

John decided to drop the subject for now. He had no wish to upset their tenuous relationship just before they were due to retire. After all, they were on their honeymoon. When they reached the cabin door, Linnet turned to John. "I shall be quite all right now, John, thank you. Please return and join the men in their brandy with the captain." She wanted to sound airy, as if it were of no consequence to her either way. John hid a smile, not fooled for one moment—he knew that she wanted him gone.

"No, my darling, I wouldn't dream of leaving you alone on our first night aboard ship."

He opened the door and went over to seat himself on the bed. Linnet, realising that she was not going to be able to check on the torn shirts that night, resignedly gave up and decided she would wait until the morning. She bustled behind the screen to use the chamber pot and wash. When she had finished, she called out, requesting that John fetch her night-gown for her. John walked over to the screen, and reaching behind it, took a gentle hold of her arm, drawing her out into the room.

"Come, my dear," he said, "I will help you disrobe. As you so rightly pointed out earlier this evening, it was I who was remiss in leaving you to cope without a maid's assistance."

Linnet reluctantly allowed him to lead her towards the bed. He turned her to face him and started to undo all the front lacing on the dress. She had chosen the front-faced opening deliberately so she could manage without assistance. She kept her eyes downcast and watched as his strong fingers deftly loosened the laces. He then pushed the robe off each of her shoulders in turn so that her bosom lay enticingly exposed. John bent his head and kissed the soft white swell of her breasts. He tilted her head back, and his mouth closed over hers possessively. He kissed her lips apart and flicked his tongue teasingly against hers.

Linnet tried to pull back. She had no wish for a repeat performance of the previous night but John slipped his arms around her, holding her closely pressed up against his muscled body, leaving her no room for manoeuvre.

As the kiss progressed, she relaxed into his arms and, somewhere in the centre of her being, warmth expanded. Mounting heat flooded through her veins. He traced his hand down her back in slow sensual strokes until he cupped her lovely, womanly buttocks; gently kneading them, he pulled her against the hard length of his body. He gazed into her eyes, which had flown open as he broke the kiss. His eyes held hers, mesmerised. His compelling stare darkened with desire as he traced the shape of her parted lips with his finger. "You are so lovely. Your body is made for love, Linnet. Do not fear, tonight will be very different from last night, I promise you."

She attempted to pull out of his embrace but he held her fast. With a backward step, he sat upon the bed, cradling her on his lap. Tugging open the front of her dress, he undid her corset, loosening her chemise until her breasts spilled free. His hands caught them as the filmy material parted. Weighing them in his hands, he moved his thumbs over her nipples, making them perk in rosy peaks. She drew in her breath sharply, feeling strange warmth spread through her limbs, making her languid. She was nervously aware that she had nowhere to escape to aboard a ship, and submitted to his attentions anxiously.

Lowering his head, John kissed her lingeringly. His hands gently caressed the erect buds of her nipples. Her arms crept up and wound around his neck as he moved one of his hands down to her lap and pulled her skirt upwards. She watched, breathless, as his hand snaked beneath the white lace of her petticoat then, sliding up her parted inner thigh, he stroked the velvet skin above her stocking, his fingers tantalisingly brushing against her womanly mound. She felt immobilised by the sensations he aroused.

Then John deftly lifted the silken dress over her head and removed it, throwing it aside. She gasped as he resumed his intimate attentions. He nipped her neck, soothing the sting with his tongue. She gasped, not ready for his next move, which was to roll her over so that she lay sprawled back upon the bed with her legs flung up over his hip. John bent his head to her nipples, skilfully tweaking and sucking the turgid peaks. His hand slipped from her knee and up her leg until he touched the skin of her inner thighs. Heat curled through her centre core, unsettling her so that she snapped her thighs together. John tutted and parted her with a knowing hand, exploring her, arousing her with gentle, questing fingers, until she was slick and wet with desire, lost in a fathomless delight as his kisses peppered her, moving down her body. He held her as she writhed, lowering his head between her thighs. His tongue probed the hot pulsing heart of her passion, finding and teasing the small nub of her desire. His searching tongue tantalised her senses, sending her spiralling into a vortex of ecstasy such as she could never have imagined. Her back arched as wave after wave of delicious pulsing pleasure washed over her. She cried out his name with a sweet surrender. Afterwards, as she lay bathed in a gleam of perspiration, her white shift screwed up around her waist, legs thrown apart, head flung to one side, he kissed her neck, murmuring his love for her.

He admired her gorgeous hair, a pool of gleaming copper. Soft silken tendrils trailed like fire over the creamy mounds of her breasts, nipples taut, exposed to his carnal gaze. He ached with the need to mate her; she was irresistible, ravishing. Standing, he peeled off his clothes, turning to face her, his manhood pulsing stiffly from his groin.

"Look at me, wife," he commanded. She gazed at him. Never having seen a man naked before, she was fascinated. Her eyes devoured the sight of his tumescent hardness that testified his desire for her. How proudly it jutted, long and thick. Were all men made so, she wondered. Her eyes travelled down his long powerful legs, covered in whorls of dark curling hair, the plane of his flat stomach, the wide, well-muscled chest, coated in the same dark hair. Her gaze took in his broad shoulders and strong biceps before finally settling on his dark, lean face.

Disconcertingly, he watched her with those hooded inscrutable grey eyes, his stare unwavering. As he moved purposefully towards the bed she shyly, nervously, shifted over to accommodate him. He gathered her into his embrace, kissing and caressing her. He began to stir her passion once more. His deft fingers worked their magic, her furrow quivering, slickly plump with desire. He slowly moved above her and this time, she parted her legs, unconsciously welcoming as he guided himself to her waiting cleft.

With a thrust, he drove into her yielding channel and she lifted her hips, bucking, meeting thrust for thrust, needing him.

"Now," he whispered hoarsely, "now… you see, you are mine."

He snapped his flanks and plunged deep inside her wetness, his strokes carrying them both to heights of ecstasy. She writhed beneath his pounding body, clinging to him—her anchor in a sea of turbulent passion. Her very consciousness fragmented; she moaned his name as she hovered deliciously on the crest of indescribable joy, his voice joined with hers as he soared, suspended in the molten heat of his climax.

Afterwards, raising himself up on his elbows, he placed his hands on either side of her face and pushed the damp hair back from her flushed cheeks. Studying her, he was delighted to have found that she possessed such a great capacity for loving. "Your eyes have changed colour, they are a smoky green… like the depths of the ocean. Do you know, sweet… you were made for love?"

She nuzzled his neck. "Is it… always so between a man and woman?" she asked.

"No, not always." he replied. "I knew it would be this way for us the first time—"

"I remember," she interrupted, pulling a face as she thought of the previous night.

"No, not last night. I was about to say, when I first kissed you on that balcony."

She was nonplussed. "But I kicked and punched you after that kiss!" she insisted.

He grinned. "Yes, you were as surprised as I at your response to that kiss—which made me realise that you were not the wanton I took you to be. You were as attracted to me as much as I was attracted to you."

Linnet nodded. "I was so confused because I disliked you so much... and actually, I think I was a little afraid of you too."

John raised an eyebrow. "Afraid, hmm, was that before or after our disagreement in the coach?"

She flushed crimson. "Before—because I hated you afterward! However," she added impudently, "I think perhaps I might have misjudged; you are a man, after all, and not the tyrant I took you to be."

"What!" he exclaimed in mock surprise. "Can I believe what I am hearing? My wife does not believe me to be a tyrant? Oh, but I must prove her wrong!"

Linnet giggled and hit him playfully. "I admit," she told him, "I may have misjudged you, but you did give me cause, treating me so abominably."

John nodded sagely. "Ah, yes, the spanking, the one you so richly deserved!"

"I most certainly did not!" she squealed.

"You most certainly did, ma'am, and I admit I enjoyed the exercise immensely, so much so that I thought it most kind of you to give me an excuse to indulge in spanking you once again. I propose to repeat the process. Come, lie over my lap and let's get this lesson over with."

Linnet's face flushed even redder than her hair. She caught her bottom lip between her teeth and began to move surreptitiously away from him towards the edge of the bed. Guiltily she remembered his damaged shirts, hidden in the chest. What on earth had she been thinking when she'd destroyed them—and, more importantly, what should she do now? Before she could even formulate a plan, John's hand shot out and gripped her wrist firmly.

"Did you think for one moment that I would let that nasty, spiteful prank go unpunished, my dear?" he asked, one eyebrow cocked. When there was no reply, he shook her wrist. "When you threw water over me today, I let your behaviour go without dealing with your bad behaviour because of the shock you'd so recently experienced, leaving behind your father and your home. I realise now that was the wrong thing to do. You thought me weak instead of kind, didn't you? If I had dealt with you as you deserved this afternoon, you wouldn't have dared to ruin my shirts. I also have to reprimand your unladylike behaviour at the dinner table tonight."

Her gaze met his, confused.

He enlightened her. "Your comments about Lord North were unacceptable—I will not have my wife repeating common gossip. You embarrassed the captain and his officers, Linnet, and I will not tolerate such bad manners. What have you to say for yourself?" His voice was as steely as his arctic grey eyes.

She licked her lips, her mouth dry. She could barely utter an audible reply; it was difficult to speak. Her stomach clenched, she was nervous. Where was the gentle lover of only moments before?

Without warning, he tipped her across his knee.

"Linnet, you are my wife and you will learn to comport yourself as such with respect and obedience. I shall be happy to teach you how to behave. Every time you disobey me, I shall be forced to take you in hand and you will end up across my knee, and believe me, you will soon learn how to conduct yourself."

He shifted her high over his lap so that she was forced to place both palms on the floor of the cabin to support herself. "Please don't do this, John, not now, after we made love!"

"I deliberately decided to punish you afterward because I wanted to show you that I love you before I spanked you, so that while I am lighting a fire in your butt, you will recall me lighting a fire in your heart. I will never harm you, Linnet, but I will school you with spankings."

She shuddered. Her backside clenched but her heart melted at his words. "I am so, so sorry about damaging your shirts, I am, truly! Perhaps you don't understand how I felt today—" She sputtered to a halt as the air left her lungs in surprise when John's hand met her bottom with a forceful smack.

At first, she expected it would be over quickly, but she soon realised her mistake. This hurt so much more than the spanking he had given her in the coach. This was a spanking she could not have imagined. As his palm fell with searing accuracy, she thought it could not become any more painful but, as spank followed spank, her burning behind became unbearable. She began to kick out in earnest, desperately trying to cover her bottom with her hand, but he smacked it keeping hold of her wrist, securing it at the small of her back, out of his way. Then he moved his leg and placed it over both of hers so that she was held fast. She bucked and churned, attempting escape.

"Oh no, my sweet, you don't get away with that little trick!" he told her, swatting her bottom and thighs until she shrieked. He paused, admiring his handiwork, taking the opportunity to lecture her again before resuming the spanking he felt she so very much required.

When he had found his mutilated shirts earlier, he had wanted to throw his spiteful new bride over his knee and tan her backside then and there but, after reflection, he decided to use her nervousness about her wicked deed to put her on edge all evening, leaving her to wonder and worry. It served the naughty wench right after such a vindictive action. Remembering his shirts again made John decide to carry on with this punishment a bit longer, and he aimed some swats across the tender area above Linnet's thighs. She let out a screech and struggled furiously until he slapped her harder than ever and she subsided, limply weeping. With a few more smacks to the tops of her legs, which elicited a howl from his young bride, John released her and rubbed her now flaming behind.

It took Linnet a minute to realise the spanking was over. She lay there trembling across John's lap a while before dropping off his knee and onto the floor on her bottom, where she instantly leapt up with a yelp. John reached down and pulled her onto his lap, where she struggled until he told her firmly that he would continue the spanking if she didn't settle down. Linnet wilted and buried her head into his chest and wept. She felt so humiliated and wanted to be alone with her embarrassment, but John was going nowhere.

In fact, he found the sight of his naked wife most enticing, and his erection surged. He was aroused once again. "There now, it is all over, sweet. Come, lift your face. Linnet, look at me now," he commanded softly, but when she lowered her head, allowing her hair to fall and screen her flushed face, he swept back the errant locks and tilted her chin upwards. Linnet tried to avoid his eyes. "Look at me!" he demanded firmly.

Linnet lifted swimming green eyes to meet his steely glare. "Your punishment is over, and it need never happen again if you are biddable and behave as my wife should. But if there is a next time, and I tell you to lie across my knee, you will do so willingly, submitting to me as your promise to obey demands of you, and I will go softer on you for your obedience, do you understand me?"

Linnet nodded and John pulled her into his embrace, murmuring endearments and kissing her passionately.

Linnet was amazed at her body's traitorous reaction to the kiss and to her husband's arousing, exploring hands. She was on fire, the heat of her bottom seeming to transfer to her sex, and she felt a wet rush of roiling desire. John rolled her onto her back and took her hard and fast he held her hands above her head and thrust deep, building a tempo that pounded her senses.

She exploded with a powerful climax, and John followed with shuddering release. Exhausted, he pulled her to him and curled his body around hers, kissing her on her temple and wishing her a good night. They both fell into a deep satiated sleep, not moving or waking until morning.

Shortly after dawn, John awoke and, slipping from the cabin, he went in search of breakfast for them both. Linnet woke and, stretching languidly, realised that she was alone in the cabin. She snuggled down and dozed contentedly until a sharp slap on her sore rump awoke her with a start.

"Come on, you lug-a-bed! I thought you would be up and

dressed by now. I have brought breakfast." John went over to the table where he had placed a large tray covered in a white linen cloth.

"It obviously escaped your notice, sir, that I had a very disturbed night!" Linnet chided him saucily.

John looked surprised and said, "Well, I thought riding always gave you such an enormous appetite. At least, that is what you told me before we left England!"

Linnet looked suitably outraged and launched a pillow at him.

After they had eaten a delicious breakfast of eggs and salt bacon, washed down with a strong aromatic coffee, Linnet began her toilette. She was behind the screen, washing, when she heard John muttering oaths from the other side of the cabin.

"Is something amiss?" she asked.

"My ruined shirts, there is not one left fit for wear. You have ruined them all!"

"I promise I will mend them. I am good with a needle. Fear not, I shall have a shirt ready for you to wear for dinner tonight."

She jumped as John's glowering face appeared over the screen, "Make sure all my shirts are repaired by the end of the week or you will find yourself across my knee again, ma'am!"

"John! I was going to repair every single one anyway—there is no need for threats!" she responded hastily.

"My darling, there is not a doubt in my mind that you will repair every single one! Now, come here." He patted the bed beside him.

She hesitated. "Now, Linnet," he grinned, "I promise not to bite."

Uneasily, she did as he asked. He pulled her down beside him and, kissing the top of her head, he put his arm around her. "Are you nervous of me?" he asked with a twinkle in his eye.

Heat suffused her face as she gave a brief nod.

"Be warned, fair wife, I won't stand any nonsense from you!" he growled.

She was shocked by the arousing shivers that pulsed through

her at his stern tone. Thrillingly, she knew that he meant every word; last night had proved that. He'd proved that he was not a man to be trifled with. She realised that she found this side of him rather exciting.

"I was so angry with you yesterday. It was dreadful having to leave Papa unexpectedly. I had not said goodbye to anyone at home, or to Pango. I blamed you; do you understand that I wanted to hurt you? I wished that I hadn't damaged your wretched shirts... afterwards."

He chuckled. "I am sure you are extremely sorry now, and I forgive you this time. However, you will have to sew all the sleeves back on, and quickly, because I do mean what I said."

She nodded, relieved by his lighter tone. She was a little put out by how condescending he was toward her and she determined that he would never ever spank her again. Indeed, her behind was so tender this morning; she would have to start her sewing standing up!

"As soon as I am dressed, I shall go in search of sewing materials," she told him cheerfully.

"I don't think so, not just yet." She noted his gaze fixed upon her cleavage. Pushing her back onto the bed, his hands grasped her wrists. Holding her arms above her head with one hand, his other roamed the swell of her breasts. She mewled softly as shivers of pleasure pulsed down her spine. Tentatively, her hand began explorations of its own, making him gasp in surprise as her fingers traced the rigid outline of his throbbing phallus through the straining cloth of his breeches. She gave a small sensuous chuckle as she deftly managed to extract his erect manhood from the confines of material and then ran her hand over the thick, smooth, velvety shaft. She was testing his self-control.

When he could no longer risk suffering her tormenting attentions, he pulled her hand away and pushed her back onto the bed. Thrusting her legs apart and then lowering himself between her parted thighs, he mounted her. He took her fiercely, bringing them both to a rapid, quivering release. She rolled away onto her stomach and stretched luxuriously.

"Hmm," she mused, "perhaps I should chop off your coat sleeves next time around!"

She shrieked as a large hand descended with a resounding slap on her naked, vulnerable derriere.

CHAPTER 7

*L*ater that day, they decided to take a stroll together up on deck, where it was a relief to get out into the bright daylight. Linnet gulped in lungful after lungful of the invigorating, salty air. Her hair was torn from its pins by the breeze and whipped around her face.

Linnet was fascinated by the sea; far around them, the green waves dipped and rolled, the occasional white foamy tip surfacing and breaking. She leaned over the ship's rail, watching the creamy froth break at the side of the ship as they ploughed through the swelling sea.

"It's wonderful!" she cried to John. "I never imagined the sea to be like this!"

John watched her indulgently. Every second he spent with her, he was falling more deeply in love with his captivating bride. With his arm around her waist, he pointed out the salient points of the ship. He told her that she must stay off the gun decks, and he pointed out the mizzen mast and the bulkhead. John explained to Linnet that the head was out of bounds to her, and once he had explained to her that the crew used it as a chamber pot, she readily agreed to avoid the area!

They looked up, shielding their eyes from the bright sun, to the crow's nest. John explained that a man was up in the tiny eyrie and that the sailors took turns at shifts the whole time, looking out for danger. "What sort of danger?" Linnet wanted to know. John, not wishing to alarm her, forbade the mention of pirates. He told her of fog and the danger of collision with other ships.

After an hour in the bracing sea air, Linnet was starting to feel chilled, so they returned below. John wanted to search out the captain to discuss navigation routes, and Linnet had a shirt or two to sew. John kissed his wife and left her to her own devices. Linnet turned out the chest that contained her clothes and items for the voyage but nowhere could she find her sewing box. Fairly certain that the efficient Lottie would have packed it, she sat back on her heels and pondered for a moment on what she should do.

While she was thinking, there was a tapping at the door and, thinking it would be Mr. Snow, she called out, "Please come in." The door opened and a scruffy individual, whose face was obscured by a large tray bearing tea things, entered.

"Oh!" Linnet was much surprised. "I thought you would be Mr. Snow."

She felt rather foolish sprawled on the floor, and scrambled to her feet. The tray was placed on the table, the person turned around, and Linnet saw it was a young lad.

"I am Pat, missus," he said. "I be the person what'll serve you, run errands and the like. Mr. Snow's right busy in the day so he's asked me, like."

"Well yes, yes of course, Mr. Snow would be," Linnet said. She was amused by the little ragamuffin. "Well, I am very pleased to meet you, Pat," she said, and looked the lad up and down. He was a skinny boy, perhaps twelve, she guessed. His whiskers had not grown yet, so she knew him to be young. He was quite filthy; his nails, she noted, were black, and so were his clothes. He wore a striped, long-sleeved top and what had once been white, tattered breeches.

Under the grime, Linnet could see the boy had delicate features and blue eyes. He stood, waiting uncomfortably, first on one leg, then the other.

He jumped when Linnet spoke to him. "Pat, I need my sewing box; I believe it to be in one of my travelling trunks. Do you know where they would be stored?"

The boy nodded vigorously. "Ay, in the storage hold, shall I take 'ee there?"

Linnet thought quickly, deciding it would be nice to rummage through her things; she could fetch other bits and bobs that she would need at the same time. "Yes please. One moment, though, while I fetch my shawl."

A second or two later they were ready to go.

"Right, lead on, Sir Galahad!" she commanded.

"What's that, missus?" Pat looked bewildered.

"Oh, never mind, just a silly saying, is all," she replied.

Pat led the way down dim passages and creaking stairways. She stumbled a few times because she was unused to the ship's rolling movement. Pat, at least, had the foresight to bring a lantern because most of the narrow galley ways were unlit. Occasionally, they came across an unsavoury-looking sailor, who would stare at Linnet with lewd interest; however, they seemed a harmless enough bunch to her as she swept past them, eyes ahead, concentrating on her mission. One or two sailors who knew Pat by name made a playful gesture, cuffing his head in rough greeting.

After rather too many narrow stairways, which were awkward for Linnet in her full-skirted gown, they came to a low ceilinged, darkly open space.

Hammocks were slung across the ship's timber joists, and one or two were occupied by snoring sailors. The overpowering smell of unwashed humanity hung heavy in the fetid air. Pat led the way between the rows of hammocks to the opposite side of the space, where another dingy galley lay. Holding his lantern high, Pat led the way forward. At the end of this passage was a small hobnailed door which Pat pushed open. He gestured for Linnet to follow him. They were in a large open space with another very low ceiling, without the lantern's glow; it would have been pitch black. Pat held the lantern up as high as he could to disperse the eerie shadows. Linnet was startled by a soft scurrying sound deep in the darkness.

"Them's rats," he told her matter-of-factly.

She shuddered, wishing now that she had waited for John's reassuring presence before venturing down here with only a lad for company.

"Where are the trunks normally stored?" Linnet asked him in a whisper.

"I don't know," came his unhelpful reply.

She resisted the temptation to clout his ears. "Well, let's start to look for them." He moved away and, in alarm, she added, "But stay close by me!" The boy moved back with the lantern.

As her eyes adjusted to the gloom, she began to make out large shapes in the deep shadows and called softly to Pat. "Over here, boy, shine the lantern here!"

He did as she bid and sure enough, a large pile of travel trunks were stacked along the wall. It was not going to be as easy as she'd anticipated. Not all this luggage belonged to her. She guessed correctly that the captain and his officers stored their own chests and trunks down here. Sighing heavily, she decided there was nothing for it, she would have to sort through them all until she recognised her own. At least hers had her family crest on the side of the trunk, which would make it easier to identify.

"Stand the lantern on a chest, Pat." He duly did as he was bid, and Linnet began to slide chests and trunks forward one by one. "Come on, lazy bones, help!"

Pat pushed the nearest trunk, then there was an almighty crash and they were left standing in total darkness. There was a moment of shocked silence. Pat's voice whined, "T' lantern fell, not my fault!"

"I am aware it fell," she snapped, exasperated. "What on earth shall we do? Can you feel around for the lantern?" She herself was feeling her way around the stack of trunks, heading towards the sound of the boy's voice.

It was totally unnerving standing in the horrible dark place, unable to see and without the comforting presence of another person to hold on to. Her foot knocked against something solid. It yielded and moved. Linnet's heart thumped. "Pat, is that you?" Her voice sounded reedy in the hollow space.

Pat's voice came from her left. "Over 'ere, missus!"

She swivelled towards the direction his voice came, but as she did so, she tripped over a large mass of something warm and moving. She shrieked.

A deep voice resonated from where she'd staggered. "*Mon dieu!*"

Pat yelled, "Missus, missus?" His voice betrayed his fright.

Linnet, more terrified than ever, blundered towards the boy's voice and they collided, each screaming at the impact.

Linnet quickly realised it was Pat. She clasped his arm. "There is someone over there!" she hissed quietly. She could feel the boy begin to tremble through his thin clothes.

"A ghosty? I isn't staying here! Come on, missus, the way out is over there." Pat grabbed hold of her and they moved blindly through the pitch black. Suddenly Linnet collided with a solid wall and she squealed in fright, truly panicked.

Stretching out her hand, she felt her way along the rough wooden ship's wall. There was a long grating noise and dim light appeared on the other side of her. Pat had located the door and pulled it open. They both scrambled through, jostling one another to be first through the small frame. The door swung closed behind them. With hands still clasped, they scurried along the dark galleys, back through the sailor's sleeping hanger, on upward to the stairway, climbing to the next level.

Hurriedly, they returned to Linnet's cabin in silence. Panting and sobbing, Linnet flung open the cabin door and they tumbled inside, still holding hands as the door slammed shut.

They drew up short when met by the astonished faces of John and Duncan Snow. "Good God, ma'am, where on earth have you been? You look terrible!" John strode over to his dishevelled wife.

He looked surprised when she flung herself into his arms and buried her face in his chest. Mr. Snow grabbed the unfortunate Pat by the scruff of his neck. "What's been going on, boy? Where have you two been?"

Pat began to howl. Duncan shook him. "Stop that at once and tell us what has happened."

"Ghosties! Ghosts, is what!" the poor boy stuttered.

"That is ridiculous! He must be hysterical!" Duncan said, releasing the boy in disgust.

John held Linnet away from him and looked earnestly into her face. "Linnet, calm down and explain to me what has happened."

Duncan Snow poured a cup of tea. "Here, John, this might help her."

John pushed her down on a chair and told her to take a sip of tea. Hunkering down in front of his wife, he ordered her to explain.

She drew in a shuddering breath. "We went down to the luggage hold to fetch my etui from my sewing box. We were sorting through the trunks when the lantern fell over and went out. We were left in total darkness!"

John ran a hand distractedly through his hair. "Why didn't you ask me to fetch the damn thing for you? Linnet, you are *not* to roam about the ship alone! Do you not possess any common sense, woman? Anything might have happened to you! In fact, what actually *did* happen?" He stood up and began to pace back and forth.

She flared up at him. "Oh, for goodness sake, stop your bellyaching and *listen.* I am trying to tell you what happened, and anyway, I wasn't alone, Pat was with me! It was totally dark. I fell over something but I don't know what!" She shuddered and wrapped her arms around her body. "It was horrible; we heard a voice, crying out in the dark." She gazed wide-eyed at Pat, who shivered and stared back at her.

Duncan Snow frowned. "What kind of a voice?"

"It be the soul of a drowned sailor," whispered Pat, unexpectedly.

Linnet stared at him, round-eyed "Yes!" she whispered, trembling. "You are right; that's exactly what it sounded like, a French sailor."

John rubbed a hand over his face, utterly exasperated. "Oh, for goodness' sake, this is complete twaddle! Duncan, I leave you to sort out this ignorant young scoundrel. What on earth did he think he was doing, taking my wife down amongst those ruffians? Anything might have happened to her. It doesn't bear thinking of!"

Pat opened his mouth to protest but Duncan Snow quelled him with a look that boded no good. Pat gulped and snapped his mouth shut.

"Come along, you young whipper-snapper," Duncan ordered, walking to the door. "Perhaps a sound thrashing will help you forget about drowned sailors and ghosts!"

Linnet leaped up. "No, please don't hurt him, Mr. Snow, I beg of you! Be kind to the lad, he's had a terrible fright—we both have."

She stretched out an imploring hand. Pat flashed her a grateful smile. Duncan Snow nodded politely but refrained from replying. As a ship's officer, Linnet feared he would do as he saw fit with Pat, her plea fell on deaf ears.

When they were alone, John swung round and immediately took her to task. "Have you any idea of the danger you might have been in?" he asked.

"John, please leave it. I have had a horrible shock. I just want to lie down."

John gritted his teeth and counted to ten. "You have had a shock through your own thoughtless behaviour. Turn about and place your hands on the bed."

She glared at him. "NO!"

It was a feeble fight, one that ended with her tossed over his knee with her skirts raised and his hand imprinting his lesson onto her bared bottom. As much as she shrieked and kicked, it was to no avail. He was bigger, stronger and much more determined. "You will not wander the ship without me and you will not put yourself in danger. Am I clear?"

When there was no reply, he doubled his efforts and soon she sang her apologies and made promises of obedience. He stood her to face the wall and think upon her actions. Calling her to him after a few moments, he asked her to tell him how she should have arranged to fetch her etui. Sulkily, she said that she should have asked him to go with her, or fetch it for her. He kissed her forehead and left her alone to dress for luncheon. When he'd left the cabin, Linnet stamped her foot and stuck out her tongue at the door before flouncing behind the screen to wash.

Later, at dinner—a meal this time with the two of them, the captain and Duncan Snow—Linnet recounted her tale again for the captain's benefit. When she had finished, he put his elbows onto the table and placed his fingertips together thoughtfully.

"Tell me, my dear, what made you and the boy suppose this ghost to be French?" he asked.

Linnet thought a moment. "Well," she explained, "for one thing, it spoke in French. It moaned horribly, calling out, '*Mon dieu, mon dieu!*'"

The gentlemen passed one another meaningful glances. "What is wrong? Tell me!" Linnet demanded, looking from John to the captain, but they both ignored her.

"Where are the new crew from?" Captain Pettigrew asked Duncan.

Duncan frowned. "Most have sailed with us for some while now, but we did press-gang a few men from Plymouth for this voyage."

The captain nodded thoughtfully, unconcerned by Duncan's revelation, for it was common practice in these times to kidnap drunken men from taverns to take aboard ships as ship's crew. Often these men were bludgeoned unconscious before they were flung into a hold until the ship was far out to sea.

Captain Pettigrew turned again to Linnet. "Ma'am, I am sure today's adventure has exhausted you. Perhaps you would like to retire now and leave us to our port."

She cocked her head to one side and smiled sweetly at him. "On the contrary, Captain Pettigrew, I am well rested and not at all fatigued."

John stood and frowned at his wife. "I think, my dear, that you would benefit from an early night, especially after your shock and the consequences of today. Come, I shall escort you back to our cabin and return, if I may, Captain, to join you for port?"

Linnet threw John a filthy look. How dare he embarrass her by referring to the *consequences*, thereby letting the other gentlemen know that she had been humiliatingly punished!

"Come along, my dear," he said, his voice brooked no discussion.

The gentlemen rose to their feet and bowed; Linnet realised that she had no option but to leave. "Gentlemen," she said icily, her nose in the air as she swept through the door.

John followed behind her stiff, indignant figure. When they arrived at their cabin, he unlocked the door and she marched inside. Spinning about, she faced him furiously. "How dare you treat me like that? I am not a child, John, to be put to bed before the adults! That was an interesting conversation which concerned me. You had no right to hint at what happened earlier. That was private, between the two of us! What on earth must have Mr. Snow thought of your arrogantly rude behaviour?"

John made no attempt to interrupt her tirade. He simply lounged in the doorway, his grey eyes twinkling, his arms folded, watching her with irritating amusement.

When at last she ran out of breath, he spoke. "My, my, we do have a temper this evening! I must try to remember not to stand too close to the ship's rail when you are in poor humour. I am sure it would not be quite so easy to climb out of the sea as it was for poor Charles from that pond!"

Then, with a grin, he ducked out of the room, slamming the door shut behind him. She heard the lock turn with a click. The bastard had locked her in! Picking up the water jug, she hurled it at the door whilst giving an ear splitting shriek.

Something smashed against the back door. A loud scream of rage echoed from within. He would let her behaviour go on this occasion; after all, she'd had a nasty fright today, and he suspected her rage was Linnet's way of feeling in control of herself again. Chuckling, he pocketed the cabin's key and went back to join the officers and drink port.

Over drinks and cigars, the possibility of a French spy being stowed aboard was discussed. It was decided that Duncan Snow should conduct a thorough search below decks as a precaution the following day.

THE DAYS ROLLED PAST PLEASANTLY ENOUGH. They even fell into a routine. They would take breakfast together in their cabin, after which they would take a stroll up on deck before returning below for a light luncheon, which was generally set out within the captain's quarters. Afternoons were spent sewing shirt sleeves in place, while John disappeared with Duncan Snow. Pat came daily to run errands, wash out their smalls, and clean. He often brought breakfast to them in the mornings and it was his job to empty the slops. They met up for tea in their cabin; this was a mutually satisfying hour in which they generally ended up in bed, slaking their honeymoon passion. Linnet was amazed at how much she enjoyed John's attentions. She enjoyed their lovemaking and was learning more about her husband. She quickly realised how easily she could manipulate him using sex to get her own way. Linnet still entertained the hope that she could persuade her husband to return to England and live at Lavenstock Hall. She thought wrongly that he had no idea of her wiles, but John was an astute man and fully aware of her plan. While it was harmless, he was happy to indulge her. For the duration of their honeymoon, he would appear to comply with his bride's whims, just so long as she respected him and did as he bid.

Linnet awoke one night to a terrible shrieking noise and a sickening rolling sensation. There was a vast storm in progress and the ship groaned, her timbers screaming under the force of the wind, bucking and dropping as she strained to ride the high boiling sea. Linnet clung to John, who was awoken by her terrified whimpers, and he reassured her and comforted her.

He began distracting her, and soon the frenzied elements were blotted out by the internal frenzy of own their lovemaking. When morning dawned, the storm had lessened considerably, but the wind still howled and the ship rocked alarmingly. For the first time since boarding the ship, Linnet felt bad. As the morning wore on, she became more and more unwell. She retched until she lay completely exhausted. John stayed by her side and held a cool, damp cloth to her forehead; concerned for his sickly wife. He was so used to her boundless energy and robust good health that he found the sight of her lying limply pale quite terrifying. He berated himself for taking advantage of her fears during the night, using her to slake his lust, quite forgetting the active role she'd played in their coupling.

Duncan Snow came to check on Linnet, bringing Pat. "She's jus' sea sick, 'tis all." He shrugged unsympathetically.

Duncan showed more concern. "I have a draught of powders in my chest that may help," he told John. "I'll fetch them. Just pour a little wine into a glass, Pat, ready for my return. The sooner Linnet swallows them, the quicker she'll recover."

As good as his word, he returned promptly and mixed a foul potion in the waiting glass. John held her head up, and Duncan pressed the glass to her lips. Linnet turned her head away stubbornly, refusing to drink.

"Right then, there's only one thing for it," John decided.

He signalled for Duncan to support her head then, taking the glass, he gripped Linnet's small nose between finger and thumb, and as soon as she opened her mouth, he tipped the liquid in. She coughed and spluttered, but most of the noxious potion went down her throat. "Good girl," he encouraged kindly as he mopped up the spilt medicine and plumped pillows to make her comfortable. She glowered up at him from the bed, too ill to complain. Duncan and Pat left quietly, closing the door behind them.

Linnet dozed, sleeping fretfully until evening. When she awoke, the horrible moaning winds had dropped, the storm had passed, and the ship lolled gently once more. She felt drained and washed out but so much better than she had done earlier in the day. When she roused, she saw that John was sitting across the cabin, reading.

"Hello. Have you been there all the while I was asleep?" she asked.

He put his book aside, walked over and seated himself beside her. "Yes, of course, I wouldn't have left you on your own; I've been worried about you. How do you feel now?" He placed his palm upon her forehead, checking for any fever. She felt warm but not feverish. He grazed his knuckles down her pale cheek in a gentle caress.

"Like a wrung-out dishcloth and utterly horrible! You absolute beast, making me drink that odious stuff of Duncan's. It tasted foul!"

John grinned and Linnet smiled back; she decided that she liked the way his eyes crinkled when he smirked. How could she have ever have feared this handsome man of hers? He who'd brought ecstasy into her sheltered life. Her eyes roamed over him, noting the way his dark hair fell over his collar. He lifted his leg and sat with his foot crossed over his thigh. She admired the bulging muscled thighs, and her gaze moved up to the exposed bulge of his loin. She licked her lips, giving a sigh, wishing she felt better.

John frowned at her in concern. "Is something wrong, sweetheart?" he asked, smoothing back her russet hair.

"No. I hate being ill, I always have done. Talk to me, John; tell me about Boston and your home there."

Linnet settled herself back against the pillows. John was pleased that she had at last asked about his home. He swung his legs up and lay on the bed, pulling her into the circle of his arm. She snuggled against him, feeling warm and safe. She could hear the soothing beat of his heart and the deep rumble of his voice as he spoke, telling her of his home in Boston. He spoke of the people he knew and of his friends and, finally, he mentioned his mother.

She jerked upright. "Your mother is alive?" she asked, amazed.

"Why, yes," he replied, surprised. "I assumed that you knew."

"No, I did not. Why did you not tell me this before? What is she like?"

John smiled at his wife's interested, animated face. She had more colour in her cheeks now. "She is a delightful woman, and I am certain that she will love you, my darling. We have a reasonable-sized, wooden salt box house and a housekeeper to run it." He planted a kiss on her nose and added, "My mother and your father have been writing to each other since my father died. They plotted our betrothal between them."

Linnet couldn't believe that her father had not mentioned this to her. "What is your mother's name?" she asked curiously.

"Louise. She is a very brave and sweet lady, and I am sure you two will get on right away," John told her confidently.

She sat thoughtfully. "My father did mention the name Louise when a letter came for him once, but I was impatient to go out riding and I just didn't listen. I suppose after that, he didn't bother to mention her letters to me again."

Linnet looked so sad that John said kindly, "Well now, how many children listen when their parents talk of their friends' news?

I for one never know who has had what baby, or whose husband has what illness. I simply cannot keep up with all my mother's friends and their doings, so why should you?" He quelled the thought that Linnet was far too self-absorbed to listen to anything not directly concerned with herself, but Linnet nodded in agreement.

"Anyway, it will be nice to have a Mamma. Do you think your mother will continue to run the house?"

John was reassuring, saying, "Well, as I told you, Mistress Plant is our housekeeper and she is an excellent organiser. She will run the house, but I am sure you could make any changes that you see fit. Mistress Plant and her husband, Ben, have been with us for some years now."

She jolted. "John, I do not even know how old you are."

He chuckled. "Twenty-six, and you are almost nineteen, exactly seven years my junior, the perfect age difference for a man and his wife!"

"Huh! I don't know about that. Why, sir, it seems to me that you are almost old enough to be my father!"

Her teasing earned her a merciless tickling. When they both lay tangled up in the sheets, exhausted and laughing, she rolled over and said seriously, "I think I may be falling in love with you, and I want to tell you that I am glad that we married. I just wish that I could tell my father so."

He cupped her face in his hands, murmuring softly, "I would have no other woman but you, my sweet. I love you so much already. Yet I find a little more to love about you each day that we spend together."

He bent and kissed her mouth with tender passion. When he finally broke the kiss, he suggested that she begin writing a letter to her father, one that they could send back to England with The Tempest on her return voyage from Boston. He fetched ink and parchment so she could make a start.

❦

THE DAYS RESUMED their familiar pattern. The stormy weather passed. Linnet felt invigorated and well again due to the bracing sea air. One day, while she was on deck, a huge grey and white bird settled upon a crosspiece. The sailors became excited; they said this bird was a lucky omen. They fetched nets for trawling fish, and she watched with fascination as the net was pulled in a short while later, laden with flapping silver fish. The fish writhed upon the open deck as the men started to salt them into barrels, leaving a small pile of writhing live fish to one side.

When the sailors moved back, the large sea bird flew down onto the deck and ate its fill. Linnet was thrilled to witness this special event; she spoke of little else for days. It also meant that their diet was supplemented with fresh fish. The chickens had long since been devoured, and the vegetable supply exhausted. The fish would be a welcome change to the ship's rations of rice.

One afternoon, on a particularly blustery day, John left Linnet on deck with Pat for company as he spoke with Duncan. The sea that day was a steely grey; "white horses" crested the waves which buffeted the ships sides. Occasionally, the waves rose high and broke over the side. Linnet and Pat decided to play ball, one that Pat had made from wound-up rags tied with string. Linnet threw the ball for Pat to catch and it flew wide, far above his head. It rolled beyond him and settled at the edge of the ship. Laughingly, Pat careered after it. He'd just reached the ship's side and was bending down to retrieve it when the ship dipped and a huge wave broke over him. Silently, he vanished, swept over the side, into the high sea. It was as if he had never been there at all.

So quickly did the accident happen that for a few seconds, Linnet stared frozen at the spot where the boy had stood. Then she screamed, hastening to the ship's side, turning her head this way and that, frantically looking into the churning waters for any sign of her friend.

"Help! Help, for pity's sake! Man overboard, help!"

Her frantic screams brought two seamen to her side and she waved at the restless sea, screaming, "Man overboard! For goodness' sake, do something! Pat, oh, Pat!"

The sailors tied a rope to a bulkhead and threw the coil of rope over the side. Duncan Snow came and, quickly assessing the situation, told the men to lower a rowing boat. Duncan himself climbed down the loose rope to reach the small vessel, which bobbed about on the swelling sea. Linnet waited, her hand pressed to her mouth to prevent her screams escaping. John arrived, pulling his wife against him. "What on earth happened?" he asked.

"Oh, John, dear God, Pat was washed overboard. He just disappeared into the sea! If only I hadn't thrown that stupid, stupid ball so high!" Her voice rose to a shriek.

John gave her a reassuring squeeze. "It was not your fault. This was an accident. What are they doing now?" he asked, gesturing to the sailors who were slapping each other on the back and laughing.

"Oh, dear Lord, let this mean they have found him," she begged fervently, craning her neck to see over the side of the ship.

John pushed his way through the crowd. "Have they got him?" he asked a midshipman.

"Ay, look for thee self." The sailor grinned, gesturing over the ship's side.

John looked down. The small rowing boat was continually knocked against the side of the ship by the relentless sea. John could see Duncan struggling with Pat's inert body. He appeared to be attempting to tie a rope around the boy's waist and chest. He waved a signal up to the men, who began to haul the boy up by the rope. Eventually, they pulled the lad over the ship's side and onto the deck. He lay there, unmoving. Linnet rushed forward and the men silently parted, letting her through. She dropped to her knees by the boy's side and put her hand over his heart. It was beating very faintly.

"Quickly, John, get him to our cabin."

She turned to the nearest sailor and shouted for him to help her husband. John swiftly picked the lad up, not requiring any help, the boy was so slight. Linnet hurried along at his side. Neither of them spared a thought for poor Duncan, who was climbing the rope to safety, but as he appeared on deck, he was cheered by everyone.

John placed Pat on their bed in the cabin. "Fetch another blanket, quickly. I must get these wet clothes off the boy."

Linnet turned away to do as he bid but turned back quickly as she heard John utter an oath. "What the heck? But this is no boy! Come here," he called his wife urgently. They both stared down at Pat. John had removed his wet shirt. It was obvious to them both that *he* was a *she* as an unmistakable pair of small but perfectly formed female breasts lay exposed to their sight.

They gazed at one another, shocked. "Good Lord, Patty and not Pat! You'd best be the one to fetch the blanket while I undress… *her*," Linnet said.

After removing Pat's trousers, they could both see the flat triangle of her sex that proved beyond doubt Pat was indeed a Patricia. John threw Linnet a blanket. "Wrap her in this, and when she is decent, I will rub some warmth into her limbs."

She did as he asked and minutes later, after a vigorous rub down, Patty started moaning softly. Linnet pulled a clean nightgown from her trunk and pulled it over the girl's head. Then they tucked her snugly into the bed and heaped covers over her. As they stood looking down at her, the door opened and Duncan strode in, wrapped in a blanket over his still soaking clothes. "How is the boy?" he asked immediately.

"You had better see for yourself," said John drily, stepping away from the bed.

Duncan joined them and stared down. Silently, John lifted the covers, then parted the nightgown, revealing Patty's bare chest and proof of her female identity.

"Good God! He is a girl? I cannot believe it!" Duncan was extremely shaken. "Are you sure?" he asked rhetorically.

"I changed her, and Pat is most definitely a Patty and a girl!" Linnet told him.

"My God, I just cannot believe it, *a girl*! How on earth has she managed to keep that secret in a ship full of men? God!" Duncan paled. "To think—" He stopped, shaking his head.

"To think—what?" John queried.

Duncan looked ashen as he replied, "The conditions that she lives in, surrounded by the roughest of men. The way I treat her! Poor girl, all those thrashings she endured at my hand."

"Duncan, you must not blame yourself," Linnet retorted briskly. "As far as you knew, Patty was a lad!"

John looked up, nodding in agreement. Turning to Duncan, he put an arm around the man's shoulders. "Duncan, you saved this girl's life. Now go and get yourself dry. You're a hero, man!"

John guided Duncan out of the room and called back from the doorway, "I will go and beg some hot soup from cook. If you have brandy, give her some of that. It might help warm her."

Linnet found a bottle of brandy and, tenderly, she helped Patty to sit up. The girl took a sip or two and lay back down with a sigh, her eyes unopened.

Linnet, watching her, noticed a tear slide down the girl's cheek. Gently, she stroked the girl's forehead and murmured soothingly to her. How could they have been all been so blind? Patty's delicate features were so obviously those of a girl. Her skin was so white, it looked translucent, the skin under her eyes shadowed, her small rosebud mouth set beneath a small straight nose. The grime that usually hid her small heart-shaped face had been effectively washed away by the dip in the sea.

She made a small sound of distress. Linnet spoke softly to her. "Patty, dear, please do not fret. You are safe now." Slowly, Patty's eyelids fluttered open, soft blue eyes gazed up at Linnet with misery. Tears filled them and trickled down her pale cheeks. "Hush, hush, it's all right now," Linnet soothed.

"How's... I mean, what'll I do now?" Patty's thin voice asked in despair.

"I don't understand," said Linnet, frowning.

Patty started to speak but the effort set her coughing. Linnet fetched a cup of water and held it while she sipped. Then Patty lay back against the pillows before she said, "Tis plain, missus, now them knows I is a girl, they'll put me ashore first chance they'll get!"

Linnet had to concede that this could be the case. She looked at the piteous girl and thought quickly. "Patty, I am travelling without a maid to a strange new land, alone except for my husband. Would you do for me, perhaps? I could train you in the ways of a lady's maid, and even write a reference as such. It would help me a great deal to have a lady's maid again, I do assure you." She looked hopefully at the sorry girl on her bed.

A small smile curved Patty's pale lips. "'T would be nice," she said nodding, "but I don't know nuffin' about dresses and stuff though."

Linnet gave a small delighted laugh. "I will teach you, have no fear. Now, you need to rest. John has gone to find you some nourishment. We shall talk when you are feeling better."

Then Linnet fussed around with the bed covers but had to turn away, lest Patty see the tears of pity that flooded her eyes.

FIVE DAYS HAD PASSED since Patty's dramatic recovery, and she had been moved into a small cabin around the corner of the passageway from Linnet's and John's. She was shy at first with them, but grew more confident with each day that passed. The first thing that changed was her name. Patty's real name was Patsy and so she became that once more. Linnet turned out a couple of suitable dresses and undergarments for the girl, altering the size so that they would fit Patsy's slighter build. Patsy showed herself to be quick and willing and was deft with a needle. Linnet discovered a great deal about the young girl from their long afternoons spent together in sewing. By now, the gradually decreasing pile of John shirts and their sleeves were sewn back together. Linnet had cursed herself for her destructive act with each shirt she mended, not to mention the discomfort she had suffered with her sore backside.

John, missing the afternoon siesta that he and Linnet had grown used to taking earlier in the voyage, was becoming increasingly amorous first thing in the morning. Linnet was not in the same frame of mind, preferring to sleep through the dawn. This caused some friction between the honeymooners, so that they spent less time together during the day. Patsy became devoted to Linnet and listened quietly to Linnet's complaints without once uttering her own opinion. Lottie, Linnet's previous maid, would have had no such reticence.

If Patsy thought privately that Linnet was an extremely spoilt young woman, she would never dream of putting that thought into words. She had by now told Linnet of her own sad past. Of how she came to be on board the ship as a ship's cabin boy. To Linnet, the tale was a terrible one, but she could not truly relate to the hardships Patsy had faced. Her own world had been so far removed from the fear and deprivation that Patsy had suffered.

Patsy had been born in the area of Battersea, a small village outside London. Her father had died when she was three, and her mother decided to take in washing for local folk. They lived contentedly enough, until their local undertaker, who had frequently used her mother's laundry services over the years, was widowed. After a very short period of mourning, he began to court Patsy's mother, Rose, still an attractive woman of twenty-nine. They were married, and Rose and her daughter moved in with the undertaker, Jonas Briggs.

Patsy hated his house and the workshop, which was always full of coffins and, of course, dead bodies. The smell of embalming fluids that Jonas used permeated every nook and cranny of the establishment. When Patsy was twelve, Jonas decided she could earn her keep and help him in his trade. She was horrified and argued with her stepfather and her mother, who took her husband's part. The outcome of this family argument was that Jonas decided to take her down to the workshop for a thrashing but, instead of delivering the expected beating, Jonas had raped poor Patsy. Upstairs, her mother, hearing screams from what she thought of as her ungrateful daughter, ignored poor Patsy's cries and pleas for help. The following day, Patsy had tried to tell her mother what Jonas had done to her but her mother, not wishing to believe such a dreadful thing, had slapped her daughter's face and screamed at her to get out.

Jonas had come up to see what the commotion was about, and when confronted, he denied all, accusing Patsy of being evil and of lying just so she would not have to work. He took Patsy downstairs for yet another promised thrashing, but once again he raped her, laughing and jeering at her attempts to tell her mother the truth. He even insisted he had the right to use her whenever he wished—after all, he told her, she should be grateful that he had provided for her and her mother. Unable to contemplate a future of continual rape, Patsy had run away.

She had found an empty cart, and the driver, having that day sold his goods at the London market, was willing to allow her to ride in the back of the empty wagon. She travelled from cart to cart until she reached the coast. Patsy had a vague idea that she could get work in a tavern. With this in mind, she had turned herself into a boy and Pat was born, with the help of clothes stolen at the sea shore from a lad who splashed naked in the surf with his friends.

That night, she had trawled the sea front taverns, asking for work. When a burly sailor and his mate overheard her talking to the innkeeper, they had grabbed hold of her arm and told her they knew of a tavern that needed a likely lad; just such a one as he. Hauling Pat along between them, they plied her with rum until she could no longer stand. Then they took her aboard their ship, flinging her into a hold with other poor wretches who had been unwittingly press-ganged that night. When Pat came to, they were far out at sea. She then discovered that she was to be the new cabin boy on board The Tempest, and here she had remained, her secret successfully hidden beneath the layers of dirt and ragged clothing until now.

Duncan Snow was devastated by guilt when John recounted the tale told to him via Linnet. Duncan had gone to see Patsy and tried to make his apologies, but Patsy would have none of it. As far as she was concerned, Duncan had always treated her fairly and well and, above all, he had saved her life.

Life aboard The Tempest settled back down again. Linnet started to notice that Patsy would often disappear at odd times during the day. One evening after dinner, when she and John were returning to their cabin, Linnet remembered that Patsy had taken her nightgown to sew it, since it had been missing several buttons all due to John's rather impatient lovemaking. She tapped at Patsy's cabin door and, receiving no reply, turned the door knob. The door was unlocked, and Linnet saw straight away upon entering the tiny cabin that it was empty.

John, who had continued along to their own cabin, wondered why his wife had not yet joined him and went back to look for her. Linnet was just closing Patsy's cabin door. She held a lighted lantern in her hand. "Patsy is not in her room," she told John. "I am going to look for her, I won't be very long."

She turned away from him but was hauled back. John took the lantern from her. "No," he told her, shaking his head, "you are certainly not wandering around the ship alone, and most certainly not at night. I have told you before, it's not safe. Patsy will be fine. She has spent the last three and a half years aboard ship, she knows The Tempest. Have no fear, she will be safe. Now come to bed." He kept a firm grip on Linnet's arm as he towed her towards their cabin.

"No, John! Come with me. We can search together," she suggested, thinking this an admirable solution. She was not pleased, however, when John, undeterred, curtly refused her request. Upon reaching their room, he deposited the lantern on the table and, mindful of his wife's wilful nature, locked the door and dropped the key into his pocket. Linnet whirled furiously to face him, her green eyes flashing. John groaned; he knew the signs of one of his wife's temper tantrums.

"You do not even care that poor Patsy could be lying hurt somewhere alone out in the dark! With all these rough sailors on board! Think of what could happen to her! She has turned out to be a pretty little thing, anything could happen. We must go and look for her, John, surely you see that!"

John took off his jacket and waistcoat, keeping his eye on Linnet as he did so. With an outwardly cool demeanour that belied his inner fear that she was about to have a full-blown tantrum, he answered her with composure. Perhaps simple reason would divert her temper.

"My dear, I repeat: Patsy, will be fine. You forget, Linnet, that up until a few days ago, she was the ship's cabin boy. Now stop your fussing and get ready for bed."

Linnet seethed, she had become used to John doting upon her. She was used to having her own way. Provoked and furious, she was not about to give in over this. She was genuinely concerned for Patsy. She stalked to the door and attempted to open it. When it wouldn't budge she spun around and stamped her foot, holding her hand out for the key. "Give me the key at once!" she demanded.

John's eyes narrowed. He had been so pleased with his lovely wife, besotted with her delightful wiles and ways. It was, after all, their honeymoon, a time he felt should be spent in cementing their relationship, a time to get to know and trust one another. He really did not want this confrontation, however, he realised that he could not go on allowing Linnet to keep defying him in this way. She was just too damn rude and wilful. He had hoped that his dominance over her body in the marriage bed would be enough to calm and subdue her arrogant defiance. As his wife, Linnet must learn to become properly submissive towards him. How else was he supposed to keep her safe in the wilds of the Colonies if she would not heed her husband?

"Linnet, do not force me to take you in hand again. Be a good girl and prepare for bed."

She didn't move, mutinously determined to win this battle. Feeling righteous, she felt that she had justice on her side. Husband and wife stood across the room from one another, eyes locked, two narrowed, implacable steely grey, the other two flashing green and haughty, each awaiting the other's move.

John was by now utterly livid. He drew himself upright and pointed to the bed. "So be it! Remove your clothes and lie face down across the bed. If you comply willingly I shall simply spank you with my hand but defy me over this, madam and I shall use your hairbrush. The decision is yours."

Linnet was astounded, this was no spanking matter! She was simply concerned for a young woman in her charge. "Surely you cannot be serious, John? Why can't you understand that I am concerned for the girl?"

John frowned, looking thoroughly foreboding. "Linnet, what did you promise me on our wedding day?"

She rolled her eyes and stamped her foot. "Oh, please, let this not be about this obedience vow again!"

His jaw ticked. "Answer me, wife, what did you promise in your wedding vow to me?"

"This is utterly ridiculous!" She stamped her foot again—a mistake, because that small act of defiance was enough to tip John's patience over the edge.

With the speed and agility of a cat, he pounced to where Linnet stood and swung her up under one arm. He reached out and grabbed Linnet's flat backed, silver hairbrush from the chest and sat down on the bed. He dumped his argumentative wife across one knee while pinioning her legs with the other. Grasping her flailing hand, he swept up her skirts. Linnet was wild with righteous fury; she fought him tooth and nail.

The outcome was inevitable. She was no match for her muscular and much larger framed husband. To her chagrin, he delivered the first of many painful swats with her own hairbrush. Linnet was not afraid of her husband. They had spent time getting to know one another and Linnet was livid with him for reverting to the vile spanking man she had known before they were married.

She struggled and tried to bite him, swearing, using words she'd learned from listening to the sailors. John, incensed by his pretty young wife's foul tongue, spanked her ever faster and harder until the swearing was replaced by sobbing pleas for mercy. John grinned wickedly. "After hearing your foul language, darling, I think this punishment should continue, and the more you beg, the harder I shall spank. Quit your wailing and take your medicine like a good obedient wife, for I am determined that you will learn to do my bidding without argument. Do I make myself clear, Mistress Foster?"

Linnet was having a hard time understanding anything other than the relentless stinging and heating of her poor, naked bottom. She squirmed sideways, attempting to avoid the slaps and swipes as they continued to rain all over her posterior and the tops of her thighs. The pain was far worse than the previous hand spankings John had administered. She regretted pushing him into this punishment. Why could she not learn to control her temper around her husband? By this point she would have agreed to anything to make him simply stop, so she promised him everything she could think of.

"I am so sorry! John, stop, I am s-sorry… Stop! Please stop! No, ouch, no-o!"

She blustered and blubbered. Her face was awash with tears, her nose ran but John was angry, he was not about to let his wife off easily. This time she would learn her lesson.

He shifted her higher across his knee and bought the hairbrush down even more vigorously. She pulled helplessly at the quilt on the bed, but John had her in an iron grip and all she could do was bury her head into the quilt, sob, and suffer her punishment. At last, John flung the hairbrush aside and hauled Linnet to her feet. He spun her around and undid her skirt, pulling it down to the floor where it puddled about her feet. "Step out of your clothes," he ordered.

Linnet did as she was bid and reached behind her to rub her painful, swollen buttocks, whereupon John slapped her hands away. "No, I want you to remember this lesson! If I see you rub yourself even once, I shall spank you again just as hard and for just as long. Now stand and face the bed. That's right. Now bend over the bed and spread your legs."

John placed his hand in the middle of Linnet's back and bent her at the waist. Then he pushed her legs further apart and stepped back, admiring his handiwork. He placed his hands on her burning buttocks, squeezing, feeling the molten heat that radiated off her skin. "You will stay here, not moving or speaking, until I tell you otherwise, is that understood?"

Linnet mumbled, her head resting on her arms, which were wet from her tears. John slapped her bare bottom sharply twice in quick succession. "Answer me!"

She jumped as tears trickled down her cheek. "Yes," she whispered.

Another hard smack followed.

"Answer properly, with yes, sir!" he commanded.

Linnet bit her lip, stiffening with temper again but another stinging slap to her rump soon had her singing. "Yes, sir!" she cried, loud and clear. A smile twisted the corner of John's mouth. He felt that finally he was getting somewhere with her.

There was a loud rat-a-tat at their door and they both jumped. John went to the door and unlocked it. Outside stood Patsy, a nervous smile on her face. She held out Linnet's nightgown, now mended with all the missing buttons replaced. John took the gown and tried to block her view into the room with his body but Patsy could see her mistress and the girl's eyes widened at the sight of Linnet bent over the bed with her bared and scarlet backside thrust up into the air. Patsy looked at John nervously, knowing instantly what had occurred. She backed away from the door and then turned, fleeing to the safety of her own little cabin.

John closed the door and glanced over at his now very embarrassed wife. She had not moved, but he could see the flush that had crept up her neck and he knew that she was mortified. Linnet might consider modifying her behaviour in future; a bit of humiliation might have been the turning point in her wilful behaviour.

He needed some air, and he wanted her to ponder on her behaviour tonight, so he took his coat and, after warning Linnet not to move from her position, he left the cabin. As a precaution, he locked the door.

As soon as his footsteps had faded away, Linnet frantically rubbed her sore bottom, groaning with the blessed relief of being able to massage her afflicted derriere, which felt as though it was a furnace. She grabbed her hand mirror and positioned it so she could see her injured behind. Apart from the scarlet colour, it did not seem to be bruised. Flinging the mirror aside, she went to stand near the bed lest John suddenly return. She wondered whether he would make love to her that night. Strangely, instead of the disgust she expected to feel, she found herself shivering with anticipation. Whatever was wrong with her? John had just spanked her with her hairbrush, why wasn't she angry or disgusted? She shook her head with confusion. Turning to the wall, she leant her forehead against the wood while she massaged her poor benighted bottom.

Up on deck, the moon was full and shone brightly, bathing everything in magical silver light. John walked to the edge of the ship and looked out at the sea. The water gleamed with an iridescent light, sparkling where the moonshine left a silver trail that led from the moon itself. A flash of light darted from the ship out into the darkness and appeared to glint back as if it were some kind of reflection. Intrigued, he waited for the phenomenon to happen again. He stood at the ship's side and looked up at the large silvery orb hanging in the sky. It reminded him of Linnet's creamy, rounded bottom, recently upended over his knee. Immediately his manhood surged to life. He grinned, thinking that, as furious as he was with his wife; he did so enjoy spanking her delectable behind.

A sailor on the other side of the ship begun to quietly whistle a familiar tune; it niggled John that he could not remember the words to the song. He gazed up at the sky where the stars glowed bright, lighting the heavens. A sailor added words to the song he'd been whistling earlier.

"*Frere Jacques, Frere Jacques, dormez vous, dormez vous, sont a laiment ti, sont a laiment ti, ding dang dong, ding dang dong.*"

Of course, that is it, I recognise it now. He felt faintly uneasy but he wanted to get back to the cabin and remedy the ache in his loins.

Linnet had obviously heard the rattle of the key in the lock, he caught her movement as she quickly placed her hands back onto the bed, thrusting her bottom up high. Glancing at her as he came into the cabin, he said not a word about her disobedience. Disrobing, he washed then seated himself naked, in a chair, facing her back. His manhood stood fully engorged, it was a relief to be out of his constraining britches. He studied the alluring sight of his wife's rosy ass. He could see the shadow of her glistening sex. She was obviously aroused, the minx! His cock lengthened to its fullest extent at the sight of the delectable tableaux she presented.

Meanwhile, Linnet held her breath as she awaited her husband's command.

He decided that tonight he would take her as a stallion takes a mare, his need to master her strong. He padded over to her and slipped his hand straight between her legs. She instinctively tried to close them, protecting her sex from his invading fingers, but John slapped her bottom sharply. Obediently she parted her thighs for him with an endearing little mew of distress. His fingers explored her soft folds, slipping up to part her blazing bottom cheeks. He circled her anal star and she jerked forward, trying to shift away from him in obvious surprise.

"There is more than one way to subdue an errant wife," he told her as he moved to her dripping sex and frigged her with his fingers until she moaned and sighed. He felt her dew flood his hand. Bending her further over the bed, he brought her bottom up toward his erection. He swiped his cock up until it pressed against her anus; he felt her suck in a breath. A mewl of distress escaped her as she attempted to shift away from the pressure he placed against her private hole. "I shall take you here if spanking does not curb your wilfulness. So be warned, this is an act that will be immensely pleasurable for me but you will find it uncomfortable. I would never harm you but I demand your respect and obedience… I'll have it one way or another."

She moaned in response to this edict.

With a final press against her anus, he lowered his shaft to the drenched entrance of her quim. One swift thrust impaled her. He watched as his cock disappeared into her luscious wet core. Exquisite pleasure pulsed through him as he pounded against her reddened arse. She shuddered at his entry, wildly churning at the sheer animal sexuality of the act. He gloried in the fact she relaxed as never before. He felt the coil of release as she, too, cried out, her own climax devouring her.

The following morning, Linnet awoke lying on her stomach. Her stinging bottom had led to a restless night. She was embarrassed by the previous evening's events and peeked through her lashes to see whether her husband was awake. She thought him handsome with his bare chest covered with dark whorls of hair. One hand was flung up over his head, the hand she realised had spanked her so mercilessly the evening before. She tingled with lust, shocked by her reaction to the thought of his palm crashing against her nether flesh. She wondered if this was because she had never been spanked before she'd met John or whether it was the use of her hairbrush last night but after her spanking, she had become so very aroused. She could not even entertain the thought that his threat to take her bottom had anything to do with the way her body now thrummed.

When John stretched and opened his eyes, he found himself staring into sea green eyes that darkened and pooled with lust as she saw that he was awake. He pulled her on top of him and kissed her, his hand sliding down the soft satiny length of her body, insinuating his fingers between Linnet's thighs and sliding inside her damp mound. He had barely moved his fingers over her sensitive bud when she convulsed violently and climaxed. John grabbed her hips and rolled her over onto her back, plunging himself into her. He rode her hard, stoking her passion so that wave upon wave of lust surged through her loins like wild fire. At last, with one final push, he spent himself into her and they lay in a tangle of sheets on the bed, both breathing heavily.

"Well, good morning, wife," he managed at last, breathing heavily. "I think from now onwards, a spanking for you last thing at night would be beneficial for both of us!"

Linnet was silent, clearly too exhausted to reply.

A WEEK HAD PASSED, and they were finally running along the coast of America. It was now seven weeks since they had left Portsmouth and, weather permitting, they should be arriving in Boston within the next two weeks. Standing on the poop deck, relieved at last to see his homeland, John slid his arm around Linnet. She leaned against him happily.

"May I ask you something?"

John looked down upon her pretty up-turned face. "Anything," he replied.

She looked surprised. "Really? Anything?"

"Of course. If you asked my permission, you wouldn't end up across my knee quite so frequently," he replied.

"Whatever do you mean?" she asked, genuinely intrigued. John shook his head; she still didn't understand what he had been trying to teach her.

"If you asked when you wished to do something and did so in a pleasant way, then obey me when I have to say no to you because what you ask for is not safe or good for you, I would reward you."

Linnet frowned. "But I asked you last week if I could go and find Patsy and you still spanked me—and with my hairbrush!"

John sighed. "Linnet, that was because you wouldn't accept no as my answer; you still wanted your own way, and you were very rude and sassy to boot! That is why I used the hairbrush. Oh, and next time you behave like a spoilt little madam, I might not use your hairbrush. I might use a strap instead. You are forewarned, my sweet."

She pulled away from him, incredulous. "Just to be sure that I understand this correctly: if I ask your permission to do anything other than breathe, you will say no, then, when I point out how unfair that is, you will spank me? Please tell me, have I got that right?"

John grinned. "Well now, I might just surprise you and say yes once in a while. I need you to breathe, after all!"

He caught Linnet's arm and turned her to face him. He put a finger under her chin and tilted her face up to his before saying gently, "Darling, I want to say yes to your requests, but I have to keep you safe. I promised your father that I would, and anyway, what sort of a husband would I be if I let you fly off into danger without stopping you when we are home?"

Linnet had an overwhelming feeling of homesickness. 'Home,' was Lavenstock Hall, oh, how she missed it! Her mind drifted off, remembering her home. Then she realised she had missed half of what John had said.

"…and if you want baubles or dresses, just ask me!"

"A horse, oh John, I want a horse! One that I choose for myself," she said, her face growing animated.

John laughed. "Then a horse you shall have, my love," he said and he picked her up, swung her off her feet and planted a smacking kiss onto her astonished lips.

LINNET WAS FINDING Patsy's behaviour increasingly odd. She kept disappearing for hours on end. She tried to speak to John about it, but he was irritatingly off hand. He couldn't see what she was worried about. "She probably has a sweetheart. Patsy is a very pretty girl," he answered dismissively.

She was indeed. Soft brown hair, although not yet grown long enough for a girl, curled sweetly around her heart-shaped face as it fell to touch her shoulders. She had lovely blue eyes and long sooty lashes. Linnet showed Patsy how to tie rags into her hair at night to produce curls the following morning. With a few days of rest and regular meals, her cheeks had filled out and held a pleasing, rosy bloom. Yes, Patsy could certainly turn a few heads now if she wanted to.

But it wasn't that which concerned Linnet. Patsy was furtive. On the deck one morning, Linnet sent Patsy to fetch her shawl. She awaited the girl's return, chatting with John and Duncan. After a long while, and feeling chilly by now, Linnet decided to go and see where Patsy had got to. As she went to the steps leading down to their cabins, she espied the ex-cabin boy coming up from the other side of the ship. Linnet waited for her at the bottom of the stairs. Patsy was startled when she saw Linnet. Flushing a deep, cherry red, she couldn't look Linnet in the eye. She claimed that she had been unable to find the shawl. Linnet asked her where she had really been, but Patsy insisted she'd been nowhere. Linnet knew she was up to something, especially when she entered her cabin and found the shawl lying in full view across the bed.

Every Sunday, Captain Pettigrew held a service for all aboard his ship. John stood with the officers up on the poop deck and, on this occasion, Patsy joined Linnet. Prayers were said and an officer —a different one was chosen each week—read an extract from the Bible. This week, however, the captain had asked John whether he would like to read. Linnet watched happily as her handsome husband stood tall and proud next to the captain. The slight breeze lifted his dark hair. The shiny brass buttons of his great coat glinted and flashed in the bright sunshine. He began the reading. "The text today is taken from the New Testament, James, chapter three, verses four to six. 'Behold also the ships, which though they be so great and are driven by fierce winds, yet are they turned about with a very small helm...'" There was a sudden shout from below. John stopped reading and looked up, a finger marking his page.

A man gestured wildly towards starboard and sailors began to run to the ship's side, gesturing and looking out to sea. More men scrambled up ropes and stood upon one another's shoulders in order to obtain a better view, there was much shouting and clamouring. Captain Pettigrew bellowed for the telescope to be brought to him. He turned the telescope toward the direction in which the sailors were pointing excitedly.

"What is it?" Linnet asked but no one answered her.

The officers started making their way to the captain's side. Suddenly, a yell came from the captain, "Muster battle stations! Man the cannon!"

All around them, chaos broke out, men dashed to and fro. Linnet and Patsy clung together, terrified. Linnet was searching amongst the mêlée, frantically looking for sight of her husband. Where had John got to? The next moment, it seemed to her, the floor under her feet gave way; this was followed by a huge explosion. She was thrown sideways where she lay in a stupefied daze. She could not make sense of what was happening around her. After what seemed like an age, but was in fact only a moment or so, strong arms lifted her and John's face framed her view.

"My God, I thought I'd lost you!" he cried, sweeping her up into his embrace. "When I saw that cannon ball hit the deck, I was beside myself. Come!" he yelled over the noise and confusion. "We have to get down below deck."

He turned, ducking and diving, while men, ropes, broken decking and thick smoke all hindered his progress. Where had the smoke come from? she wondered, shocked by this frightening turn of events. She kept asking John over and over what was going on and what had happened to Patsy. Had he seen her?

He pressed onward, trying to find somewhere away from the chaos and confusion that surrounded them. Eventually, they stumbled down the steps that led to their cabin. John shoved open their door and they tumbled inside.

They stood holding one another and listening to the dreadful sounds coming from above them. Awful screams and yells accompanied the sudden and shocking pounding of a ship's cannon. Then it dawned on them: they could hear guns from another ship.

"We are under attack," John stated heavily.

Linnet's eyes widened with shock. She bit her lip to stop it trembling, she was afraid. "Who would want to attack us, John, the French? The one you spoke of to my father? Why would they attack an English ship? We are not at war with the French at present, perhaps they haven't heard that the war is at an end," she babbled with fear.

John hugged her briefly then set her aside. He spoke rapidly over his shoulder as he strode to the chests. Lifting the lids, he rummaged inside, scattering clothes as he hunted frantically within. "They probably are French; I cannot tell as yet. Their privateers are still attacking merchant vessels, as are the English privateers. We must hide as much of our valuables on our persons as we can, Linnet. Find your jewellery and put as many of the good pieces as you can into your underclothes, wedge them in tightly. I have a money belt here for the paper. Quickly!" he snapped. He felt sorry to sound so harsh but he wished to rouse his wife from the stupor of her innate terror.

She wrung her hands in panic. "Linnet!" John's voice penetrated her frozen brain, propelling her to the wooden chest. Pulling her jewellery cask out, she lifted the lid and selected the finest pieces, emeralds and pearls, a diamond ring with matching bracelet and ear bobs.

John turned to her and removed a chain and locket.

"No, my dear, we have to leave the rest; otherwise, when the pirates search, they will know we have taken all the best pieces and search us."

Linnet put the rest back in the casket. "You think they will board us then?" she whispered, trying to keep calm.

"Undoubtedly, and I'm afraid our guns will be no match for theirs. Put on another layer of clothing, but try to conceal the fact that you are wearing two sets of clothes."

So saying, John began to pull on more clothes over his present outfit. Linnet did as she was bid, thankfully without question, for once. Finally, he stepped back and looked her over critically.

"Hmm, your neckline isn't right." He reached out and undid the buttons of her gown about her neck then, turning up her lace collar so that the dress beneath was hidden, he re-buttoned her. "No one would know, I think, you still appear trim even wearing two sets of clothing. Now for your warm cloak…"

The ship tipped suddenly and Linnet stumbled. John caught her and held her close. "They are boarding, that is why the ship dipped. They have grappling irons and have placed boarding planks from across their ship to ours," he explained.

Linnet pulled herself from his arms and ran over to lock their cabin door. When she returned, her eyes were wide with fear. "Oh God, John… what are we to do?"

John sighed and shrugged, resigned. "We wait. There is nothing more we can do."

Linnet dropped into a chair and gripped the arms. "Will they kill us, do you think?" she asked tremulously.

John looked at his beautiful young wife; so young, only eighteen, with almost no life experience. She had no idea that her fate could possibly be worse than death. He knew for a fact that young women caught by French pirates were often shared among the crew. "I am sure that they will not harm us." He spoke with a confidence he didn't feel. If he had to, he would kill her rather than watch her suffer. He fingered the small pistol hidden in his coat pocket. Linnet relaxed slightly, believing and trusting in her husband.

The noise above was harrowing. Linnet covered her ears then jumped, startled by a particularly loud bang. The two of them remained there, silent and tense, waiting for what seemed an eternity. They listened to the dreadful sound of battle and the death cries of men, the ear-splitting shriek of tearing wood as the guns found their mark. All they could do was listen and wait for the appalling noise to cease. Neither spoke of the friends they had made who were now fighting for their lives. Each prayed quietly for their safe deliverance. The sounds above began to sound less frenetic and the pounding of the guns ceased. There were a few isolated screams, then the sound of pounding feet overhead.

The minutes ticked slowly by, and when finally there came a pounding upon their cabin door, they both started with shock. Standing beside her, both facing the door, John placed his arm protectively about his trembling wife. He knew how little protection he would actually be able to afford her against the rabble.

The door suddenly crashed inwards and two men, bare-chested and smeared with blood, pushed their way into the cabin. Linnet screamed and turned her face into her husband's shoulder. It was only a second of comfort before she was wrenched away by rough hands that dug into the tender flesh of her upper arms as the pirates manhandled them both up onto the deck.

The scene that met their eyes was one of almost total devastation, the broken and blood-stained bodies of sailors lay everywhere. Mutilated remains lay where they had fallen, hideous wounds and unseeing eyes stared blindly at the sky. Even in her worst nightmares, Linnet could not imagine such horror. Her eyes were drawn to a small group of figures hanging in a line from the main mast, swaying heavily in the sea breeze. A slow dawning, realisation of what she was looking at suddenly hit hard and she spun quickly around, doubling over as she was violently sick. When she was done, the pirate holding her punched her hard in the small of her back, disgust written across his face. The sudden shock of the impact knocked Linnet to her knees. Through a haze of pain, she heard two shouts, one she distinguished as John's, cut-off mid-yell; the other she recognised as Patsy's.

Gentle hands smoothed back her hair and helped her to rise, and she turned towards the kindly person. "Patsy? Is it you? Oh, thank God, I thought you dead… John, John! What have they done with him?" Linnet twisted around to look for her husband. He lay slumped upon the deck, he wasn't moving. "Oh God, they have killed him!"

She dropped to her knees beside him and placed her hand over his heart. To her relief, she could feel the steady beat. Stroking his dark hair back from his forehead, she bent her head and pressed her lips to his temple. She realised she was shivering violently, trembling as if she suffered a fever, her teeth chattering uncontrollably. She was finding it hard to gather her wits.

Patsy stood beside her and she yelled across at someone close by, "'Ere, you promised me these two wouldn't be 'urt, an 'ere they are, all bashed about!"

"Merde, cherie, zees is war an' zere are casualties! What I said was I would not 'ave 'em keeled!" A large pirate stepped into Linnet's line of vision. She attempted to focus on him but found it hard to control the dizziness that threatened to overcome her. She saw he wore a red and white sailor's cap which flopped jauntily to one side and, like the other pirates, he wore no shirt. His arms and chest were covered in tattoos. He had on dark blue breeches that ended at the knees; below these he wore dirty, striped red and white stockings.

"Patsy?" Linnet croaked. "I don't understand... do you know this-this person?"

The pirate gave a coarse bellow of laughter. "Ah, oui! Ze madamoiselle knows me verra well! Do you not, ma petite choux?"

"Stop it, Henri!" Patsy said and turned to Linnet, a pleading look on her face. She reached down to where Linnet crouched over John and took hold of Linnet's hand. "It was after I fell into the sea, missus, I met Henri below deck. I was crying, and he was very kind to me. Well, we fell in love, we did. Don't be mad at me, missus— Linnet. I didn't want no one hurt, he promised me that you, Mr. Foster and Mr. Duncan would go free. Them's plan was all set up anyways so there was nuffin' I could do to stop it."

Linnet jerked her hand away from Patsy's. "You helped him? You knew that a pirate was aboard this ship and said nothing?" Linnet was incredulous; Patsy flushed and hung her head.

The pirate strode forward and spoke to Linnet. "Ma femme! Of course elle would not betray me! Elle knew I would cut her preety throat if she did zuch a zing! Mais, I will keep ma word; you will go free!"

Linnet stared into the heavily lidded, dark brown eyes and unshaven face. A livid scar ran down one cheek. "It was you in the luggage hold." She said it as a statement, for she knew his answer."

"Mais oui, madam. Also, I had zee pleasure, non, zee *verry* great pleasure, to watch your lovely self and your 'usband, in zee moonlight one night, being so very romantic, hmm?"

Linnet looked at him with horror. "You were spying on us?"

The pirate gave a lascivious laugh, revealing a few missing teeth as he did so. "Oui, madam, certainement! I compliment vous, vous ete tres belle, madam!"

He continued to chuckle while Linnet closed her eyes briefly, willing herself not to swoon.

"What are you going to do with us?" she asked in a low voice.

The pirate, Henri, looked serious. "I keep ma word, petite. Vous et votre marie… alle!" So saying he turned and raised his arm, signalling to two of his men.

Then a pirate ran forward, talking in French to his leader. She saw that he held her jewellery casket. The man opened it and showed the contents to Henri, whereupon the large pirate scooped out the valuables and handed them all to Patsy. The girl stood there, her hands cupped, holding more wealth than she had ever seen in her whole life before, her mouth hung open like a fish.

Linnet was livid. "How dare you! Those belong to me, you nasty little thief!"

The French pirate's heavy brows lowered, and he snarled at Linnet. "Merde! You are verra lucky, madam, zat your jewels are all zat we take, you understand ma meaning, I am sure. Maintenant, ferme la bouche!"

He gave a typically Gallic gesture and turned away. Linnet had to know what had happened to Duncan. "Where is Duncan? Have you seen him?"

Patsy lowered her eyes as she replied, "Yes 'm. I'm real sorry, missus, but he were killed in the fight, a clean wound straight through his chest. I was with 'im when he died, comforting him was the least that I could do."

Linnet pressed her hand to her mouth and bit down hard to stop herself from screaming. No, please, not Duncan! Not sweet, fresh-faced Duncan with a wife and baby daughters in Plymouth. How would they cope without him to support them?

The two ruffians who had fetched them up from the cabin were dragging John, still unconscious, over to the port side of the ship, that side remained relatively undamaged. They tied a rope around his body.

"What are they doing?" Linnet asked Patsy in a whisper, her

heart beating jarringly in her chest as her mouth filled with fear. She stood and ran over to her inert husband.

Patsy followed Linnet, who was now pulling at his arm, trying in vain to get him away from the pirates. Patsy caught up with Linnet. "They is going to lower Mr. Foster 'cos he's not awake."

Linnet frowned in puzzlement, asking, "Lower him where?"

Patsy shuffled uncomfortably. "Into the row boat," she said.

"But you assured me that we would remain safe!" Linnet shrieked at her in rage.

Patsy paled and stumbled back. "I saved your life! If Henri 'ad his way, you and your man would be dead now!"

Linnet lunged, her hand lifted to slap Patsy's face, but a vice-like grip upon her raised arm prevented her from following through with her action. Her arm was twisted up painfully behind her back. She was frogmarched to the side of the ship, where John was already being lowered over the side. Linnet turned her head and spat at the pirate gripping her arms. "You traitorous bitch, I should have left you to drown!" she screamed at Patsy. Then, to her fury and shame, she burst into noisy, gasping sobs of misery and rage, the horror and the fear completely overwhelming her.

She found herself flung over the shoulder of a foul-smelling pirate, who made his way over the ship's side, where he began the fearful descent to a small rowing boat bobbing about at the side of the ship. From her upside down position, Linnet could see John's body slumped in the bottom of the boat. When the pirate carrying Linnet was at the bottom of the rope ladder, he swivelled his shoulder and dropped her down into the stern.

"Land is zat away," he told her, jerking his thumb away from the ship. He gave Linnet a leering grin from under a greasy blond fringe, then shinned back up the rope ladder onto the ship.

Patsy's voice floated down to her. "There is a flagon of water under the seat of the boat. Land is about twelve miles to port. I am sorry, truly. You was kind to me. Farewell, missus!"

Linnet slumped dejectedly on the seat of the boat, wondering what she should do next. She looked down at John. He appeared to be sleeping but Linnet knew that the blow to his head meant that he was unconscious. She tore off some of her second petticoat and dipped it into the sea, then lifted her husband's head gently onto her lap where she tenderly mopped his wound. John groaned, and she called his name but there was no other response. She held his shoulders, the cool wet cloth laid across his forehead.

The boat bumped gently against the side of the ship but it was now beginning to float away from the side. Linnet noticed the oars on the floor of the boat; she would have to move John off her lap if she wanted to use them. Perhaps she should try to move the little boat away from the ship, just in case the pirates changed their minds about killing them. A vision of Captain Pettigrew and the ship's officers hanging from the masts sprang unwanted into her mind. She hastily suppressed the images; she must not think about the things that she'd seen on the ship, not yet. Linnet knew that she had to remain calm; their lives were in her hands. If she moved the boat away, they might blow them out of the water with cannon fire. She was petrified about which decision to take. Glancing up the wooden side of the ship, she saw that nobody appeared to be watching them. She decided she would row; they had to get away from this ship of death. At least if they were to die, they would be alone together on high seas with only the Lord and fish for company.

She rebelled against the thought of death, for she—they—were too young to die! Awkwardly, she extracted the oars from under John's prone body. First, she used an oar to push the boat away from the ship's side, then she placed an oar on either side of the boat, slipping them into the rowlocks. Clutching one in each hand, she dipped the paddle ends into the sea and pulled back with all her might. One oar slipped from her grip and hastily she caught it, only just saving it from disappearing into the ocean depths. She took a deep breath and started again, eventually building up a rhythm: pull back and stroke, pull back and stroke.

Sweat dripped down her face and between her breasts, yet she struggled onward.

When she finally broke for a rest, wiping her hot face with the back of her forearm, she looked back at the ship and was surprised by how far she had managed to row.

"I am only just realising what an amazing woman you are, Mistress Foster."

Linnet started, and then squealed with joy, reaching for John, helping him upright. She covered his face with kisses.

"Steady on, now!" He swayed, holding his head with both hands.

"Thank goodness you are all right!" Linnet gasped with relief.

"Well, I wouldn't say that, exactly," John quipped with a weak grin. He gazed about, frowning. "So, here we are then. I take it we are the only ones blessed with this particular fate?" He arched a questioning brow. Linnet hung her head; her hair tumbled forward in a curtain of honey which screened her face.

"Linnet?" He reached out a hand and gently raised her head. Her face was awash with tears. She was unable to speak.

John's face hardened. "All dead?" he asked, hazarding a guess. "Captain Pettigrew—dear God, not Duncan too?"

She suddenly spluttered into gut-wrenching sobs, her body folded double, her head dropping onto John's lap. He gently laid his palm on her head and stroked her hair. Sorrowfully, he sat, thinking about the good men he'd come to like and respect, all so needlessly slaughtered. He wondered how this disaster had come about, and recalled the strange darting light from the ship the other night. He remembered the French song being sung by a man hidden from his view on the deck.

He looked up at the sky and saw it was still blue; the sun shone and it remained quite warm. The sea looked pleasant and although there was quite a swell, it was reasonably calm. They must make use of this fine weather to row as far as they could. It was their only chance of survival.

Linnet had subsided into hiccups. John mopped her cheeks with his handkerchief. Holding her face between his, he spoke tenderly, "We will talk of what has happened later, once we are safe. Now, we must row to survive—or rather, you must row. I shall have to rest and then hopefully I can assist you."

John pressed his lips against her forehead gently. Linnet nodded grimly and settled herself back on the boat seat to row once again. She found it a relief to do something physical and put all her strength into it.

After an hour, she stopped, absolutely exhausted, and sitting where she was, she bowed her head, her chest heaving from her exertions. She was disappointed to see the ship still in view even though they were some way from it.

John watched her sadly. What terrible dangers he had exposed her to, a young gentle-born girl of not even nineteen years. She should not have seen such terrible atrocities. He knew that he would never forgive himself for dragging her into this nightmare. If only he had heeded her wishes, she would still be safe at her home in England.

Gingerly, John felt his injured head and then stretched, reaching out to touch Linnet's arm. "I will row now, sweetheart. Can you move over here so that we can switch places?"

Awkwardly, they shuffled around one another so that John was able to row. The first five minutes were hell for him. His poor head pounded and his arms throbbed with the effort of rowing, but then he managed to find a good rhythm.

Linnet settled into the bottom of the boat and rested her head on her arms while leaning against the seat. She fell into a doze, and when she awoke, The Tempest was no longer in sight and the sun was low in the sky. John was rowing still.

"Have you been rowing all this time?" she asked him with concern.

"No," he replied, shaking his head. "I stop every hundred strokes for a rest. Is there any water? I'm parched."

Linnet turned from side to side, looking for the flagon of water that the pirates had given them. She finally found it under the seat and passed it to John. He drank deeply and wiped his mouth with the back of his hand.

"I had hoped we were near enough to shore so that we could land before night came but we are farther out than I had estimated," John said.

Linnet reached out to take the water from him. "How do we know if we are even rowing in the right direction?" she asked dejectedly.

John pointed beyond her. "Turn your head and look," he urged. Linnet turned to see. What she saw made her eyes liquid with relief. For there in the distance lay mountains and, wheeling in the sky, coming from that direction were birds. "Land, oh John, land! How long will it take us to row there?"

"It's much farther away than it looks. I can't say how long but we will get there, I promise you that!" John grimly rowed onward, determined to land the small boat before night fell.

It was fully dark and still they had not reached the shore. The sea began to rise and the waves tossed their small craft from side to side. It was almost as though the sea were playing catch-a-ball with them, only in this case it was catch-a-boat. Linnet was terrified, her teeth chattering, her lungs jarring with each ragged breath. John abandoned rowing as darkness descended. He tried to use one of the oars as a rudder to keep their course true but the sea swelled until it became an impossible task and he gave up. He stowed the oar in the boat alongside its partner. A small sail was folded under the boat seat, and he wrapped it about the two of them so they could snuggle together in the bottom of the boat and attempt to keep warm. They were at the mercy of the elements. All they could do now was pray, which they both did silently, each imploring God for their beloved's survival.

After a while, it may have been minutes or hours, they had no way of knowing, it started to pour with rain. The wind gusted and the little boat was thrown about like a bobbing cork. Linnet clung to her husband in terror. John held her tightly and cursed himself for ever bringing her on this wretched voyage. He now believed they were doomed, he expected the boat to pitch over as each new wave buffeted them. How long the storm lasted, neither knew.

The long night finally passed. They had survived but morning bought no joy. Thick fog had fallen and they had no way of telling in which direction land lay. John dared not row, lest he take them far out to sea by mistake. They lay listless in the boat, dozing, overwhelmed with fatigue. As the day passed, Linnet began to shiver. Soaked to the skin, cold and hungry, she had given up all hope of them ever reaching safety. Finally, she fell into a deep, unhealthy sleep. John roused himself enough to give her the last of their water, dribbling it between her salt encrusted lips before he, too, was overcome and fell into an exhausted slumber.

CHAPTER 8

*T*he first John knew of the following day was a rough shaking of his shoulder. A deep male voice shouted in his ear, "Mister, mister! Wake up, mister!"

He groaned and tried to push the man away. He just wanted to be left alone to sleep. He felt himself shifted into an upright position. Opening his eyes, he quickly shut them against the brightness and the salt that stung. He rubbed them with the back of his hand, and as he did so, a wet rag was placed into his palm and a deep, calm voice spoke to him. "Use this. It is fresh water."

Gratefully, John wiped his eyes and face. At last able to open his eyes, he saw a sturdy arm covered with curled, white-blond hair, holding out a drinking canteen. He drank deeply. Never before had water tasted so sweet.

"Thank you." He handed the flagon back, his voice hoarse.

John blinked and gazed around. He was sitting on the sandy beach of a cove, and his rescuer was a huge blond giant of a man dressed in thick outdoor clothing. At his side was a small blond boy so like him that John surmised that it must be the man's son. John smiled at the boy then, suddenly, he remembered Linnet. "My wife!" he cried, attempting to stand but the exertion was too much and he blacked out.

The blond giant sighed heavily and turned to his son. "Peter, go to the cart, un-tether old Bess, and bring her here to me."

"Yes, Pa!"

The boy ran as fast as his thin legs could carry him up the beach to the track where they had left the horse and cart tethered. In the cart, covered in a warm home-knitted blanket, lay the feverish Linnet. Together, the man and his son managed to get John slung over the horse's back and up into the cart, where they placed him next to Linnet. Slowly, they set off up the earth track towards the man's home.

He wondered what his wife, Sarah, would say when he returned with two more mouths to feed. He frowned, shaking his large shaggy head with a sigh. On the beach, sea birds flew back down, landing on the now deserted shore to scavenge in the surf once again. Undisturbed by man, gulls perched on the wreckage of the small rowing boat, which lay just beyond the tide's reach.

THEY HAD by now been staying with the family Lammers for a month on their farmstead near Ogunquit, Maine, so named by the Abenaki, the local native Indian tribe. Hans explained the name meant 'Beautiful place by the sea.' By this time, John was more than seriously concerned about Linnet. After their ordeal, John had spent a couple of days in bed suffering from mild chills and exhaustion, but with Sarah Lammers' excellent cooking and dedicated care, he was up and around in no time. Linnet, however, was suffering from fevers and chills and had been extremely ill indeed. Even now, she protested that she was too weak to leave her bed. Sarah Lammers, a shrewd woman, suspected her house guest was stronger than she let on, but after what that lass had been through she wasn't about to complain, so she kept the knowledge to herself.

Their hosts were kindly, down-to-earth farming people, who had settled on their land ten years ago, only months after they had married. Hans Lammers was Dutch; he was brought to America by his father after his mother had died in childbirth in their native Netherlands. This was to be a new start for the family, and although it had been a hard struggle, the tough, honest man had made a good life for himself and his small son. He ran a supply store in Boston and that was where Hans had grown into a fine, strong young man.

Sarah had caught his eye when she had visited the store with her mother, the local school teacher. Both her mother and her father were teachers and ran the local school in a kindly but firm manner. Sarah's quiet character, her brown eyes and prettiness attracted the big man, and he had courted her with gentle determination, his polite, calm manner finding approval in the eyes of Sarah's parents. They were wed, and with the monies given them by both families for their wedding present, they had bought a plot of 180 acres of fertile land and woodland situated near the coast, almost a hundred miles north from family and Boston.

At first, Sarah's parents were appalled. They had envisaged a life with Sarah and Hans running and perhaps extending the Lammers' store, their grandchildren visiting daily, the family all living safely nearby. Peter Lammers was startled but then pleased by his son's decision to move on and to farm. And it was only after the birth of Hans and Sarah's son Peter that Sarah's parents finally reconciled themselves to their daughter's move.

Hans and Sarah had travelled down with a wagon train of people wishing to build a new life and community near the land Hans had bought. Now a small township was settled some five miles away from the farm's boundary. The farm was hard work, but both Hans and Sarah loved it. The house was made from the trees cut from their own land and was a spacious, if not large, comfortable log house.

Downstairs was simply one large open room, with the cooking and eating area to the back of the house. A large black cooking range stood against one wall, and a big, well-scrubbed pine table stood in front of that with six beautifully carved chairs around it. Hans had made them the first winter they had moved into the house. He loved to carve, something his grandfather had taught him as a small boy in the Netherlands. Hans had made the farm house unusual and beautiful with his carvings. All the shutters at the windows were carved with leaves and flower designs. The stairway that ran up the left hand side of the large downstairs room displayed carved animals from the local area, including squirrels, deer, racoons, and even snakes, from one end to the other.

There was a large stone fireplace on the right hand wall and, on the floor in front of it, a bright circular wool rug, which Sarah had lovingly made. Four carved rocking chairs were placed around the rug, enticing a person to sit and enjoy the roaring log fire that the Lammers generally kept ablaze in all but the hottest of summers. Upstairs were four rooms; Hans had planned for a large family, and neither he nor Sarah ever mentioned the fact that, so far, only Peter had come along. Sarah used the spare rooms for when their respective parents came to visit.

Of course, to Linnet, used to the large stately houses of England, two extra bedrooms did not merit comment. John had come to an agreement with Hans over payment for their room and board; however, in the first instance, Hans had refused to discuss such a thing. But Sarah's quiet good sense had prevailed, and a sum was agreed upon between them. John helped Hans with the farm and was learning a great deal about the land from him.

John remained extremely concerned about Linnet. At first, he had been nearly demented with the possibility that he might lose her, but as time went on and Linnet began to improve, he relaxed, happy to know his beloved wife would live. However, it was now the end of August, and soon it would be too late to travel across land to Boston. Winter could be fierce, and with Linnet's health so poor, they would be foolish to risk trying to reach Boston before the spring. John had tried to talk to her, but any discussion with him seemed to tire her and she would tell him to leave, asking for Sarah to come to her. The truth was that Linnet was afraid of the journey. She felt safe in the pretty farm house, and Sarah reminded her a little of her maid Lottie, not in looks but in temperament.

Linnet assumed, quite wrongly, that John had sent word ahead to Boston, and daily she expected to be told that a coach had arrived to collect them. She had no concept of how wild and rugged the country was in the Colonies; her expectations were based on her knowledge of life in England. When she was well enough to sit up and think rationally, she found that she harboured a deep resentment towards her husband—so much so, that when he entered her room so full of vigour and vitality, she felt an overwhelming rage towards him. She tried to stay away from him as much as she could. Being young and confused, she had no idea why, after feeling so much love for her husband when on board the ship, she should now have developed such an intense dislike of him.

The family and John were sat around the table, finishing super that night. Linnet had taken her supper on a tray in her room. Hans was quietly filling his pipe with tobacco while Sarah cleared the dishes from the table. Peter was chatting excitedly once again about his discovery of the small boat wrecked on the beach and of finding the two bodies, who had turned out to be John and Linnet. He was just getting to his favourite part of the story, where he had run to tell his father about his discovery, when the bell upstairs could be heard tinkling yet again. Sarah sighed heavily. Since Linnet had recovered, she had been ringing that bell all day, off and on. She set aside the plate she had begun washing and started towards the stairway.

As she passed her husband, he put out his arm and held her back. Surprised, Sarah glanced down at him. Hans shook his head.

"Nee, leave her," he commanded. "The girl will come down herself if what she wants is urgent."

Sarah looked dubious. "But she has been so very ill, Hans."

He nodded. "She has indeed, but she is better now and only a sickness of the soul remains; so leave her, Sarah. Only she can heal the rest." He patted his wife's bottom. "Coffee would be nice."

Sarah flushed; she wished her husband wouldn't be so familiar with her in front of their guest. Glancing at John, she found him looking at her with kind understanding in his eyes.

"Hans is quite right, Sarah. You must not wait on Linnet anymore. You have been wonderfully kind, and I am in no doubt that she owes you her life." He held up his hand as Sarah denied this. "There is something troubling her," he told them. "I like the way Hans described it, as a sickness of the soul. God knows, she has seen some horrible things, enough to turn a man's stomach, let alone a young girl of eighteen." John fell silent, frowning. Hans put a comforting hand on his friend's shoulder.

"Peter, you go now and fetch some water for your mother." He nodded at his small son, who was listening round-eyed to the adults' conversation.

He wriggled crossly on his seat. "Not yet, in a minute, Pa," he whined.

Hans took his pipe from his mouth and regarded his small son steadily. An awkward silence fell, until Peter reluctantly got up to fetch the bucket from his mother. She smiled at him fondly and ruffled his hair, but Peter jerked away as if he had been scalded. "Mind your manners, son." Hans's deep voice held a warning. Peter flushed and reached up to peck his mother's cheek with a brief kiss before grabbing the pail and running out of the house.

As soon as the door had banged shut behind him, the room filled with laughter. "That boy!" said Sarah, wiping tears of laughter from her eyes.

"He is a lovely lad. You should be very proud," John told her, chuckling.

Hans looked thoughtful and said, "He is becoming spoiled. He needs brothers and sisters."

An awkward hush fell as Hans realised what he had said, but into the hush came a frantic jangling of the bell upstairs.

John stood up, it seemed an opportune moment to leave. "Excuse me, Hans and Sarah. Thank you for a delicious dinner. I will see to my wife's needs and then retire. I shall bid you both a good night!"

Hans slapped John's shoulder. "Good night, my friend."

As John disappeared up the stairs, Hans turned, took the dish cloth from Sarah and scooped her onto his knee. Holding her face between his large callused hands, he kissed her soft mouth. "Ach, you know I didn't mean that as it sounded. There was no criticism meant. I love you and our son. Both of you are all I need."

Sarah nodded. "I know, I know."

She laid her head against his chest and they sat in companionable silence until young Peter banged back indoors again, struggling with the heavy pail of water.

JOHN OPENED Linnet's bedroom door quietly and stepped into the room. Linnet was standing by the window, gazing out at the moon. She turned, expecting to see Sarah, and frowned when she realised it was John.

"How are you feeling?" he asked her gently.

"Perhaps a little better," she replied, picking up her hairbrush and brushing her hair.

"We have to talk, Linnet."

"Yes, about what?" she said, turning her back to again to continue her brushing. John felt irritated. He took a steadying breath, reminding himself to be patient—she had been very ill.

He moved over and stood behind her. Firmly, he turned her around and sat her down on the bed then sat beside her. "You have been through a terrible ordeal, and you have been very ill, but you are over both now. It is time for us to make our plans."

He waited for his wife to reply, but after an uncomfortable couple of minutes had passed without her saying a word, he tried again. "Linnet, what is wrong? You can tell me, I am your husband and I love you."

Linnet made a small sound like a snort. John frowned. "Do you doubt me?" he asked.

She tossed her head, her hair rippling silkily down her back.

"*Love?*" Linnet sneered. "Was it *love* you sought to show me, with men hanging from the ship's mast, kicking their legs, their poor tongues sticking out like huge purple plums from their mouths?" Her voice began to rise hysterically. "Poor mangled bodies, screaming in agony? Luck brought us here! Not you! We should have died along with Captain Pettigrew, Duncan and all those poor brave sailors, and you speak of love?"

She began to laugh horribly, hysterically, shaking her head from side to side in a wild motion. John sat frozen, shocked by her strange reaction, yet how could he deny her words when they held so much truth? Ashen and guilt-ridden, he stood up and quietly left the room.

When he had gone, Linnet flung herself down onto the bed and sobbed herself to sleep. At some point during the night, she woke shivering with cold, and crept miserably under the covers, eventually falling into a fitful doze.

In the cold grey light of dawn, for the first time since their arrival at the homestead, Linnet rose with others in the house. She dressed, joining the others for breakfast. She helped to lay the table and to clear it but made little effort to help Sarah in any other way. Linnet spent her time alone or with Peter, she was much taken with the small boy, delighted with his fresh clean youth and innocence, a balm to the horrors that had stolen her own childish innocence forever.

He in turn, adored Linnet with a calf-like devotion which

amused his father and worried his mother. "I don't like it, Hans," Sarah told him. "Peter has chores to do and Linnet distracts him."

Hans shook his large shaggy blond head and grinned at his anxious wife. "Woman, you worry too much. Linnet has much healing to do, ja? Our boy's youth helps her, I think."

Sarah banged the pastry she was rolling hard down upon the table. "Don't call me woman! You know how much I dislike it. I am worried though, Hans. I mean, how long are they going to stay here? They barely talk to each other. Has John mentioned what he intends to do now they are both recovered?"

Hans pulled up a chair and sat down. Sarah was right; winter was on its way and now Linnet was up and about, the two of them should be making plans to leave. He took out his pipe and rummaged in his pocket for tobacco. "I think tonight that I will suggest they winter up at the old cabin. It will need some minor repairs to the roof and some supplies taking up there but it will be cosy enough for the two of them until spring."

Sarah nodded. "Sometimes, Hans Lammers, you are very clever. I wonder why you are not involved in politics. I had forgotten about our cabin. Whatever is between them, they are sure to have resolved it by the spring. Yes, that is a very good idea."

Later that evening, after they had all sat down and partaken of Sarah's delicious pie, Hans cleared his throat. "We are so glad, Sarah and I, that Peter found you both and that you are now fit and recovered once again. I have given some thought to your predicament."

He paused and started to get out his pipe. John, thinking Hans had said all he intended, spoke up, "We are very grateful to you and Sarah for your kindness and hospitality, indeed, for saving our lives."

Linnet, sitting across the table, added her own thanks. She looked down at her hands, which were trembling. She was so afraid they were going to be asked to leave here. All at once, she felt guilty for not having helped Sarah with the chores, but she had no knowledge of how to do housework.

Hans raised his hand and shook his head, smiling. "Ach, I fear you have misunderstood me. We do not need your thanks; we are friends, ja?"

They both nodded.

"We have a cabin which was our home for a while before we built this house. It is a few miles away, up high on the side of a hill in woodland. It is very small but sturdy and snug through the winter months. We would like to lend it to you until you can start your journey in the spring." Hans sat back a satisfied grin on his open face.

They were all surprised when Linnet interrupted. "That is most kind of you, Hans, but I am sure the coach will be here any day to collect us. We would be only too grateful if you would continue to give us shelter, just until it arrives. I was so fearful you would ask us to depart before it could get here."

There was an awkward silence as the others glanced at her in surprise. "What coach is it that you speak of, my dear?" John inquired.

Linnet stared back at him. "Well, you have surely sent word to your people in Boston to alert them of our troubles? Surely they will have set out to collect us?"

John gazed at her pityingly. "I am sorry, my dear, but I have not been able to send word to Boston." He watched her face become pinched as she paled. "Linnet, there is no possible way to get a message to Boston until the spring. There are no roads to Boston, only a rough trail which is best travelled on horseback. That is how we will have to travel when we leave. It is much too late in the season to risk such a journey now. The winters here are extremely harsh. That is why I think we should gratefully accept Hans's generous offer of overwintering in their cabin."

He turned and put his hand on his friend's shoulder, giving a hearty squeeze of gratitude. There was a sudden crash as Linnet leaped to her feet and knocked over her chair.

"Well, I won't stay here!" she shrilled before spinning away from the table and flying out of the door, which banged shut behind her.

Sarah stood up. "I'll go after her," she said, but John put his hand on her arm.

"No, thank you, Sarah. I should like to talk to her."

Hans nodded in agreement. "Ja, this is for John to solve. Come sit with your old husband and tell me how much you love him." He patted his knee invitingly.

Sarah harrumphed but nevertheless she sat on his lap.

John found Linnet sitting on a log beyond the barn, looking at the moon.

"Can I sit down?" he asked, doing so before she could answer. Linnet shrugged, turning her face away. John studied her profile for a moment. "America is a young country. There are so many hazards, quite apart from the weather which is so much more extreme than the English climate. There are Indians: wild native people, with occasional savage behaviour. The animals here are much fiercer than anything you would find in England. There are bears, mountain lions, wolves and snakes. This is not a safe and ordered country like the one you are used to, it is wild and untamed. I thought you understood that."

Without turning or looking at him, she said flatly, "You know, I believe at one point I really did want to be a part of this adventure but after what happened on the ship… all I want is to remain safe."

John was filled with pity. "Oh, my dearest girl, I am so sorry to have put you in so much danger. It was not my intention. I would die rather than expose you to risk. It is why it would be foolish to risk a long journey at the start of winter."

He slipped his arm around her shoulders and attempted to draw her to him but Linnet drew herself away. "I do agree that for a woman to try and ride all that way at this time of year would be foolish. However, a man alone could get to Boston before winter sets in, surely? You could have gone already and come back with help before any snow fell."

John sighed. "I suppose I could have risked the ride but I too was unwell and afraid to leave you, you were so very ill, Linnet. I will ask Hans tomorrow if it would be possible to leave soon and perhaps borrow a horse and supplies. You do understand, though, that if I cannot get back for whatever reason, you would be stuck here, possibly never knowing my fate?"

She merely nodded. "I understand." She stood up. "Well then, I shall bid you good night, husband." She turned with a gentle swish of skirts and walked back toward the house.

John watched her go but remained seated on the log, dejectedly. Hans appeared beside him and sat next to his friend, quietly smoking his pipe. John sat silent for a while before turning and speaking to Hans. "Linnet wants me to try and reach Boston before the winter sets in. She thinks if I travel alone I can get there and back to collect her before the spring."

Hans nodded thoughtfully and said, "I see."

John looked at him and asked, "Hans, what do you think? Should I attempt it?"

Hans cleared his throat. "Nee, you do not know the trail, there will be hungry wolves and big cats eager to attack a lone traveller such as yourself, and what if you are caught in a white-out? Once the snow comes, all landmarks disappear and the trail will be covered. I would not attempt such a journey at this time of year and I know the trail. What would become of your wife should you never return? Why do we not travel early tomorrow, leave at dawn to go and see the cabin, then you can decide what is best for you both?"

John nodded thoughtfully. "Linnet seems to want me gone. I think she blames me for putting her in danger. I should never have bought her to America!"

Hans put his hand on his friend's shoulder. "But you did bring her, my friend, and you are not to blame for the actions of others.

Linnet is still so very young. I think she behaves as a child does when things go wrong and they blame their parents or God. She is your wife, John, but she does not know how to behave as such, you must guide her. You both need to look forward and not back. Come now, it is late. We shall leave at daylight tomorrow. We go to our beds now."

Both men stood. John stretched and yawned. "Thank you, Hans. You are right. I will see what this cabin of yours is like and then decide what is best to do."

CHAPTER 9

*W*hen Linnet came down to breakfast the next day, she found that only Peter sat at the large table. He was eating freshly baked bread and honey. "Good morning, Peter. My word, that looks good! Where is everyone this morning?" she asked while helping herself to a cup of milk.

Peter gave her a friendly grin and repeated what his mother had told him. "Pa and John got up early and went riding off. Mother is gathering blueberries for a pie and I have to feed the chickens. Will you help me, Linnet?"

Linnet became still. A dreadful thought occurred to her; had John left already without saying goodbye? "Peter, may I ask if John has gone on a journey?" she asked.

Peter frowned. "Well, I think so. Mother said they wouldn't be here for lunch and that Father will be back tonight."

Peter looked pleased with himself for remembering exactly what his mother had told him. Linnet bit her lip; she had urged John to go, so why did she feel such a dreadful sense of loss now that he had? She sat down, feeling wretched.

Peter looked concerned and asked, "Is there anything wrong?"

Linnet looked at him sceptically. "Peter, are you sure your

mother didn't say that John would be back tonight with your father?"

Peter thought hard. He had asked his mother if Pa would be back for lunch and she had definitely said, "No, not until supper time." She hadn't mentioned John at all. "No, she only said Pa. Will you help me with the chickens now?"

"Sorry? Er, I will be along in a little while. You go and get started," Linnet told him distractedly.

"All right but don't be long!" Peter shouted as he rushed off, banging the door behind him.

Linnet wasn't even aware the boy had gone, so deep in thought was she. Amazing, but now that she knew John had gone to Boston for goodness knew how long, it was as clear as day to her that she did, in actual fact, love him. Supposing the snow lasted all winter; he might not be back until the spring. A dreadful thought crossed her mind: suppose he didn't come back at all? What would she do, perhaps never knowing what had happened to him? Oh, she should never have spoken to him the way she had last night, urging him to go alone to Boston.

She had to go after him. She was his wife and she should be by his side. She had to tell him she loved him, that she was sorry. It would be all right; they would travel on together. She would need food, a blanket, and some clothes—and a horse, perhaps. Peter would saddle one of Hans's for her. Linnet ran to the door, calling frantically for Peter. She must be gone before Sarah returned, for she knew Sarah would try and stop her from riding out alone.

Fifteen minutes later, Linnet mounted a pretty brown mare called Penny. She had rolled everything she thought she might need into a blanket from her bed and tied it onto her saddle.

Peter was not happy with her plans. He had been faintly shocked when she had come out wearing a pair of men's britches and had mounted Penny astride. He thought he ought to be going with her, however, Linnet was adamant that he should remain behind to help his mother and to explain to his parents where she had gone. As she galloped away from the homestead, she felt a wonderful sense of freedom and exhilaration. Linnet loved riding; it had been too long since she had been in the saddle.

Although not in the same league as her thoroughbred, Pango, the little mare was sweet-natured and willing. She and Linnet soon left the homestead far behind. As she rode, Linnet studied the countryside, finding it quite beautiful, much more open than England, rugged and wild with tall trees and rocky outcrops. Land just as God intended it to be, unspoilt by mankind. The trees were magnificent. They seemed so much higher than the trees back home, but perhaps that was because she had been at sea for so long, she had forgotten. They cantered along, Linnet enjoying the feel of the warm sun on her face. Peter had given her directions. It was simple; all she had to do was follow the Webhannet River inland, then follow the river fork to the right until she met up with John, which she guessed would be at nightfall when he made camp.

It was so good to be out again alone on a horse, her hair flying behind her. All the horrors and fears she'd witnessed seemed to be a thing of the past. She laughed aloud with the joy of it as she urged Penny into a gallop. The horse obligingly raced ahead, seeming to enjoy the freedom as much as her rider. Linnet slowed her horse when up ahead she saw the wide sparkling expanse of the Webhannet River, its water glinting brightly in the sunlight. The river was much wider than any others she had known at home. It was flowing much faster than she'd expected, too. Linnet walked Penny to the river's edge and dismounted. The thirsty horse lowered her head and drank greedily. Linnet found a boulder to sit on and viewed the river, it was so delightfully peaceful.

On the opposite bank, the trees grew almost to the water's edge. A long ridge of pine trees rose high above the river, covering the side of the steep hill. Linnet held up her face to the warmth of the sun and breathed in the sharp, astringent scent of the pines. A flock of birds flew up into the air, startled by the gentle whicker Penny gave after she had drunk her fill. Linnet watched them fly high and circle, disappearing into the distant blue sky, and wondered what sort of birds they were. After a while, she rose and brushed down her clothes, calling Penny to her. She mounted and swung right as they set off, the horse picking her way along the river's path.

MEANWHILE, John and Hans had arrived at the cabin mid-morning. They'd travelled steadily uphill for the last half hour of the hour long trip. The cabin was set in a wide clearing surrounded by tall broadleaf trees. A fenced corral stood to one side, and a small barn stood beyond that. In the far distance on the other side of the hill, John could see snow-capped mountains. The view from the front of the cabin through the clearing entrance was breathtaking.

"Let's put the horses in the corral first," Hans instructed as he dismounted.

They unsaddled the horses, shooed them in and then barred the entrance to the paddock. John checked that there was water in the trough before walking over to the cabin. Hans proudly pointed out the well dug above an underground spring he had followed from farther up the hill. The cabin was low and solid with an apex roof, which hung wide over the cabin walls, giving maximum protection from the weather. It had one sturdy wooden door and two front facing windows that were shuttered.

Hans unlocked the door and shoved it open with his shoulder. Once inside, he flung the shutters wide open so that the sunlight poured through the square openings. *I wonder what you would call them, because really they could not be called windows, not without glass,* John mused.

He looked about the rectangular room. A large wooden bed without a mattress stood in one corner, a table and two chairs in another. Two carved wooden candlesticks stood on the stone mantel above a broad stone fireplace. It was basic but dry and reasonably clean. There was dust, a few dead leaves which had blown inside beneath the door and John noticed a few spiders lurking in thick webs in the corners of the cabin, otherwise the homestead was sound.

"We took everything useful with us to the farm house when it was finished. It will be easy to bring the wagon up here filled with the items you need. Well, what do you think of it, my friend?" Hans stroked his hand down a window edge. "I built this with my own two hands, no help I had with this cabin. It is very cosy in snow, ja. Like the houses of The Netherlands, I built the roof so the build-up of the snow is not so dangerous. We were very snug here for three years, Sarah and I."

John was impressed. "It is certainly an achievement. There is no damp that I can see either, the floor is quite dry. I think it would be ideal for us; the only problem I can foresee…" he hesitated.

Hans noted that his friend looked anxious. "You don't think Linnet will like it?" he queried.

"Ah well, that is more than a possibility but no, my friend, it is not that," John reassured him. "No, it is the fact that she cannot cook."

Hans chuckled. "Sarah will have to try and teach her the basics before you leave us."

John frowned and said, "That would be kind of her, but will Linnet want to learn? She is a very spoiled young lady. In fact, I am only just realising how difficult that fact is going to make living our lives together."

Hans went over to the table and sat down, gesturing towards the empty chair. John pulled out the chair and sat down.

Hans looked at him thoughtfully while filling his trusty old pipe. "John, Linnet is your wife, and it is up to you to set some rules for her. She is young, and as you said yourself, she has been spoiled, but that can change. I have always found a woman's bottom to be her weak point, and the best lovemaking is always after she has had a spanked bottom. Perhaps time up here alone will bring you closer together. You will have more time to get to know one another, and if you feel the need of company, you can ride down to visit us, weather permitting, of course. It is all down to you, my friend. I will make a beautiful map to guide you to Boston. It will be ready for you to use come the thaw, and it will be a pleasant way for me to spend the dark winter evenings. I enjoy drawing and writing."

John said, "That would be most kind, thank you, Hans. You have been a good friend to us. I think you may be right about the time spent up here together, and who knows, perhaps I underestimate Linnet. She is very brave but much too impulsive. She just needs a little guidance. How I wish she had some of your Sarah's good sense."

Hans threw back his head and roared with laughter. "John, when we first lived here, Sarah was a sore trial to me. I cannot tell you the number of times she got herself into mischief. Make no mistake, I had to warm her backside for her plenty, plenty times! She would wander too far and get herself lost while she was sketching and forget she had a stew cooking, until I would find the pan burned over the fire and no sign of my Sarah. She was bitten by a snake during our first year, and we had no idea whether the snake was poisonous or not. We waited for a reaction, not knowing if she would live or die—it was the worst day of my life, I think. Fear not, Linnet will do her growing up in good time with her good husband to guide her. Now let us inspect the barn and then we will see what delights Sarah has packed for our lunch."

Linnet had been travelling for about three hours when she saw a plume of smoke rising into the air from trees ahead and slightly to her left. Excitedly, she turned Penny in that direction and picked her way forward slowly. She wanted to surprise John and so went as quietly as possible. As she entered the tree line, she dismounted so that she could walk under the low branches. She crept towards the camp. As she came to a clearing in the trees she saw a fire burning merrily and a horse tethered nearby.

A saddle and a blanket roll were on the ground to the left of the fire, and she noticed that, oddly, another bed roll lay a few feet away. Linnet frowned, but then her face cleared as she realised that of course it must be for Hans. He obviously planned to show John the route and travel a little farther on with him. She crept over to one of the blanket rolls, giggling as she planned how she would surprise them.

She tethered Penny back in the trees so that she was out of sight of the camp and then went and unrolled the blanket. Wrapping herself up, Linnet lay on the ground and waited. After a few minutes, she heard male voices. She sniggered and scolded herself; fearing that she would spoil the surprise for John. She lay very still, her heart racing as the men entered the clearing. One of them went to the fire and Linnet could hear wood cracking as he threw kindling onto blaze. Then it went very quiet. *Oh ho!* she thought, stifling another giggle but failing. *They know I'm here!*

She waited expectantly. Suddenly, there was a vicious kick to her side and a male voice shouted, "Bastard, up yer get!"

Shocked and groaning with pain, Linnet threw back the blanket and found herself staring up the end of a musket. "Well, what 'ave we got here. God damn it… a female! Will… lookee here, there's a doxy in me bed, just a waiting f' me t' give it to 'er!"

Linnet scrambled to sit up. She was shocked and couldn't speak. A second man ambled over, she noticed he carried a musket as well. She stared back at them in horror. They looked very similar to one another with scruffy beards and dirty, odd-looking clothes made up of a mixture of leather and fur. One of the men was slightly thicker set than the other, and he wore a fur cap that seemed to have the tail from the animal still attached. It was this man who spoke to her. "Well now, where did yer hail from, little lady? Come t' warm our old bones at night, 'ave yer?"

Linnet swallowed, she tried to speak but when she finally found her voice it sounded unnaturally high. She cleared her throat and tried again. "I am really most terribly sorry, gentlemen. I thought to surprise my husband who is, um, camping somewhere in these parts. I actually thought this was his camp. Please excuse my error."

The two men looked at each other and stared at Linnet. They began to grin. Linnet shifted uneasily, disliking like their horrible leers. "Hoity-toity... English are yer, an' is yer husband English, too?"

The man who had spoken pronounced 'husband' with a fake accent, mimicking Linnet. She nodded. "Why yes, I am, but my husband is American. He was only a small boy when he moved to Boston."

"Boston, yer don't say! Long way from home, ain't yer?"

Linnet tried to smile breezily. "Please, no need to concern yourselves; I'll just be on my way! I expect my husband is camped a little farther on and he will be wondering where I have got to."

The man who was doing all the talking frowned. "There ain't no one camped around here, missy. We'd know, see, this is our regular trapping area. I'm Ned and this ere ugly bugger's Will. I hope I didn't hurt yer none miss, when I kicked yer arse? I thought you was another trapper, takin' advantage, like."

Linnet had no idea how to reply, she simply shook her head. What on earth was she going to do? More to the point, what were they going to do with her? She shuddered with a mix of fear and disgust.

CHAPTER 10

*J*ohn and Hans arrived back late afternoon. As they were getting nearer to the farm, they could see someone approaching them rapidly on foot. They realised as they drew closer that it was Sarah. It soon became apparent that she was running whilst waving her arms frantically at them.

"What do you mean she's gone?" John hadn't intended to sound sharp but he was stunned.

"As I said, she is gone and Peter, too."

It was Han's turn to look shocked as he breathed out his son's name. "*Peter?*"

Sarah sighed. Really, men could be so obtuse at times. "Linnet left here this morning. As I explained, apparently, she thought you had left to travel to Boston. Peter went after her at lunch time when I returned from berry picking. He felt bad about telling Linnet you had gone on a journey, and when my back was turned, he left here to go and fetch her."

Hans looked thunderous. "Why did you let him go?" he yelled.

Sarah flushed with temper. "I did not *let* him go, Hans. Peter left here without my permission! I told him he was to stay here and wait for you both but the next thing I knew, he was galloping off towards the river."

The two men dismounted. Hans muttered furiously in Dutch, something he rarely did nowadays and only when he was extremely agitated.

MEANWHILE, Linnet was feeling rather pleased with herself. She had left Penny tethered a little way away from the camp, initially because she thought she was surprising John, but now it was to be her salvation because when the men were asleep, she planned to escape quietly. They wouldn't even hear Penny riding off until it was too late for them to give chase. She'd been lucky so far, the men had argued over her fate. The talkative man insisted that he wanted to bed her, but to her huge relief, the thinner man, Will, had protested. Linnet heard him say that he thought they should wait until they were certain that John and his friends—Linnet had told them there was a whole party of men out hunting together—were not in the immediate area. Will didn't want any trouble. His partner, Ned, finally agreed with him and shrugged, admitting it might be better to wait and see.

Linnet was relieved to have overheard the men, she felt slightly less afraid than before. She tried to endear herself to Will, smiling at him whenever he glanced at her, in order to show her gratitude and enlist his support. The men cooked some fish they had caught earlier over the fire and gave her a stick with a burnt fish speared onto the end. She had nibbled dubiously at it, but was surprised to find it tasted good, and she was so hungry, she devoured every last morsel. She tried to stay awake while the men made preparations for the night, building up the fire and tending to their horses.

She must have fallen asleep at some point because she jolted awake suddenly to the most terrible screams—a horse, she surmised. The noise was punctuated by the fearsome roars and growls of some fierce, wild creature. Petrified, she scrambled to her feet. Will ran across to her, signalling for her to stay quiet. He grabbed hold of her, towing her along with him. They ran into the darkness and the terrible racket followed them, echoing loud in the still night air. With the horrible shrieking still ringing in her ears, Linnet stumbled and staggered along in wake of the men. Finally, they reached the river, where the men urged her into the shallow water, dark and oily in the faint light cast by the moon. She shuddered with cold and fear as she put her foot into the icy, fast-flowing water. It was horrible not knowing what was underfoot. They began to push their way against the current, upstream in single file, stumbling on slippery moss that covered the stones under their feet.

Linnet whispered to Will in front of her, "Whatever was that creature?"

Will turned his head and she saw the pale oval of his face in the faint moon light. "Bear," he whispered. Linnet was none the wiser.

The water was so cold, the strong current tugging at her legs. She was thankful she had had the foresight to put on a pair of John's trousers that morning, it would have been impossible to walk against the swift waters with long heavy skirts weighing her down. They trudged on for what seemed like an age before they scrambled out of the water onto dry land. The men knew where they were going. Soon they stood before a large rock face. Will started to climb and then it was Linnet's turn to follow. When she refused, Ned wasted no time in argument. He simply grunted and picked her up, slinging her over his shoulder, climbing slowly up behind Will, who had already reached the top, whereupon he leant over the lip of the rock and grabbed hold of Linnet under her arms, hauling her up onto the flat top of the huge rocky outcrop. At last, they were all safely up. Linnet shivered from the wet, she was so very cold.

"What was that creature?" she managed to ask again between chattering teeth.

"Black bear, perhaps a grizzly, a nasty one, too," said Ned.

"What is a grizzly?" Linnet asked.

"Yer a real green horn, ain't yer, girly? Bear, a big ol' grizzly bear, been tracking it nigh on a week now. Clever old bastard, this un is too!" Ned spat sideways to emphasize his point. Linnet gagged with disgust as the phlegm blob hit the rock beside her.

Will grunted in agreement as he unrolled a blanket that he'd had the foresight to grab before they had left their camp. The two men seated themselves on either side of Linnet and wrapped the blanket over all of them. Although grateful for the warmth, she was embarrassed to be sandwiched between the two rough men. She covered her confusion with chatter. "A bear, you say? Well, what was all the screaming? I thought it sounded more like a horse, and why did we walk in the river?"

Will answered her questions. "A grizzly tracks by smell, and can't smell our tracks in water, an' this 'ere rock bein' high enough up, will carry our scent in the opposite direction to the camp where the bear is now, see? We should be safe enough 'ere till mornin'."

Linnet felt relief. "So what shall we do in the morning?"

Ned put his arm about her waist and gave her a squeeze. "Don't yer worry, darlin', the bear will be long gone by dawn. Mostly bears sleep durin' the day at this time o' the year, they is ready to hibernate. Anyways, yer got Ned t' keep yer safe and cosy, eh?"

Linnet shifted, uncomfortably aware of his arm snaked around her waist. "Ah, hmm, good, thank you," she muttered uneasily. Despite everything, she was beginning to feel sleepy. Anxious that she might lean into one of the men if she fell asleep, she sat with her head resting forward upon her knees, her arms clasped around her legs. She had no intention of giving these men any ideas.

MEANWHILE, John and Hans decided to ride out despite the evening gloaming. As it darkened, they found that they could follow the trail by pale moonlight. Once they reached the river, it would be easier to keep on track, marked by the course the river took. They rode silently, each man with his own grave thoughts. Hans led the way.

John realised after a while that he could hear a faint sound. He stopped his horse, listening hard. He thought he could hear a distant voice calling—yes, there it was again. "Hans, listen!"

Hans drew in his horse; he, too, could hear the faint shout for help. "It means us leaving the river path. I do not like it, we could get very lost in the dark."

John was desperate to follow the voice; he was frantic with worry for Linnet but he knew that Hans must be equally worried about his young son. John was a sensible young man and he knew that Hans would have more luck tracking the two miscreants than he.

"I'll stay here by the river's edge while you go and search, Hans. You know the country better than I. If you get lost, fire your pistol, then I will fire mine in response—that way, you can trace the sound back."

Hans reined his horse in and turned it so that he could put his hand on John's shoulder. "Are you sure of this, my friend? Would you rather go and I wait?"

John shook his head. "Go. As I said, you know this area of country." John reached out and slapped Hans's horse's rump, then horse and rider disappeared into the darkness. John stilled his horse, listening to the sound of hooves receding into the distance. Dismounting, he tethered the animal. He might as well try to rest; he might be in for a long wait.

Hans, meanwhile, drew in his cantering horse. Moving forward slowly, he listened intently for the sound of the cries but now there was only silence. He went some way ahead and reined in, listening, but still nothing. "Peter? Linnet!" he called into the night, his voice sounding hollow and strange.

He heard the whisper of the night breeze and the faint rustling of grass and trees but no voice replied. He tried again, "Peter! Linnet! Answer me!"

Hans listened. This time, he heard it, a reedy voice, slightly louder now but unmistakably that of his son. He trotted his horse for a short while, following the direction of Peter's voice. He stopped to listen, calling again, and this time there was no doubt about the reply. "Pa! Pa! I'm over here! Pa!"

Hans jumped down from his horse, running toward the sound of his son's voice. "Keep calling, son, so that I can find you. Just keep calling!"

"Pa! Pa! Over here, Pa, I'm under a tree!"

Hans saw movement under a large, looming tree, then he spotted his son. Gathering the boy into his arms he clasped him to his chest. "Peter, oh thank the Lord!"

He loosened his hold and took the boy's pale cheeks between his palms, gazing anxiously into his small face. "Are you hurt?"

Peter tried to nod. "My leg, I think it's broke, Pa! The horse was snake-bit, I think, he threw me, bucked and bucked and then he collapsed and, Pa, he *died*! Oh Pa!" Peter's small face was awash with tears.

His father rocked him, crooning to him in Dutch. Then he lifted him onto his horse and turned back towards John.

LINNET AWOKE TO SUNSHINE; she was curled up on the sun-warmed rock. It took her a moment to realise where she was, and she was surprised to find herself alone, with no sign of the two trappers. After scrambling back down the rock's steep side—much easier in daylight than the climb of the previous night—she decided to pay a call of nature and bathe quickly in the river. She needed to wash away all the grime of the last couple of days. She was drying herself with the blanket in seclusion, surrounded by low shrubbery, her clothes placed on a bush beside her, when she heard the unmistakable crack of twigs and the sound of stealthy footsteps. She froze, holding the blanket high under her chin. Ned appeared, his eyes narrowed lustfully at the sight of her near nakedness. His thin lips slackened with desire and his feral gaze boldly raked Linnet's semi- naked body.

"What d' we 'ave 'ere then?" he drawled.

He placed his musket carefully against a tree trunk, his eyes not once leaving her body.

Linnet glanced over at her clothes. Could she reach them? "Why, Ned, you startled me. Is-is Will with you?" she stuttered, looking beyond Ned to find Will.

"He's off tracking that old bear, determined to get it, he is. Damn thing killed all our mules last night."

Linnet wished Will was there, she was becoming increasingly uncomfortable with the way Ned was staring at her. "Could you hand me my clothes, please?"

He ambled over to them, scooping up her things. Holding them in his hand, he grinned at her. "These, yer mean? Come an' get 'em, girly." He swung his arm so the clothes swayed slowly to and fro.

"Please, Ned, this isn't funny. Give me my clothes."

"Yer won't be needing them fer a while." Ned flung the clothing far out amongst the shrubbery.

Linnet spun about and took off at a run, stumbling over her blanket as she went. She gathered it higher, trying to wrap it about herself as she fled. She sprinted as fast as she could away from the river's edge, low branches of the Aspen bushes stinging her face as she blundered through the undergrowth. Her heart pounded, racing painfully in her chest, and she ran until the agonising pain tore at her ribs. She had a stitch. Glancing behind her, she tripped over a tree root, falling face down in the dirt, her breath knocked painfully from her lungs.

Immediately, she felt rough hands on her, turning her over onto her back. A heavy weight landed on top of her, crushing what little air she had left in her chest. Ned was slobbering over her, his foul breath making her gag. His filthy hands mauled her, digging painfully into her most tender parts. He grunted and muttered thickly as Linnet struggled helplessly beneath him. Finally, she managed to twist her head free of his slobbering mouth. She screamed, attempting to bring her leg up to knee him in the groin. He grabbed hold of her thigh and forced her legs apart, inserting his knee between. Linnet screamed again, louder this time, and sank her teeth into his ear, hanging on with her teeth. Ned bellowed in agonised rage and pulled back, splattering Linnet's face with his blood, then he raised his arm, ready to hit her across the face. Linnet flinched, screwing her eyes shut, tensed, ready for the blow.

When it failed to fall, she opened her eyes and stared into his face. It had contorted, twisted into a horrible grimace. Slowly, he slumped forward, falling inert on top of her. She screamed. Scrabbling frantically, she pushed at the sudden dead weight crushing her. When all at once the burden was lifted from her, she squinted up, shielding her eyes from the sun, and found she was looking into the stark and furious face of her husband. He stood, glowering down at her.

"John! Oh, darling, you saved me! Oh, thank God!" She flung her arms around her husband's neck.

He helped his wife to her feet, disentangled her arms from his neck and, picking up the blanket, he wrapped it swiftly about her nakedness.

"Goddamn it, Linnet, what the hell are you playing at?" he yelled, grabbing hold of her, his fingers biting into her shoulders.

Linnet looked back at Ned. Trembling with shock, she realised that he was dead. A dagger protruded from the middle of his back. She pointed a shaking finger at his body. "He is dead! My God, John, you *killed* him!"

John shook her so hard that her teeth rattled. Her head snapped back and her hair flew forward, stinging her eyes. "Of course I killed him, you little fool! He was about to rape you!" John suddenly groaned and yanked her hard against him, coiling his arms around her tightly. "Linnet, Linnet, thank goodness I found you, darling, you are safe now, are you hurt?"

He tipped up her chin in order to study her face, which was covered in spots of blood and any number of tiny scratches. He traced a thumb across her cheek, which was smeared with leaf mould. "Linnet, you look terrible, such a mess and dang it, woman, where are your clothes?"

She gazed back at him numbly. "My clothes are by the river bank. I was bathing when Ned..." She turned to walk slowly back towards the river's edge. John followed her.

He tenderly washed his wife's scratches in the cool water, his emotions swinging between compassion and rage. He built a fire and brewed coffee from the small supply provided by Sarah for the men's search.

John watched Linnet as she recounted her adventures to him, excitedly waving her hands about to express herself, just like a child. He sighed to himself; his wife had absolutely no sense of responsibility. She was utterly oblivious to the worry she had caused, yet he was bemused by her lack of consideration.

"What became of the horse you borrowed?" he asked when she had finished her tale.

Linnet's hand flew to her mouth. "Oh, how dreadful of me, I had forgotten all about her! Poor Penny is tethered in a clearing over that way. Oh John, she will be so thirsty! I shall go at once to fetch her." She leapt to her feet, agitated.

John rose. "No, you stay warm by the fire. I will go and find the horse."

He turned to walk away then hesitated. He spun back to face her. "Do not move from this spot, Linnet. I mean it, for I have no wish to hunt for you again. Do you understand?"

She looked at him, surprised by his stern tone. "Of course."

"I mean it, madam. If I return to find you gone, I swear I'll take a strap to you. *Now* do you understand me?" He waited. When she failed to reply, he snapped, "Linnet!"

She scowled at him. "Yes, I have said that I shall remain here. Now go and fetch poor Penny, she will be thirsty!"

John strode away. He was not happy letting her out of his sight. He surmised, from her tale about the bear attack, that Penny had been a casualty, and if he was right, he didn't want Linnet to see what was left of the poor creature. He replayed the scene he had come upon by the river. Having heard Linnet's scream, he was now thankful that he'd been nearby to hear her. He couldn't begin to think what would have happened if he had arrived a few minutes later than he had. When John thought about that man with his filthy paws all over his wife, he ground his teeth and wished he could kill the bastard all over again. However, he was also absolutely livid with his naive wife; she had brought all this trouble down upon herself.

He'd run out of patience with her. This time, she would learn her lesson and as her husband, he would be the one to teach it to her!

CHAPTER 11

*W*hen Hans rode up in the grey light of pre-dawn carrying Peter's small body, John had thought the boy was dead. The relief he'd felt when he realised Peter was alive had been huge. He knew a broken leg was a serious injury for such a small child. Linnet had caused all this trouble, yet she still seemed to be totally oblivious of the fact. Hans told John he was going to travel straight back to the homestead with Peter. He turned his horse around and left without even acknowledging Linnet.

John found Penny, or rather, what was left of the poor creature. There was no point in him going any closer; the wolves would finish her remains. He swatted at a cloud of flies that had risen from the carcass and buzzed around him. Walking back to where he'd left Linnet, he remembered that he had still had to bury the trapper. His expression grew grim as he recalled the man astride his wife's nude body. By God, she would have some explaining to do before he was through with her. The problem had always been that she was too damn wilful. He would have to bury the body now before they could head on back to the farm. He'd already decided that upon arrival, he needed to take Linnet in hand.

He arrived back at the small camp. The fire was burning merrily, his horse nearby, contentedly grazing on the patchy grass but of Linnet, there was no sign. Where the devil was she now? Twenty minutes he'd been gone, just twenty short minutes, and yet she'd defied him! He stood stock still, a nerve twitching in his clenched cheek.

"Linnet!" he barked. He listened hard, but there was no answering call, not a whisper. He slapped his leg, agitated. Perhaps the second trapper, what was his name… had taken her? Anxiously, John hurried towards the river looking for signs of his errant wife.

Linnet had patiently waited for John. They would need to get started on their journey as soon as he returned; she wanted to get away as soon as possible. She folded the blanket and added it to the pack on John's saddle. She noticed the water bag was hanging limp and empty. Sighing, she decided that she would fill it, they would need water on their journey. Linnet built up the fire and set off with the leather water bag swinging by her side.

It was only when she had reached the water's edge that she recalled John's instruction not to leave the camp. Well, she reasoned, she hadn't really left the camp area; she was just fetching water for their journey. She knelt and filled the bag until it was full to overflowing. As she straightened, she caught sight of something moving on the opposite side of the river. She shaded her eyes from the bright sunlight but, even squinting, she couldn't tell what it was. She noticed that slightly down river, there were overhanging branches that created shade. Perhaps it would be easier to see from there. Linnet made her way along the river bank toward the trees.

Suddenly from across the water, there was a roar. Crashing sounded in the undergrowth; a man's high-pitched scream rent the air. She froze in her tracks, staring at the place the commotion was coming from. A man burst from the foliage and flung himself into the river. Linnet gasped as she recognised Will, the second trapper. From behind him came another deafening roar, then a huge black bear crashed from the undergrowth. The bear stood up on its hind legs and its enormous shaggy arms pawed the air.

Terrified, she drew back into the deep shade of the tree. She saw Will frantically trying to swim across the fast flowing water. The bear dropped to all four paws and waded in after him. Linnet moaned in fear for the trapper, pressing her hand to her mouth to stifle the sound. The bear walked easily against the swirling current, the fast flowing waters parting on either side of the huge body, the sheer size of the beast anchoring it to the river floor. It reached out one huge paw and scooped Will up into its arms, bending its massive head and jaws toward him. Linnet fainted.

John heard the horrible noise and made his way warily toward it, watching in helpless horror as Will was attacked by the bear. There was nothing he could do to save the poor man; he was just too far away across the river. John's concern was focused on finding Linnet but where on earth was she? He made his way along the riverside, trying to keep himself hidden from the bear, which seemed to be fully occupied with Will. John was careful all the same.

He stumbled across Linnet quite by chance, she was folded in a heap under a tree and for one devastating second, he thought she was dead. As quietly as possible, he lifted her into his arms and carried her back to the safety of the clearing and his horse. Cradling her, he found mounting difficult but, finally, he was astride the horse with Linnet secured against his chest. Ned would have to remain unburied; they had no choice but to leave now. Linnet came to, feeling groggy and nauseated. She turned her face into John's shoulder and wept.

They stopped to rest briefly, mainly so that John's horse could recover from carrying them both. Linnet clung to John, weeping piteously for much of the time. As darkness began to fall, John reined in and handed her down to the ground. They silently searched for wood to make a fire, and John saw to the horse's needs. He rolled out the blankets and put water on to boil for coffee. They ate the last of the bread and cheese Sarah had packed.

Linnet, exhausted, fell asleep rolled up in a blanket within seconds of lying down. John watched his young wife sleeping. He contemplated the dark, star-lit sky. Sleep seemed a remote possibility; his stomach was knotted with a deep, burning anger at his wife's repeated foolishness. At last he fell into a fretful sleep, punctuated by horrific nightmares, all involving Linnet facing some terrible danger from which he failed to rescue her.

Exhausted and hungry, they rode into the farm late the following day. Hans was outside the barn when he noticed the tired trio heading in; the gallant horse's head hanging low with thirst and exhaustion. When they drew level with him, John lowered Linnet to the ground but Hans made no move to help her. He stood regarding her beneath a stern brow. Linnet was unsure of how to approach him, it was obvious that he was very upset with her. She stood still, chewing her bottom lip indecisively. John dismounted and went straight over to Hans.

"How is Peter?" he asked immediately. Hans glanced at John and reached out to take the horse's halter. "He is much improved but it will be a while before the poor lad can walk again. I see that you found your wife."

Linnet flushed at the tone of his voice. She spoke to him falteringly, "Hans, please understand that I did not ask Peter to follow me... I wasn't even aware that he had done until John told me. I have had the most dreadful time..."

Hans looked incredulously at her. "You really are the most self-centred creature, Mistress Foster." He turned to lead the horse away, muttering furiously in Dutch.

John barely glanced at Linnet. "Wait here," he instructed curtly, striding after Hans. The two men spoke intently together for a moment. Linnet strained her ears but they spoke too quietly for her to hear what was being discussed. Finally, they both turned and looked at her. Hans slapped John on the back and walked away to stable the horse. John walked back to where Linnet stood waiting.

"What was all that about?" she asked anxiously.

"I was explaining about poor Penny," John told her. He took hold of her arm, leading her toward the barn.

"Where are we going?" she asked in surprise. "I'm tired and I want to go to bed. Oh no, surely Hans hasn't decreed that we sleep in the barn because of this misunderstanding?"

John didn't reply but led her inside and pulled the doors of the building shut behind them. He dropped the wooden bar across to lock them. Linnet watched, baffled. He turned to her, his face stern and forbidding. An uneasy apprehension filled her. When he spoke, it was brusquely to the point.

"First of all, I want you to understand that I love you and to have lost you or to have seen you suffer at another man's hands would have killed me. You have caused a huge amount of suffering these past couple of days. I wonder if you have any idea of the anguish you have put everyone through. A man and two horses are dead because of you. A small boy has come close to death. The son, I might add, of the very people who saved our lives and took us into their home!"

He stopped speaking as he turned away from her, shrugging off his coat. Linnet watched in astonishment as, next, he rolled up his shirt sleeves. When he marched to the side of the barn and lifted a long leather strap from a hook upon the wall, an anxious chill trickled down her spine. She backed away from him.

"John, what is happening?" she asked, her voice hollow and quavering. "You do know that I am *truly, truly* sorry about everything that has happened? You must realise that I intended no harm, especially to young Peter."

John sighed heavily. "I am sure you are sorry in your own way, but Linnet, you have to learn to take responsibility for your actions which have consequences. You have to learn how to acquit yourself in this land. You must think before you act rashly, putting yourself and others in danger. Last, but certainly not least, you must to learn to obey me as your husband!"

She was indignant. "That is absurd. I have obeyed you! When I left here, it was to find you! How can you blame me for what other people choose to do? I didn't ask young Peter to follow me."

John snorted, and his words cut sharply across her outburst. "Linnet, I do not intend to stand here arguing the point with you. Tell me, what was the last thing I told you to do before I set off to look for Penny?"

He frowned as he noticed his wife trying to edge her way towards the barn door. "Linnet," he barked, "stay where you are and answer me, madam! *What did I tell you?*" His voice was cold with steely resolve.

Linnet stammered, "I-I, look here, I didn't actually intend to *leave* the camp. I went to fetch water for our journey! This is utterly ridiculous. You are treating me just like a child, and I *insist* you stop scolding—you are frightening me. I am, after all, your wife!"

"Yes, madam, you are indeed *my* wife, and as such, I have every right to punish you as I see fit. I fully intend you to remember that fact from this moment on!" John looped the strap double in his fist. Crooking his finger, he beckoned to her. "Come here."

The slim line of the strap rippled in his hand, swatting nastily against the leather of his boot. Linnet blanched. "John, you cannot be serious. I do not believe you would do this, y-you cannot, I won't let you!" she shrieked and stepped back.

He shook his head. He was tired, it had been a stressful day, and he was becoming irritated by her histrionics. "I intend spanking you, young lady, do not be so melodramatic."

A cold shudder ran through her as she noted the unyielding set of her husband's face. Incredulously, she realised he meant to do just as he said. John intended to spank her with the strap. Obviously the thing was hung in the barn for that purpose. It dawned on her that Hans must have used it upon Sarah. Well, she wasn't about to surrender her derriere that easily! She pivoted, making a dash for the barred door.

John strode grimly after her. While she struggled fruitlessly with the heavy bar, he grasped her about the waist and swung her off her feet. In vain, she kicked and bucked against him but he hauled her over to a pile of hay where he threw her down. As he stood over her, his eyes narrowed to steely slits. His face was set hard and his gaze pitiless.

"Dammit, I warned you that I would take a strap to your disobedient backside if you left the camp and you dared to defy me yet again!" he growled. "It has become a habit for you to ignore my instructions; you put yourself and others in serious danger. I won't have it. I intend to remedy your thoughtlessness; you are about to learn that actions have consequences. Now roll over onto your stomach!"

Still having no intention of submitting to such callous treatment, she started to scramble away on all fours. John grabbed one of her legs but she fought like a wildcat and managed, by twisting her head around, to sink her teeth into his forearm. He let out a harsh bellow of pain. "Darn it! By God, you deserve this lesson and you're getting it, my girl!"

Despite her desperate struggles, John flipped her over so that she lay face down in the hay. With a hand square in the middle of her back, he held her squirming body fast. He took delight in the sight of her bucking posterior—clothed in his own breeches no less, whereupon his rage intensified. How dare she gallivant about the country displaying her curves to any man who cared to look? Dammit, no wonder she was almost raped! He laid the strap aside and, reaching for the offending garments, he yanked them down to her knees, revealing her naked, rounded buttocks.

Linnet immediately shifted sideways, hurling abuse at him using every expletive she knew, most gleaned from sailor's curses she'd heard aboard the ship. Her cursing did not help her cause but merely galvanised John into furious determination.

Taking a firm hold of the leather, undeterred by her struggles, he grabbed her arm. Twisting her ignominiously back onto her stomach he held her in an inexorable grip. The first painful lash across her bottom was such a shock, she opened and closed her mouth in a silent scream. The second cut roused her into defiant action, kicking and bucking.

Unrelenting, he held her fast and spanked her with ruthless resolve. As each stinging swat found its mark, she screeched and hollered, alternating between begging him to stop and wailing abuse at him. Had she remained silent, he might have stopped after only a few strokes with the doubled over strap but her continuous abuse only served to make him more determined to punish her thoroughly. Relentlessly, he brought the strap down, cutting across her backside time and again, impervious to her pleading cries until her bottom was criss-crossed with crimson marks. Eventually, she lay limply, submitting to her punishment. She wept genuine tears and spouted apologies.

At last he released her, his chest heaving. "Perhaps now, ma'am, you will reconsider before recklessly defying me. No more putting yourself into harm's way, or running headlong into danger."

She rolled away, weeping, her rounded bottom flaming red. Sobbing uncontrollably, she gazed up at him resentfully from a tear-streaked face. "I hate you!" she cried, without any real conviction.

John's eyes narrowed, his lip twitched. "Why, darlin'," he drawled with tender malice, "I love you with all my heart an' soul. In fact, I've a mind to show you just how much I love you."

He advanced purposefully toward her. She attempted to stand but, hampered by the breeches lowered about her knees, she fell backward onto the hay. She had no idea of the provocative picture she posed with her hair in tumbling in disarray and her clothing revealing far more than it covered. Her swelling bosom was exposed by the gaping shirt, her shapely limbs sprawled upon the bed of hay.

John, fully aroused by the sight she presented, strode over, throwing himself down beside her. She cringed away from him, trying to roll out of his reach, but he held her fast, entwining his hand in the loose cascade of her hair. He pulled her unceremoniously against his chest, his arm clamped tight about her. His mouth found hers, silencing her protests with a demanding kiss. His tongue raked the soft inner flesh of her lips. Breaking the kiss, he lifted his head and his gaze met her tear-flooded eyes. When he spoke, it was with deep conviction. "You are my wife, Linnet. It's time you accepted the fact. Learn to know me as your husband. There is no going back from here. Mismatched we may be but I love you regardless, my spoiled, aristocratic lady."

He reached down to wrench the breeches from her ankles, ignoring her shriek of pure rage. He avoided her clawing hands. He administered a couple of hard slaps to her scalded posterior, then grabbed her knees and pushed her legs apart, yanking her spread-eagled body toward him. Using his heavy weight to subdue her resistance, he penetrated her easily, impaling her with a snapping thrust that caused her to gasp his name aloud.

Always, in the past, John had considered her pleasure before his own. This time was to be very different, he meant her to know her master. He smiled—as he expected, she was slick with desire. Her body wanted him even as she struggled against him.

"Shall I take your bottom, is that what you need in order to mind me?" he growled into her ear. She froze, and he chuckled as she moaned.

He pressed her down against the scratching hay, ramming into her with an unrelenting force. Sliding his hands beneath her, he ignored her whimpered reply. "No, please, not my bottom!"

He clutched her smarting buttocks, raising them to meet the full force of his thrusts. "I shall take you in your final virginal place. Tell me you need me to tame you, tell me you want me in your ass." He glared down into her wide, sea-green eyes. Oh, the signs were all there, she was fully aroused. "Make no mistake, Linnet, you have met your match. I intend to make you mine, *in every way,*" he whispered, his voice a hoarse growl in her ear. His teeth grazed her neck, his body demanded surrender. She whimpered, her hands clutched at his shoulders. She slid her arms down over his back, digging her fingers into his taut buttocks. He rode her hard and she was with him, her hips rising to meet his thrusts as she fell voluntarily into the rhythm of his onslaught.

His deep hammering brought her to the edge of a shattering and surrendering climax. "Oh, oh, my, J-John!" she keened with quivering ecstasy. "Yes, yes—oh yes!"

With deep satisfaction, he heard her cry of supplication before pulling suddenly from her body and flipping her over onto her stomach. He put his mouth to her ear. "Tell me to take your virginal ass, prove that you submit to me and that you are mine and mine alone."

She quivered at the picture his words painted in her mind. "I-I do," she whispered quietly.

"No, ask me to take you... *there,*" he persisted. His finger slipped into the crease of her buttocks and rested against her puckered hole then, gradually, he increased the pressure. She clenched against his invasion.

"P-please," she whispered shakily, "t-take my bottom. I am yours, *only yours,*" she agreed nervously.

"Good girl," he praised as he pushed his fingers into her slick channel, gathering her dew. Coating his finger, he eased it into her tight little anus. Scissoring his fingers within her, he opened her passage, widening her, ready to take his girth. She mewled and shifted away from him. "Hush, do not pull away from me; push your rump back to meet my hand. Trust me, it will go easier for you if you do that. I shall not harm you—remember, I love you— but you need to learn that I am in charge of you and your well-being. This base act, this taking of your backside, will brand you as fully mine. I promise you shall remember the lesson and that it will keep you safe in future. If I am to protect you then you have to learn to obey me, Linnet. Prove to me that you can do that, obey, and trust me now. Let me take your wicked little ass." He relaxed as she did as he asked. Lifting her hind end, she pushed back onto his hand.

When he felt she was ready, he gathered more of her leaking moisture to lubricate his throbbing cock. Pressing his manhood into her small puckered entrance with gentle pressure, he halted, holding still as she cried out at the rude invasion. He whispered reassurance then continued to ease himself inside her, gradually, until his cock was fully pressed deeply within her passage.

She complained, whining as he remained still, deep seated within her heat. She shifted with a groan that sounded more aroused than punished. He grinned into her hair. She was ready, more than ready. He slipped a palm underneath her, covering her slick mons. His digits tormented the raised nub of her hardened clitoris. Her groans became moans; she was definitely a woman aroused.

Slowly he withdrew his length from her tight warmth. Then, gently, he slid back into the tight and greedy grasp of her virginal back passage. As he pushed himself through her tightness, the pleasure of his gripped manhood felt indescribably good. Gradually he increased his pace until he was pounding against her fiery butt cheeks, his flanks slapping against her yielding flesh. Frenziedly, he gave one last snap of his hips, thrusting deep within her, using her unremittingly for his own pleasure. Moving the hand that cupped her sex over her taut nubbin, he pinched.

She howled her release, the sound a frenzied mix of pleasure. Roughly, he branded her as his. Arching against her, he convulsed with a surge of roiling rapture as his seed spilled into her hot dark vessel.

Together, their laboured breathing slowed to a normal pace. He withdrew slowly so as not to hurt her. Lying beside her, he smoothed the tangle of titian hair back from her flushed face.

He leaned in and grazed her lips with his, studying the depths of her unfocused, smoky green eyes. "Do you know me now?" he asked huskily.

She nodded, hesitating briefly.

"*Tell me,*" he commanded.

"Yes, husband, I know you," she whispered, relishing her deeply primeval need to give him her submission, accepting finally his dominion, and glorying in his possession of her. She recognised him finally as her match, her mate—her *master.*

CHAPTER 12

*S*he opened her eyes; turning her head to look at her husband's pillow, she saw that he was gone. Stretching out her hand, she felt the sheet. Cold. He must have risen early.

She'd spent a restless and uncomfortable night, her body sore from the spanking of the previous evening. She'd accepted the fact that she alone was responsible for the horrible misunderstanding. She'd created havoc and paid the price for her foolishness. She also realised that, after last night, their honeymoon was over; their marriage had truly begun.

She shuddered as she remembered her punishment. She'd made an enormous error of judgement but John had corrected her and forgiven her mistakes. She dreaded facing the Lammers, although her guilt had receded in the knowledge she'd been properly chastised for her stupidity. Ruefully she rubbed her chastened buttocks. She was sore inside and out. Last night was not a punishment she would ever forget. It had been intense, both dreadful and wonderful, a powerful reminder to her to take the dangers of this new world seriously and to follow her husband's guidance.

Attempting to sit, she found it impossible, her bottom was too tender. So she rolled off the bed, wincing at the movement. Standing, she gingerly soothed her scalded rear end. A soft tap at the door had her hastily reaching for her hairbrush, whereupon she began to nonchalantly brush out the snarls in her hair.

As she worked at disentangling her curls, Sarah Lammers walked in holding a china jug.

"Good morning," she greeted Linnet brightly. "John said to let you sleep in this morning; I hear that you have had an uncomfortable night."

Linnet flushed hotly, she wished he'd not shared such information.

Sarah grinned. "Relax, my dear. I understand. Here, I have made you some balm to soothe the pain. It is what we use for burns but it has always worked for me in this situation. Just rub it in gently and it should help to soothe, it stops the stinging."

Linnet looked at Sarah with surprise. "You mean?"

Sarah chuckled and sat down on the side of the bed. "My dear, surely you don't think you are the first young woman to receive a licking from her husband?"

Under Sarah's gentle, questioning gaze, Linnet pondered on how to reply. "Well, I have no idea... but I guess not." Her voice trailed away as she flushed with shame.

Sarah shook her head, clucking her tongue. "Linnet, what a sheltered life you must have lived! Now, child, you listen to me: there is always a period of adjustment in any marriage. It is difficult to accept that your husband now has the ultimate say in all that you do. Especially living here out in the wilderness, but you must accept that John has your best interests at heart. Your safety is his sole responsibility. Do you understand that?"

Linnet nodded and asked curiously, "Does Hans, er... perhaps I shouldn't ask?"

Sarah quickly interrupted Linnet's stumbling question. "I was a young bride, like you. When Hans and I married, I knew nothing of men, other than my father. Boston is not like the wilderness where we have chosen to live. I had grown up in relative safety whilst living in Boston. My schoolteacher parents encouraged me to learn, to read and to sketch. Oh, how I loved to draw. I hardly ever have the time now."

She paused, staring dreamily out of the window; finally, she sighed and picked up her tale again. "Hans was such a handsome devil and he is such a giant of a man. When he began courting me, I felt I was in seventh heaven!

"We were soon married and moved out here. It was an adventure for me. It was like all the books that I had read at home of explorers and travellers, but I had no idea of the dangers that surrounded us. We built the cabin first up on the ridge and lived up there for a couple of years while Hans built this house.

"I used to wander off to sketch. Hans was a very understanding young husband, he liked to see my drawings of the forest and wildlife. He told me that, provided I stayed within shouting distance of the cabin, he had no objection to my hobby."

Sarah broke into a chuckle. "I remember feeling so indignant at that. I thought that he had no right to even think of objecting to wherever I wished to roam. Anyhow, I wandered farther and farther afield each day. Hans kept telling me that I must stay close by the cabin but I ignored him.

"Then, one day, I was sitting on a log, drawing, when I felt a sharp bite on my leg. A snake had bitten me; the pain was dreadful. I screamed for Hans but of course I was too far away for him to hear me. I was outside all night. Luckily for me, Hans found me early the following morning. I was very unwell for several days. We had no idea if I was to live or die.

"When I recovered, Hans told me that it had been the worst week of his life. He told me that I was never to go out of sight of the cabin again. At that time, I was still weak and frightened. I made the promise easily, never thinking that I would want to go farther away after my terrible fright.

"Some weeks later, Hans had been out cutting wood for our

176

new house. He came back at dusk; the fire in the stove was out with no meal cooking. He thought perhaps something must have happened to me, that I was hurt again. He searched and called for me for an hour or so.

"In the meantime, I walked home from my wanderings and lit the fire to begin our supper. Hans arrived back from his search fearful that I was dead. When he heard me singing happily with no thought at all of the worry I had caused him, well, he soon made it very clear how worried he'd been!"

Sarah looked at Linnet impishly. "I couldn't sit for a week! It was then I went through the book of recipes and herbal remedies my mother had given me for our wedding. I found a recipe for balm made with wintergreen to help soothe burns and bruising. Never again have I wandered away from home without first telling Hans where I am going.

"So there you have it; you are not the first, and you certainly won't be the last to suffer from a sore bottom! I still have to remember to obey, otherwise, well, you know!"

Sarah stood up and handed Linnet the bowl of medicinal-smelling balm. She reached over and gently kissed Sarah's cheek. "Thank you," she said simply.

Sarah patted her hand. "When you are ready, come down. Apparently I am to teach you how to cook."

Linnet frowned. "Oh?"

Sarah shook her head when she saw the mulish expression settle on Linnet's face. "I wouldn't deny this request from your husband, not just at the moment, *hmm*?"

Linnet nodded, she understood. Sarah smiled and left, closing the door quietly behind her. Linnet lifted the pot of balm and sniffed it. She found it smelled pleasant, slightly medicinal. She scooped some out then rubbed it gingerly over her sore buttocks. Sarah was right; it would not do to test John today, and probably not for some while.

She pondered over the story Sarah had shared with her. Perhaps all wives were regularly spanked by their husbands? Women promised to obey their husbands in their wedding vows, and she realised she had not been very obedient to her husband. She decided she would make more effort to listen to him—after all, she didn't want a repeat of last night and the ghastly strap. She shuddered.

Linnet was still pondering her marriage when she made her way downstairs. Sarah had placed two steaming cups of coffee on the table and when Linnet arrived, she placed a cushion on one of the chairs. Giving Linnet a cheeky grin, she gestured for her to sit, which she did, wincing even with the cushion under her.

"Now, I want you to know that I bear you no grudge for what happened to Peter. I knew he had gone off by himself and he has explained that you didn't know that he'd followed you. Thankfully, his leg is sprained and not broken. I should like to know what happened. Why did you run away?"

"I think I should explain something of my background to you so that you can understand what led to my decision to leave here. My father is Sir Edward Wainwright; my family home is Lavenstock Hall in Devonshire in England. My mother, Arabella, died when I was small, and so I suppose I was a little indulged by my father and used to having things mostly my own way..."

Here Sarah tried to hide a smile, for she privately thought Linnet the most spoiled young woman she had ever met. "That explains your accent."

Linnet nodded. When she'd finished her tale of woe, she told Sarah that she very much doubted that John still loved her. Sarah reached across the table and, taking Linnet's hand in her own, she gave it a squeeze. "You cannot doubt his love; he was distraught when he discovered that you had gone. His anger toward you was because he feared for your safety, and his fury at your disobedience was because your wilfulness placed you in danger."

Linnet nodded and sighed. "I seem to have a knack for making the wrong decisions."

"We all take time to adjust to a new way of life, and you have had an enormous change to your own, so try not to be so hard on yourself. I always think that one of the good things about a spanking is the clearing of the air and the fresh start it affords us."

Linnet nodded, slowly understanding. "Hmm, I hadn't thought of it quite like that. Thank you, Sarah."

A comfortable silence settled between them as they drank their coffee and reflected upon the relationship each wife had with her own husband, pondering the uncomfortable circumstances that arguments with their men sometimes led to, and the private but rather delightful side effect of the spankings they occasionally received—namely bedding their men.

Linnet came out of her reverie first. "Now, where were we?"

"I think you were about to tell me how you came to be upon the ship?" Sarah prompted.

Linnet sipped her coffee and nodded. She began her tale, finishing with her spanking in the barn the night before.

When she came to a halt, Sarah grinned. "I have to tell you that I am feeling a great deal of sympathy for John right now!"

Linnet cocked her head and gave a sheepish grin. "No need. John had his revenge, believe me."

"Yes, I know, and you are... *uncomfortable.*" Sarah winked and the women began to giggle together, which soon morphed into howls of mirth. Sarah had to mop her eyes, she was laughing so much. For Linnet, the laughter was emotional balm to her soul, she had never had a close friendship with a woman before. She had hoped to find friendship with Patsy but then the girl had betrayed her, and that had hurt more than she cared to admit. She realised that she wanted Sarah as her friend but she was nervous of how to proceed.

"Sarah, I want you to know that I totally regret running off and leading Peter into danger. I am so sorry; please, can you ever forgive me?"

Sarah saw her sincerity. "Of course I forgive you, but why did you run away? I still don't understand."

"I thought that John had set out to Boston without me. I was simply attempting to follow him, to catch up with him. I had no idea that your son would follow me, honest to goodness, I did not!"

"It's all right, Linnet. Your husband punished you; it is over, you are forgiven, and there is no more to be said on the matter. Hans and I *both* forgive you. We shall put the matter behind us."

"Thank you, Sarah. I feel so much better now that we have spoken."

Sarah sat and looked at the beautiful young girl before her, wondering how she herself would have coped with everything this eighteen-year-old girl had gone through since her marriage. Not very well, was her conclusion.

"Well, you have certainly had some terrible adventures, my dear. It seems to me that you are a survivor and a very brave girl. You have a husband who knows how to love and protect you, and friends here in us. Your life can only improve and you can be happy again."

Sarah stood and made her way around the table to where Linnet sat. She wrapped her arms about her, holding her close. After a moment, Linnet buried her head in Sarah's shoulder and sobbed. Sarah stroked her hair and held her until the cathartic emotional storm had passed.

"Right. Now, we work!" she stated briskly after Linnet's tears had ceased. "To begin with, we shall bake. You are going to learn how to make bread."

Linnet smiled tremulously. For the first time since she'd been aboard the ship, she felt hope that her marriage might work.

CHAPTER 13

*B*y the time the men returned that evening, Linnet had ruined two loaves of bread and burned two batches of biscuits. But she had learned how to make a bed and milk a cow, and she had even helped with some of the laundry.

She felt very guilty that up until now she hadn't lifted a finger to help with the heavy domestic chores. Insisting that Sarah sit down with a cup of coffee, she attempted to prepare some vegetables for their evening meal. Even that simple task proved difficult, since she had never prepared a vegetable before.

She followed Sarah around diligently, trying to learn the tasks she needed to run a home. Several times throughout the day, she'd winced as she sat, turning her face away from Sarah's shrewd gaze.

Linnet was nervous when the men came home that evening. She took a deep, steadying breath and went directly to Hans, apologising profusely to him for what had happened to Peter and to poor Penny. He had been magnanimous in his forgiveness. As far as he was concerned, Linnet had been punished. Justice had prevailed and so he could forgive her. He accepted her apology, patting her bottom robustly in a fatherly manner as she turned away. She winced at the contact.

"*Gehoorzamen*, Linnet, *gehoorzamen!*" he boomed.

Sarah translated for her: "Obey, Linnet, obey!"

Sarah, who knew her husband only too well, hid a smile, knowing that he had made the gesture simply for the purpose of causing Linnet a discomforting reminder to obey the rules.

John was pleased to see that his wife had taken his instructions seriously and that she'd made progress with learning domestic chores. He'd worried that she would remain sulky and resentful all day. Hans had assured him, when he'd fretted, that a sore backside never harmed anyone. He'd also added that Linnet's chastisement was long overdue.

While the punishment still caused her some discomfort, the thought of what might happen if she failed to follow John's instructions ensured Linnet's complete compliance—she had no wish for a repeat performance in the barn.

She asked if she could ride with him up to see the cabin but he'd told her that only when she handed him her first properly raised loaf, he would take her. Try as she might, every loaf came out like a brick. She even asked Sarah to help her cheat, to bake one for her. Sarah had only laughed good-naturedly but refused.

When her first properly raised loaf of bread finally came out of the oven, large, crusty and golden brown, she was glad Sarah had not let her cheat. Her achievement was her own. John was absolutely delighted, he told her how proud he was of her.

Straight away, they made plans for their journey to the cabin. Hans suggested that first of all, they take his wagon, packed with various items they would need for furnishings. That way, when they permanently moved, they could travel on horseback and leave the wagon where it belonged, on the farm with Sarah and Hans.

Linnet was devastated at the thought of not being able to ride as she'd planned but kept quiet. She felt constrained around her husband since he'd punished her, wary of him. John had seen her face fall with disappointment when the wagon was decided upon. He fully expected her to speak out, voicing her complaint.

When she quietly stood up and left the room, he was amazed, and rightly guessed the reason why. The last thing he wanted was for Linnet to feel that her wishes must be supplanted by his own. He brooded over the change in her, finally deciding to ask Sarah for advice. He knew the two women had forged a bond of friendship. He was pleased that his wife had made a friend and confidant of Sarah.

He waited until Linnet was outside, helping Peter feed the chickens and pigs. The boy was able to hobble about using two sticks that Hans had crafted for him. Then he approached her. "Sarah, I wonder, could you spare me a minute or two? I need to ask some advice."

Sarah turned and looked at him in surprise. John had always struck her as a supremely confident man, even arrogant. Intrigued by his sudden need for advice from a woman, she gave him her full attention.

"Of course, how may I help?" she inquired with her gentle smile.

John ran a hand distractedly through his hair. "I am not sure if you can help. I am sure you know what happened the night I brought Linnet back here?"

Sarah nodded, blushing.

John grinned broadly at her. "I see that you do. Ever since I punished Linnet, she has behaved responsibly and sensibly, yet she is distant and even seems to be a little afraid of me. Do you think she is?"

Sarah looked at John, dumbfounded. Men! "John, you strapped her. What did you expect?"

John was affronted. "Well, you aren't afraid of Hans, and he told me that he has warmed your backside for you!"

Sarah flushed, embarrassed.

"I shouldn't have said that, please forgive me." John was instantly contrite. He was genuinely fond of Sarah and had no wish to embarrass her. "You must have found life out here quite difficult to begin with," he suggested gently.

"I-I'm surprised that Hans shared something so personal with you." She took a deep, flustered breath. She was disappointed with her husband, she would complain to him about his loose tongue but then she remembered that she had talked to Linnet about Hans taking her to task; perhaps she should keep quiet, after all?

She couldn't meet John's eyes, and when she began to talk, John had to strain to hear her, shy, reticent voice.

"It took me a while to understand the dangers of life here in the wilderness. My father was a schoolmaster and he never spanked me as a child. The first time Hans spanked me, I confess that I was a little afraid of him for a while. I expected him to punish me every single time I disagreed with him. It took a while to adjust and to realise that he was a fair and just man, that what he required from me was normal loving respect and obedience due to him as my husband."

John looked thoughtful. "So what should I do to convince Linnet that I am not some kind of monster, about to thrash her every time she disagrees with me?"

"Have you tried simply talking to her?" she asked.

"No, I just don't know where to begin." He spread his hands helplessly.

Sarah pondered for a moment or two. "I know! Why don't you make her a small gift? Perhaps then you could find a way to open the conversation."

"What an excellent idea. I promised to buy her a horse when we arrived on dry land. You aren't just a pretty lady but a wise one, to boot! Why didn't I think of that?" He planted a kiss on Sarah's cheek. "Hans is a very lucky man to have you, and I shall tell go and tell him so too!"

He turned and strode out of the house, leaving Sarah shaking her head, a delighted blush suffusing her cheeks.

A trip into the local settlement was required in order to stock up on supplies for winter. After much discussion, it was decided that, instead of a visit up to the cabin, John and Linnet should move up there as soon as they'd bought their supplies. They talked about who should go to buy the goods and who should stay behind at the farm. Finally, it was decided that Hans, John and Linnet would go.

The morning of the trip dawned crisp and clear. The first warning of the winter to come was in the cold fresh bite of the bitter wind. They set off with John and Linnet riding the buckboard and Hans on horseback. The journey took a good hour, and Linnet was chilled to the bone by the time the small wooden township came into sight.

Linnet looked around with interest at the rough wooden buildings with their covered walkways. Many had a horse or small wagon tied to a hitching rail out at the front on the dirt road. The little town seemed packed with people, and the atmosphere seemed almost like that of a fete or carnival. Whole families wandered the street together. Small children rode on their fathers' shoulders. Hans looked at John, his eyebrows raised questioningly. John shrugged in return, both men nonplussed by the unexpected crowds.

Penman's General Store was in mid street, and they pulled up outside the store in a line with three other various types of wagons. John helped Linnet down and, curious, she went inside the strange-looking store. It was full of every type of household need, from pots and bowls, pans, cups and utensils, to grain and coffee, cloth and even children's candy. Everything, in fact, a family could need. Linnet spotted some stacked bolts of cloth and went over to study them. Sarah had asked her to buy something warm to make winter clothes for her and shirts for Peter and Hans.

As she fingered the serviceable material, John came and stood behind her. "You'd better choose something for yourself, as well. You need warm clothing for the winter. I have an errand to run with Hans. Do you think you will be all right here alone for a little while? Select what you need and Mr. Penman will add it to our bill."

Linnet looked up at him, surprised. "Yes, of course, I'll be fine. How long do you think you'll be?"

John had already turned to walk away but answered, "Only about half an hour, perhaps, no more." He paused and turned, his gaze directed to his wife as he said, "Oh, and do not stray from the store, do you understand me, Linnet?"

She could not meet her husband's eyes because oh, yes, she understood his meaning—only too well. "Yes, sir," she answered quietly.

John gave her a brief kiss on the forehead. "Good!" was his reply. Then he called over his shoulder for Hans and the two men left.

Linnet turned back to the pile of cloth, immediately engrossed in the selection of colours and texture of the materials. She decided on strong serge for skirts, along with a blue and cream checked material for Sarah to make into a dress. Mr. Penman, a tall, thin, stooping man with thinning grey hair, took the cloth away to cut the lengths she required.

While she was waiting, Linnet's eye was caught by a beautiful deep, emerald green velvet bolt of cloth, virtually hidden under a pile of other materials. She eased it out from the stack and ran her fingers over the soft folds. It was surprisingly good quality, thick and rich, the pile of the velvet weave close together. Should she buy a length? It certainly wasn't suitable for farm living but it would look wonderful against the green of her eyes. Would John approve? She thought not, sure that he would tell her to wait until they reached Boston before indulging herself.

She hesitated, heaved a sighed and put the bolt back on the pile, deciding she had no wish for another spanking from her husband if he didn't approve. She reached for woollen flannel in a dull grey and took it to Mr. Penman for cutting.

He took the bolt of cloth from her and gave her an indulgent smile. "I saw you looking at the velvet," he said, measuring out the serge. "It is very fine quality but unfortunately not practical. I ordered that for an elderly lady last year but blow me if she didn't go and die the very week it arrived. I can do you an excellent price on it, Mistress, er?"

"Foster, Mistress John Foster. You would need to ask my husband's permission on his return, Mr. Penman," she replied absently as she fingered lengths of green ribbon. Linnet bought thread and needles for sewing and some velvet ribbon for trimming, in three different colours. She turned her attention to the purchase of some readymade undergarments. Finally, all her packages were wrapped and stacked with the household order.

Awaiting the return of the menfolk, she went out onto the sidewalk. Crowds milled in the street; obviously something was going on in the small town to be attracting so many people. Linnet hesitated but decided to join the throng to find out what was happening for herself, she hoped it might be a fair or some such event like the ones held on the village green near Lavenstock in England. She decided to tell John that the crowd had simply swept her along with them.

People gathered at the edge of the street where a large rough wooden structure stood. Linnet thought it might be some sort of a stage and waited, watching along with the happy, jostling people. There was a commotion to the left of the structure and an expectant hush fell over the gathering. A priest appeared on the platform, followed by a young, fair-headed lad who stood with his hands behind his back. Linnet wondered whether a sermon was about to be preached.

It seemed she might be correct when the priest started saying prayers and the men in the crowd removed their hats and everyone joined in the Lord's Prayer. She murmured the familiar words and then looked up to see what would happen next. Two older men appeared on the platform, they manoeuvred the young lad to the middle. One placed a thick rope about the lad's neck. Linnet's eyes widened with dawning horror of what she was about to witness.

Frantically, she cast her eyes about her, looking for a way out of the crush. She caught sight of John at the edge of the crowd, waving at her, trying to catch her attention, a worried frown creasing his forehead. She lifted her hand to wave to him and began to push her way over to where he stood.

There was a shout from the crowd and a woman's sharp cry. Her gaze was involuntarily drawn back to the platform and its fatal drama. The young lad stood straight, his head held high with the thick rope twisted about his throat. The breeze stirred his blond hair. Linnet could see that tears flowed down his cheeks, yet he made no sound. A deadly hush fell, save for the wailing of a single woman whom Linnet could not see.

She held her breath; there was a sudden loud crack and the boy fell feet downward, kicking grotesquely at the end of the rope. Mesmerised, she was unable to look away. She watched his purpling face and protruding tongue. Then promptly, blessedly, she fainted.

John shouted for Hans to follow him as he pushed and shoved his way through the melee, elbowing people aside in his desperation to get to his wife. What on earth was she doing out there in the middle of the crowd? *Dear God, will she never learn to stay where I leave her?* Finally, he reached her unconscious form. Stooping, he lifted her into his arms and pushed his way back through the press of people who politely parted to let him through.

Hans hurried over, patting at Linnet's pale cheeks. "What a thing to happen. Why was she not safely waiting in the mercantile?"

John shook his head. "I don't know." They reached the cart and he placed Linnet on some rough sacking in the back of the wagon. "Here is the cash for our goods. Would you mind settling my account with Mr. Penman for me, Hans? I need to remain here with Linnet." He handed some cash to Hans.

"Of course I will, my friend, and I will load the goods too, *ja?*"

Linnet stirred. She stared up into John's anxious face. "My head is aching. "Oh my word, that poor boy—*just like on the ship…*" Her voice faltered.

John helped her up so she was sitting with her legs dangling over the tail gate of the wagon. He leaned forward and pulled her against his chest, wrapping his arms tight about her. He kissed her pale forehead and smoothed back the tendrils of hair fallen around her pinched face.

"Linnet, listen to me, it was *not* the same as aboard the ship. Do not grieve for that young man; he was a killer and a rapist. He deserved his end."

Linnet raised her head and gazed intently at her husband. "Really? That young lad was a murderer?"

John held her eye. "Yes. You are to put all thoughts of what you saw out of your lovely head... I would like to know what on earth you were doing there, though!" He put his face close to hers and growled, "*I told you to wait for me inside the store!*"

She tensed. "You knew there was to be a hanging?"

"Yes, that's why I wanted you safe inside while you waited for me."

"I'm sorry. I suppose now you will strap me?" she asked in a hushed tone.

John groaned and hugged her to him tightly. "No I shan't spank you but I just might decide to take that naughty bottom of yours again! Come now, you've suffered a nasty shock. I want to get you away from here. Do you feel strong enough to walk, darling? We are going to find something to eat and allow you time to recover. Later, I have a surprise for you, which will cheer you up and take your mind off the hanging."

She frowned. "No, John. How can I relax when you threatened my," she lowered her voice to a whisper, "*bottom*?" she hissed.

He pinched her cheek. "I am not like to do so in daylight, and if I recall correctly, you quite enjoyed the experience. Methinks the lady complains too much? Relax and try to enjoy the rest of today." He kissed the tip of her nose.

She scowled. "I-I *need* to talk."

John saw that she was serious. He held up his hands. "Okay, if you need to talk, we shall. I think you need to forget the hanging and the heinous events aboard the ship. It does you no good to dwell upon these things."

She shook her head. "I am not going to dwell upon them!" she snapped. "I just want us to talk quietly about the awful things that have happened to us, and about how we now feel about each other."

He took her arm and turned her to face him. "I know how I feel about *you!*" He planted a soft kiss on her lips. "I love you, Mistress Foster," he whispered into her ear.

Linnet drew away, looking searchingly into his eyes. "Do you, John, truly?" she asked earnestly.

He studied her face for a moment. "You're serious. We do need to talk. Come along."

He grasped her arm and lifted her down, carrying her around to the front seat of the wagon. He climbed up beside her. "This is as good a place as any to talk; we cannot be overheard if we talk quietly." He turned to face her, taking both her hands in his. "All right, sweetheart, tell me what it is that troubles you."

She dipped her head and chewed her lip, gathering her thoughts. "After we were safe ashore, I felt guilty about the gentlemen who died on the ship, Captain Pettigrew and D-Duncan Snow." Her voice broke. He squeezed her hand and she took a deep breath before continuing. "I couldn't stop thinking about how we were sitting safe in our cabin while our friends above were fighting for their lives! We might have helped them but we didn't even t-try."

"But in all probability, darling, had we been there, we would have perished alongside them," he reasoned.

Linnet wrenched her hands from his. "But you can't be sure of that! Anyway, I have other concerns." She wondered how best to explain to him how she felt. "You see, when I asked you to go alone to Boston, it was because I couldn't face seeing you every day. I felt such guilt that we'd survived and they had not. I prayed when you were unconscious, *begged* that you would live. Yet, when you did, I resented you for actually still being alive when they were all dead. It made me feel so guilty that we were saved. I *hated* you for not helping them. I *hated* you for not protecting *me* from the pirates! Oh, John, I was so *confused*!

"Then, afterward, I thought you had left me behind and gone on ahead to Boston and I realised how much I actually did love you. I regretted sending you away. That's why I took off to find you, so that I could make everything right between us." She dipped her head. A tear trickled down her face.

John realised how very young and vulnerable she still was. He was determined to put this matter right. "Sweetheart, don't you realise that I feel terrible guilt for not joining the crew and fighting alongside my friends? Instead I chose to stay below and protect you, who have become the most precious thing in my life! I am also guilty of putting you in terrible danger by bringing you so far away across the sea. When I think of what might have happened to you on board the ship... how close you came to drowning and afterward, when you rode off, the danger you faced from wild animals and that trapper, Ned. Dammit, I still get mad when I think about the fact you were very nearly raped!"

He caressed her cheek. "Sweet girl, you have no need to feel any guilt. It is I who feel guilty because I didn't fight, and even though I know it wouldn't have changed the outcome, I shall live with the guilt gladly because the alternative was to leave you alone and unprotected in the cabin and I just couldn't do that to you."

"I didn't realise that you felt that way," she whispered, her eyes welling with fresh tears.

He gathered her close, allowing her to weep. "Why do you think I was so harsh with you after you wandered off? It was because I love you very, very much. I cannot stand the thought of losing you. I had to make sure you would never risk your life again."

She sniffed and gave him a watery smile. "Really, and here I was thinking it was only because you enjoyed spanking me!"

John chuckled. "Well, since you mention it, I do. You have such a cute butt!"

She pinched his arm. "Swine." She giggled. "What on earth is a 'butt'?"

It was his turn to smile. "A bum," he said, pinching hers lightly.

She wriggled. "Honestly? I was glad you punished me. I felt exonerated somehow for what had happened aboard the ship."

John was shocked. "Darling, no, that's dreadful! What happened between us has nothing whatsoever to do with The Tempest. If I'd known that was how you felt—"

She interrupted him. "What difference would it have made? You were furious because I'd disobeyed you. You would have punished me anyway."

He frowned. "No, Linnet, had I realised the amount of guilt you were carrying, I would have talked to you about it. You should have spoken to me about this instead of foolishly trying to send me off into the wilds to Boston."

Her temper flared. "Well, I might have done if I had been given half a chance to *speak*!"

He sighed. "Look, that spanking wasn't just about obeying. It was about keeping you and others around you safe. Your repeated defiance endangered yourself and young Peter. A valuable horse died because of your ill-considered action."

Her eyes flashed. "Really? What about at Lavenstock Hall then, after the ball, inside the coach? I was in no danger then, except from you!" she retaliated.

"This is absolutely ridiculous; you are behaving like a spoilt child. You *bit* me and, come to think of it, you bit me again in the barn. You darn well deserved everything you got!" he replied brusquely.

Incensed, she twisted, attempting to slap his face but he caught her wrist and yanked her forward. Crushing her to him, he kissed her grindingly upon her mouth. He kept a firm grip of her hands. "That's enough, unless you want another spanking and in public!

Stop! We're supposed to be *talking*, not arguing. I've explained how I feel and why I took the actions that I did. I think perhaps I understand how you were feeling. However, I will *not* apologise for punishing you, however resentful you feel about it. Darn it, you're my wife, and should you defy me, I will punish you. Mark my words, that's the way it is, without discussion. Now, do you wish to talk about anything else?"

She nodded vigorously. "Just this: you're wrong if you think I'm resentful about the other night. The coach, yes, that was high-handed of you." She took a deep breath. "But after everything that has happened, I am relieved that you have placed limitations on my behaviour. In the past, I did everything I wanted, no matter how dangerous or stupid it was, no one stopped me and no one interfered. They certainly never disciplined me, not until you came along. At first I was livid that I couldn't bend your will to mine but after a while, I rather enjoyed the fact that you would put a stop to my wilder behaviour. Am I making any sense at all?"

John's eyes twinkled, his lip twitched. "I think I follow you perfectly. Your father spared the rod and spoilt the child. I knew you needed a strong man for your husband, one who would stand up to your stubborn wilfulness. Had you married that poor boy Charles, you would have run rings around him! The marriage would have been a complete disaster. You would have had little or no respect for him and he would have had no idea how to deal with a reckless little minx such as you!"

She flushed scarlet and muttered under her breath.

He grinned at her. "What was that, my love?"

She glowered at him. "I *said*, Charles was far too much of a gentleman to behave the way you do!"

John threw back his head, laughing delightedly. "I think it's just as well you married me then!"

She suddenly gurgled with laughter. "Actually, I happen to agree! Poor dear Charlie, I would have made his life utterly miserable, although I hate to admit that you are right and swell your arrogant head further! Seriously, though, John, I do love you. I am beginning to understand what you need from me as your wife. I promise not to knowingly put myself in danger, but only if you will promise me the same. I should be utterly helpless should something happen to you."

He nodded. "I hope you mean your promise, Linnet, because, in return, I promise to protect you however I can. If occasionally that means risking danger, then so be it. I also promise to blister your sassy butt whenever I think you require a reminder!"

She pouted prettily, wrapping her arms around his shoulders.

He scooped her to him and held her tight, kissing her soundly before he released her. "Now, can we find this eating house that Hans mentioned? Because I am absolutely starving and my ribs are sticking to my vitals."

'Aunt Bessie's' eating house was glass fronted; very few establishments could boast such refinement in such a small backwoods town. The glass was the thick green variety, unlike the fine thin glass to be found in the more sophisticated buildings of New York and Boston. Nevertheless, the presence of glass at all gave the eating house a prestige that owners of the other premises within the town envied, and business was booming.

Inside, there were a series of long wooden benches and trestle tables set in lines across the width of the room. When someone vacated a space, the next man in line sat down and was served. There was no varied menu; the meal always consisted of soup, fried chicken or stew and a hunk of bread, followed by a cup of strong black coffee. Pie was optional when fruit was in season.

Linnet was surprised at how tasty the meal was. The girl who served them smiled too much. She simpered at John and asked him if they were there for the hanging and whereabouts they were from.

He sat back in his chair, stretched his long legs and told her they were staying with Hans Lammers. The girl, a pretty fair-haired, freckled-faced young miss, with wide blue eyes and an overdeveloped bosom, pressed herself far too close to John for Linnet's liking. She then proceeded to gush with verbal enthusiasm about Hans's size and good looks, asking John whether Hans would be joining them for lunch, batting her pale eyelashes at John as she spoke. *Just like a demented house fly hovering over something sweet,* Linnet thought, bitterly jealous.

She rolled her eyes as her husband puffed out his chest and told the girl the tale of the shipwreck that had landed them there. She kicked his leg under the table, giving him a sharp shake of her head. John glanced up at her in surprise. He raised an eyebrow at her and then turned away to listen to some flippant comment the flirt made about the hanging.

It seemed that the lad who had been hanged was one Tom O'Cleary, who had come upon a half-caste girl who'd rejected his advances. In a fit of drunken rage, he'd raped and murdered the poor girl before being caught red-handed by her father who had been looking for his daughter, concerned that she'd not appeared for her supper. The town had been in uproar ever since. Half the town's folk thought that the lad should be hanged; the other half did not, based on grounds that the girl was half Indian. In the end, a trial was held, and Tom was sentenced to hang by a jury of twelve men.

As they were finishing their meal, Hans strolled in to join them. He greeted the red-head with a big hug and she squealed with delight, kissing his cheek and pulling his whiskers. Linnet glared at them both and pushed up, ready to leave. "Are you coming, John?" she asked regally.

He regarded her with surprise. "Of course I'll come with you," he said, immediately standing.

He followed her retreating back, shrugging at Hans, who laughed, calling after him, "I will see you back at the wagon, my friend, just as soon as I have eaten my fill."

John caught up with her. Catching her by the upper arm, he

stopped her in her tracks. "Whoa, what's got into you all of a sudden?"

She raised her eyebrows. "Into *me*? By Gad, that girl couldn't keep her hands off you or Hans and you just adored flirting, didn't you?"

He looked incredulous. "So that is what this hissy fit is all about? You're mad just because I talked to a pretty serving wench?"

She flushed, sneering scornfully. *"Talked?"* Her voice dropped an octave, copying John's deep drawl. *"Let me take those heavy plates for you there, missy,"* she mimicked before she spun away, marching off at a brisk pace.

John grinned, watching her shapely form appreciatively for a second or two before he strode after her. Catching her by the arm, he guided her down the narrow opening between two buildings. Once screened from the street, he pushed her roughly up against the wall, intending to kiss her.

Her hand flew up and slapped him hard across the cheek, leaving a livid palm impression. John's eyes smarted but, ignoring the sharp pain, he spun Linnet around and landed two heavy swats to her already burning bottom. He spun her back to face him and, placing his hands on either side of her furious face, he forced her head up, kissing her thoroughly. Linnet hit the back of his shoulders with her fists. She tried to bring her knee up between his legs but John forestalled her by quickly pushing his own leg between hers. Breaking the kiss slightly, he grinned down at her. "Uh-uh, naughty," he murmured before resuming the kiss. His lips moved in a sensuous slow rhythm that spoke of a passion shared. Her legs turned weak, her body wanting. He drew slightly away, whispering huskily into her ear, "Don't you know yet, you *impossible* woman, that you are the only one for me?" He lowered his lips to hers, kissing her searingly. His hand roved up over the slope of her hip, moving inexorably upward until he cupped her breast.

Anxiously, she broke the kiss, twisting her head aside. "Stop, John, someone might see us! Halt, *please!*"

His hand whipped up to grasp her chin. "Let them stare, you are my wife and if I choose to kiss you then, dammit, I shall." He lowered his head, his fingers twined in her silky hair. To his surprise, her arms wound themselves sinuously about the thick column of his neck, her hands stroked the thick dark hair, her lips parted under his, her tongue darted teasingly between his lips.

He crushed her hard against his length; they stood locked together in a passionate embrace. When at last he broke away, he gazed down into her unfocused, sea green eyes, turned misty as they did whenever she was aroused. He smiled at her dreamy sensual expression and kissed her small nose. "We shall finish this conversation later, my love, in private. Now come, for I have a gift for you."

She began tidying her mussed hair. "A gift, for me?" She looked astonished. Reaching out, she patted his pockets.

He laughed. "Stop that, you minx, I don't have the gift on me! Come, follow me."

Taking her hand in his, he towed her back along the way they had come, eventually stopping outside the livery stable. He hailed the hostler and the man appeared, leading out a pretty russet mare with a jet black mane and tail. John took the reins from the man and led the horse over to where Linnet stood. "Yours," he said simply, handing over the horse's reins.

Linnet lifted her palm to allow the horse to sniff her hand before turning shining eyes to him. "I can't believe it!" She flung her arms about her husband's neck, pressing her lips to his. Spinning back to look at the horse, she shook her head in disbelief. "She's absolutely beautiful! Thank you, my darling, *thank you!*"

John looked more than a little embarrassed. "She hasn't the pedigree that Pango had but she is the best I could find at short notice."

Linnet lifted her glowing face to his. "John, she is perfect. I *love* her, look at her colouring and her beautiful intelligent eyes." She admired her new horse, lifting her hooves, running her hands over her fetlocks, all the while talking soothingly to the gentle creature that stood obediently by her side. The horse followed Linnet's progress with a tolerant eye, blowing softly through her velvety nose.

John helped her to mount the mare and she rode up the street with him walking alongside until they came to the now fully laden wagon.

"So what are you going to name her?" Sarah asked her as the two women walked back to the house after stabling and settling Linnet's new mare for the night.

"Oh, that's easy, Amber, because of her colouring," Linnet replied chirpily.

"My, but you're a happier soul than left here this morning!" Sarah noted.

"I am, but it isn't just receiving Amber, although I just cannot get over John buying her for me. It's just, well wonderful! We actually spoke about *everything* that still lay between us. I believe we have reached an understanding."

Sarah patted her friend's arm "I'm so glad, he is a lovely man, your husband. We are lucky women to have found such gentlemen as your John and my Hans." She linked her arm cosily through Linnet's.

"You're right. We *are* lucky ladies," Linnet confirmed happily. They smiled warmly at each other and walked on in companionable silence back to the house to make supper.

Later that evening, Sarah and Linnet spread dress patterns and material across the table in order to make a start on the warm clothing they would need for the cold winter ahead.

John and Hans sat in front of the fire across the room, talking of the political news they had gleaned from Mr. Penman that day. It seemed that various skirmishes had broken out between the colonists and British troops based in Boston; ill feeling was flourishing amongst local people, who were fast turning against the British.

As they worked together, Linnet answered Sarah's questions about her trip into town.

Sarah shook her head sadly when she told her about the hanging. "That poor, poor girl, it is so very sad. What a savage place the world can be."

The two women worked together in silence, each wrapped in her own thoughts of the winter to come. Linnet reached out impulsively and placed her hand over Sarah's. They smiled at one another. "I do wish we could stay and spend the winter here with you. I shall miss you so much, Sarah!"

Sarah smiled warmly back at her young friend. "Aye, I'll miss you, too." She reached over to give Linnet a swift hug. "It wouldn't work, though; you have no idea the strain a long winter can take. To be snowed in for days at a time with a lack of privacy. I use that time to teach Peter his lessons. If you stayed with us, Peter wouldn't concentrate, and neither would I. Probably you and I would be at each other's throats by the end of the winter. It's far better that you overwinter at the cabin. You and John will have the privacy a newly wedded couple requires to be able get to know one another properly. Actually, it's the one thing I like about the winter months. Hans and I seem to become closer during the enforced confines of the house."

Linnet smiled sadly at her friend. "I understand," she agreed but she didn't, not really. How could she, never having experienced the long winter months trapped inside a small cabin.

Later, in their bedchamber, John pulled out a package from beneath their bed. "For you. Happy nineteenth birthday, darling!" He handed her the parcel.

"My birthday was a month ago," she cried, reaching for it excitedly.

"I know, but you were too ill to know anything about it."

"What is it?" she asked curiously.

"Open it and see." He perched on the edge of the bed, watching as she tore open the package, revealing the soft, shimmering folds of green velvet that she had admired in Mr. Penman's mercantile.

"How did you guess?" she asked, fingering the soft material lovingly.

"Mr. Penman. I asked him to take note of anything that you particularly liked." John smiled at her response. "Are you pleased?" he asked.

"*Pleased*? I am thrilled! I wish I had a gift for you though." She flung her arms around her husband's neck.

"Oh, I'm sure if I put my mind to it, I could think of something I want," he said dryly, his eyes narrowing as he reached out and drew her to him, his hands sliding down to her tender bottom cheeks. He squeezed them gently as he pressed her body to his. Linnet sighed as the heat from her smarting bottom seemed to curl exquisitely through her loins. She melted sensuously up against him, ready to thank her husband prettily for his gifts. He wasted no time in scooping her up and throwing her squealing form onto their bed. He joined her and, placing his arms on either side of her head, he lowered his mouth to hers.

$\mathscr{T}$he day that John and Linnet left for the cabin dawned chilly but bright, the sky pink with the early flush of dawn. They'd loaded the wagon the previous evening, so the goodbyes were heartfelt but brief. Hans handed Linnet a package just as they were pulling away. Intrigued, she opened it to find a lovely carved wooden horse, the lines so smooth and fine it matched the real thing for perfection. She swung Amber around and cantered back to where Hans and Sarah stood. Leaning down from the horse, she kissed Hans's cheek and thanked him with tears in her eyes before riding after the wagon and John.

John drove the wagon with the cow tied onto the tail gate, whilst Linnet rode Amber. Sarah turned her head into her husband's broad chest and wept. The sense of sadness dropped away from Linnet as her youthful exuberance and sense of adventure bubbled to the surface.

She sent Amber into a gallop and raced the horse up the grassy slope ahead, feeling the wonderful sense of freedom as she rode. The journey was uneventful and they reached the cabin before dusk. Linnet went straight to the cabin and unlocked the heavy door. She was rather shocked at the total lack of rooms. One large space was not what she had been expecting but it was sound and sturdily made. Importantly, it looked to be draught proof.

Hans had visited the place on a couple of occasions to prepare it for the young couple; he had swept it, so it was relatively clean. He had also refurbished where necessary, then placed rag rugs, homemade by Sarah, upon the floor. A lantern hung from the ceiling and a large lamp sat on the table by the side of the large, sturdy wooden bed.

John had enjoyed watching his wife as she'd ridden to the cabin, admiring her prowess as a horsewoman, as horse and rider gracefully merged as one. He wished that he could have joined her and ridden beside her on horseback himself but he'd been tied to the cumbersome wagon. He was pleased to see his wife's enjoyment of the pretty mare he'd bought her.

The door banged open as he struggled in with armloads of household items.

"Where do you want these? I think they are mainly bedcovers and such."

"Oh just pile them all on the bed, I shall put covers on in a moment," she told him as she busied herself around the cabin.

John followed her instruction, watching with amusement as his previously spoilt girl made the place into a home. It took a couple of hours to get reasonably straight; they fed, then bedded down the animals for the night.

At last the small dwelling was organised, at least for that night. John lit the stove to heat the stew that Sarah had made for their first night together. As soon as they'd eaten, they dropped exhausted into bed and slept dreamlessly until the first light of dawn. Linnet awoke to the sound of John feeding wood into the stove. Although the sun shone without, the cabin was bitterly cold.

"A sharp frost overnight," John called over his shoulder. "We must keep the stove in at all times. From now on, if you leave the cabin, even for a short while, check the stove is full first."

Linnet shivered, and snuggled back down into the quilts,

squealing as John stalked over to the bed, yanking the covers away from her, leaving her curled and shivering in the centre of the bed.

"Oh no, you don't," he scolded. Grabbing her ankle, he hauled her over to his side of the bed. "Get up, lug-a-bed, I want my breakfast!"

She squealed and tried to grab the covers back from him but he held them out of her reach with one hand while he slapped her rump with the other. "Up!" he ordered again.

She smacked his offending hand away and rose, hurriedly wrapping a blanket around herself. "Bully!" she muttered as she banged a pan down onto the stove.

Linnet spent a busy morning rearranging the furniture to suit herself. She stored all the spare bedding in chests and stacked their supplies of jars and dried goods onto shelves. Then she made bread dough and set it to rise while she hung curtains at the glassless windows. Placing the two cushions she'd helped to embroider upon each rocking chair, she hung two brightly coloured woollen shawls, both of which Sarah had knitted, over the back of each of the two rockers that Hans had crafted himself.

When John returned for lunch, he looked around in astonishment, for Linnet had transformed the cabin into a welcoming and cosy homestead.

They ate a lunch of pickled eggs from a jar packed by Sarah, meant to last them until their own three chickens had settled into their new home and started laying. The eggs were accompanied by the fresh baked bread and some of Sarah's delicious cheese.

"I really wonder how we will manage when Sarah's generous supply of food stock has gone," Linnet confided ruefully.

John hummed thoughtfully. "We should really have our own eggs. Chickens won't lay regularly through winter months but we do have enough vinegar for you to pickle a few before they stop. Did Sarah show you how to make butter and cheese?" he queried.

Linnet looked uncomfortable. "Well, yes," she said doubtfully. "I am not sure I will be able to get cheese made, it needs time to mature."

John smiled at her and said, "We can have a practice at churning butter and see what we can produce."

Linnet nodded, feeling relieved. "I am sure it will be fun!" she enthused.

John cast her an anxious glance. Did she not realise how much hard work was ahead of them if they were to stock the larder before snow came?

"Y-yes, but also hard work if we are to stay fed all winter. I want to hunt for a couple of days to stock up on meat. We will have to smoke it so that it will stay fresh, although once it freezes, meat will stay fresh if it is hung.

"Before I leave here, I need to mend the corral fences. Hans thinks that I should take down a tree, the fir next to the barn. It has grown over tall, if we suffer a heavy gale, it could easily land on top of the barn."

Linnet looked anxious. "Can you manage a tree that size all by yourself?" she asked.

"I think so. It's not a thick trunk but it is tall enough and heavy enough to smash the roof of the barn, should it topple in a gale. We can't afford to risk leaving it where it is. I will probably tackle it tomorrow or the day after."

With so much to do, it took a few days before John finally found the time to cut into the tree base. Linnet came out to watch as he tied rope around various places along the tree trunk, then pulled and pulled until the sweat stood out on his bare back. The tree stood unmoving.

"What's wrong?" Linnet called as John walked over to her, wiping the sweat from his brow with his discarded shirt.

"I think I need to chop the notch into the trunk much wider. The thing is, I don't want the damn thing to drop onto the barn, but should I cut too deep, it might fall in that direction. I want to pull it so that it goes over away from the barn."

"Well then, I can help you pull." She strode towards the tree without awaiting his reply.

John gave her two of the ropes to hold. "No pulling until I say so. If I tell you to stop, you must stop! Understood?"

Linnet braced herself with the ropes wrapped around her back as John had shown her. "Understood and ready!" she called.

He stood in position and took up his own ropes. "All ready?"

She nodded.

"Pull!" he cried. They strained on the ropes; each leaned using all their strength. There was an easing in the ropes and a groaning crack as the tree began to move.

John shouted, "Run away, move left. Go!" They both threw themselves out of the line of the falling tree, which fell with a satisfying crash of cracking branches and fallen cones. Linnet squealed. Clapping her hands, she ran over to where the tree lay horizontal, the branches quivering.

John picked up his shirt, grinning hugely, and walked the length of the tree, running his hands over the knotted bark of the prone trunk with satisfaction. "There's enough wood here to keep us warm all winter. It's very green right now but it should burn in a month or two."

"What do you mean 'green'?" Linnet asked, seating herself on the fallen tree.

"Green wood is unseasoned wood, it still has the sap inside and so it burns with a lot of smoke. Wood should be left to season for a year or two, ideally, before you use it as fire wood."

He was standing with his back to her. Naked to the waist, he surveyed the tree while he explained. Linnet cast her eyes over her husband's bare torso. Beads of perspiration stood proud on the skin of his taut muscles across his shoulders, and she watched, mesmerized, as a line of moisture trickled down the base of his spine and into the waistband of his trousers.

He turned and caught the sultry look upon her face. Flinging aside the shirt he held, he padded towards her, his body loose limbed with predatory lust. "Turn around and lift your skirts," he growled, turning her shoulders so that she lay stomach down over the fallen tree.

She shivered, excited but confused. Her mind raced over the past few days, she could find no fault with her behaviour which might require punishment. She trembled with anticipation; what did her husband have in mind? He exposed her shapely legs, baring her curved behind. Looking around, she saw he was gazing lustily at the provocative sight she presented. He ran his work-rough hands up her smooth skin, his palms outstretched so that his thumbs caught the edge of the mounds of her creamy buttocks. She quivered with desire.

John held the two orbs of her rump within his hands and kneaded them, letting his thumbs drop down between her legs where she felt her body's natural dew gathering. He spread her legs wide then dropped to his knees behind her, she felt him press his face into her glistening folds. Parting her with his tongue, he worked his magic, making her hot and fierce with spiralling need.

She lay with her cheek pressed against the rough bark of the tree trunk. The overwhelming lust that seared between her legs caused her to bite the soft flesh of her forearm as she pushed her hips back against her husband's questing tongue.

She moaned his name as he gripped her thighs, holding her firm while he continued his oral ravishment—frustratingly, he halted before she'd reached her climax. She groused as he stood to loosen his breeches, sighing as she felt him shift behind her, his shaft nudging at her slippery core. Then he drove his erect manhood deep into her sweet, waiting cleft. Holding her churning hips still against his pelvis for a moment, he forced her to match his own steady pace, moving inside her with strong, gliding strokes. She dug her nails into the tree bark and bit down again on her arm.

She barely felt John sweep the soft skein of her hair aside, kissing and nibbling her neck. His hands slid beneath her breasts, gripping them as he increased the tempo of his thrusts. She quickened under him as he pounded into her, fierce and hard. Her climax came as a searing rush of exquisite pleasure that spilled over, her cries blending with his shout as he sang his own cry of release.

It was a few moments before John lifted his body from hers and swept down her skirt, lifting her off the tree. "You will wear me out come spring!" he complained. "I only have to look at you and I want to take you then and there."

She gave a low and sensuous chuckle. Her finger trailed across his naked chest, his copper-coloured paps budded to her touch. He clutched her hand in his and lifted it to his mouth, where he placed a kiss upon her open palm before turning her toward the cabin, giving her a little push in that direction. "Go get your man some victuals, strumpet. I need to keep my energy up if I'm to service such a rapacious wench!"

THE FOLLOWING WEEK passed in a haze of activity. Linnet took out the cut material for her dresses and began the process of making her clothing. The never-ending chores of the homestead kept them both busy as they prepared for the harsh winter soon to come. She successfully produced a pat of butter, hardly able to contain her excitement when, turning the handle of the wooden butter churn, there came the thump, thump, thump of the butter as it finally formed inside the barrel. Cheese took her longer—although she did attempt a roundel of cheese, she decided that since they planned to leave here in the spring, it was pointless to make more. It needed too much time to cure.

CHAPTER 15

*T*he weather grew colder. Leaves fell as morning frosts became bitter and sharp. John finally set off on a three-day hunting trip. He planned to stock their winter larder with fresh venison. It was so cold that the meat would stay fresh once it was hung.

Linnet was not at all happy with the idea of spending three days alone in the cabin, despite John's reassurances that she would be safe if she did as he bid and stayed put. In the end, they were barely speaking when he set off, having kissed his sulking wife goodbye.

John rode Amber, another reason why Linnet was upset. Amber was *her* horse and yet, the first chance he got, John took her horse for his own use. Linnet moped around the cabin on the first day of John's absence and did little, other than keep the stove in.

That night, she awoke alone in darkness. She lay still, listening to the strange sounds outside the cabin, the distant hoot of an owl, the lonely cry of a wolf and the scuffling of small creatures nearby. She dragged herself from the bed to feed the fire.

When she awoke again, it was broad daylight. Refreshed and full of energy, she built the fire, dressed and went about her usual tasks, setting the dough to rise and sweeping out the cabin.

She decided that because the day was sunny and breezy, feeling warmer than it had the day before, she would take the dirty laundry to wash in the nearby stream. She recalled John reminding her to stay inside the cabin while he was gone but she was certain that since the stream was so nearby, she would be safe.

She felt annoyed with John for commandeering her horse; this little act of rebelliousness satisfied her vengeful streak. She gathered the stiff brush that she used for washing the clothes and a bar of strong soap, threw them into the clothes basket, and set off.

It was still a chilly day, despite the sun, and she was glad of the thick shawl she'd wrapped about her. The stream water was freezing but thankfully not actually frozen. She was able to scrub the clothes and rinse them in the clear, swift-running water. Task completed, she stood and rubbed her icy hands, tucking them inside her shawl for warmth.

Gazing hypnotically into the sparkling, spilling water, she heard a high-pitched squeal. She stared around her but could see nothing unusual along the banks of the stream or on the nearby bushes. She stood and listened intently; a snuffling noise appeared to come from inside the nearby shrubbery.

Cautiously, she walked over, her heart racing as she knelt down and gingerly parted the bushes. At first she could see nothing; then, as her eyes adjusted to the gloomy interior, she detected a pair of dark eyes gazing at her. Leaning in toward them, she realised the eyes belonged to a small, rounded brown face—it was the face of a very young child.

Shocked, she stepped back to look about her, expecting a parent to materialize close by, but there was no sound save the tinkling of the stream and the calling of the birds. Linnet bent again into the dark recess of the bush and reached for the small child. Her arms closed upon a surprisingly warm little body, and she lifted it out. "Why, you're only a babe!" she exclaimed as she held aloft a child who was no more than eighteen months and strangely dressed in a pale, soft leather tunic, sewn with small, brightly coloured beads.

On the babe's feet were soft shoes made of the same material, held on by soft strips of leather that criss-crossed the plump little legs. A native infant, perhaps?

The babe regarded her solemnly with large, dark, expressive eyes.

"Goodness! Where on earth have you sprung from?" she spoke aloud, hoping for some response but the baby continued to regard her with an unblinking stare.

She pondered. She could put the child back, hoping that his parents were nearby, watching, and come back in a little while to see if he had gone, but she was concerned about the stream being so close by to where the baby was hidden, she worried he might crawl to the stream and drown. Finally, she decided it was a risk she would have to take—after all, the babe had not attempted to move from the hidey hole in which she'd found him.

Parting the bushes, she placed the baby back onto the ground and the child began to wail. She steeled herself to walk away then turned to glance back. The baby was crawling toward her.

"Oh no," she muttered and returned to pick him up.

As soon as she held him in her arms he leant forward and buried his face into the hollow of her neck. His fat little arms reached up, grabbing fistfuls of her hair. In an instinctive rush of tenderness, she hugged the little body to her and patted the small back. "Hush there, little one," she soothed as she walked up and down the side of the stream, looking around for signs of the child's protectors.

After a few moments, she came to a decision. She absolutely refused to leave such a small baby outside, all alone and unprotected. If the parents of this child wanted him back, they could come to the cabin and ask for him. With her rather cumbersome load of a baby on one hip and the washing basket on the other, she made her way slowly back into the welcoming warmth of her small home.

Dropping the basket into a corner, she turned her attention to the child. First, she attempted to disentangle the child's hands from her hair in order to place him on the bed but like a small leech, he clung to her fiercely. She gave up and, 'wearing' the baby, she poured out a small cup of milk.

She sat in one of the wooden rocking chairs and pulled the shawl from the back of the chair to wrap it around the pair of them. After a minute or two, the child relaxed his hold. Letting go of her hair, he slid down into Linnet's lap. She crooned gently, offering the milk, holding it up to the babe's lips.

The child drank thirstily, finishing the cup and wailing for more. "All right, fear not, there's plenty more, hush now," she soothed. After a second cup of milk, the child plugged in a small thumb then snuggled against Linnet, rapidly falling asleep. She gazed down at the small, round face with its sweep of long lashes and was choked with emotion; how endearing, how trusting.

She lifted the sleeping child to the bed and laid him in the middle, well away from the edge, tucking the shawl tightly around the baby. Straightening up, she put a hand to the small of her back, massaging the ache that sitting in a cramped position with the child had caused.

She looked down at the sleeping babe and realised she didn't know for certain what sex it was. Carefully, so as not to wake the child, she lifted the tunic. Definitely a boy and one with no napkin, which was perhaps not a problem for a native child but a huge one for her!

She remembered the pile of extra bedding that Sarah had insisted she bring and ran to the chest at the foot of their bed. Flinging up the lid, she pulled out the oldest and softest blanket she could find. She tore it into as many napkin type squares as the blanket's size allowed and ended up with eight decent-sized squares and a couple of oblong pieces. She swaddled the babe's nether regions with one of the improvised napkins, covered him up warmly, and left him to sleep.

By the time the child awoke, she'd made porridge with oats for a meal. She had improvised toys, putting together a few safe household items onto a rug in one corner. She'd put a large pot of water on to heat for the babe's bath. The tiny boy sat up and blinked owlishly at her from the bed.

She hurried over to him, crooning baby-talk to soothe him. He watched her solemnly as she changed his makeshift napkin, which was soaked through. She dropped the soiled napkin into a pail.

Feeding the baby was extremely difficult for Linnet, who had no previous experience of small children. She became quite flustered as he kept grabbing the spoon, tipping the contents on Linnet, the floor, or all down the front of himself. Eventually, he seemed to have eaten enough, so she deposited him on the floor while she went to set up a bath for him.

She'd only taken a couple of minutes to organise the filling of the tin and yet, when she turned her attention back to the baby, there was mess everywhere. He'd found the basket of wet washing she had dumped in the corner on her return and pulled all the clothes out onto the floor, then crawled through them with a very dirty napkin, one which failed to contain the contents.

She groaned, picking up the unsavoury little character. His face split into a huge grin as she bent down to him and he lifted his chubby little arms to her. Linnet's heart missed a beat with a flood of tenderness. "You little darling," she purred.

Regardless of his disgusting state, she hugged him, and then quickly stripped off the offending garments, dropping them all into the napkin pail. "I shall be doing nothing but washing at this rate," she muttered as she lowered him into the tub of warm water. The boy adored the warm bath and splashed, chuckling with glee.

She was absolutely enchanted by him and played with him for a while before reluctantly turning her attention to clearing up the mess he'd made. The once clean washing from the basket now joined the overflowing pail of dirty clothing that she placed outside the cabin door to remove the pong of the soiled clothes from the room. When the cabin was straight, Linnet turned back to the tub and retrieved the child.

She dried him in another of Sarah's soft blankets and swaddled him in another makeshift napkin.

"What can I dress you in?" she asked his owlish little face. He grinned, showing several small, even, pearly-white teeth. "Ah, bless, you have toothy-pegs," she crooned. "Auntie Linnet must give you something harder than porridge for your breakfast to keep those little teeth nice and strong."

"Tong," the child repeated happily.

"Oh, you can talk." Linnet was startled.

"L-i-n-n-e-t" she said slowly and then repeated her name several times over but he gave no response. She reached for one of her clean chemises, popping it over his head. With the drawstring tightened, it would do for him to sleep in.

"Ah well, come along, baby, let's put you to bed."

She carried the babe and tucked him in on John's side of the bed. After a moment's consideration, she fetched another, thicker blanket, folded double to place beneath the child.

"Net!" the baby called.

She stopped what she was doing, delighted. "That's right, darling, my name is Lin-net."

"N-n-itt," replied the boy, "an da ka ga gwa," he crowed and reached out, his fat little hands grabbing for her hair.

"What does that mean, poppet? Hair. Come on, little man, say, *hair.*"

"Ay-ah," repeated the child obediently, "ayah."

She laughed and bent, kissing his plump golden cheek. "Go to sleep now, you little rascal." She tucked him firmly into the bed. He plugged in a small thumb; his sooty lashes drooped with tiredness. Soon, he was fast asleep.

As she stroked his forehead tenderly, she wondered where on earth he had sprung from. Hans had told them that there were no native settlements nearby. John had told her not to fear the local tribes since their only interest with them was in trade. It was impossible for a child this age to crawl or toddle any distance. He must have been brought here by someone; the question was, who? They could be outside right now, Linnet realised. Hastily, she went over to bar the door. She closed the shutters, barring those as well. "I wish John were here!" she whispered aloud. Shaking herself out of her reverie she set about making preparations for the morning. Making dough, she set it to rise overnight, then, exhausted by the day's events, she fell onto the bed next to the sleeping child, promptly falling asleep herself.

Linnet awoke at dawn with a small fist lying in her face. She still felt exhausted. The child slept like a small crucified being, spread out like a star, forcing her to cling to the edge of the large bed. Sleeping with a small child was worse, she decided, than sleeping with a man. They both broke wind as frequently, true, a man snored and the babe snuffled. This little boy seemed to take up the entire bed, moving about the space restlessly all night long.

Linnet spent the entire day clearing up after the child. As she struggled back up from the stream with the re-washed laundry, the little child toddled or crawled by her side, slowing down the process considerably. She eventually managed to peg the clothes on the washing line that John had rigged up for her. All day long, the child clung to her skirts as she moved about the business of her daily chores. By the end of the day, she was physically exhausted, yet she felt surprisingly content. She found to her amazement that she enjoyed household tasks. Looking after a small, demanding tyrant was a joy in itself and she found herself hoping that the parents of the babe would not come looking for their child just yet.

For the first time since her marriage, she seriously considered the arrival of children and what might mean for their marriage, with the relentless hard work and lack of privacy, the constant demand on her time and attention. She wondered if John liked children, she supposed that she'd assumed that he wanted children.

Linnet knew that however demanding looking after a child might be, she wanted a baby of her own.

She gave the small boy the small wooden horse that Hans had carved for her to play with. He was delighted with it and crooned lovingly to it. The boy seemed to have a name for it, 'Ko si.'

Linnet taught him the word "horse," he dutifully repeated it and then promptly returned to saying "Ko si." He was now garbed in his original clothes, which Linnet had carefully washed and dried. She marvelled at the intricate bead work, the meticulously sewn quills and little feathers that decorated his tiny tunic. Whoever this child belonged to must love him very much indeed to have spent so much effort decorating his clothes this way, she surmised.

CHAPTER 16

*J*ohn had a successful hunting trip; he'd stalked and shot a young stag, which would provide plenty of meat to last them for a while. He was unaware that his movements were being tracked. Breaking camp in the clearing of a forest, he packed and prepared to leave. Tightening the girth on Amber, he turned to collect his bedroll. When he straightened, he sucked in his breath. He was faced with three native braves.

They were similarly clad in deerskin leggings, all bare-chested except one, who had a breast plate made of quills. This man was exceptionally tall and well-built. He sported a necklace of what looked like claws. All had shaved heads with a line of hair running from the front to back of their skulls, and their hair stood upright, not unlike some crested bird.

John held out his palms to show he held no weapon. He nodded to them, stood still and waited. The large Indian raised his hand in greeting. He nodded at John, then he touched his eye and pointed to John, holding his hand down at knee height. John followed the pantomime and realised straight away these men were looking for something of a small height, possibly a dog or perhaps a child. They wanted to know if he had seen one. John shook his head. The native mimed hunger, rubbing his belly in circles as he gestured to the deer carcass. John nodded and patted the thigh of the animal, gesturing to the man to come forward and cut off a haunch for their use.

It would have done him no good to have refused their request; he was outnumbered three to one.

MEANWHILE, Linnet had spent a much better night with her young charge. She'd decided to make the baby a bed in the tin bath, and he had snuggled down in there quite comfortably. Consequently, she had slept through the night, awaking refreshed. She'd just finished feeding the child his breakfast when she heard what she thought might be the approach of horses. Sure enough upon, opening the shutter to peek outside, she saw John dismounting from Amber. Delighted, she was about to run out and greet him when the boy gave an excited cry. She swept him up into her arms then stepped outside.

She spotted them immediately: three native men. They sat silently mounted upon their horses, watching her with dark, unblinking stares.

Instinctively, she clutched the child tighter, clasping him to her in a protective gesture that was not lost upon the natives watching her.

She stood frozen to the spot as the child called to the natives in an excited babble. His small hand reached up and wound itself in Linnet's loose hair, he bounced excitedly on her hip.

Linnet spotted John by the fence, standing motionless where his horse was tied. If he was startled to see his wife emerge from their home carrying a small native child, he made no sign of it as he stared anxiously at her. She tried to smile at him to reassure him, but she felt too nervous to make the gesture.

One of the men rode forward a few paces while the other two

hung back. He stopped and waited. She glanced down at the child's animated face. He was still bouncing up and down in her arms, oblivious to the tension surrounding him.

Making a decision, she took a deep breath and walked up to the large, muscular native. His skin was a darker bronze than the child's. His dark eyes betrayed nothing of his inner thoughts, let alone his intentions. His nose was slightly bent, as if it had been broken at some point. Bizarrely, his head was shaven, save for a middle strip of hair that ran from his forehead to neck. It appeared to be coloured with ochre paste, which caused the ruff of hair to stand stiffly. He wore a necklace of what looked like animal claws strung about his neck. One ear sported an earring of silver from which hung three small feathers.

He stretched out his arms to take the child. She searched his face to assess his intentions but she could read nothing there, his expression was blank. She realised there was nothing else to do but to trust the child's happy response at seeing this man. She shifted the boy toward the terrifying man. The babe suddenly grabbed her about the neck, snuggling his face into her shoulder, holding her hair tightly.

Gently, she withdrew his arms then, kissing his cheek, swiftly handed him up to the native, who took him in a firm grasp. Holding him against his naked chest he smoothed the child's hair back and spoke gently to him in a soft rumble. The child twisted in his arms and called to Linnet, "Ko si. Mi he wi!"

She held up her palm to the Indian. "Wait, please, wait!" She ran inside quickly and came back clutching the carved wooden horse.

The natives were in the process of turning their horses so she was forced to run alongside, stretching out a restraining hand to the large Indian as she held up the carved figurine. The child reached for it but managed to grab a fist full of her hair at the same time. The native Indian spoke sharply to the child but he clung on tightly and began to wail. With a swift movement, the Indian withdrew a dagger. Before she had time to register fear, he'd cut off the length of hair the child clutched. Man and horse moved swiftly away from her, the child waving the toy horse and a long gleaming rope of Linnet's hair. A thin wail carried back on the breeze as the boy suddenly realised that Linnet was not attached to the hair he squeezed in his tiny fist.

She stood still, staring into the distance long after the natives had disappeared, silent tears slipping unnoticed down her cheeks. She was startled out of her reverie by John, who had come up behind her. He placed his arms about her, holding her close, his chin resting atop her head. After a while he turned her around and led her indoors. There, he settled her into a rocking chair and bade her stay while he went to stable Amber.

Making short work of un-tacking the horse, he settled her down, fed the animals and returned to the cabin. He found his wife sitting silently in the rocker. She appeared to be deep in thought. Hunkering beside her, he took her hand in his. "Where did you find the child?" he asked.

Linnet told him the whole tale, John listened without comment. When she'd finished, he explained about his meeting with the three natives and of the mimed conversation. "Hans told us there were no natives living nearby; I wonder where those three braves came from?" he pondered. "I think, from their attire, they were Abenaki. We were lucky; they are the most warrior-like tribe in these parts. I had the shock of my life when I turned around and there they were, silent and watchful."

Linnet nodded. "I know, the baby was so quiet at first, not at all like any other children I have come across—mind you, I have had very little contact with babies." She sighed. "He was so sweet. I am going to miss him so much!"

John pulled her to her feet and wrapped his arms about her, holding her close. He looked down into her miserable face. He hated what he had to do next, but she had disobeyed him once again and the consequence of her actions had put them both into grave peril. He set her from him and went to the bed, where he seated himself. He saw her watching him with a questioning intensity. "When I left here the other day, I told you not to leave the cabin, yet—"

"If I'd stayed inside, that poor baby might very well have died!" she interrupted.

"Regardless, you should have obeyed me and stayed put. You have put us both in peril because, once again, you did not listen to my instructions. Show me that you understand your error, prove to me that you have matured enough to accept punishment and come and place yourself over my knee and ask me for a spanking. Either that, or you may fetch your hairbrush. The choice is yours."

He could see the internal struggle as her emotions flitted across her face. He had to press his lips together to stop himself from smiling when she stamped her foot, glaring at him from across the room. Not so biddable then. He crooked his finger at her, eyebrow raised. He felt a sense of relief when at last she took a faltering step toward him, sidling closer, her hands behind her—already protecting her threatened derriere.

He patted his lap. "Come, darling, you know that you will feel better afterward. A spanking will help you to release all that pent-up emotion over the child."

Her chest heaving, she took a deep, shaky breath and almost flung herself across his lap.

John flipped up her heavy skirt and thick flannel petticoat, baring her curvaceous bottom. He rubbed the soft peachy flesh, kneading and stroking. He began by peppering her with small smacks, landing the swats ever faster and closer together as he set a cadence, covering the whole area of her bottom. She squirmed and gasped but did not throw back her hands to protect her rear. He slowly turned her cheeks from blushing pink to crimson red.

He knew that she was determined to stay proudly silent throughout her ordeal but as the spanking progressed and he landed more and more heavy spanks on the tender spots at the tops of her thighs, she gave into her grief. Weeping loudly, she wailed her regret.

Up until now, she had been just too damned wilful. She needed to learn that there would be consequences each and every time she disobeyed him. He had to remain consistent if she were to learn to mind him, even though in disobeying him on this occasion, she may well have saved a small child's life. She needed to understand it could have gone horribly wrong. If those natives had decided to see things differently, they might have attacked. They could be lying dead right now. Linnet needed to understand that. He halted the spanking in order to explain what might have been. She simply sniffled, listening but making no reply to his explanation. He continued to slap her pink, quivering cheeks.

He surmised she needed the release a spanking would give her to help with coming to terms with handing the child back to his tribe. He did not intend for this to be a long punishment, just a short, sharp reminder of what she could expect when she disobeyed him, regardless of the circumstances. He was delighted that she'd come willingly across his lap. Perhaps this might be a turning point for them both; maybe she would be more inclined to obedience from here on in? He sincerely hoped so.

Her wails turned into earnest sobs and he tipped her upright, cradling her in his loving arms, smoothing her tangled hair back from her hot, tear-drenched face, wiping her wet cheeks with his thumbs. "It looks as though I shall just have to give you a baby of your own to love. Would you like to make a child with me, dearest girl?"

Her mouth curved into a sweet smile, "Oh, I should adore a baby, Joh—I expect you would want a son?"

His eyes twinkled. "I would love either, but what I shall most enjoy is conceiving one with its very beautiful mother!"

He lowered his head to kiss her with all the passion of a man who has abstained for a number of days. She clung to him and they tipped sideways onto the bed, entwined together. He prayed that their lovemaking would bear fruit.

$\sim$

THE DAYS PASSED by in a whirl of activity, there were so many preparations to make before the snows came. Both of them were exhausted when they fell into bed at night, all thoughts of making babies were forgotten.

The day came when they awoke to a white covering of powdery snow. Linnet was thrilled with how pretty everything looked. The air had a scent to it that only a fall of snow can produce: sharp, clean, brittle and bright.

They fed the animals and set off for a stroll. "We won't be able to walk through the snow soon, not once it falls heavily," John told her. "It will be far too deep; it will turn very, very cold."

Linnet skipped ahead of him and gathered up a handful of the soft snow, throwing it at his head. John charged after her and there followed a fierce snowball fight which left Linnet gasping for breath from giggling. They trudged home, wet, tired, but blissfully happy.

During the next few weeks, the temperature dropped, the weather froze and a thick snowfall covered the ground. As John had predicted, the snow was so deep it was difficult to walk at all, even over to the barn to tend the animals. John struggled daily to see to their needs and kept clearing the never-ending falls of snow from the path he had dug to the barn and outbuildings. Despite the struggles, Linnet was enjoying the closeness brought about by the harsh weather, and the covered landscape was stunning in its cloak of dazzling white.

Inside the cabin, it was always cosy, and the aromatic smell of Linnet's daily baking wafted through the warm indoor air. The fire was constantly in, giving a cheerful glow to their small abode. Thick snow on the roof insulated the cabin from the worst of the cold. The evenings were spent happily in front of the fire. John would read aloud to Linnet or he would continue her lessons in the game of chess. He had started to teach her aboard the ship, but it had been some time since their last lesson and Linnet had forgotten many of the moves he'd taught her. John had to begin again and teach her from scratch.

He watched her as she frowned in concentration, her pearly teeth catching her bottom lip. Her lovely thick, red gold hair swung forward as she made her move and placed her bishop in jeopardy. Her hair caught the light from the fire, burnishing her locks to liquid gold. John's eyes travelled downward over the swell of his wife's breasts. All at once, he wanted the game over. He moved his queen and took her bishop.

Linnet flung up her hands with a sigh, shaking her head. "I swear; I'll never understand the moves that each piece can make!"

John moved the board aside and stood behind her. "You will, given time. You already know most of the pieces. I am very impressed with how quickly you've mastered the game, my love."

He bent forward, kissing her neck, running his hands through the soft skein of her hair. He slipped his palms lower until he cupped her breasts through the fabric of her dress. She turned her head and her lips met his in a lingering kiss. He stood and pulled her to her feet, sat down upon the chair and attempted to pull her onto his lap but instead, she slid to the floor before him. She placed her hand over the swelling in his groin. "Hmm, I have another sort of game in mind," she purred.

"Certainly, my love. I think you need tutoring in the art of pleasing your husband."

She cocked her head to one side. "Oh, really?" Her hand slid boldly downward, massaging the hardened bulge inside his breeks. Stilling her hand, he loosened his breeches, releasing his throbbing organ. Coiling a hand in her hair, he guided her downward toward his cockstand.

It seemed that Linnet understood what it was he desired from her because without hesitation she took his firm shaft into her mouth. He cradled her head in his hands, groaning in pleasure as he wondered how long he could withstand the exquisite waves of pleasure that the suction of her mouth created. Jerking suddenly, he almost reached release. He yanked Linnet away before it was too late. She gave a soft, throaty chuckle.

He turned her swiftly, pushing up her skirts, uncovering her long slender legs and creamy bottom. Fondling her between her divide, he parted her legs and his fingers readied her, fluttering over her folds and tapping her ridged pearl, reducing her to a quivering wetness. With a sharp tug towards him, he pulled her down onto his lap, impaling her with a quick upward thrust. She gasped as she sat back and he sank deep into her soft flesh.

Holding her firmly, with both his hands either side of her waist, he lifted her up and lowered her again onto his thrusting shaft. He pushed himself deep up inside her slippery mound. Linnet moaned, writhing as her sheath convulsed around his manhood.

He made quick work of the fastenings at the neck of her gown, unlacing the front of her dress so her breasts spilled into his waiting palms. He teased and tormented her burgeoning nipples as she began to gyrate over his lap, abandoning herself to the enjoyment of his embedded shaft.

John lifted her up and held her high in the air, turning her about so that she faced him. He lowered her slowly back over him, allowing his erect length to slip sensuously into her wetness. She shuddered as he filled her deeply, lowering his face to her bosom, suckling first one breast and then the other, biting and nipping each budded nub in turn.

She wound her arms around his neck. He raised his head to kiss her, stifling the little cry she made as he snapped his hips demandingly. His tongue flicked in and out of her mouth, matching the rhythm of his internal onslaught. She threw back her head, arching back as he increased his tempo.

Suddenly, they were both thrown to the floor as the chair gave way beneath them. They clutched one another as they were spilled from the chair, Linnet giggling helplessly.

He rolled them over until she lay on top of him. He gently smoothed the snarled mop of hair away from her smiling face.

Becoming serious, she stared deep into his eyes then lowered her mouth to his. His thumbs caressed her cheeks as they kissed languorously. Their passion rekindled, Linnet slid down the length of his hard body, astride him. Raising herself above his swollen staff, she lowered herself onto him, sliding down his length. He filled her completely.

She rode him hard. John held his hands on either side of her waist, holding her steady as he ground himself upward into her yielding warmth. The exquisite sensations building within him flooded through him, finally exploding into a kaleidoscope of fathomless delight. He gave one almighty thrust, convulsed with a shout, and relaxed into a shuddering release. He watched her face as she came apart, her spent cries a thing of beauty to his loving ear.

He pulled her down to lie beside him, his arm circling her, a hand cradling the back of her head. Gently, he stroked his wife's hair, letting the burnished curls slip through his open fingers. When he felt he could speak again, he whispered into her ear, "Your secret is out: you are a wicked hussy but I love you!"

She gave a throaty chuckle and, turning her head into his shoulder, she nipped him. "I am your hussy, 'tis true. I love you too."

He wrapped his arms tightly about her as she gave a shiver. "Oooh, it's turned so cold!"

John lifted her onto the bed. "Tuck your hands under my arms." She did as he bid and pushed her hands deep under his armpits, where he was cosily warm. He wrapped the covers around them in a tight cocoon. Gradually, she grew warm and they lay together, savouring the delicious heat, gazing into the hypnotic flames of the fire before drifting into sleep.

CHAPTER 17

One night a few days later, Linnet awoke in the dark. She lay still, listening to the familiar sounds of John's breathing. As she snuggled drowsily into the warmth of the bed, she heard a scraping noise at the cabin door. Alert now, she listened but heard nothing. Then she heard it again, an odd, scrabbling sound. Could it be the natives back again?

She patted John on the back.

"Mm, huh?" John mumbled, half asleep.

"Wake up!" she hissed urgently. "Listen!"

There was the scraping noise again. They lay still, both listening intently.

"Wait here," John finally whispered.

"No, if you're getting up then so am I!" She hastily scrambled after him.

He went to the stove first, throwing more wood on, then he lit a taper for the lantern, which he handed to Linnet.

"All right, you hold that for me. I intend going outside."

She trembled. "No, don't open the door; there is no need to go outside." She gripped him fearfully.

"We have livestock, I need to make certain are safe. They are vitally important to our survival and our way out of here come spring. Be a good girl and follow my instructions even if I am still outside. If I order you to bolt the door, do as I say without argument. All shall be well, calm down!" He reached out and traced his knuckle down the side of her anxious face, his voice softening. "I am just being cautious. The noise is probably only a wolf scratching his back on our cabin wall." He pulled on his boots and reached for his coat and muffler.

He took down the musket and shot, priming the gun. She stood and watched him uneasily, shaking with cold and fright. "Be careful. Perhaps we should just wait until it is light?"

He shook his head. "No, I would rather take a quick look and ascertain that all is well with the livestock."

At the door he put his ear to it, listening, but the sound outside had stopped. Cautiously, he opened the cabin door and stepped out. Linnet stood in the doorway and held the lantern high, the flickering light turning the white snow to gold. John walked a little way from the cabin, where he stood still and glanced both ways along the walls. "I can't see anything here… ah…"

He hunkered down on one knee, studying the snow.

"What have you found?" she called anxiously.

He straightened up with a look of terror on his face then immediately began to run towards the door of the cabin. "Cougar! Be ready to shut the door!" he bawled.

There was a terrible snarling roar as a huge dark object flew through the air from around the corner of the cabin. John was already halfway inside the doorway when the mountain lion slashed at him, knocking his legs out from under him. He fell to the floor with a thump and gave a terrible shriek. Linnet leapt to the stove where she grabbed hold of the iron skillet and swung the pan at the terrifying sight of the big cat's snarling face, catching a blow to the end of the creature's nose. The animal roared with pain and reared back, which gave her the moment she needed to drag John. Desperately, she attempted to pull him into the safety of their cabin, sobbing with fright; the cougar was so close that she could smell its fetid breath. The creature raised a huge paw and slashed at John's leg once again. He screamed in agony.

Galvanised by his terrible cry, she rolled John inside the cabin, fighting the cat for her husband's life. The feline lunged forward with a lash, the vicious claws of its paw fully extended. Linnet reacted instinctively, smashing the animal hard on the head with the skillet once more, scoring a direct hit. There was a split second where the cougar dropped to its haunches and appeared stunned, whereupon Linnet slammed the door shut and threw down the heavy wooden cross bar.

For a terrifying minute or two, the large cat battered at their door, raging with growls and roars of impotent rage. Finding that this achieved nothing, finally it gave up, slinking off into the darkness. John lay writhing in agony on the floor. His leg was a bloody mess, his breeches in tatters.

Linnet, shaking, ripped a blanket off the bed and tossed it about his shoulders. "Can you move?" she asked.

John shook his head, his eyes held tight shut, his face white. "Water…" he whispered.

She spun away, quickly returning with a ladle of water which she held to his lips. "I will make you as comfortable as I can but then I must tend that wound." She remembered Ned telling her that bear scratches were poisonous and the best cure was to wash them in alcohol. She assumed cat gouges should be treated in the same way. She placed a pillow under John's head and left him on the floor where he lay.

She heated water, gathered clean cloth and picked up the bottle of whisky that John had bought from Mr. Penman's shop. She poured an equal measure of whisky into a pan of boiled water, hoping it was enough—she had never seen anything like this wound before. Swallowing the bile that rose in her throat, she cut away what was left of John's breeches.

He was floating in and out of consciousness, obviously in a fog of pain. Linnet tore up a sheet ready to use as bandages then, when she was ready, she began to swab out the dreadful wound. John gave an agonized yell then, thankfully, blacked out. She worked quickly before he could regain consciousness. Whole lengths of flesh hung loose from his leg. She cut the smaller shreds of flesh away while moving the larger pieces back into place as best she could.

Finally satisfied that the wound was thoroughly clean, she bound his leg up firmly with the strips of clean sheet. She scrubbed the blood from the floor and from her hands. Stripping off her nightgown, which was also covered in blood, she replaced it with a day dress. She tucked quilts about her patient then put the pail full of its gory water and rags in the corner of the room. She felt nauseous at the sight of it but knew she daren't venture outside to dispose of the contents, not with a lion in the vicinity. She fought against the faintness and lay down upon the bed, shivering violently with shock.

Only an hour ago they had lain in this very bed, safe and warm lovingly together. If only John had listened to her and not stepped outside. She had trusted his judgement but look what had happened. She had believed that John had known what he was doing when he'd ventured out. Oh, why had she put such trust in him and not insisted that he remain safe inside with her?

Round and around in her head this jumble of confusing thoughts churned until, eventually, unbelievably, she must have slept, for she awoke late to the bright light of day and a reedy voice calling her name. John was awake but in agony. She checked his swathed wound, it was seeping blood.

"John, do you think you could make it up onto the bed?" she asked.

"I can but try," he returned bravely.

She hooked her arms beneath his and pulled him into a sitting position. His face ran with perspiration, his teeth gritted with effort. "Are you sure you can do this? Would you prefer to lie back down on the floor?" She worried it was too much for him but he shook his head.

"No to both. I cannot stay on the floor—for one thing, my back is hurting like the very devil and for another, I am blocking the route to the door. Let's just get this over with."

She nodded. Tucking her hands under his arms, she struggled to get him on his feet but finally, he stood, although he swayed alarmingly, leaning heavily on her. They made slow progress even though it was only a step or two to the bed. When they reached the bedside, John sank onto it gratefully. She let him rest for a second or two before lifting his legs up onto the bed. She was anxious. John lay gasping, perspiration peppering his forehead. His eyes were closed, the pallor of his face matched the sheet he lay on.

Gently she placed a pillow beneath his head and drew the covers over him. "Would you like a drink?" she asked as she smoothed the mass of dark hair away from his clammy forehead.

With a slight movement, he shook his head. "No, need sleep," he mumbled.

Linnet frowned, concerned. "Well, if you are sure, then I shall quickly check on the livestock but when I return, you must drink. I shall tend to that dressing on your leg as well."

He merely grunted.

She watched him anxiously for a while. Once satisfied that he was merely sleeping, she built up the fire, put more water on to heat, and ate a little bread and butter then drank some milk. She wasn't particularly hungry but knew she knew she ought to keep up her strength. Wrapping herself warmly, she cast an anxious glance over John before setting off to feed the animals in the barn. Closing the door behind her, she halted. The sight confronting her caused her to gasp.

The snow was splattered red, presumably with John's blood. There seemed to be so much of it, she was dismayed. No wonder John was desperately weak, not simply from the terrible wounds he'd sustained but also from the loss of so much blood. She fetched the shovel and cleared the blood-soaked snow as far from the cabin as she dared walk, throwing it under the trees then piling fresh snow over the bloody snow to cover it. She didn't want the smell of blood attracting more predators. She worked steadily, keeping a wary eye out for cougars.

She noticed the musket lying in the snow where John had dropped it the previous night. Picking it up, she kept it close as she made her way to the barn. There had been no fresh snowfall since John had last cleared the path, although it remained slippery.

When she opened the barn door, she found Amber grateful to see her; she swung her head toward her, ears pricked eagerly as she whickered a soft greeting. Linnet went straight to her horse and petted her soft nose, soothing the troubled mare. Both the horses seemed nervous, they had obviously heard the disturbance during the night. The other horse snorted and pawed the ground, determined not to be left out of any reassurance. Linnet soothed her until she, too, was calm.

She mucked out the horse stalls, laid fresh hay and gave the animals a feed. The water trough she filled with snow which would soon melt in the warmer temperature of the barn. She settled down on the small wooden stool to milk the cow. The gentle creature stood patiently while she rested her cheek against the animal's warm hide and tugged her teats with gentle firmness. Before long, the milk pail was half full of frothy milk. Linnet moved the pail out of the cow's kick range, covered it with a clean cloth used for the purpose, and went to perch on an empty trough. She watched the three animals contentedly chewing their food.

A small shuddering sob escaped her and soon she was weeping wretchedly. She threw herself down upon the pile of fragrant hay and gave full vent to her misery. When at last she was completely drained, she dried her eyes and rolled onto her back. What on earth would she do if the worst happened and John died?

She shied away from such an unbearable thought. He wouldn't die, she would make certain of that! She realised that part of her misery was sheer rage with John for making such a dangerous mistake. Yet, he was as human as the next man, so why did she expect perfection from him? Was it because he seemed to expect perfection from her and punished her for her mistakes? The wound he'd received could very likely kill him, the shock alone could do that, and then where would she be?

Fresh tears welled and impatiently she brushed them away. It was strange how important John had become to her, so much so that she could no longer imagine life without him. Yet she had been bitterly opposed to their marriage. She realised that, quite simply, he was everything to her now. He was her life now and without him, she would struggle to go on alone.

Not for the first time since their arrival at the Lammers' cabin, Linnet felt a wave of homesickness for Lavenstock Hall. She liked this country with its wilderness and wide open spaces, yet she yearned for the softness of England's rolling countryside, for the temperate climate of that pleasant isle. She wondered how long it might be before she saw her homeland again, if ever.

She found herself wishing for Sarah's sensible presence. She wondered if she could make the journey back to the farmstead in this snow. Almost as soon as the thought entered her head, she dismissed it, she knew the snow lay too thick upon the ground. She would have to manage alone; she had no choice but to make her man well.

This time she would be the strong one and he, in his weakness, would learn to lean upon her. Other than the vow of obedience that John constantly reminded her of, she had also promised to care for him, in sickness and in health. She straightened her shoulders. Now was the time to leave that spoiled English aristocratic girl behind; she was a woman and no longer the proud, 'green' girl that John had married. It was imperative that she succeed in nursing him back to health, for both their sakes—the alternative was unthinkable.

She stood, determined, a new mantle of maturity settled upon her. It was time to get on with the tasks. She had to take on all the chores now, there was no time for her to sit and mope. There was bread to bake, the blood-soaked clothes from last night to wash. John must have some wholesome broth to help him build up his strength. With a new resolve, Linnet petted the beasts one last time and checked that all was as it should be before she locked the barn and made her way back to the warmth and security of their cabin.

John was asleep when she returned, which enabled her to complete her chores. By the time he woke some hours later, the cabin was straight and the aromatic smell of the cooked broth and the homely smell of freshly baked bread wafted about the cabin. Far from whetting his appetite, however, the smell made him nauseous. He lay quietly and watched his wife move efficiently around the cooking stove; she looked beautiful and fully in control.

Her hair, hastily pinned up earlier in the day, tumbled free of its pins, wisps curled damply around her flushed face, pink with exertion, a film of perspiration glistened upon her brow. Who would have thought that the haughty, spoiled Miss Linnet Wainwright—correction, *Lady* Linnet Wainwright, John grinned— would make such an able and domesticated wife? He praised himself for seeing through her veneer to the potential of her strength. This woman was everything he'd hoped for… and more.

He shifted, wincing; giving an involuntary groan as pain sliced through his damaged leg. Immediately, Linnet was beside him. "How are you, my love?" she asked, placing a concerned hand upon his forehead, checking for fever.

"Thirsty," he croaked, his voice ragged with pain.

She went at once and fetched him a cup of fresh milk to drink. "When you have quenched your thirst, I have some broth ready for you."

John pushed the mug away. "No. I'm not hungry." He lay back against the pillows, his eyes closed.

He was surprised when, a few moments later, he was eased forward as more pillows were tucked behind him so that he was raised almost upright. Linnet settled beside him, a bowl cradled in her hands. She tucked a cloth under his chin and raised a spoon to his lips. "Come now, open your mouth," she ordered crisply. John did as she bid. To his surprise, the broth tasted good and he found he was able to eat almost the entire contents of the bowl.

Linnet calmly removed it and fetched a bowl of hot water. "What is that for?" John enquired suspiciously.

"For your wash," she replied briskly. He shook his head. "No, I'll attend to that in a day or so when I am feeling able."

She ignored him, pulling the covers back. She unfastened the buttons of his shirt, all the while, his hands slapped at hers crossly.

Finally, she stood. With her hands on her hips, she glared down at him. "Now you just listen to me, John Foster. You will tire yourself unnecessarily with this futile behaviour and then, when you are exhausted, I shall wash you anyway! So let us just make this easy on the both of us and get it over with quickly. I have a lot to do and you are not helping."

John glowered at her. "I am not a child and I will not be bathed like one!" He glared at her mulishly.

Linnet considered him for a moment or two before dropping to her knees beside him. "Listen to me, darling, when I was sick, you took care of me. Now that you are sick, allow me to care for you. You are my husband, in sickness and in health, under the eyes of God. Now please, let me fulfil my obligation to you as your wife. Please, do not resist the help that is my duty to give and yours to receive. After all, I allowed you to care for me when I was ill."

He gave her a rueful look but he finally nodded. "Get on with it then," he said, resigned, "and you can stop looking so damned smug about it!"

He lay with his eyes closed throughout the entire proceedings, only wincing once, when she jarred his wounded leg. Once he was clothed in a clean nightshirt, Linnet placed the bedcovers over him, turning back the material at the end of the bed that covered his legs so that the air could circulate around them. She fetched a bowl of clean, freshly heated water and more cloths.

John watched her suspiciously. "What torture are you planning?"

She wagged her figure at him then brought him a large pewter goblet filled with rye whiskey. "Here is your reward for being so brave."

He appeared to cheer up immediately, sipping gratefully at the liquor she handed him. Linnet left him to enjoy his reward in peace. She gathered up the pot of herbal, medicinal ointment that Sarah had given her for healing wounds. Glancing across at her husband, she saw that he finally slept; she hoped the effect of the whiskey would ensure that he stayed asleep while she changed the dressing on his leg. Gently, she wet the bandages until they were soaked and would peel away from the wound easily. Then she very carefully lifted the first of the dirty dressings away from his leg.

"Sly vixen!"

She almost leapt out of her skin with surprise, glancing up into a pair of twinkling grey eyes. "Oh, you startled me! Your wound cannot be left or it will fester, do you wish to take some more whiskey? It might help with the discomfort."

His gaze held steady as he shook his head. "No, I'll not take any more liquor. I can see you're determined on this and so your lovely face will have to distract me from the discomfort."

"Are you sure? This is going to hurt." Linnet turned pale, she trembled.

"Do what needs to be done, I know you will be as gentle as you can be," he reassured her.

"Oh, darling, I promise I will try not to cause you unnecessary pain," she said as she tried to control her distress. But her hands shook as she continued with her ministrations.

John was very brave and did not move a muscle as she removed the final strip of cloth. His leg was a ghastly sight; the flesh still vibrantly mottled and swollen. The wound seeped but at least it did not smell putrid. Linnet was apprehensive. Knowing that the worst was yet to come, she hesitated to continue.

John encouraged her gruffly. "Get it over with, there's a good girl… just get on with what needs to be done." She poured whiskey into the water as she had done the previous night then, resolute, she began to gently wash the wounds.

He flinched, gritted his teeth, beads of sweat standing out on his brow.

Linnet carried out the task with speedy efficiency, then began to coat the wounds liberally with the herbal ointment. John ground his teeth, muttering under his breath. She bound up the wounds and he visibly relaxed.

"Fetch me that damned whisky!" he gasped. She did as he bid and held the jar out. "No, you first," he said, "you look as though you need it, love."

She nodded and tipped the jar, taking a large swig. Coughing, she swiped the back of her hand over her mouth then passed the bottle to John.

"I wonder how many married couples have their first year spent in the company of pirates, are shipwrecked, meet natives, and are attacked by wild bears and mountain lions?" she mused solemnly.

"Not that many, I think we might have been singled out for the pleasure," John rasped wryly before falling back onto the pillows and losing consciousness.

She retrieved the whiskey and smoothed his dark hair away from her husband's chiselled face. "Who wants a conventional marriage? Not I, at any rate!" She kissed his forehead.

CHAPTER 18

"What is the date today?" Linnet asked some weeks later.

"The twenty-third. Good grief, do you realise that two days' hence, it will be Christmas Day!" John exclaimed in surprise.

Over the past few weeks, John's leg had healed well. Although it was still very painful, the wound had scabbed over nicely and he had no fever or infection even though the scratches were deep. John assured Linnet that this was solely due to her meticulous care and cleansing of the wounds. Mountain cats, he informed her, had very dirty claws, and most who survived their initial attack died later from the infection that followed.

He sat in a chair, whittling himself a pipe and marvelling as he watched Linnet competently kneading dough for bread. He still found it astonishing that his defiant girl had become such a domestic and efficient wife.

"Christmas will seem strange with only the two of us. I loved Christmas at home with all the spicy smells, the dancing and the giving of gifts. The balls..." Her voice trailed away wistfully.

John rose awkwardly and hobbled over to her. Slipping an arm about her waist, he hugged her. "Our first Christmas together, and we shall make the most of it because it may be the last we ever spend alone together."

He arched his brow, and Linnet blushed and sighed. He knew how much she wanted a baby. "John, we could visit Hans and Sarah!"

He hated to disappoint her. "I'm sorry, darlin', but quite apart from the snow, there's my darned leg."

She nodded, crestfallen. "Oh yes, your poor leg, I'd quite forgotten but never mind. You are right, it might just be the last Christmas we spend alone together. We shall make it special! This afternoon, I will start baking some tasty cakes and tarts."

He chuckled, relieved by how well she had taken his refusal to travel. "I'll fetch some greenery to decorate the cabin. I want it to feel like a proper Christmas for you."

She hugged him. "Are you sure you want to risk your leg walking outside?" she asked with concern.

"Yes," he affirmed. He was tired of being an invalid, cooped up inside all day.

She kissed him on the cheek and danced away coquettishly. "I must go and tend our animal friends. I have named the pony Pickle because she's so very naughty. At home, Cook always called me *Pickle.*"

"I wonder why?" John answered facetiously.

She ignored his comment. "Do you know that Pickle crept up behind me yesterday and pushed me flat on my face with her nose?"

He chuckled. "That's because you spoil those darn horses."

"I treat Amber and Daisy the cow in exactly the same way as I treat Pickle, and they are perfect ladies! I'm sorry, but Pickle is a monster!"

Linnet left to make her way over to the barn to begin her daily chores, which always started with mucking out, then milking. John waited a moment before going over to the largest chest, where he had hidden the small wooden casket that he was carving for

Linnet's Christmas present: a box in which to keep her jewellery. She'd lost most of her finery aboard the ship, but the best and most valuable pieces they had saved. Hans had tutored John and he had carved the top of the casket with fruit and entwined leaves. He was pleased with the way it was coming along, and hoped he would be able to finish it in time for Christmas Day.

Linnet, meanwhile, had finished milking Daisy, covered the pail of milk, and gone to a pile of hay in which she had hidden her Christmas present to John. She'd taken some of the green velvet that John had given her for her dressmaking and was in the last stages of making him a fine waistcoat. She'd almost finished the embroidery work on the front panels of the garment. When that was complete, all that was required to finish it off was the addition of five buttons. It was the buttons that caused her the most concern. She had no spares available, and she couldn't take any from John's clothing without him noticing. What to do? She would just have to give him the gift minus buttons, he could choose which of his garments to take some buttons from or wait until they were in Boston and able to purchase some.

After an hour of sewing, her hands felt frozen. She'd had enough of sitting in the chilly barn. She petted the horses and left them to their hay, closing up the barn. She stepped into the warm cabin, the wonderful astringent scent of wet woodland wafting over her. Tangy and fresh, the smell of spruce and ivy mixed with the heavier lingering smell of wintergreen and fir. John stood over a pile of freshly cut greenery, obviously trying to decide where to place it all.

"It smells heavenly!" Linnet exclaimed, delighted.

He looked up from his labours. "Thank goodness you're back. I have absolutely no idea where to put the stuff," he confessed, wiping his brow.

She could tell that it had been a little more tiring than he'd care to admit, cutting and dragging back branches. He rubbed his leg and she realised it must hurt. She hung up her cloak and examined the fragrant heap of greenery. "Let's keep some outside to replace the dead as it dries out," she suggested. Gathering up an armful, she placed it beside the door, ready to store outside.

Linnet pulled out a chair, clambered up and John handed the greenery up to her. Once they'd finished, she thought the cabin looked quite festive. She dug out some red ribbon from amongst her sewing then tied bunches of greenery together with it; the splash of red enhanced the green foliage. Then she and John spent a busy couple of afternoons preparing for their special Christmas Day. Linnet baked and cooked while John stocked up the firewood and melted snow over the fire for their water supply.

Christmas morning dawned. They made slow, sweet love, wishing each other a Happy Christmas in their own unique way. After breakfast, John said a prayer for their family and friends. He asked the Lord to keep them safe and in good health. They even sang a carol, but then decided they should complete all their morning chores. Survival meant their routine was as any other day and certain tasks, such as tending to the livestock, still needed to be done, even though it was Christmas.

Later, Linnet changed into her newly finished, green velvet gown. She had set a hunk of venison to roast, taken from the kill that John had made when the natives had appeared. The icy weather had kept the meat fresh. She'd made an herb suet crust to accompany the meat and soaked dried peas overnight to prepare them to have with the meal. John changed into in dark breeches and a fine lawn shirt.

Linnet excitedly fetched him her gift, wrapped in a piece of plain calico and tied with a red bow. She placed the package on his lap. "Merry Christmas, my love!" she said, watching as he carefully unfolded the cloth and lifted out the waistcoat. He held it up so that the delicate embroidery on the front panels gleamed in the flickering light. The rich embroidery thread of the yellow ivy, entwined with flowers of shades of gold and russet reds, glinted sumptuously in the candlelight. It was a beautifully made garment, and he knew that Linnet must have spent many hours on it to have produced such fine work.

He was deeply touched, and he gathered her in his arms and held her close. "Thank you, my darling, it is the most beautiful waistcoat I have ever seen and I shall treasure it always. Now my gift to you, I hope you will not be too disappointed when you see it. I am afraid it lacks the skill and beauty of your waistcoat. Sit down and close your eyes."

She did as he bid and John placed the casket on her lap. She opened her eyes and exclaimed with delight, "Oh my, John, it is lovely, a jewellery box, it is so beautifully carved! Thank you, darling!"

He grinned, delighted by her response. "I have been frantically carving the lid every time you went and saw to the stock. I was so sure that you would come back and catch me at it!"

Linnet giggled. "And I sat freezing cold in the barn each day sewing until my fingers were too numb to sew anymore!"

He acted startled. "So you haven't been feeding the stock? Poor creatures will be dead from starvation!"

She smacked his arm playfully. "You... They are pampered, spoiled beasts that seem to demand more of me each time I visit them!"

He leaned in and kissed her cheek. "I know because it is you who spoil the wretched creatures, they will be totally unmanageable come spring. How is that meat coming along? It smells absolutely delicious and I am starving!"

She hopped up and checked on the progress of their meal. "All's well," she reported. "Shall we play a game of chess and you could nibble on a tart while we play? The meal will not be ready for us to eat for at least an hour."

John winked. "Nibble on a tart, eh? I'm not sure I'd go so far as to call you a tart, wench!" She smacked his cheek playfully and he hauled her into his lap, kissing her until she stilled, acquiescing to him. He finally shoved her off, giving her rump a resounding slap.

"We will continue this later, you voracious strumpet!" he promised.

She giggled and went to fetch the chess set Hans had carved for them.

They spent a happy day just enjoying being together. After the chess, which John won, as he had won all their previous games, they played parlour games that Linnet had learned to play as a small child, giggling as they teased one another, each becoming more physically acutely aware of the other.

It had been a few weeks since they had last enjoyed conjugal relations due to John's damaged leg but he was determined that, wound or no, he was going to pleasure his wife that Christmas night. The meal of roast venison, glazed with honey, was mouth-watering, and the accompanying suet crust and peas complemented the venison perfectly. The two of them made complete pigs of themselves, so that they had no room left for the English plum pudding that Linnet had made for their dessert, using a mixture of dried fruits that Sarah had packed for them from her own stores.

"Never mind the pudding, keep until tomorrow." He was more concerned with another kind of dessert.

Linnet pouted prettily. "You do not even love me enough to sample my puddings," she huffed petulantly.

His lips twitched. "Oh, I'll sample your puddings, milady!" He caught her to him and swiftly eased her down on her back. She squealed as he bent his head, burying his face into her cleavage. He understood her tepid reaction. She was concerned for his injured leg.

He grasped her chin, turning her so that she was forced to look at him. "I want you. I will be careful of my wound, but I can wait no longer. I mean to have you tonight."

He bent his head to her lips, and this time she wound her arms sinuously about his neck without complaint, proving to him that her need was as great as his for her. John enjoyed her plump sweet lips but he wanted more. Sliding the sleeves of her gown down her arms, he trailed kisses over her shoulders, licking her soft décolletage. He unlaced the front of her gown, baring the pale mounds of her breasts. Her nipples hardened under his gaze. Mesmerised, he drew one burgeoning nubbin into his mouth, giving a delighted husky sigh as his tongue curled around the sweet morsel of raised flesh.

She moaned. His manhood leapt with excitement, impatient to get to the main dish, but John wanted to savour this, it had been a long time since he'd taken his wife. He started to remove her clothing completely. Lowering the velvet gown, he slid the soft material over her contours, stopping to kiss each part of her body as it was painstakingly revealed. Her breath hitched as he removed her petticoat and unlaced her stays. Her naked skin was burnished by the flickering flames from the fire. He removed his shirt, savouring the sight of her voluptuous body as she lay on her back with one leg bent, shadowing her sex, watching him, waiting patiently for his attention.

Her copper hair spilled around her like a halo, the richness intensified by the fiery light thrown from the fire. Her eyes morphed into the misty sea-green that he now knew indicated arousal. She stretched seductively under the warmth of his gaze, a small sensual smile played across her lips as she watched intently as he unbuttoned his breeches. As he released his engorged phallus, she stretched out a languorous hand, running her fingertips lightly up the length of him. He pulsed at her touch. Sliding her palm down, she cupped his aching sac in her hand.

"Why do you not remove your breeks?" she asked throatily.

"I thought to leave them on as protection for my leg," he replied.

She nodded. Rising up to kneel before him, she tossed her head. Her hair cascaded and rippled down her back like molten gold. She opened her mouth and ran her tongue over the head of his cock. He cupped her face between his palms and leaned toward her as she drew his shaft deep into her mouth.

Her breasts thrust forward, her nipples taut. John slipped his hands down and cupped them in turn, twisting and rubbing her nipples, eliciting small mewls and grunts from her wet mouth, which vibrated deliciously around his cockstand.

He watched her parted lips working him, teasing his swollen member, the sensation an exquisite torture, causing a flood of delight to course through his manhood. He immediately freed himself from her tender ministrations and pushed her onto her back. Holding her legs apart, he moved between her thighs then, setting her legs either side of his head, he laid them over his shoulders. Her cleft splayed open and he wasted no time in claiming her, glorying in her mewls and cries as she came apart, spending against his rapier tongue.

Her hands entwined in the thickness hair of his head as she tried fruitlessly to pull away. "Hush, love," he soothed. "I intend to build another fire within you."

He lowered his head to his task, tongue and fingers playing her slick furrow until, sure enough, he felt the arousing quiver of her flesh as she pulsed and cried out his name. The erotic reaction to her orgasm empowered him, urging him to wring the same cry of pleasure from her once again. He ran his tongue through her glistening furrow once more, enjoying her quivering reaction to the rasp of his tongue. Then, traversing the length of her torso, he took a nipple into his mouth, worrying the swollen peak, taunting her sensitive buds with his circling tongue. He petted her, whispering his love into her ear, mastering her body with his.

His manhood was heavy, aching with the need for release, but he resisted the urge, waiting for her to recover. He ran his hand up the length of her arm then, grasping her wrist, he drew her hand down between their bodies, placing her palm on his aching phallus. Her fingers closed over his throbbing manhood caressingly. Sliding down the turgid thickness of his shaft, she cupped his tightened sac, rubbing the soft area beneath until he groaned with delight.

Gently, he frigged her quim until she was slick, drenched with desire for him, ready for his mount. His breath became an urgent groan. A simple shift of his hips and he was aligned with her folds, easing his flanks forward, finally mating her—one sure thrust sheathed him to the root.

Beginning with slow strokes that encouraged her warm, wet welcome, he gradually increased the tempo which carried her with him to the edge of ecstasy. They hung together at the precipice, experiencing the overwhelming emotion that comes to those who truly love. Gazing deep into one another's eyes, each lit by ecstatic delight, they fully recognised the deep love and trust that was between them, bound to one another body and soul as they climaxed together, their loving cries echoing loudly within the confines of their snug cabin.

Afterwards they remained conjoined, holding one another close as they drifted into sleep with the knowledge that they were as one.

CHAPTER 19

*T*he weeks following Christmas were extremely cold. They experienced severe blizzards that lasted two full days. The wind howled, shrieking around the outside of the cabin. The force of icy gales drove the snow to pile high against the cabin door. It required a lot of digging to free up their entrance when the blizzards had finally passed. They were thankful the animals had survived without their attention, they did at least have water in their troughs. The cow was in some discomfort for the period that they could not get to her for milking. None of the creatures seemed to be the worse for their period of slight neglect. The winter seemed to continue interminably until early March. Linnet noticed the faint sound of running water. The stream had started to thaw. She ran excitedly into the cabin to tell John but met him returning from the barn.

"Listen!" she yelled excitedly.

"Is something wrong?" He limped over to her with concern.

She shook her head, eyes shining. "Just stand still and listen, tell me what you hear."

He did as she asked, with a dawning realisation. "It's finally thawing!"

She nodded excitedly. "Isn't it wonderful? We can visit Sarah and Hans and travel on to Boston!"

John kissed her swiftly, walking back toward the warmth of the cabin. "I want to brush the snow from the cabin roof before it slides and catches one of us unawares."

She caught up with him. "When do you think we will be able to travel, when can we go, John?"

"Not for a while yet, love, the mud is almost as dangerous as the snow, besides, although it is thawing now, the snow could still return. I should think perhaps we could leave at the beginning of May."

"Not until May!" She was bitterly disappointed. She had thought they would leave soon, perhaps even the following week.

"Well, I suppose we could risk a visit to the Lammers as soon as the snow melts," John reflected, noticing his wife's disappointed expression.

"I guess so." She shrugged dispiritedly and went into the cabin to place the risen dough in the oven to bake. How nice it would be to see Sarah again and share their winter experiences.

John's leg healed, the scars growing paler by the day. He was able to clear the cabin roof of snow and they waited to see if the thaw would continue. It did—by the end of the week, they'd made plans to travel down into the valley to visit the Lammers family on horseback. Linnet cooked provisions for the journey and baked a seed cake for young Peter, knowing it was his favourite.

She'd made Sarah a pretty purse, using a piece of left over green velvet. The winter days of enforced inactivity had proved a blessing as far as her dressmaking was concerned. She'd made a serviceable riding skirt and habit for herself from the grey serge.

Between them, they'd made Hans a tobacco pouch. John had prepared the hide from a piece of deerskin, scraping it and soaking it, drying and oiling until it until it was supple enough for Linnet to sew.

The day before they were due to leave, John wrapped Linnet's jewellery cask in cloth and buried it beneath the wall of the barn, then covered the area with debris.

Finally, with preparations for their brief journey complete, they went to saddle the horses. Saddling Amber was rather like trying to hold onto a slippery, wet fish. Linnet waited for her naughty horse to breathe out so she could tighten the girth but Amber was skittish after being enclosed for so long.

The horses had become very spoilt during the long winter months and Amber filled her lungs with air so that her mistress couldn't tighten the girth. Linnet knew that if she rode her with a loose girth, she would fall off as soon as Amber let out her breath.

"You are a bad girl!" Linnet scolded the horse as she rolled her eyes and danced sideways. "Oooh, if only I could spank you!" she exclaimed, exasperated.

"I don't know why you bother to scold her, Linnet; both she and I know you don't mean a word of it! Here, let me try." He strode up to the horse and slapped her rump. "Behave!" he instructed firmly.

Amber seemed to know that her master meant business. She let out her breath, allowing him to tighten the girth.

"Well!" Linnet spluttered with disgust. "I've been trying to do that for an age, and all it took was one smack on the rear end from a man!"

"Women and horses, much alike," he assured her smugly.

Linnet bristled but couldn't help chuckling at her puffed up husband. "Sometimes you're such an arrogant swine!" She grabbed hold of a handful of hay, deftly thrusting it down John's neck. He spun about, catching her as she attempted to scuttle towards the barn door. Swinging her hard against him, he captured her wrists behind her back, leering down at her, one eyebrow cocked. "A spanking or kisses are forfeit, which does my lady choose?"

She pursed her lips, thinking, and he lowered his mouth to hers. His hands dropped to her bosom, tweaking her burgeoning nipples through her gown. Linnet deftly stuck her foot through his legs and hooked it up behind his knee, unbalancing them both. They overbalanced and fell into a heap, ending up in a tangle of arms and legs upon the hay-covered floor. John tipped her face down across his thigh and smacked her bottom then began to tickle her unmercifully. They were both laughing so hard that their sides ached and they fought to get their breath back.

Eventually, he managed to stand and helped Linnet back to her feet. They brushed the hay off one another and John emptied his shirt of hay. Then they returned to the task of saddling up and tying on their bundle of provisions. Once the fire was fully doused and the cabin secure, they wrapped up warmly and mounted, setting off. Daisy the cow was tethered to John's horse, as they couldn't leave her behind on her own.

The snow had receded but there were still patches, making the ground slippery underfoot and the journey tricky. They had left in the early morning, but because they had to travel so slowly, they didn't reach the farm until the afternoon. Linnet's heart raced as they rode up to the house. She was slightly nervous about the reception they would receive, arriving so unexpectedly.

She had been hurt that Sarah hadn't wanted them to stay with them throughout the winter. Although, now that she had experienced the isolation of a winter, she could understand Sarah's reservations. Linnet need not have worried; the door to the farm house was flung open and Peter ran out shouting with excitement, followed by a beaming Hans and a waddling Sarah.

Linnet gaped.

"Well, are you getting down or staying up there all night?" Sarah asked, grinning up at Linnet's astonished face.

"You're with child!" Linnet squealed.

Sarah nodded delightedly. "Yes, isn't it wonderful? I didn't realise at first! Hans noticed that I was unwell most mornings and suggested that I might be with child. I snapped the poor man's head off but it turns out he was right after all!"

Linnet dismounted and hugged her friend, careful not to squeeze her too tightly.

"What are you doing here? You are both mad to travel yet!" Sarah scolded.

Hans came up behind Linnet and gave her a great bear hug, swinging her up off her feet. "It is wonderful to see you. Is that man of yours keeping my cabin in good repair, eh?" he asked jovially.

John answered. "It is in excellent repair. No thanks, though, to a large cougar that tried to destroy both me and the cabin!"

Peter caught John's hand excitedly. "A real mountain lion? Did you kill it, Mr. Foster? How big was it?"

"Peter, enough, John can tell us the story over supper." Sarah ushered them all into the warmth of the house.

It was wonderful for all of them to have company and conversation again. The evening turned into a party. Each couple shared their winter experiences, but Hans and Sarah seemed to have had rather a quiet time of things compared to John and Linnet. Sarah was intrigued by Linnet's encounter with the native child and asked no end of questions. Hans was concerned by the sighting of natives so close to the homestead. He'd heard that a number of attacks had been levelled at white settlers farther inland, but John assured him that these natives had been reasonably friendly. Sarah's talk was of her coming babe, which she judged would arrive sometime around the end of May. She was full of surprise that, after all this time, she should conceive again.

Sarah observed a new maturity in Linnet and a new closeness between Linnet and John that had been lacking when she had last seen them together. She was relieved that they had achieved a good bond and wished them the good fortune that she and Hans now shared. Hans was delighted with his tobacco pouch and she with her purse. She insisted that John keep *The Iliad* as a gift, and presented Linnet with a needle case that she'd made herself and filled with different sized sewing needles.

Linnet gave the cake she had baked to Peter, he insisted on cutting it up and sharing it out between them all. Finally, full of cake, he went cheerfully out into the cold, slamming the door as he disappeared outside. The adults settled down to more serious conversation, sharing news they could not in front of a young boy. Hans presented John with a beautiful map he'd drawn to help them on their journey to Boston, and the two men pored over that while they sipped whisky together.

Linnet and Sarah discussed children and men, fashion and remedies. Sarah suddenly reached out and placed Linnet's hand on her swollen belly and Linnet felt the miracle of life moving within her friend. Bumps moved across the tight surface of Sarah's belly, rolling from side to side. The two women smiled at one another. Linnet leaned over and gently kissed Sarah's cheek.

"I am so happy for you," she told her softly.

Sarah nodded and smiled. "It will be your turn soon, Linnet, don't fret, just wait and see."

"Oh, I hope so! Ever since I held that little one in my arms and cared for him, I've wished for a child." Linnet sighed.

"Much better to wait until you are returned to Boston, carrying a babe while on such a journey would be risky," Sarah told her sensibly. Linnet knew her words to be true.

The door opened, letting in the fresh, icy evening air. They all turned to see Peter standing holding something that wriggled determinedly in his arms. Linnet gasped. Recognising the creature straight away, she flew to Peter, who, grinning widely, presented her with a fat pink piglet.

Linnet took the small, wriggling bundle and spun around, laughing, holding out her prize for John to see.

"Linnet has a special affinity with hogs," John told Hans and Sarah proudly. "When I first met her, she showed me her pig, an enormous hog that was tame enough for Linnet to pet!"

Peter wandered over to Linnet's side and watched as she scratched the piglet's soft ear. "She's yours if you want her, my Christmas present to you!"

Linnet placed her free arm about Peter and gave him a hug. "Of course I want her, Peter; she is so adorable, thank you!"

"The *varken* must stay here with her mother until she is bigger, but you can take her to Boston when you leave," Hans told them, reaching for the now squealing hoglet. Sarah translated the Dutch word *varken* as pig. "I'll go and return her to her mamma. We don't want her rejected because she has been missing from her side for too long." Hans left the house with Peter trotting at his heels, clutching a pig bucket full of kitchen scraps to feed to the '*varken* family.'

"John, this is so exciting. My very own pig! I just can't wait to mate her and have more piglets!"

John laughed. "Poor little thing, she's only just been born, let her grow up first!"

John and Linnet spent two days with the Lammers. Starved as they had been of company over the winter months, it was balm for both couples to enjoy renewing the friendship that had developed between them in the early fall. They stayed two days at the farm but too soon the time came for Linnet and John to return to their cabin. They took the maps as guidance for the long journey to Boston packed safely in their belongings.

A deep sadness prevailed upon them all, knowing they might never have the chance to meet up again.

"When you leave for Boston, just set the cows free to roam. They will wander and find the rest of the herd," Hans instructed. They were taking two cows back with them this time because Hans knew that two would have a better chance of finding the herd. Linnet and John rode with a cow each, tethered to their horse for the return journey. It would be slow going, matching their speed to that of the cows' gait.

Finally, they made their tearful farewells. "Write to us in Boston when the baby is born and tell us whether it is a girl or a boy. Perhaps you could come and stay when the child is a little older?" Linnet asked hopefully as she hugged her friend goodbye.

"Perhaps," agreed Sarah, knowing even as she said it she could never leave the farm to travel all that way to Boston.

Linnet drew Peter to her and kissed his forehead. "Look after your mother, Peter, and perhaps you could visit us in Boston when you are older."

Peter's eyes shone. "Can I, Mother?"

He turned excitedly to Sarah, but it was Hans who answered. "Perhaps in a year or two when you are a little older, *lieveling*!" he told his son, ruffling his hair. Amidst the chorus of goodbyes, Linnet and John rode off, back to the solitude of their mountain hideaway.

John was anxious to return to the cabin; he'd enjoyed their visit immensely but longed to have Linnet all to himself again. Seeing Sarah large with child made him want to plant his own seed; he so longed for a child of his own.

They broke the journey once they were over half way. Sarah had packed them the usual generous supply of food, so they lunched well on fresh baked bread, cheese and cold chicken. "I long to gallop for a little while, the ground is softer and there is hardly any snow about. May I ride ahead a little way and leave both cows with you? I could light the stove and start boiling water if I arrive back before you," Linnet asked pleadingly.

John hesitated. He hated her roaming alone. Ever since he had come across her being attacked by Ned, he feared for her safety. "I don't know, it's not safe here like in England."

"Well, I know that now! I will be very careful and keep to the trail. Please, John!"

She knelt in front of him and grasped his hands, raining kisses on them. He tugged his hands away, chuckling at her antics. "Enough! Very well, then."

"Thank you, thank you!" she cried, delighted.

"Wait a moment… this is on the condition that you keep within my sight," he ordered sternly.

Linnet's face fell. "That's not necessary!"

"Nevertheless, those are my terms, take them or leave them. Either that, or you ride with a sore butt."

She scowled. "Since I appear to have no choice, I agree."

John grinned at his wife's sulky face. "Oh and Linnet, darlin'?"

"Yes?"

"Disappear from my sight for more than five minutes, and I promise you'll not be able to sit for at least a week!"

She stuck out her tongue playfully at him then turned to mount Amber, riding away with a flourish.

She kept her word, returning to the horizon to wave at him every time she rode out of sight. When she realised she had almost reached the cabin, she cantered on ahead, intending to relight the stove and set their meal to cook.

As she rounded the crest of the hill, she noticed a black plume of smoke rising over the trees. The smoke appeared to be coming from the direction of their cabin. Linnet kicked Amber into a canter, moving into a gallop, riding hard until the cabin came into sight. Flames poured from the windows and licked up over the eaves. Shocked, she slowed Amber to a walk, drawing to a halt as she stared incredulously at the fiery destruction of her first ever marital home.

Had they left the stove in? She recalled John saying that he'd raked the embers over but perhaps not? With a cry of dismay, she leapt from Amber's back and ran to the front of the cabin.

She was almost at the door when strong arms swept her up and back away from the inferno. She screamed in horror as she turned and found herself looking straight into the red and black painted face of a native warrior.

CHAPTER 20

*H*e was a huge man, well over six feet. Bare chested, despite the cold. His face and body were painted red and black. His dark eyes bored into Linnet's as he spoke, his voice deep and guttural. *"Mi he wi."*

She shook her head to show that she could not understand him and tried to pull her arms free of his grip. The man tightened his hold on her, swinging her up into his arms. Linnet punched his shoulders, shrieking, absolutely terrified. Where was John? She craned her neck, looking around to see if he had arrived. It was then that she noticed four or five other braves sat quietly mounted on horses, waiting at the edge of the forest.

The large Indian walked over toward them, he threw the now screaming Linnet up over his horse, face down. Swiftly, he mounted behind her, his arm resting solidly upon her back. Shocked and terrified, she struggled, kicking wildly as the horses and riders melted away into the trees.

They travelled onward for an hour or more before coming to a halt in dense forest. Linnet had ceased her struggles after the native man had wound his hand in her hair and yanked hard each time she kicked. All she could think about was how worried John would be when he found the cabin burning and her missing. Perhaps he would think that she'd perished in the fire—dear Lord, he might not search for her. Then she realised he would undoubtedly see Amber, untethered and still saddled. Hopefully that would be enough of a sign that she had not even made it into the cabin before being spirited away.

She was spilled unceremoniously to the ground and lay winded in a tousled heap. Once she'd managed to get her breath back, she sat up and scraped the dirt and leaf debris from her hair, deliberately pulling her hair out with it and throwing the lot aside to leave as a sign for John should he track them. The natives hunkered down on the other side of the horses, their guttural voices murmuring in conversation. Stealthily she climbed to her feet and edged away from them, creeping deep into the dark thicket of trees. Once she was sure she was well screened by undergrowth, she fled as fast as she could, running through the forest, where branches whipped her face and sharp brambles caught at her skin and clothes alike.

She recalled running from Ned, and wondered why she could hear no sounds of pursuit. Perhaps the natives thought they'd be better off without her. With this in mind, she slowed her pace, eventually coming to a gasping halt.

She stood, doubled over, attempting to catch her breath. She listened: silence. Nothing. Starting to walk, she picked her way more discriminatingly through the tangled brush. She noticed a particularly nasty scratch across her forearm and bent to lick the stinging wound. Suddenly, without warning, she walked smack into the solid chest of her native captor.

She recoiled in shock; where on earth had he come from? The brave raised his hand, smacking her, open-palmed, across the cheek. Stumbling back, she fell to the ground. The man bent over her and said something in his guttural tongue. She stared into his dark, glittering eyes, giving glare for glare, then spat full in his face. He wiped the spittle away and back-handed her across the face again, this time splitting her bottom lip.

"You utter *b-bastard!*" she screeched.

Ignoring her, he reached down, painfully yanking her to her feet by her hair, winding it around his hand to keep a firm hold of her. He strode off, dragging her along in his wake. Linnet pulled back, resisting, but it was useless; her tactic barely touched his superior strength. Tears of pain and fear welled in her eyes.

They arrived back at the clearing, the other natives having simply vanished. Linnet tried to kick her tormentor as she struggled to break free but the man gave an evil sneer. He picked her up as though she weighed nothing and threw her face down over the horse before leaping up behind her. This time, however, he swung her upright then, grabbing her ankle, he turned her so that she sat with her back against his chest. She sat up straight, bent slightly forward so that she did not touch him, but as the horse leapt forward, she was jolted back against the solid slab of his naked chest, his steely arm coiled around her, holding her firmly in place.

Linnet had no idea how long they'd travelled for. Once it had grown dark, time ceased to exist and she fell into a fitful doze, waking and dozing, depending on the jolting movement of the horse.

Just as dawn streaked the sky, they approached habitation. There came the sharp barking of dogs, jolting her out of her stupor. The horse picked its way amongst clusters of strange rounded earthen dwellings. A mangy collection of assorted dogs ran in between the horse's legs, whining, yipping their excitement. Otherwise, the place seemed deserted. There were almost no people about, although she noticed a couple of elderly women tending to fires. She assumed that most of the inhabitants of this community were still abed.

The native pulled his horse to halt outside one of the lodges. He pushed Linnet to the ground, where she landed like a sack of grain. He leapt deftly from the horse himself and disappearing into the opening of the humble dwelling, entering through a flap of hide that covered the entrance. Before he disappeared inside, he gestured impatiently at her to follow him. She stumbled to her feet and followed him inside, dazed, unable to accept this kidnapping, the event seeming unreal.

She saw that a fire burned in a hollow pit dug in the centre of the dwelling. It was a relief to be inside with the welcoming warmth. Despite her exhaustion and fear, she gazed about curiously. Above the fire hung various things; smoked roots, strips of meat, a whole fish, plants, or perhaps they were herbs, strung across the width of the lodge. The floor of the enclosure was covered in braided matting. Large baskets hung lashed around the walls of the enclosure. On the opposite side of the structure, furs lay on the floor, covered with woven blankets in bold patterns.

Linnet's captor took her arm and led her to one of these blanket piles, he gestured for her to sit. She lowered herself gratefully onto the bedding, pulling one of the brightly woven blankets around herself. She lay on her side with her legs tucked up to her chest. Closing her eyes, her last coherent thought was of her husband. She was concerned for him and how frantic he must be feeling.

She was awoken by small hands patting her at her cheeks and even lifting up her eyelid. Opening her eyes, she stared into a pair of wide, shining eyes that belonged to the small golden-skinned child. The boy grinned at her. She immediately recognised him, it was *her* native baby, the one she had found and cared for. Sitting up, she pulled him into her arms, delighted to see the child again. The small boy scrambled about on her lap, getting comfortable, then he held out his hand to show her the carved horse he was clutching. He still had it with him. She hugged his warm body and he cuddled into her, plugging in his thumb.

Linnet smiled, entranced. "Well, I see you haven't changed, my little suck-a thumb!" She spoke aloud, noticing for the first time that they were alone in the lodge. She settled back, enjoying the warmth and companionship of the child, his innocent presence relieving some of the exhausting terror she felt. He was the only person in this place whom she knew intended her no harm. Why had she been brought here? Were white women kidnapped on a regular basis by natives? Would John be able to track her from so far away? Would he find the carefully placed strands of hair she had deliberately pulled from her head and dropped discreetly along the route? Question after question tormented her.

There was movement from without, then a large figure stooped in through the flap at the doorway—her captor. Today, he was clear skinned, free of the terrifying black and red paint that had coated his face and body yesterday. He'd obviously bathed, for his hair was damp and the cock's-comb on the top of his head soft and fluffy, although there was nothing 'fluffy' about this man. Linnet regarded his harsh, arrogant face nervously. She noted the high planes of his cheekbones and the black eyes that appeared so arrogantly cold.

He nodded to her, and she thought she saw his cheek twitch at the sight of the child curled in her lap. She drew the babe protectively against her and lifted her chin defiantly, staring him down, refusing to allow him to intimidate her.

He sneered, and with a jolt she recognised him: it was the broken nose. This man was the child's father, the same man who had come to their cabin to fetch him. Her hold on the child relaxed slightly as she realised that he wouldn't harm his own son.

There was a shout outside, the native spun around as another person entered the dwelling. She gasped in shock as the second man straightened up. She recognized him!

"Will! Oh my God, Will, it *is* you—*you are alive!*" she cried, both amazed and delighted. Amidst the trauma, here was someone she knew. Someone who could help her, someone who could explain what on earth was happening!

She was astonished. She'd assumed that Will was dead, killed by the bear she'd witnessed attacking him.

He nodded. "Yup, 'tis me, Will." He came and hunkered down beside her, chucking the small boy under the chin.

"B-but I saw the bear pick you up, it was attacking you! How on earth did you get away?"

He grinned. "It attacked me all right, tore my left arm clean off!"

He turned to show her his armless shoulder. The skin had grown over the wound that was pink and puckered. "Yaogah saved me. He still wears the claws of that mean old bear strung about his neck."

Linnet peeked sideways at the enormous native man. He certainly looked savage enough to kill a bear. "Yaogah, that is his name?" she asked.

"Aye, 'tis. That child you hold is his son, *Aweont*."

She nodded. "I guessed as much. Aweont… what does his name mean?"

Will pondered before answering. "The nearest translation is Growing Plant or Growing Flower. The meaning is a little different, though; it implies a strong, healthy, thriving growing being, whether it be plant or mammal."

"I see. *Aweont*." Linnet rolled the name around, trying to get used to the strange sound.

The small boy sat up, pleased she had used his name. He nodded, repeating his name himself. She smiled down at him and stroked his cheek with her finger. Then she pointed to her own chest. "Linnet."

She noticed that they were both being closely observed by the child's father, and Will. The father's features appeared to soften at the obvious rapport between her and his son. She turned again to Will; there was so much she needed to ask him. "Why has *he*," she nodded at Yaogah, "brought me here? My husband will be frantic with worry by now. I have to get back home."

Will put his hand over hers, giving it a firm squeeze of reassurance.

"Now, girl, you aren't going to like what I'm about to tell you, but just be calm and hear me through. Yaogah lost his wife when his son was born. Some eighteen months later, he was out hunting. He'd taken the boy with him on the trip but the child wandered off and got hisself lost. You found the child and, by all accounts cared for him, probably saving his life."

Linnet nodded. Will continued, "The child has missed you. He cried for you for many days after they returned him to the village, crying, '*Mi he wi! Mi he wi! Mi he wi!*' That means Sun Woman in their language, that is what the boy has named you," Will reached out and touched her hair, "due to your sunset red hair."

She smiled at the child she held and the little boy grinned back. "*Mi he wi,*" he stated firmly, reaching for a strand of her hair.

Will coughed. "The long and the short of it is this: you have been chosen to become his new mother. Yaogah means to take you as wife, as his squaw—"

She interrupted violently. "No! He cannot do that; I am already married! Tell him—explain to him!"

Will shook his head sympathetically. "White man's law means nothing here. Do you have any children?" he asked.

Her eyes narrowed suspiciously. "No, why?"

"You might have stood a chance of convincing the council that you needed to return if there were children missing their mother."

"It will be easy, then, we'll tell them that I have children!"

Will shrugged, looking uncomfortable. "No, I cannot do that. Sorry, girl. You see, Yaogah saved my life and he has made me his blood brother, which makes me not only a member of his family but of the tribe. I owe him my life; I have pledged an oath of loyalty to him. I'm sorry, but I'll not lie to him for you."

"You would betray your own people for *savages?*" She was incredulous.

Will sighed. "Not savages. If I had to stake my life upon which nation is more savage, it would not be the Abenaki."

"Honourable you say, snatching a married woman from her home to take as a slave?" she spluttered, enraged.

"Be reasonable, girl, you wouldn't be a slave! I promise you that. You are miles from your home, your husband will never find you here, and anyway, the man should have taken better care of his wife! On both the occasions I have met you, the man was miles away from your side, what kind of protector is that?"

Linnet hung her head, tears flooding her eyes. "It was *my* fault, not his. If only I hadn't been so stupidly wilful and headstrong!"

"I'd best warn you now that here, a headstrong girl will suffer punishment. You would have more freedom and respect in the tribe if you marry Yaogah, more than any other squaw. He is the strongest and richest warrior in the village. He is much sought after by the other women as husband. He is a good and fair man, but I warn you, girl, hurt his pride by showing bad behaviour and you will be *severely* punished. The worse thing for an Abenaki is to lose face in front of his companions."

"What about my rights!" she demanded indignantly.

"Women here have no rights, they are squaws. You are allowed no pride; in fact, you don't count at all." Will explained.

She whipped back her hand and cracked him across the face. Will didn't move except to lift his hand to halt Yaogah—who had taken a step forward—from interfering. The child sat up, startled. He stared wide-eyed at his father but when his father didn't move, he settled back against Linnet.

There was silence. Will smiled. "It's been a long time since a beautiful woman slapped my face. No woman would dare to do that here, their hide would be beaten from them! The only way for women to have a voice in the tribe is to be elected onto the council but that only happens when women become older and wiser, like Small Speech. She will be the council's spokesman."

A despondent tear slipped down her cheek.

Will swiped his thumb across her damp cheek. "Girl, believe me, I do understand why you are upset... I am only telling you these things to make your life easier."

Linnet stretched out an imploring hand. "I am sorry I hit you, Will, I understand that this is not your fault but I am so frightened! This is just too ridiculous, it's just so, so, impossible! I am *English*, I cannot marry a heathen! I am married, and happily, too! I love my husband, he loves me. This is *insanity*, it makes no sense! This cannot be happening to me!"

Will frowned and shook his head. "Well, I have done my best for you, my girl, the rest is up to you. The council will speak with you shortly. If you wish, I'll translate for you." He stood up.

"Yes, please translate for me. Tell them to let me go, Will, I beg of you, please, please tell them to let me go home!"

"I have a pretty young wife, Iniabi, her name means 'homemaker.' We have a babe on the way. I'm telling you to show you where my loyalties lie. These people are *my family*."

"I understand," she muttered, incredibly downhearted to hear this statement. She realised that Will was telling her he would only help her if it didn't interfere with his own special relationship with this tribe.

"Be careful what you say to the council. Remember to show respect. I will tell you this, though: one of the old men on the council has a daughter, Running Deer. She is a pretty little thing, and before you obsessed his son, Yaogah fully intended to take her to wife. I have no doubt that her father would support you in your wish to leave here."

"Thank you." She felt there was some hope left. "Is there anything else I should know, Will?"

"No. Although, I should like to know what happened to my partner, Ned."

"I am so sorry, Will, but he is dead. He-he tried to *rape* me. Luckily my husband John came upon us just in time and saved me.

It was my husband who killed Ned… but I cannot say I am sorry he died, not after he attacked me."

He gave a brief nod, pressing his lips into a thin line before turning towards the entrance. Just before he stepped outside, he turned. "Darn it all, I don't understand why Ned just wouldn't listen! I knew he'd wind up dead one of these days. I don't rightly blame your man for killing him. Jus' so long as you don't go counting on your man to save you this time around, 'cause I can assure you, he won't!"

CHAPTER 21

*S*he was left alone with just the child for company, and stared down at his glossy black head in disbelief. Who would have thought that her simple act of human kindness would cause so much grief and trouble? Still, even if she'd known the outcome, she wouldn't have left the child to die.

But what on earth was she to do?

She wouldn't marry this Ya-whatever-his-name-was, that was for certain. Will had said that he'd represent her at the council, but could she trust him? He'd also said that he considered himself a relative of this native tribe. The bear man was enormous! She shuddered. He wanted her to take her as his wife but that couldn't happen! She was married to John under God's holy law, surely God would not allow this bigamous marriage to take place?

There was a commotion outside the lodge; an elderly woman entered the dwelling. She held out a soft suede native dress toward Linnet, who reluctantly accepted the gift. The woman then spoke with the child, holding out her arms to him. He clung to Linnet, burying his face in her neck. She smiled despite the situation and eased him upright then, smoothing his hair; she kissed him on the forehead. "Come along, it is time for you to leave, but I will see you again soon."

She placed him on his feet, pushing him away from her. The small boy turned back and wrapped his arms about her neck, giving her a swift hug before he toddled over to the elderly woman. He reached up to take her hand. The woman smiled a toothless grin and left, taking the child with her.

The entrance darkened again as Will entered. He coughed. "Put on the dress, girl, it will honour the Council."

He turned his back as Linnet did as he bid, stripping quickly out of her torn and muddy clothing and pulling the soft, beaded garment over her head. It was beautiful, a very soft, a pale buttery colour decorated with a fringed hem. It was shorter than any dress Linnet had ever worn before, ending at mid-calf. It showed her ankles and fitted her curves like a second skin. It felt indecent yet strangely liberating to be free of her petticoats, stays and underclothes which normally hampered her movements.

"Time to go." Will lifted the hide flap for her to step through. She took a deep breath and followed him. They passed through the press of Abenaki natives and he directed her towards a long wooden cabin. When they reached the steps, Will cried out in a sing-song voice to the entrance of the building, and a voice from within replied. Will entered first, lifting the hide for Linnet to pass under.

Inside, a group of mainly elderly women sat in a semi-circle around a fire. Opposite them sat Yaogah and his son. Linnet noticed that the elderly woman who had collected the child moments before sat in the centre. Will bowed his head to the council before sitting down cross-legged beside Yaogah. Linnet also bowed her head in greeting but she remained standing.

Yaogah's dark eyes raked over Linnet's body and he began to speak in a deep and guttural tongue. Linnet studied his thick, bulging muscles. His veins stood out like small snakes upon the surface of his muscular arms and his skin resembled the colour of tea.

He stopped talking and the elderly woman who seemed in charge smiled at her. The woman's skin was creased, weathered with age, yet she looked wise. Linnet felt some hope that all may yet be resolved to her advantage. The old woman spoke, gesturing for her to sit, but Linnet remained standing until Will yanked her down onto the floor beside him. Once she was seated, the woman began to talk. Will translated her words.

"Ever since Aweont was found, he has longed for his chosen mother, Sun-Woman. You are to be honoured by Yaogah, who wishes to take you into his lodge as mother to his son."

Linnet nodded, willing herself to remain silent and not interrupt. When the elderly woman finished speaking, she spoke up. "My name is Linnet. That is the name of a bird that lives in a land far away across the sea where I come from. Please may I ask your name, wise lady?"

Will looked at Linnet with surprise. Smiling, he gave a nod of approval as he translated her words. The wise woman glanced sideways, nodding approvingly to other council members. "You are right; introductions should come first. I, *Soaewaah*, Small Speech, representative of the Supreme Council, sit among the famous League of Nations. We, the council, enforce law in our villages. You are welcome here, Linnet-bird."

Linnet smiled and waited for Will to finish the translation before continuing.

"I thank you, Small Speech, for your welcome and hospitality. I am pleased to see Aweont again, for he is dear to my heart, but I already have a husband, one whom I love dearly and who will be missing me. I do not know this man. I cannot marry him for I have sworn a holy oath to forsake all men but my husband."

Will translated again and a murmur went up from the assembly. Finally, Small Speech spoke. "You have no children who wait for you but this child needs a mother. He chose you, he honours you,

Linnet-bird. His father is a great warrior; he wants you to warm his bed. I cannot understand your objection."

Linnet took a deep breath. Placing her hands protectively over her belly, she answered, "I am with child. I carry my husband's son." Will raised a brow but she glared at him. "Make sure you tell them exactly what I said," she hissed. He nodded but before he could speak, her kidnapper, Yaogah, leapt to his feet. Grabbing Linnet, he held her in front of his body, placing one large hand over her belly, kneading her flesh. He growled at the council, whereupon one of the women stood up and begun arguing with a man whom Linnet assumed was Running Deer's father. A furious row broke out amongst the gathered council.

Amidst all the shrieking and growling, a rattle sounded, and suddenly silence fell. Everyone settled down as Small Speech stepped into the fray.

She focused her stare upon Linnet as she spoke, and Will translated. "I am sorry for the behaviour of these dogs. Will you allow me to feel for the child you claim lives within you?"

Linnet could only agree, giving her a nod of assent, whereupon the old woman came forward and felt over her womb area. As she pressed and prodded, she muttered to herself, shaking her head. Will translated. "She says it is impossible to tell whether you are with child, it is too early."

Small Speech turned to Yaogah and spoke with him at some length before turning back to Linnet. "Yaogah wants you even though you might carry another man's child. He says that you cared for his son, and he will care for yours. The spirits alone will decide whether you shall bear the child.

"The council will talk of this; you will be told of our decision once it is made."

Again, Will translated then, bowing to the council, he took Linnet's arm and guided her away.

The wait seemed interminable, the afternoon dragged on. Linnet paced inside the lodge. She looked at the dirt floor and dropped to her knees. In desperation, she began to scrape the soft earth away from the wall of the lodge, hiding it under the bedding. No one came to speak with her all afternoon. At one point she heard a noise and hastily seated herself on the bed as though resting. A beautiful young woman peered inside the entrance, a furious scowl marring her pretty features. When Linnet called to her, she ran away. Will appeared to have vanished. She lifted the entrance flap to look outside for him, whereupon she discovered two Indian braves, presumably guarding her. Surely the council would find in her favour? She was a married woman, she might very well be carrying John's child, for goodness' sake!

She wished now that she had voiced her suspicions to her husband about the baby but she'd been waiting to see if her courses had really stopped. She guessed she could be at least three months with child. *Dear Lord,* she prayed, *let John find me!*

As the glooming settled and darkness fell, Will returned to take her back to the council. Small Speech was there alone—Bear Man and everyone else, including the child, were gone. As before, Will bowed and Linnet copied him. He translated for her as Small Speech spoke. "We have not taken our decision lightly. We have not taken into account your oath, for it is a white man's oath and not applicable to us. We can find no reason why Yaogah should not take you to live in his lodge, if he so desires."

Stunned, Linnet dropped to her knees, pleading with Small Speech to set her free. Will tried desperately to translate all she said but for the most part, Linnet was incoherent with shock.

He gave up, lifting her to her feet. "Come on, girl, really it's not so bad. Yaogah is a good man. He will look after you. The other squaws will be envious of you. He is considered a great catch."

She rounded on him. "Let them have him! I have a husband; do you hear me? Why will no one listen? *I-have-a-husband!*" she shrieked. Yaogah appeared from the shadows and scooped her up, carrying her back to his lodge where he dumped her uncermoniously onto the furs. Then he turned to Will, they spoke together in hushed tones.

Finally, Will hunkered down by Linnet. "I'd advise you to cooperate with your new mate. These people have some very nasty ways with those who won't comply. I cannot help you any more, girl, now it is up to you."

She closed her eyes. "I would rather die than submit to rape. Just go away!"

Will shook her by the shoulders. "Damn it, woman, that's just what you will do, *die*, and none too pleasantly, either! At least while you're alive, there is hope. You're no good to your unborn child or John if you're dead. Think on that, woman!"

He stood, nodded to Yaogah and left them alone. The huge native stood like a statue, watching her thoughtfully. Suddenly, with the speed of a mountain lion, he reached out, grasped her arm and hauled her up against his chest. A hand gripped her chin.

Staring down into Linnet's green eyes, his free hand slid over her breasts, squeezing. It felt as though he was assessing her assets. Insulted, she drew back her head and spat in his face. Releasing her, he ran the back of his hand across his face to clear her spittle. She took the opportunity to bolt but as she made her escape, a large arm snaked about her waist and hauled her back inside the lodge.

He twisted a hand in her thick hair, pulling her head back, forcing her chest out. Her bosom jutted, her nipples outlined by the tight leather dress. His ham-like hands mauled them, pinching her breasts, kneading the tender flesh. Without thinking her action through, Linnet twisted her head and sank her teeth deep into his arm. He immediately let go of her hair. Giving a guttural curse, he sucked his injured wrist. Linnet dropped onto the furs behind her with a whimper of fear. She glanced at his face then blanched at the expression of fury she saw there. No longer inscrutable, she could see that he was livid with her.

Yaogah dropped beside her on the bedding. Reaching out a huge hand, he grabbed the skein of her hair and, wrapping it around his fist he tugged her face down across his enormous thighs. She struggled in vain; she knew this position only too well, recognising her predicament would bode ill for her.

He shifted slightly and produced a large dagger from the sheath tethered to his thigh. He proceeded to slit her dress from waist to hem, exposing her bare bottom. Linnet let out a banshee wail of fury and frustration. Only her husband had the right to punish her, this savage had no right! This indignity should not be happening to *her*, especially not with a barbarian!

She froze as she felt his large hand roughly exploring her hind end, stiffening as his fingers dipped between her legs, thrusting into and invading her private furrow. She kicked frantically, attempting to struggle free, but he pinched the inner flesh of her soft thigh, twisting the tender skin viciously.

She gasped with the pain. Thrashing her head from side to side, her mouth searching for flesh to sink her teeth into, she wished to bite, to tear, to vent her fury. When a loud slap and a sharp pain sliced across her buttock, she shrieked with rage, bucking. She gasped as a volley of powerful, painful slaps scalded the skin of her tender bottom.

The spanking was harsh, with no reprieve. Relentlessly the native beat her rump until she lay sobbing, her body jerking as each heavy blow fell. Finally, he halted. His hand moved purposefully between Linnet's thighs, thrusting into her channel brutally, he shoved his fingers inside her, roughly fondling her sex, violating and humiliating her. This continued, and she assumed his next move would be to rape her.

He startled her by pulling his hand from her channel. He shoved her roughly off his lap. Standing, he licked at his bleeding wrist, cursing as the blood flowed steadily from the bite wound. He stared at her with unblinking eyes, dark and coldly furious. Then he spoke harshly in his guttural tongue before he turned fluidly, disappearing through the entrance flap, still clasping his injured wrist.

After he'd gone, Linnet dropped sideways with her arms clasped around her upper body, legs drawn up. She lay curled into herself, weeping bitterly. Shifting, she felt a sharp object dig into her flank. Reaching beneath the blanket, she pulled out Yaogah's dagger. She stared at the blade, pondering. Why did this native man want her so much?

Any young woman of the tribe could mother his son. Was he, like his small son, drawn to her because of her red hair? He certainly seemed to be fascinated by the colour. She twirled the knife in her hands, then, before she could change her mind, she reached behind herself and grabbed her hair. Twisting it at her neck, she drew the blade across the wedge she'd created. A cascade of rippling russet fell into her hand. She placed it on the fur bed she sat upon.

Perhaps if he found this gift from her, he would let her escape, and not pursue her. If he did give chase and he caught her, perhaps, without her hair, he might release her. Anyway, she needed to get away quickly before the man came back to finish what he'd started.

She took several calming breaths before using the dagger to scrape at the mud and rushes that were the main components of the wall's construction.

Due to her previous efforts of digging that afternoon, it wasn't long before she'd made a hole large enough for her to wriggle through. Terrified that at any moment Yaogah would return to rape her, she frequently glanced over her shoulder, her heart racing, beating so loudly she was certain that someone would hear.

Lying on her stomach, she squirmed through the small gap. Once outside, she ran lightly from lodge to lodge, keeping to the shadows. A snarling dog appeared but all at once a small, shadowed form caught hold of the dog, whispering a command. Immediately, the dog fell silent and flopped onto its belly.

Linnet wondered if this person was about to give her away, but as the form moved close to her, she realised it was Running Deer. She recognised her as the girl she'd seen peeking into the lodge earlier. The girl took hold of her hand, quietly leading her around the perimeter of the encampment, keeping any dogs that growled quiet with a softly spoken command.

Once they were at the edge of the village, she pushed Linnet toward the cover of trees then melted away into the darkness. Linnet didn't look back. She crept quickly through the undergrowth. When she was deep enough into the forest, she sprinted.

It was pitch black so she couldn't see her feet, let alone where she was going. After struggling downhill, constantly tripping over tree roots, her head whipped by low branches, she became exhausted. Eventually, she had no choice, her legs turned to jelly and she collapsed in a heap upon the ground, her chest heaving painfully from her exertion.

After a brief rest, she stood up, determined to get as far away as she could under the cover of darkness. She continued to push her way through the press of trees, heading to a lighter area of ground that she hoped might be edge of the woodland. Disappointingly it turned out to be simply another clearing in the forest. Linnet crept around the edge, unwilling to risk exposure. Without warning, she was grasped from behind and lifted clean off her feet. A hand clamped itself over her mouth before she could scream.

CHAPTER 22

*S*he fought with every ounce of strength she had until a familiar voice cursed her and delivered a stinging slap to her bare rear end. *"Nee, lieveling!"* a man whispered in her ear. Not Yaogah, then, but Hans. She fell limp with relief. Hans carried her through the darkness and handed her up to John, who sat astride Amber, clutching the reins to Hans's own mount.

She pressed her face into her husband's shoulder and breathed in the safe familiar scent of him. Her relief made her boneless. She felt him kiss her face and sighed. *Safe, at last I am safe...*

Linnet awoke from her deeply healing sleep. It was the morning after they'd arrived back at the homestead. Sarah sat next to her on the bed. She stroked the short fair hair back from Linnet's face.

After they had arrived back at the Lammers' house the night before, Linnet had given a brief version of what had occurred at the native village. After feeding her oats and brown sugar in warm milk, John had carried her upstairs, where he'd gently tucked her into bed. She had fallen instantly into a deep, restorative sleep.

"I should stay in bed today if I were you," Sarah advised, handing Linnet a cup of steaming coffee.

"I need to get up. I want to talk to John as soon as possible," she replied, looking expectantly at the door.

"I don't think that would be a very wise idea," Sarah replied firmly.

"Why ever not? I feel just fine!" she assured her friend.

"Believe me, Linnet, you won't feel fine for long. Now that you are safe and sound again, John is *livid* with you for riding away so recklessly the way you did. I would stay in bed today and let him calm down a bit before you get up. It won't save you from a spanking but he might go easier on you once a day has passed!"

"*Sarah!*" The women jumped and looked to the doorway where Hans stood, looking thunderous. "I told you before *not* to interfere in their marriage! You will go to our room and await me there."

Sarah gave Linnet an apologetic look. Flushing guiltily, she squeezed her heavily pregnant body past her furious husband.

Hans looked severely at Linnet. "Get up and go and find your husband, or pack your bags and leave. I have had enough of your selfish behaviour. You put everyone around you in danger and all because you cannot learn to do as you are told!" He turned away, banging the door shut behind him. Linnet felt ashamed. Dear Hans must hate her to talk to her that way.

Hastily she donned her clothing and went out onto the landing. She could hear raised voices coming from Hans and Sarah's bedchamber. She paused to eavesdrop, concerned that Hans might spank his heavily pregnant wife.

"...because you carry our child, I shall not risk spanking you, which you richly deserve. I am making a note in the family bible of each transgression, so that when you are recovered from the birth, you will go across my knee for the tally. Now, you will stay in our chamber and rest until I tell you that you may join us downstairs."

"Yes, Hans," came the very meek reply.

Relieved that Sarah's behind was safe, at least for the time being, and recognising the love that Hans had for his wife, Linnet left them to it and made her way downstairs.

John sat at the table, cradling a cup of coffee between his hands. He gestured for her to sit at the table opposite him. His eyes were steely.

"John, I—" she burst out, but her husband interrupted her, holding his palm up for silence.

"I don't want to hear it! I intend to punish you and then tomorrow we are leaving on horseback for Boston. I won't put these wonderful people in any more danger because of your thoughtless escapades. We are leaving tomorrow and that is final."

She tried again. "No, you must *listen* to me, you don't understand, John... I have learned my lesson—"

"I said, ENOUGH! I mean ENOUGH! Now come with me!" He stalked around the table and pulled her to her feet, towing her towards the door.

She cried out at the top of her voice. "Stop this! I am with child! *I am carrying our child!*"

He dropped her arm, staring at her incredulously. "What did you say?"

"I am going to have our baby," she repeated softly. She smiled at the bewildered expression on her husband's face.

"Are you sure?" he asked, bemused.

"Well, as sure as I can be. My courses have ceased."

She waited for him to respond but he simply stood still. She went and leaned against his solid form. "I realised while I was kidnapped that I had brought all this trouble on myself and I promised that if I ever got back to you safely, I would become a good and obedient wife and not rush off to do what I wanted, *whenever* I wanted. I have learned the hard way that I *have* to listen to you, the voice of experience. I have never been more terrified in my life than I was stuck in that native camp!" She shuddered, remembering Yaogah's unwanted advances and the liberties he took with her body.

She'd decided not to reveal what had happened between her and the huge native. She would take the shameful knowledge with her to the grave.

John wrapped his arms about her and kissed her forehead. Tilting her head back, he gazed down into her swimming eyes. It was obviously taking him a moment to get his emotions under control. "Linnet, if you ever do *anything* that endangers you in any way again, so help me, I-I promise I'll switch you every day for the rest of your goddamn *life!*"

He lowered his head and kissed her, all his love and pent up fear and frustration were in his kiss. She responded as though her breath was bequeathed by John's sensual mouth. Finally, he broke away. Pulling out a chair, he sat with her cradled on his lap.

"I was beside myself when I arrived at the cabin to find the natives had deliberately burned our nest to the ground and you were missing, gone! Linnet, I thought I might have lost you forever and I so might have, if it hadn't been for Hans and his tracking skills! Clever girl, for dropping those strands of your hair, we'd never have found you without your forethought. However, I *refuse* to be put through anguish like that again and I won't let you drag other people into danger because you refuse to learn from your mistakes!"

"Oh, John, I'm sorry. I truly thought I would never see you again. I *swear* to you that this fright has put paid to my defiance. I finally understand the lessons you have tried to impress upon me since we were married. I realise the wilfulness I possessed and acted upon caused myself and everyone around me such terrible trouble and anguish! I intend to become a *perfectly* biddable wife from this day forward, I promise!"

She burst into noisy sobs and he clasped her to his heart, comforting her as she sobbed, releasing the dammed-up shock from her system. Shushing her, he rocked her like a child in his arms, kissing away her scalding tears.

"Tell me true, darling, did any of those natives harm you?" he asked softly. "I know you said you cut your hair as a gift to them, something I still don't quite understand… but did any of the men put their hands upon you?" he pressed. She knew he was watching her intently.

She felt his tension. Unblinking, she denied any misuse, only explaining about the child missing her and telling him that, amazingly, Will the fur trapper was alive and he had helped her to escape. She went on to explain that he was living with a squaw who was expecting their first child and that he was happy living among the natives. She knew her husband would try to exact revenge on Yaogah if she told him the full story behind her kidnapping. She was certain that Yaogah would win any fight between them and that John would die, never to see his unborn. She could not allow that to happen. She resolved never to reveal the truth to him.

Reassured by his wife's guileless gaze, he tucked her head under his chin and stroked her soft, shorn head. Given time, her lovely hair would grow back.

Rocked safely in her husband's arms, Linnet knew she was home at last. Lavenstock Hall and England were a thing of the past, a happy memory. Reality was John and this amazing, wildly beautiful country. This was her future—their future—and her place was by her husband's side. Together they would build a family, John would guide their children, helping them to flourish and grow into strong independent young people, just as he had helped her to become an adult woman.

She'd learned that actions have consequences and she had finally learned to consider other people. Most of all, she'd learned about love—true love, which she now realized knew no selfishness.

Later, John took a stroll around the farm alone. He wanted to contemplate the arrival of a baby. He pondered about this exciting development and the fact that it would change their lives forever. He'd told Linnet that he had decided they should stay at least another week at the Lammers' homestead, there was much to do and arrange before they could think of leaving. Leaving, was that what he really wanted?

The following day, they both took a trip into town. Sarah lent Linnet a bonnet which hid her lack of hair. They went to see the town doctor, who confirmed that Linnet was indeed expecting a baby.

While they were in town, John had left Linnet in the general store with instructions to buy whatever she needed. He went to set in motion some of the business transactions he had been secretly organising.

He hired a man to ride to Boston to deliver a packet of papers and letters to his mother, explaining all that had passed since they'd sailed from England. He included a package to be forwarded to England that contained letters to the families of the crew who had died aboard The Tempest. Linnet had written to her father, telling him that she was alive and well and expecting his first grandchild.

After collecting his wife from the mercantile, John packed the cart with supplies and Linnet's packages. They set off back to the Lammers' homestead at a calm pace. John felt enormous contentment.

That night, Sarah prepared a celebratory meal at the homestead. The men made toasts to their pregnant wives with Han's homemade brew. After they'd finished eating, Hans stood and held his hand up for silence.

"I would like to say a few words. Firstly, formal congratulations to you, dear friends, on your wonderful news. I thank the Lord that Peter asked me to take him to the beach that day when we found you both half-drowned on the sea shore. I am proud to call you my friend, John Foster. I turn now to you because I believe you have some quite exceptional news for us."

Linnet looked at her husband curiously. He winked at her and cleared his throat. "First of all, we owe you our lives and nothing can ever repay your goodness to us, Hans, Sarah and Peter—however, should you need us for *anything*, we will be there to support and offer our help in any way we can."

Linnet nodded her head vigorously in agreement.

John turned his gaze on her. "I have purchased a large parcel of land along the shoreline, near Ogunquit. I intend to start a boat building business there. I think this area would benefit from such a business and flourish. I know shipping and I have helped to build boats in the past. In time, I intend building a large house for my family to live in."

Silence fell as all eyes turned to Linnet; they waited, openly gauging her reaction. She stared at John, her mouth slack with shock.

"So, darling, what do you say?" he coaxed, looking at her anxiously.

She pushed back her chair and ran around the table, flinging her arms about him. "Oh, thank you, darling! John, this is *wonderful* news!"

He kissed her, looking relieved. "You have no idea how pleased I am to hear you say that. I thought you had your heart set on travelling to Boston. What changed your mind?"

"All I could think about before I was taken by the natives was returning to Lavenstock Hall and going back to England, but while I was in the tribal camp, I realised that all I really wanted to do was spend the rest of my life with you. It does not matter to me where we are, just so long as we are together. I love it here, and I would really like living nearby to Sarah, especially when our babies are both due!"

She turned a shy smile on her friend but she noticed Hans's sombre face, whereupon she turned to him anxiously. "You don't want me here, do you, Hans?" she asked, her eyes pleading with the stern Dutch man.

His lip quirked, he shook his head and Linnet's heart plummeted. "Mistress Foster, we should like to have you living close by, my Sarah would love to have her friend near so that she can gossip and talk babies with you. You are our very dear friends —almost family—but, Linnet, I do think that trouble is thy middle name. However, John and I have reached an agreement about you staying here in my house. I am most happy to offer you both a home with us until your own house is ready."

She ran to Hans and planted a kiss on his cheek. "You mentioned an agreement. What is it that you both agreed?" she asked suspiciously.

Hans winked at John. "Ja, well, after your child is born and you live under my roof, John has granted me permission to give you a sound switching every time you step out of line and, knowing you as I do, *lieveling*, I look forward to the day I can enjoy giving you your comeuppance!"

Everyone laughed except Linnet. Indignant, she fell silent. Surely Hans was joking? She jolly well hoped so. How dare John give him permission to chastise her! She was about to become a mother and she intended to behave appropriately from now onwards. She determined to be both a good mother and a biddable wife to her husband. She certainly never wanted Hans to take her in hand—nor John, no, not ever again!

She calmed herself, took control of her emotions. Smiling absently about the table at her friends, she listened to their conversation and enjoyed their banter. John winked at her. She smiled back, remembering the first time he had kissed her on the balcony, during the ball. Comparing herself to that green girl who'd married a man she did not love and crossed the Atlantic Ocean as a new bride, she recognised how much she'd changed. Chewing her bottom lip thoughtfully, she relaxed, realising that she had nothing to fret about.

She determined to evolve, to become a sensible, mature matron. It was entirely possible for her to become the woman she wished to be, especially with the help of her husband, the man she loved beyond all others, the man who had unerringly proven to be her match, her mate, her master.

THE END

VANESSA BROOKS

International bestselling author Vanessa Brooks lives in Sussex, England. She has a lifelong love of history, most especially English and American. She has written a few western tales, one notably for the Red Petticoat series, which was such a huge success in America. Her Georgian series, Masterful Husbands, set in the 1700's, also proved highly successful on both sides of the Atlantic

Vanessa's novels are generally historically based; she has a knack of bringing authenticity into the eras in which her novels are set. She carefully researches every time period, and strives to ensure that any historical facts she uses are correct.

More importantly, Vanessa likes writing entertaining books that her readers will enjoy. She includes passion, adventure, romance and domestic discipline – de rigueur within past times.

If you read it and enjoyed it, please leave a review!

Thank you!

Don't miss these exciting titles by Vanessa Brooks and Blushing Books!

Sunny's Safe Haven

Cowboy Caveat

Twin Turmoil

Corbin's Bend

Sub-Divided

A Shift in Time Series

Lightning Switch, Book 1
Wylde Switch, Book 2

Masterful Husbands Series
His Colonial Rose, Prequel
Sir Thomas's Bride, Book One
Viscount Weston's Bride, Book Two
The Colonel's Bride, Book Three
The Smuggler's Bride, Book Four
Masterful Husbands Tame Their Wives (Complete Series)

Victorian Melodramas Series
Elspeth, Book One
Amanda, Book Two
Victorian Rogues Compilation (Complete Series)

The Adventures of Linnett Wainwright
His Spoilt Lady, Book One
His Defiant Wife, Book Two
Her Match, Her Mate, Her Master, Complete Series

Anthologies
Historical Heroes
Sweet Town Love
12 Naughty Days of Christmas 2016

Audible Books
Sir Thomas's Bride
Viscount Weston's Bride
Cowboy Caveat
Sunny's Safe Haven

Connect with Vanessa Brooks:
vanessanovels.wix.com/vanessanovels

vanessanovels@inbox.com

BLUSHING BOOKS

Blushing Books is one of the oldest eBook publishers on the web. We've been running websites that publish spanking and BDSM related romance and erotica since 1999, and we have been selling eBooks since 2003. We hope you'll check out our hundreds of offerings at http://www.blushingbooks.com.